MW01119914

Major Gutenthal Family Bushes

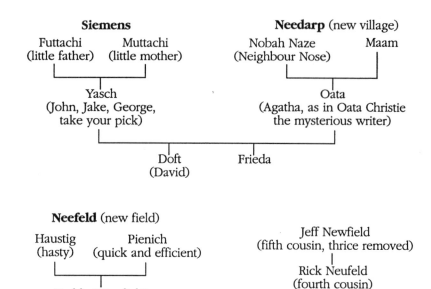

Siemens

Futtachi (little father) — Muttachi (little mother)

Yasch (John, Jake, George, take your pick)

Needarp (new village)

Nobah Naze (Neighbour Nose) — Maam

Oata (Agatha, as in Oata Christie the mysterious writer)

Doft (David) — Frieda

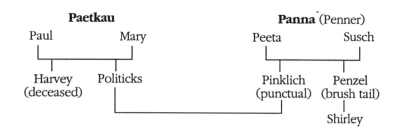

Neefeld (new field)

Haustig (hasty) — Pienich (quick and efficient)

Neddy "Needich" (necessary, as in need to go to the beckhouse haustig)

Jeff Newfield (fifth cousin, thrice removed)

Rick Neufeld (fourth cousin)

Nettie Neufeld (second cousin)

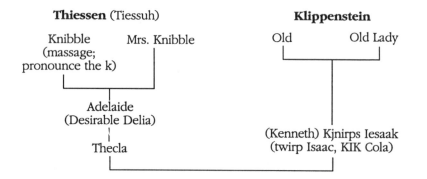

Paetkau

Paul — Mary

Harvey (deceased) — Politicks

Panna (Penner)

Peeta — Susch

Pinklich (punctual) — Penzel (brush tail)

Shirley

Thiessen (Tiessuh)

Knibble (massage; pronounce the k) — Mrs. Knibble

Adelaide (Desirable Delia)

Thecla

Klippenstein

Old — Old Lady

(Kenneth) Kjnirps Iesaak (twirp Isaac, KIK Cola)

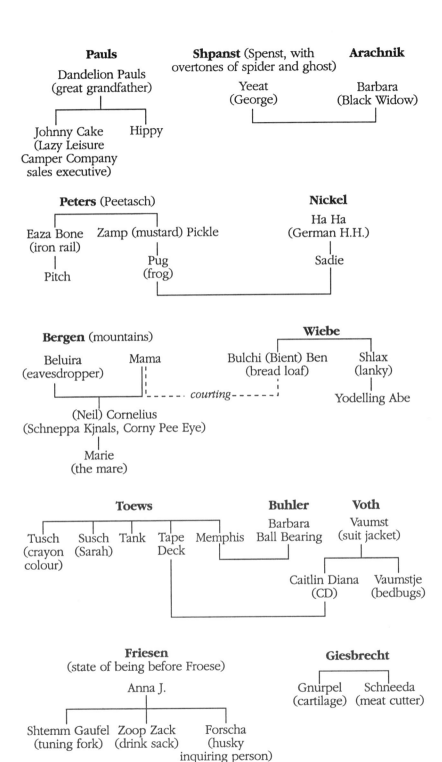

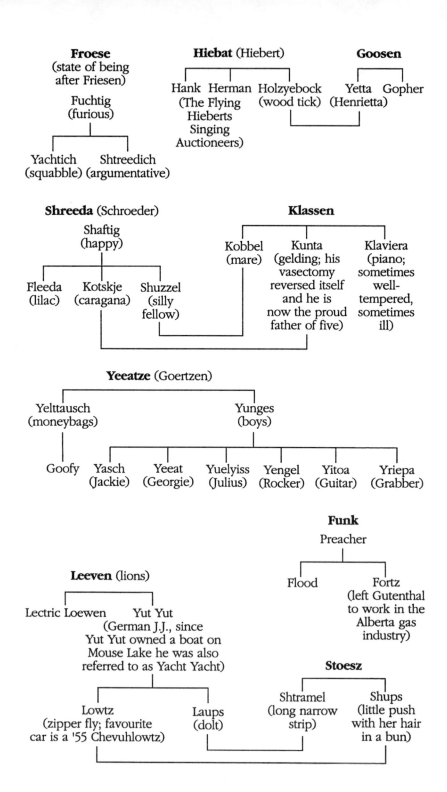

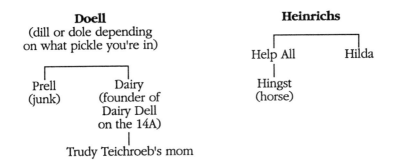

Doell
(dill or dole depending
on what pickle you're in)

Prell   Dairy
(junk)   (founder of
               Dairy Dell
               on the 14A)

Trudy Teichroeb's mom

Heinrichs

Help All   Hilda

Hingst
(horse)

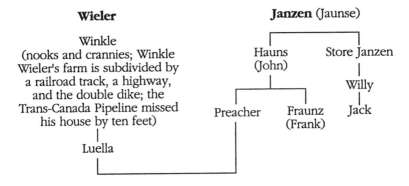

Wieler

Winkle
(nooks and crannies; Winkle
Wieler's farm is subdivided by
a railroad track, a highway,
and the double dike; the
Trans-Canada Pipeline missed
his house by ten feet)

Luella

Janzen (Jaunse)

Hauns   Store Janzen
(John)
                Willy

Preacher   Fraunz   Jack
               (Frank)

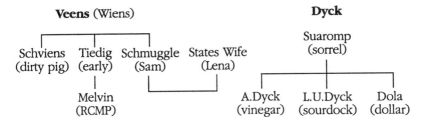

Veens (Wiens)

Schviens   Tiedig   Schmuggle   States Wife
(dirty pig) (early)   (Sam)   (Lena)

Melvin
(RCMP)

Dyck

Suaromp
(sorrel)

A.Dyck   L.U.Dyck   Dola
(vinegar)   (sourdock)   (dollar)

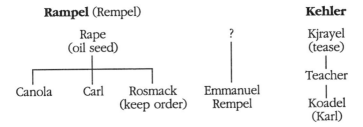

Rampel (Rempel)

Rape
(oil seed)

Canola   Carl   Rosmack
                  (keep order)

?

Emmanuel
Rempel

Kehler

Kjrayel
(tease)

Teacher

Koadel
(Karl)

Sawatsky

Simple Hein
(Henry)

Eaton

Eaton's Trienkje
(famous Gutenthal mailorder
catalogue, now defunct)

The Second Coming
of Yeeat Shpanst

From Heaven

Armin Wiebe

The Second Coming of Yeeat Shpanst

Armin Wiebe

Turnstone Press

Turnstone Press gratefully acknowledges the assistance
of the Canada Council and the Manitoba Arts Council.

Cover art: David Morrow Illustration/Design

Design: Manuela Dias

This book was printed and bound in Canada by
Kromar Pinting Ltd. for Turnstone Press.

Canadian Cataloguing in Publication Data

Wiebe, Armin

The second coming of Yeeat Shpanst

ISBN 0-88801-197-0

I. Title

PS8595.I5311S4 1995   C813'.54   C95-920149-1
PR9199.3.W543S4 1995

for Mildred and Jenny

Acknowledgements

I would like to thank the Canada Council and the Saskatoon Public Library for their support during the writing of this novel.

Excerpts from early drafts of this novel have been previously published in *Prairie Fire, the magazine Community Arts,* and *Zygote,* and broadcast on CBC Radio's *Arts Encounters.*

TABLE OF CONTENTS

Part One

Chapter 1
Beetfield Chorus 3
Chapter 2
The Prime Minister's Dark Day
for Canada Speech. 5
Chapter 3. 8
Chapter 4. 14
Chapter 5. 17
Chapter 6. 22
Chapter 7. 25
Chapter 8. 27
Chapter 9
Beetfield Chorus 39
Chapter 10. 41
Chapter 11
Beetfield Chorus 44
Chapter 12. 46

Part Two

Chapter 13. 53
Chapter 14. 67
Chapter 15. 81
Chapter 16. 98

Part Three

Chapter 17. 105
Chapter 18. 116
Chapter 19. 120
Chapter 20. 123
Chapter 21. 137
Chapter 22. 148
Chapter 23. 156
Chapter 24
Beetfield Chorus 163

Chapter 25. 167
Chapter 26. 171
Chapter 27
   A Politicks Paetkau Flatdeck Reading. 173
Chapter 28. 176
Chapter 29. 179
Chapter 30. 188

Part Four
Chapter 31. 193
Chapter 32. 197
Chapter 33. 208
Chapter 34
   A Politicks Paetkau Flatdeck Reading. 217
Chapter 35. 220
Chapter 36. 225
Chapter 37. 231
Chapter 38
   Beetfield Chorus 238
Chapter 39. 247
Chapter 40. 255
Chapter 41
   Beetfield Chorus 268

An Illiterate Hitch-Hiker's Guide to the Gutenthal Galaxy
Thesis Statement 279
Antithesis Statement. 280
Synthesis Statement 281
Phrases and Froeses Fuchtig and Otherwise 282
And a Paddle Across the Lexicon 284

PART ONE

*Even if I started at the beginning some big banger
would come along and tell you different.*
                    —*Koadel Kehler, the teacher's son*

1 BEETFIELD CHORUS

Yoh, do you remember?

Remember what?

Shpanst.

Yeeat Shpanst?

Yeah, Yeeat Shpanst
who febeizeled himself
in Ottawa.

Febeizeled?

Yeah, febeizeled.

Feschwunge.

Vanished into thin air.

In Ottawa?

Yeah, where Trudeau lived and
had children on Christmas Day.

In Ottawa Yeeat Shpanst febeizeled himself?

But no children on Christmas Day.

No children?

For sure not, Yeeat Shpanst is
not Trudeau.

You mean that Yeeat Shpanst who preached in the curling rink?
  I heard him.
      You and all of Gutenthal.
Not me, I had to baby-sit.
  He talked about weeding beets.
So?
  It was so sad.
    What?
  We'll never finish this field now.
What you mean, never finish?
        Only he could have
        saved us.
Huh? That was so long ago it's not even true anymore.
        He had another way.
  He was one of us. But now we'll never
  finish.
You mean weed beets forever?
      Forever and ever, amen?
       Unless . . .
  It's such a dark day.
And yet the sun shines.

2 THE PRIME MINISTER'S DARK DAY FOR CANADA SPEECH

Fellow Canadians, this is a dark day for Canada. We began by committing ourselves to the truth—the truth of our two nations warring in the bosom of a single state. We found the truth and spoke the truth, and now our desire to live the truth has been thwarted by those with a vested interest in error, those with no literature and no history. I shall not mingle conjectures with uncertainties—the dice of God are always loaded. We cannot escape history. A house divided against itself cannot stand.

A great Canadian poet once said, "Something there is that doesn't love a wall. Good fences make good neighbours. A gift to last. But I am done with apple picking now." I prefer the dollar sign, the symbol of free trade, therefore, of a free mind. Fellow Canadians, we stand today on the edge of a new frontier; therefore, I say to you, ask not what your constitution can do for you, ask what you can do for your constitution.

Consider the option. A government big enough to give you everything you want is a government big enough to take from you everything you have. It is the absolute right of the

State to supervise the formation of public opinion. Public opinions wins wars. Why should we subsidize intellectual curiosity? Madame, I cannot conceive, but in the kingdom of the blind the one-eyed man is king. After three days men grow weary of a wench, a guest, and rainy weather. I deny categorically that there is a deliberate conspiracy, by force, by fraud, or by both, to force Canada into the American union. The stupid speak of the past, the wise of the present, fools of the future. I offer neither pay, nor quarters, nor provisions; I offer hunger, thirst, forced marches, battles, and death. I offer the end run; government by football players. Let those who love Canada in their hearts and not with their lips only, follow me. It's not the size of your caucus, it's how you use it. By strengthening the strong, we can help the weak. Man is an animal that makes bargains; no other animal does this—one dog does not change a bone with another. I make deals; therefore, I am.

And I say to the provinces, you may have all that the hen lays, except for the eggs. And I say to the aboriginal people, you may have all the freedom and self-government of a dog at the bottom of a well. When the rooster crows on the manure pile, the weather will change or stay as it is. In this world we have people, turtles, and three-sided iron files. I say, patience and good eating carry a man farthest. Patience, and men will work and women will weep. When everything is eaten from the table, we'll have good weather. A tree is never too old to bend. It will cost, yes, but it will taste, too. If you buy what you don't need, you will soon need what you can't buy, and this country could not survive with a policy of unfettered free trade. But that was so long ago, it is hardly true anymore. I'm not denying anything I didn't say. These hands are clean!

And I say to you with absolute sincerity, whether I will or not, I must . . . constitute this country. Either it comes with me, or it breaks! For *our* country, wrong is right! When men are well-governed, they neither seek nor desire any other liberty. The bullet is stronger than the ballet. Get rid of the devil, and the priest will have nothing to do.

If I could save the country without agreeing to an equal senate, I would do it; if I could save it by agreeing to an unequal senate, I would do that. What I do about the constitution, I do because I believe it helps to save Canada; and what I forbear, I forbear because the world envies us; therefore, we must destroy what we have. All things come to an end—except a sausage, which comes to two ends. Join me on this day in singing our great national anthem. Give me your tired, your poor, your huddled masses yearning to breathe free, the wretched refuse of your teeming shore, send these, the homeless, tempest-tossed, to me. I lift my lamp beside the true north strong and free. O say, can't you see?

3

Later, Oata couldn't prove that the Prime Minister had really said those same words, but that was how she would remember the speech. As the Prime Minister turned away from the TV cameras and ducked into his black limousine, Oata said, "With him it wouldn't be comfortable eating macaroni," and she wanted to throw an egg at him. She shuddered and switched the television off. As she put on her garden hat she felt a Weltschmerz so heavy she almost sat down on the lawn swing Yasch had built beside the Chinese elm hedge. She wanted to sit down on the swing and schuckel herself out of this world.

> Schuckel schuckel Scheia
> Oostre ate wie Eia
> Pinjkste ate wie wittet Broot
> Stoaw' wie nijch
> Dann woa wie groot.

Almost she sat down on the lawn swing after she heard

the Prime Minister speaking on the television while she was ironing. Oata liked to iron in the afternoon while *Coronation Street* was on, only the CBC *News* butted in to say that the Prime Minister wanted to address the nation. The CBC reporters had such truarijch looks on their faces that Oata at first thought somebody hartsoft important had died. And the Prime Minister, too, had such a schwierich face that Oata figured maybe a war had started, but soon his words sounded like he was peeving himself like a little boy who couldn't have his own way.

Later, Oata would write that she couldn't remember ever having been made to shiver by a Prime Minister before, not even Trudeau with his red red rose. But on this June Saturday she almost burned a hole in Frieda's white Sunday blouse because the Prime Minister's speech made her feel like the time when her mother first went to the mental home and her father hadn't known how to make the washing machine work and they soon got vaumstje bugs in the beds. And when she walked outside into the yard she felt a little like she maybe wanted to die and she almost sat down on the lawn swing Yasch had built to shuckel herself away from the world.

> Schuckel schuckel scissor legs
> At Easter we eat eggs
> At Pentecost we eat white bread
> Die we not
> We won't be dead.

Later, Oata wrote that she would have sat down on the swing, only a white butterfly fluttered past her and she turned back to the house to get the cabbage duster. And once she had dusted the cabbages, she filled the sprinkling can. As she watered the tomatoes Oata worried she was getting to be like her mother in the mental home, feeling all creepy and crawly over something as silly as a Prime Minister's speech, and she wondered if it had really been necessary for her mother to stay in the mental home all these years. I mean, Oata thought, is my mother in the mental home more crazy than this Prime Minister? Then she shivered herself in the hot garden sun, remembering the beetfield yeschwieta about Yeeat Shpanst that had been ringing in her ears just before the Prime Minister butted himself into *Coronation Street*. What might such a thing mean about a person's own head? Then she tasted rainbow ice cream on her tongue. And as she dipped the sprinkling can into the barrel on the manure sled at the end of the garden, she remembered the excitement in Gutenthal when Yeeat Shpanst was running for the PC leadership, the hope people had felt working together to send one of their own to the convention in Ottawa, and she remembered, too, how during those few weeks she had felt like a child getting a double-decker rainbow cone from Hi-Way Inn every day. But then Yeeat Shpanst had febeizeled himself at the convention, just disappeared there in Ottawa, gone like he was no more than a joke told by beetweeders under a burning sun.

Oata saw herself at the bottom of the water barrel and remembered her mother's well with the syrup pails of cream hung on ropes to keep cool, remembered how she'd almost seen her own little head way down at the bottom, and as she'd leaned farther to better see herself between the syrup pails, her mother had screamed and grabbed her with both arms. The memory was so clear, so real Oata herself screamed when something touched her as she leaned into the barrel. The sprinkling can sank down until only the saltshaker spout stuck out of the water. Oata looked behind herself and screamed again at the green hair, green eyebrows, green lips smiling.

"Frieda!" she fuscheled after her scream died. "What have you done with yourself?"

"Do you like it, Mom?"

"Ach, meyall, it is still four months till Halloween. And you have to be bridesmaid yet at Thecla Thiessen's wedding."

"Oh, that's okay, Mom. Thecla coloured hers red."

"Well, red . . . lots of people have red hair and anyways Thecla's is reddish already."

"Thecla coloured it red to match her mother's cherry-red Toyota Camry. They're going to use that for a wedding car. Everything has to match."

"And you're supposed to match the onions in the potato salad . . . or maybe the undertaker's green grass around my grave when I die from shaming myself about my daughter?"

"Oh Mom, it's just the style nowadays. A woman can't wear braids or a bun all the time. Besides, if we don't like it we can wash it out just like that. It's not dye like Anne of Green Gables."

"Frieda come. I must sit down on the swing. I don't think I can take this world standing up today."

For a few minutes they sat, pushing their feet against the floor of the lawn swing, listening to the wooden squeak. Oata stared at her daughter, stared at the green hair. It maybe didn't look so bad, a person could get used to anything nowadays, and Frieda had said it would wash out. Frieda, only fourteen. Maybe if a person did crazy things at fourteen, she wouldn't have to do crazy things when she was older. Oata was happy that Frieda's figure had taken after Yasch's, even if she had come crying home from the school bus because some kjnirps had called her bony maroni. Oata figured Frieda would have an easier time skinny than fat like Oata had been. But she was worried that her daughter was growing up too fast, especially this bridesmaid business when she was only fourteen. It bothered Oata a little that Frieda had gotten so close with this Knibble Thiessen's granddaughter who was eighteen already and now was going to get married in the fall. Oata figured eighteen was too young to get married, for sure when a girl would still paint her hair cherry red to match the colour of a car.

"So tell me," Oata said, "what does Thecla Thiessen's mother think about this red hair business?"

Frieda stared at a plastic necklace hanging on a Chinese elm branch beside the swing.

"Has Adelaide seen her daughter's hair yet?"

Frieda shifted herself sideways, lifted both legs up onto

the seat, and picked at her fingernails. Oata noticed that those at least weren't painted green.

"You know, Mom," Frieda said, looking her in the eye, "I don't think Thecla is going to go through with it."

"What do you mean?"

"Get married. I don't think Thecla wants to get married."

"But they're having a wedding and everything, and you already bought cloth for the bridesmaid dress. What you mean Thecla doesn't want to get married?"

"I don't know for sure, Mom, it's just that I think Thecla is doing this stuff like the painted hair to get them to call the wedding off."

"You mean she doesn't like this schaps she is marrying herself with?"

"I don't know for sure, Mom. I mean, she says she loves him and talks about how good-looking he is and how his family has lots of money and she'll be able to live in a nice house right away with a dishwasher and a jacuzzi and satellite TV. Only, when Thecla tells me this stuff I almost get the feeling that her mom is pushing her into this."

"Well, can't a girl say no nowadays?"

Frieda stood up on the moving swing and stumbled onto the seat beside Oata. Oata put her arms around her, put her nose into the green-apple hair. Frieda didn't cry, but she whispered, "You know, Thecla makes lots of jokes and laughs all the time and she looks so happy like she doesn't have a care in the world, and she's so pretty, so beautiful. She never steps in cowshit, if you know what I mean . . . but every once in a while when I'm with her she makes me feel like she's scared of something."

Oata cradled her daughter and pushed at the swing. From the back of her mind she hoped that Yasch and Doft wouldn't come home for a while yet because she didn't want to have to let Frieda out of her arms. A mother's arms would have been good to have when Oata was fourteen.

"Does it make any sense what I'm feeling about Thecla? Could it be that she is scared of something?"

Oata kissed Frieda's forehead, stroked the green hair. "How can a person know what another person is afraid of? There is so much to be afraid of in this world today. So much." Oata felt her eyes getting wet, and she felt Frieda's body shudder, and for a second Oata didn't feel like dying quite so much anymore. But then the Prime Minister's voice seeped into her head again and she wished she had tape recorded the dark day for Canada speech on a VCR because she could hardly believe he would have said such things to the people. For a second she tasted rainbow ice cream again and then in her head she was on the wine sofa playing with her bride doll, the white hole-candy stinging on her little tongue as she heard her mother rummaging through the junk drawer muttering, "Where is that Yeeat Shpanst anyways? How come Life Savers always have to febeizel themselves?"

On the other side of the Chinese elm hedge Oata heard the rumble of the old one-ton truck her father, Nobah Naze Needarp, had left behind when he died. At breakfast Yasch had complained that the old crate was more trouble than Stanfield's underwear with no trapdoor buttons, and for a second Oata had a strange picture in her head of Haustig Neefeld washing his three-ton grain truck at Postanack Pankratz's Jet-Spray Car Wash and Video Rentals place. A strange picture to have, Oata thought, when she was trying to keep her arms around Frieda as long as possible.

Then the truck rumble stopped and a voice on the crackly radio said: "Fellow Canadians, it is the summertime; a time to relax and enjoy this great country of ours; go see our Canada from sea to sea to sea; go see the mountains; go swim in the beach; go see a baseball game."

4

If Haustig Neefeld hadn't washed his truck that June Saturday afternoon he never would have seen the flyer stuck under his windshield-wiper blade. He had been thinking about maybe selling his three-ton grain truck with hoist to Yasch Siemens who had asked him for it three times already, so he decided to try the Jet-Spray Car Wash and Video Rentals place Postanack Pankratz had opened up with his pension money after the post office redunded him and moved itself into the Flatland 7-Eleven. A vehicle gets a better deal if it is clean, and for sure only the rain had washed Haustig Neefeld's three-ton since his son, Needich, went off to Chartered Accounting school and didn't use it anymore for picking up girls on Saturday nights.

Haustig Neefeld saw the flyer after he came out of the crop insurance office where Insurance Panna had showed him the satellite infrared photograph the RCMP used to catch this farmer out by the Pembina Hills who was cheating the crop insurance after he got hailed out. Haustig had just climbed into his freshly cleaned cab and was reaching for the ignition key when he saw the folded-up gold piece of paper under the windshield wiper. When he unfolded it he saw a message written in green letters the same style as in a German Bible:

> 𝕷et not first your heart sag down into your pants. 𝕴f your stomach hangs bent about the world today come to the 𝕲utenthal Curling 𝕽ink at 8:00 tonight. 𝕭e the solution.

Haustig Neefeld wasn't hungry as he backed out onto the main street away from the crop insurance office, but his stomach hung bent. That RCMP infrared picture that had caught the farmer cheating the crop insurance bothered him. It bothered him the way it had sometimes bothered him when a preacher preached about sin and tried to bring it by to the people snoring on the church benches that God could see everything and knew everything, that there was no point in trying to hide anything because God even knew what a person was thinking, knew even what a person was afraid to think, but Haustig Neefeld had never let that bother him all the way because he figured the preachers were just guessing and maybe just trying to scare people into behaving themselves. But now the RCMP had this infrared Sputnik satellite camera counting the aphids crawling on each leaf on a wheatfield, and that made the preacher business about each hair on a person's head having numbers a pretty simple job maybe Preparation H & R Klutz would have trouble with, but for sure not a chartered accountant like his son, Needich.

Then he saw the For Sale sign on the Pool elevator and his stomach felt like a beer can feknutsched in a drunken fist. The pain was so bad he stopped the truck right in the middle of Main Street. He stared at the For Sale sign, big as four sheets of plywood, huge yellow letters on green, and a phone number with two zeros in the middle like a pair of eyes. For a second his stomach pinched so sharply he thought he would die there in the cab. And then, as quickly as it had come upon him, the pain was gone and a young bengel with a ponytail was honking a rusty red half-ton behind him.

Haustig pulled over to the curb and carefully copied off the For Sale sign phone number. Then he laughed at himself, like a person would have to have a screw loose to even think about buying a grain elevator. Only a Hutterite Colony would have the cash for such a thing. But, even so, it was hard to feel funny as he slowly drove away past the Paterson elevator now trimmed with Cargill green. The Pool elevator had been moved to town from English Siding twenty years before because the Pool figured it would be more profitable in Flatland. But now it wasn't any use here either. And there was no other place to move it to. It was like the world was at the end of the road. Maybe he should go to the Gutenthal Curling Rink at 8:00.

5

There was a brown spot where the silvery stuff behind the glass was rusting. The brown spot blocked out Thecla's right eye whenever she leaned forward to smear on her cherry-red lipstick. Above it, in the true section of the mirror, barely large enough to reflect her face, the spikes of her cherry-red hair kinked and rippled when she moved. Below her neck her freckled body bulged and ballooned and she thought of her grandmother kneading dough for brown bread. It amused her to see herself sort of blobbing away in the old mirror, and when she turned to look in the unblemished full-length mirror beside the four-poster bed, she stuck her tongue out at the slender naked girl and said, "You're not me!" And Thecla remembered the curved mirror in the Black Hills that summer she was fourteen and her mother had insisted she go along with her grandparents to the Black Hills that weren't even black to see a bunch of old geezers carved into a mountain.

She had slept every night in the same kind of motel with one room and two double beds, except for that one night in Spearfish when Grandfather rented this cabin and she had a bedroom all to herself. That had been the only time she was alone for that whole week, unless you counted going to the toilet. But that mirror in the amusement park in the Black Hills that weren't even black had made her look round and tubby like a roly-poly doll, and as she had looked into it she had seen a different person, a person other people couldn't see, a person who could have rolled away from everything that was holding her soul nailed down, and she remembered how while she was looking in the curved mirror at her self that wasn't herself she had been humming, "Rolled away, rolled away. All the burdens of my heart rolled away."

And now, as she stuck out her tongue at the slim naked girl in the mirror, she thought she should get a curved mirror for herself like the one in the Black Hills and she would never have to look at the person again who was going to fit into the lacy white wedding dress lying on the four-poster bed, the dress that Grandfather Knibble Thiessen was going to lead down the aisle of the biggest Flatland church to the front where Kjnirps Iesaak Klippenstein and his seven best men would be waiting for her while Klaviera Klassen played that wedding stuff on the organ. And as Thecla stood there in the upstairs bedroom of Grandfather Knibble Thiessen's house between the muzharich mirror on the dresser and the clear mirror on the wall, with the lacy white wedding dress spread out on the four-poster bed, she had a dream.

She dreamed how it could be at that wedding, how she could drop pieces of the wedding dress along the way from the time she stepped out from her mother's cherry-red Toyota Camry and climbed up the steps of the big Flatland church, in through the double doors where Grandfather Knibble Thiessen would take her arm. Thecla smiled, thinking maybe she would be a bird dropping white feathers as she glided down the aisle on her grandfather's arm, and when she got to the front where Kjnirps Iesaak Klippenstein waited with his seven pastel-blue best men, at that moment when Kjnirps (his mother called him Kenny) would turn around to catch his first wedding-day glimpse of the bride, she would reach up and pull the veil off her red-spiked hair and let it drift over to the Klippenstein side of the church. With one quick twist Grandfather Knibble Thiessen would be left clutching her white-lace elbow glove in the crook of his arm and then, with her teeth, she would pull off the other glove and drop it at Kjnirps Klippenstein's pastel-blue feet. For an eyeblink she would stand there below the pulpit, her naked cherry-red spike-haired freckled self as it would appear in that Black Hills curved mirror, Kjnirps Iesaak Klippenstein and his seven pastel-blue best men straining to keep their eyeballs from spilling out of their sockets, Grandfather Knibble Thiessen standing there with the empty white elbow glove still clutched in the crook of his arm, his now arthritic knibble hands sweating to reach out for her roly-poly skin. And then Thecla would wink at Frieda Siemens, her one bridesmaid, her one green-haired bridesmaid against seven pastel-blue best men, and Frieda would drop her green bridesmaid gloves, and they would turn into green palm leaves. The white glove at Kjnirps Iesaak's feet, the pieces of white wedding dress would be palm leaves strewn on the red carpet, and Thecla Thiessen would roly-poly back up the aisle to a congregation of hosannas and the only one who would dare to kiss her would be Frieda Siemens, her green-haired bridesmaid, leaning into the open window on the driver's side of the cherry-red Toyota Camry, the warm vinyl seat sticking to Thecla's freckled roly-poly bum as she turned the ignition key. And then she would drive away from the church, across the railway tracks, past the boarded-up post office with its limp tattered maple-leaf flag, past the Paterson elevator trimmed with Cargill green, and on to the highway.

But standing there in the upstairs bedroom of Grandfather Knibble Thiessen's house between the muzharich and the clear mirrors, with the lacy white wedding dress spread out on the four-poster bed, Thecla knew that even if her dream came true she still wouldn't know where to go as she sped down the highway in her mother's cherry-red Toyota Camry. She wouldn't know where to go, she thought, but at least she would be going. Going going gone, like a doll at an auction sale, and for a second she wondered how much old Klippenstein had bid to have a bride for his son?

So what if Kenneth Isaac Klippenstein, or KIK Cola for short, made dirty phone calls to the women in Puggefeld and Gutenthal and was trapped when Mrs. Daughters Derksen, with six daughters to protect, arranged to meet him by Winkle Wieler's empty yard? Klippenstein's lawyer managed to keep the whole thing out of court by threatening to smear it all over the court page in the *Echo* that she had been leading Kenny on, such a young bengel who maybe had a fan belt slipping, and so Mrs. Daughters Derksen had withdrawn her complaint on the condition that old Klippenstein make sure that his son didn't play around on the phone anymore.

Soon after that Kjnirps Iesaak Klippenstein had come to see Grandfather Knibble because his back was to nothing from bungee jumping by the Red River Exhibition. Thecla, who had seen bungee jumping on TV, thought it was cool and made sure that Kjnirps Iesaak Klippenstein noticed her before he left her grandfather's Holistic Massage Clinic. Sure enough, two nights later he came back when her grandfather was making some house calls in the States of America and Thecla had proved to KIK Cola that she was Knibble Thiessen's granddaughter and had the right stuff in her fingers to make Kjnirps Iesaak Klippenstein's back feel a lot better, and for a while it had seemed like a real lark to steal one of her grandfather's customers that way. It had felt like more than a lark, it had made her feel full of power, the same kind of power she saw her grandfather had when he got his hands on a person's body, especially when he got his hands on a person's feet and found the pressure points for all the vital organs, knowing how to create just enough pain and discomfort and then provide relief and pleasure, then pain and discomfort again, finally ending almost in relief, but always leaving a bit of an itch unscratched, to guarantee a repeat customer.

And it was a way of protecting herself, or at pretending she was protecting herself, against the power Grandfather Knibble had over her when he got his hands on her feet, when his fingers dug and rubbed and sent pain and pleasure to parts of her that had been feeling just fine before she climbed up on the massage table. She didn't know when exactly fixing up her wrecked ankle turned into something freaky, how he knibbled her differently than the States of America women who kept coming back to him, only she knew for sure on that night in the two-bedroom cabin by Spearfish in the Black Hills that aren't really black Grandfather Knibble Thiessen had crawled into the bed beside her and had mumbled that Grandmother wasn't feeling well and couldn't lie still enough so he could sleep. And for sure Thecla lay stone still with her eyes frozen open, heart hammering against her nightgown, fists gripping the sheet the whole night through, Grandfather's breath whistling through hairy nostrils.

The next day at the amusement park she had seen herself in the curved mirror that changed her body so it didn't look like her, and she wished she had such a mirror hanging beside the white lacy wedding dress lying on the four-poster bed. Thecla faced the full-length mirror straight on and stuck out her tongue, then tried to wrench her slim freckled body into gruelich shapes as she chanted a rhyme Grandmother used to say when she crossed her legs and rode her little Thecla on the instep of her foot.

> Iesaak, Shpriesack
> Schlenkjafoot
> Schleit siene Brut
> Em Kjalla doot.

Suddenly, in the middle of her wrenched pose, Thecla shivered and in the mirror the goose pimples on her freckled skin made her look like a plucked rooster.

> Isaac, Shucksack
> Stumble foot
> Beats his bride
> In the cellar dead.

6

Box 70 in the Gutenthal Store post office hadn't been crammed so full since Knibble Thiessen's daughter advertised herself for a husband and *The Western Producer* printed 70 instead of 7. How was Store Janzen's Willy supposed to know that Desirable Delia was really Adelaide Thiessen and that those letters were supposed to go into Thiessens' Box 7 and not Bergens' Box 70? Schneppa Kjnals Bergen had figured that his Mama was onntoofrade with her man, and when you were nine years old and your father, Beluira Bergen, was still very much alive listening on the party line, the idea that Mama might think of herself as Desirable Delia made the world look pretty schwierich.

For sure, Mama didn't know what to make of all these letters, not that she didn't get a kick out of one bachelor who offered a promising bride his late mother's thousand-set saltshaker collection. Kjnals sometimes thought maybe Mama would have answered that letter if the next week *The Western Producer* hadn't printed a correction right on the front newspaper page. Then everybody in Gutenthal knew that Desirable

Delia lived by Knibble Thiessen's place and for sure people soon figured out why Adelaide Thiessen was advertising for a husband.

But on this June Saturday all the letters were addressed to Neil Bergen, Investigator, the box number and postal code correctly typed by a computer, except on one manila envelope from the Department of Justice which was hand addressed with a black fountain pen. It was stamped DO NOT BEND!!! but that hadn't stopped the post office from bending all four corners and the middle both ways. Schneppa Kjnals looked at the purple words stamped under Department of Justice— Private Investigators' Registrar—and his heart murmured just a little, but before he could tear open the envelope, Store Janzen's Willy said through the bars of the wicket, "Kjnals, there's lots more mail for you yet!"

Willy handed him three large envelopes, each about an inch thick, the top one from The Hollywood School of Detection. "Well," said Willy, "as long as you keep getting so much mail maybe we can keep the Gutenthal post office open."

"Sure, only now I probably won't get another letter till Christmas card time."

Outside, in his grey Volkswagen, Kjnals carefully cut open the Justice Department envelope with his jackknife. At last, his private investigator's licence with his name spelled almost right. So what if they had put the *i* before the *e* in Neil. In a world where most people called him Schneppa Kjnals or Corny Pee Eye, "Niel Bergen" looked kind of classy on the maroon-trimmed licence signed by the Justice Minister and the Private Investigators' Registrar. The bullet wound in his buttocks itched slightly, reminding him of the hassles he had gone through to get the licence.

But now it seemed the whole world recognized his new official status. Only, as he opened the letter from the Minister of Finance advising him that he needed to register for the Provincial Sales Tax, he began to twievel a bit, and when he opened the letter from Revenue Canada Excise Branch instructing him to register for the Goods and Services Tax, the twievel grew into a doubt. But it wasn't just the government. The Telephone System wanted him to get a business phone and Yellow ads in the Pages; the Holding Pen Company wanted him to order ten thousand invisible-ink pens imprinted with his name and phone number; the Snoopy Software Company wanted him to install SnoopWindows Version 6 on his hard drive; and seventeen detective agency associations wanted him to buy exclusive memberships with fees going all the way up to $1929.50 U.S. for the Dirty Collar Crime Writers of America Association annual conference in Hawaii. As well, the Hollywood School of Detection had finally got his name right and re-issued a corrected Certificate of Honor suitable for framing, and now offered him a discount on an advanced correspondence detective-training course including a special supplement on snooping in Canada (the trouble spot of the future now that the evil empire had become a free market).

One plain white envelope with no return address had his name printed in block letters with a cheap ball-point pen that had leaked for the postal code. Schneppa Kjnals slit open the flap with his forefinger and pulled out the gold-coloured paper. His first thought was a complaint that no one had told him about a meeting at the curling rink. As caretaker-watchman, it was his job to open up the waiting room.

7

"When the rooster crows on the manure pile, the weather will change or stay as it is." Derksus Obrum, his father's oabeida hired man, used to say that. "Wan de Hon kjreit oppem Mest, dan endat daut Wada ooda blift aus et ess." And now on the television Pierre Anchorbridge was trying to get this business administration professor to explain what the Prime Minister meant when he said, "In this world it gives people, turtles, also three-sided iron files." Derksus Obrum, at least once a day: "Et jeft Mensche, Schiltkjrate, uck dreekauntje Fiele." Politicks Paetkau almost laughed when he thought maybe one of the Flat German MPs from Kitchener or BC or Steinbach must have helped write the Prime Minister's speech, but the Prime Minister had also said, "It is the absolute right of the State to supervise the formation of public opinion," and on this particular day in Canada quoting Goebbels was not a laughing matter. The *Air Farce* couldn't save the country, though Politicks was the first to admit that the *Royal Canadian Air Farce* sure was a help. Politicks liked laughing at politics and he liked thinking about it, and if his father hadn't had his stroke just before the October Crisis, Politicks Paetkau would have finished his Ph.D. and become a political science professor. Who knows, he himself could have been punditizing on Pierre Anchorbridge's *News Special.*

But now Politicks Paetkau was an egg producer worried about eggs from the States of America flooding the Canadian market. He was worried about the low price of wheat. He was worried about the health care system the government was trying to level with the States of America which didn't have one. And he worried about the environment, too. But what really worried him was that even though there was lots of ranting and raving against the Prime Minister's policies which were driving the country to hell in a manure-spattered wheelbarrow without clearance lights, nobody else was long-sighted enough to see past next week. Politicks figured that Canada needed to search its soul: Why is it when we have such an abundance of resources that we can't make a go of it in such a way that there is enough for everybody? Even Funny Money Bible Bill Aberhart had asked such a question.

But on this dark day for Canada, with Pierre Anchorbridge and his pundits buffooning themselves over the Prime Minister's speech, there didn't seem to be much hope and Politicks reached for the TV switch. The picture changed from Pierre Anchorbridge to a man with long black hair slicked back holding a feather in his hand, and for a moment hope glimmered. But the Prime Minister's words had pumped up the cynicism in his veins and Politicks clicked the TV off. Instead of entering the egg barn to begin the afternoon collection, he stepped out of his little office into the sunlight and as he blinked his eyes Politics Paetkau spotted a gold piece of paper stapled to his yard-light pole.

8

It was the top of the second inning with Gutenthal at bat when Oata looked away to slap a mosquito on her arm and saw the black Lincoln roll into the curling rink yard. Later, she would write in her Farmers' Union notebook that the car seemed still as a ghost, a geschpenst, like the disciples feared when they first saw Jesus walking on the evening water, and yes, Oata thought that after Jesus had said, "Peace, be still," the Sea of Galilee must have been as still as the wind was right there on the Gutenthal Curling Rink baseball diamond, and she wondered if in that long-ago still peace there had been so many mosquitoes, too.

The black car rolled into the yard like a sailboat or maybe an eagle gliding through the air. Oata thought of a sailboat and an eagle, even though she had never seen such things in Gutenthal. The Lincoln rolled to a stop beside Schneppa Kjnals's grey Volkswagen. Prachadarp people, Oata thought, and maybe after those people found themselves seats on the bleachers she could sneak down to schneppa their car out just in case a bumper crop with 1974 prices let Yasch afford such a car for visiting her mother on Sundays in the mental home, and maybe even giving her a ride through the Pembina Hills.

But before the Lincoln people got out, a blue Hyundai Pony with a *Winnipeg Daily Witness* sticker on the door parked beside it. Right behind came Haustig Neefeld with the three-ton grain truck that Yasch wanted to buy. To Oata it looked like Haustig Neefeld had just washed his truck. Behind Haustig Neefeld came Tape Deck Toews and his wife, CD, in their Carpet Cleaning and Audio van, followed by a cherry-red Toyota Camry. The girl in the Toyota had hair that matched the car.

A short man got out of the Lincoln, well maybe not really so short, but somehow he looked like the kind of person who would buy shoes with elevator heels. A flower pinned to his dark lapel made Oata think about Trudeau and his rose, only this was a pink rose, a wild rose, the kind Oata ate the petals from when she was a little girl. For a second she wondered if her children, Frieda and Doft, had ever eaten wild-rose petals. He kicked his door shut, his hands full with a black book and a half-eaten banana.

A woman dressed in black slipped her arm through the man's elbow hole, her dark glasses behind the veil of her black hat making Oata think about President Kennedy's wife at the funeral. Her black gloves gripped a shiny black purse, and in the shadow of the sundown her lipstick looked black, too. Later, in the curling rink waiting room, Oata saw it was a very dark red, like chokecherries almost ripe.

The couple crossed the gravel to the curling rink, the man eating his banana, the woman stumbling along beside him in her black high heels. Oata slipped off her bleacher seat. Yasch and the children didn't even notice as she bumped her hip against Simple Hein's three-wheeler bicycle, rattling the empty beer bottles in the basket. Her family was all yralled up with watching the baseball game, and later that was a problem because nobody from the game would agree that they had seen a black Lincoln that June Saturday evening. No ball fans saw Schneppa Kjnals holding the Gutenthal Curling Rink door like maybe he was waiting for Queen Elizabeth and Prince Philip to walk through. The wild-rose man shoved the last bit of banana into his mouth, dangled the yellow peel upside down for a second, then flexed it away. Oata saw it land in the patch of pigweed in front of the curling rink. With a slight bow to Schneppa Kjnals, the wild-rose man led his woman in through the curling rink door.

Schneppa Kjnals watched a fly ball arc into centre field and drop to the grass a foot away from the Gutenthal fielder's reaching glove. Then he stepped back into the waiting room and let the door close behind him even though he had seen Haustig Neefeld sauntering toward the curling rink, with Thecla Thiessen and her cherry-red hair about three steps behind.

After seeing Frieda's green hair that afternoon, the red hair wasn't so shocking, though Thecla's style was a lot wilder than Frieda's and it made Oata think about a rooster comb the way it spiked up almost straight. Oata glanced back at the bleachers to see if Frieda had noticed her friend, but even as she saw Frieda jump up and cheer a fly ball into the sky Oata also saw Thecla Thiessen in her bedroom, naked beside the lacy white wedding dress spread out on the four-poster bed. Oata blinked and hurry turned to see Thecla slip into the curling rink after Haustig Neefeld.

Politicks Paetkau clattered his cream-yellow half-ton into the yard and, as he got out, a woman in pink skirt-shorts with nylons and white runners climbed out of the *Winnipeg Daily Witness* car and slipped her arms into a navy-blue blazer. She paged through a notebook as she walked, stumbling into a qwaulem of mosquitoes in the foot-high grass beside the curling rink. She slapped at the bugs and ran after Politicks Paetkau who smiled as he held the door for her.

Oata hadn't heard anything about a meeting in the curling rink, but it looked more interesting than the ball diamond so she schluffed across the grass toward the door. Hippy Pauls bounded into the yard on his Japanese jeep with no roof and stopped beside Tape Deck who was crawling out of his van with a tape recording machine slung over his shoulder. CD hopped down from the other side with a ball microphone in her hand. As Oata held the curling rink door for them she wondered if CD had to pay sales tax on her tiny clothes. Half a dozen dusty 100-watt bulbs shone from the low ceiling onto three rows of stacking chairs. On the platform behind a folding table Schneppa Kjnals poured water from a peach Tupperware jug into an avocado Tupperware tumbler. The wild-rose man rested one foot on the platform, elbow on his knee, cheek on his fist, the black book still in his other hand. He winked at his woman sitting in a front-row chair, and Oata thought the woman pulled something black out of her purse. Schneppa Kjnals fingered the ring of keys hanging from his belt. Then he remembered something and hurried under the washrooms sign, down the connecting passage to the skating rink. Oata sat down on the end chair in the last row so the platform wasn't cut in half by the telepost. Schneppa Kjnals returned with a varnished portable pulpit sporting a Gutenthal Community Centre crest and set it between the Tupperware jug and the tumbler.

Politicks Paetkau got a quick glance at the newspaper woman's nylons as she sat down in the second row just in front of the left telepost. Later, Oata wrote that Cora Lee Semple had been in Politicks's History of Western Civilization class in first-year university and he remembered her because she always asked at least one question in each class. Even then, Cora Lee had been wearing the navy-blue blazer. And now Politicks liked to read her column in the *Winnipeg Daily Witness*.

Tape Deck Toews set down his tape machine three chairs away from the black-dressed woman. CD sat next to him and later she would tell Oata that the woman had been crocheting with black yarn. Hippy Pauls turned a chair around in the last row and sat down, resting his elbows on its back. Thecla Thiessen hugged one knee and made a quick face at her reflection in the dark spectator windows, and in her head Oata saw Thecla sticking out her tongue at her naked freckled self in the mirror beside the four-poster bed. Haustig Neefeld leaned against the right telepost, carpenter's pencil behind his ear, Farmers' Union notebook sticking out of his shirt pocket. Oata thought he looked like he wasn't quite ready to commit himself by sitting down, and in her head she saw him back away from the crop insurance office with the freshly washed grain truck, then stop in the middle of Main Street beside the Pool elevator. She saw the elevator shadow cut the truck in half.

The wild-rose man stopped whispering as Schneppa Kjnals stepped down from the platform and leaned against the wall next to the light switches. Lips twitching slightly, the wild-rose man counted the people, boosted himself up onto the platform, and laid his black book on the little portable pulpit.

Just before he began to speak, Oata recognized him. She wasn't altogether surprised and she remembered how the waiting room had been packed so full Haustig Neefeld had moved the meeting into the ice part and hurry wired up some loudspeakers so everybody could hear this candidate who was running for the leadership. For sure it was him, even if then he had been dressed in a windbreaker and baseball cap like a farmer going to a meeting. It was him, even if his hair was fixed by the hairdressers and his suit sure hadn't come from the cheap end of Vaumst Voth's Men's Wear store. Oata was almost figuring out the woman in black when the man opened his mouth, and another memory flitzed through Oata's head that made her smile and go red at the same time. But when a man opens his mouth behind a pulpit, a Gutenthal woman knows enough to listen, or to keep quiet at least, and Oata tasted rainbow ice cream as she heard his words.

Ladies and Gentlemen, fellow Canadians, Manitobans, Westerners, Gutenthallers—my name is Yeeat Shpanst.

Haustig Neefeld almost fuhschlucked himself when he heard Yeeat Shpanst come right out and say his name. His fist went up to his mouth to stop the combination cough and burp that rose from his throat. Politicks Paetkau, too, brought his hand up to hide a quiet laugh. He had still been in university when Yeeat Shpanst had run for the leadership and he had never quite believed that such a thing had really happened. Even as he looked at this man on the platform he waited for him to smile at his own joke. Oata Siemens shivered just a little, for even though she had recognized him, it wasn't until he said his name out loud that she was forced to deal with the reality of who he really was and what that could mean.

On the platform Yeeat Shpanst cleared his throat.

It has been almost seven years, since I last addressed you here in this, your two-sheet natural ice curling rink. I commend your courage and determination in keeping this tiny rink open, despite all the pressures impacting on your community today. I hold your hard work in the highest esteem. And it is in efforts such as yours that I find the inspiration for a new vision of Canada.

Thank you all for coming. I could understand if none of you had come. I failed you in 1983. I fell from my purpose and gave in to the wiles of a beautiful woman. I forgot my faithful supporters here in Gutenthal and disappeared in a Triple E van. I know how you must have felt betrayed, embarrassed, humiliated, relieved that I never got to the convention floor, never got on TV, never made the cover of *MacLean's*. Absolutely! You had absolutely every right to feel that way! Absolutely!

Haustig Neefeld's cheeks went red and Oata thought about how smeared on her neighbour had felt when Yeeat Shpanst febeizeled himself in Ottawa at that convention. Haustig's wife told Oata that during that whole leadership campaign when

Haustig had worked for Yeeat Shpanst, never once had he shaken the man's hand.

But I can explain all that. Yes, I did disappear from the convention in the Triple E van with a beautiful journalist named Barbara. Barbara and I have travelled all over Canada and we have visited every continent during the last seven years—yes, I'll admit, we visited a game farm in South Africa, but we visited the black townships, too. That's why it is so wonderful to have a woman like Barbara who knows how to find the out-of-the-way people and places mostly ignored by the media. In Asia we talked with women forced to be prostitutes in the streets after being discarded by multinational electronics companies operating in "free trade zones." We talked with Barbie Doll company workers who were given bonuses if they underwent sterilization. My point is that my apparent fall in 1983 was no fall at all, but rather a new beginning, a period of inner growth and outer awareness.

I have returned to Gutenthal tonight to present you with a new vision for Canada. And I chose the Gutenthal Curling Rink deliberately, with extreme care, because in this two-sheet natural ice curling rink I see Canada—a distinct society. In this curling rink I see a people determined to preserve their culture. Artificial ice isn't all that it's cracked up to be. And it's not distinct. You can have artificial ice in Los Angeles, but how does that help curling in Gutenthal? My friends, you have decided that curling in Gutenthal is important. It is what you want. And you have fought to keep what you value. This is what Canada must do.

The plan I will outline for you tonight will help to bring this about. It will help us to survive under the free trade deal. It will strengthen our distinct society. It will wipe out the deficit and free the First Ministers from the stress of having to go to the lake and leave them with the energy needed to attack the problem of the survival of the planet.

This afternoon you heard the Prime Minister declare that

today was a dark day for Canada. Why? Because the scheming plans of his government were toppled. A dark day for Canada, he said. But we Canadians know better. We Canadians know this is a glorious day for Canada, a glorious day because the scheming plans of a government were toppled, not by a band of thugs with guns, not by politicians making deals, not by invading foreign troops. No, this is a glorious day for Canada because the scheming plans of a government were toppled by one man holding an eagle feather, shaking his head.

My friends, we live in a great country. But it is in grave danger. That is why I have decided to devote my life to saving this great nation, this nation too important to be left to the politicians. I have a vision! I have a vision of a future for . . . uh . . . a future for . . . ugh . . . a future . . . oh, my heart . . . a future for . . . Can . . . I-I-I can . . . t . . . reach . . . water . . .

Politicks Paetkau didn't actually see Yeeat Shpanst grip the little pulpit on the table in front of him and drag it with himself when he crumpled down to the platform. That much Oata could say for sure. Tape Deck Toews said Yeeat Shpanst's face was milk white when he reached for the water glass; Hippy Pauls insisted it was beet red when he fell, for sure a lot redder than the wild rose in Yeeat Shpanst's lapel. Hippy didn't say it, but he had been wondering if wild-rose petals would make good wine. Politicks Paetkau looked up only when Yeeat Shpanst hit the planks and then he was sure Yeeat Shpanst's face was coloured more like a striped watermelon. Politicks didn't see the fall because he had been looking at a tiny run in the nylon on the inside of Cora Lee Semple's upper knee, the one she was leaning her notebook on, the notebook she was writing in while Yeeat Shpanst was speaking. Politicks Paetkau had always been interested in runs in women's nylons. That much Oata could say for sure, too.

But Politicks Paetkau saw Yeeat Shpanst when he was crumpled down on the platform. He saw Yeeat Shpanst's black book slip between two planks and disappear.

For a minute it was so still a person could have heard a bobby pin drop onto a feather pillow. Then a bat knacked a baseball on the diamond outside. Ball players cheered, and just before Schneppa Kjnals jumped onto the platform and crouched over Yeeat Shpanst, a woman screamed, "Slide home to the base! Slide home to the base!" Schneppa Kjnals felt for a pulse on Yeeat Shpanst's neck. "Get me the plunger from the toilet!" he yelled. Thecla Thiessen, cherry-red hair spiking up like a rooster comb, ran out of the waiting room. Kjnals laid Yeeat Shpanst out on his back, pulled off his tie, and tore open his shirt. When he found the breastbone he started pumping down on it with the heel of his hand.

"Sure you know what you're doing, Schneppa Kjnals?" asked Hippy Pauls, a bit of spit dripping down his lip into his bird's-nest beard speckled with grey like his ponytail hair.

"Took mail-order CPR, Hippy," Kjnals muttered.

Thecla Thiessen's rooster hair combed back into the waiting room. Schneppa Kjnals grabbed the plunger from her, put the suction cup down on Yeeat Shpanst's heart, and started plunging like there was three-ply paper stuck in a flush toilet.

"What you do, Schneppa Kjnals? What you do?" Haustig Neefeld waved his Farmers' Union notebook.

"It was in the newspaper yesterday," Schneppa Kjnals gasped. "A plunger is better to use than a hand!"

This much Oata was sure of, she wrote later. Schneppa Kjnals pumped away like his mail-order book and the newspaper had learned him. He pumped so hard he almost had a heart attack himself, but he didn't stop.

After that, though, it gets kind of muzharich. Haustig Neefeld said he heard the bat knack the baseball again, and Thecla Thiessen, eyes earnest as her cherry-red hair, said she heard a little boy scream, "Holy doodles over the fence!" And Politicks Paetkau was sure he saw Cora Lee Semple stepping with one runner on the platform so she could balance her notebook on her knee to write. Later, Cora Lee would write in a newspaper column that never got printed how the scene had made her think about assassination, like what happened to Kennedy and Reagan, how a troubled politician's reputation can sometimes be rescued with a well-placed bullet. And Schneppa Kjnals remembered plunging on Yeeat Shpanst's bare-naked chest, thinking how it was interesting that Yeeat Shpanst only had hair growing on the heart side of his chest, the other side as bald and smooth as a baby's bum, and then the next thing he knew the plunger was fortzing on the bare wood and no Yeeat Shpanst was lying there on the platform.

No Yeeat Shpanst.

Haustig Neefeld said that one second he had been glutzing at Yeeat Shpanst's nose, then suddenly he had been glutzing at a knothole in the plank. Hippy Pauls remembered for sure that Yeeat Shpanst's left foot had moved itself just a little bit and then he was looking at a black streak, the kind made by the rubber heel of a Sunday shoe. Thecla Thiessen remembered staring at Yeeat Shpanst's fingers and for sure she would affirm in court that Yeeat Shpanst's fingernails had clear nail polish on them, and all of a sudden she had been staring at the row of nails in the plank. Later, with a carpenter's pencil, Oata Siemens would write in a Farmers' Union notebook that the wild rose had closed up and turned black at the tips of the petals just before Yeeat Shpanst vanished, but of course she didn't write it down right then because Haustig Neefeld still had the notebook himself and anyways Oata hadn't started writing in Farmers' Union notebooks yet. Tape Deck Toews, who had been recording Yeeat Shpanst's speech, was sure he left the tape machine running when Yeeat Shpanst fell down and that if only he could find his tapes he would be able to prove that Yeeat Shpanst and the little pulpit had crashed down. His microphone was so sensitive, for sure the fortzing noise of the plunger would be on the tape. But, like Yeeat Shpanst himself, his tape was gone, his recording machine and cassette bag empty, only he didn't notice that until after everyone had left the curling rink without saying a word to each other.

When they came out of the Gutenthal Curling Rink the baseball game was still on. Oata was sure Thecla Thiessen saw

Ylips Loeppky slide into second base, but afterwards, when Oata started fuscheling around a few careful questions, those who had been at the ball game maintained that nothing was going on at the curling rink that evening and First Base Banman, who ran to the curling rink door three times because of Pitch Peters's foul balls, said for sure the curling rink had been locked the whole evening, even the extra summer padlock had been hanging on the hasp. The only thing to match up was that First Base Banman slipped on a banana peel on his second chase after Pitch Peters's foul ball. He noticed the padlock on the curling rink door because that's what he was looking at when he was getting up off the ground. And Oata Siemens had one recall as clear as Clear Lake: when Yeeat Shpanst had crept out of his black Lincoln he had been eating a banana and he had dropped the peel on the pigweed in front of the curling rink door.

Remembering the banana peel made her recall, too, Yeeat Shpanst's girlfriend, Barbara, the hartsoft beautiful journalist, sitting in the front row with a black dress and sunglasses on, and Oata was sure Politicks Paetkau had seen her nylons were black; Thecla Thiessen had noticed the chokecherry-red fingernail polish; and Haustig Neefeld, who usually didn't notice anything about women except if his wife didn't have faspa ready on time, even he had seen the woman's little black hat, useless for holding off the sun, with black mosquito netting yet hanging down over the face, just like the hat Mrs. Diefenbaker wore the time she and Honest John visited by the Waffle Shop in Steinbach at the Dodge Penner garage. And Haustig had remembered, too, that her name was Barbara from the leadership in Ottawa when Yeeat Shpanst had febeizeled himself the first time. Oata was sure Barbara in the black dress hadn't come outside with them when they stepped out of the Gutenthal Curling Rink. And she could still see a black spider crawling out of the banana peel lying on the pigweed beside the curling rink door. Later that same night Oata felt something crawling over her bare leg and she woke up from a dream about a black spider with fuzzy legs disappearing into the crack where Yeeat Shpanst's black book had fallen when he crumpled down.

What could they say to each other? They were like civil servants afraid they might uncover their behinds if they admitted they were having trouble convincing themselves that they hadn't febeizeled their brains. They were scared to speak until they had tested some things out for themselves. Hippy Pauls hurried himself to the beckhouse beside the curling rink to see if he could still hit the left hole by aiming only with one hand, and Tape Deck Toews schluffed off to his audio van to make sure his Carol Baker gospel tape still played. And then Oata felt herself stumble into the three-wheeler bicycle basket and the clinking of the empty beer bottles brought Simple Hein running from his spot by first base where he was coaching stolen bases for both teams.

"Oata! What the heck you do with my beer bottles?"

Oata blinked her eyes and looked along the row of parked vehicles. The black Lincoln wasn't there. None of the vehicles whose drivers had been in the curling rink was on the yard. Oata thought Haustig Neefeld's three-ton grain truck was just driving onto the road but, looking against the setting sun, she couldn't say for sure.

Yasch Siemens and his children didn't even notice Oata slip back onto the bleacher beside them to sit through the bottom of the ninth inning, which took a long time because of all of Pitch Peters's foul balls. And for the second time that day Oata felt like she maybe wanted to die, and she heard her mother's voice muttering, "Where is that Yeat Shpanst anyways? How come Life Savers always have to febeizel themselves?" Only, just before the sun hid itself behind the world for the night, it sent one golden streak upward just as Pitch Peters knacked the baseball high into the fading sky, and a long-ago beetfield chorus schwietered through her head, making her believe that wonderment was possible even on such a dark day with the ball dropping itself right into the centre fielder's waiting glove.

9 BEETFIELD CHORUS

That blue car has driven by here two
times already.
Who is that anyways?
Who?
That blue car there.
Which blue car?
That one over there,
Politicks.
It has driven by here two times already.
You don't know who that is?
No.
Never saw that car before.
(whisper) That's Yeeat Shpanst.
I know who it is.
(whisper) Mayor von Altbergthal.
You mean you know who it is?
Yeah.
Well, tell us then.
That's Yeeat Shpanst.

Yeeat Shpanst?

Yeah, Yeeat Shpanst, the mayor von Altbergthal.

                    Altbergthal doesn't
                    even have a mayor.

           What kind of name is Shpanst anyways?

What? You nevers to school went?

                    What's that got to do
                    with anything?

Lots. You nevers heard about Sir Patrick Spens?

                    Sir Patrick Spens, like in the litterchure
                    book?

Yeah sure, Shpanst is Flat German for Spens, and Yeeat
Shpanst is the mayor von Altbergthal.

                    I got cousins by
                    Altbergthal and they
                    nevers said nothing
                    about any Yeeat
                    Shpanst that is the
                    mayor.

Aw, your cousins are probly too busy kissing frogs by Buffalo
Creek trying to change themselves boyfriends from Puggefeld.

                    You just hold your
                    frate shut, Politicks
                    Paetkau, or I'll close it
                    with a handful of frogs
                    yet.

Best jealous! Best jealous!

Oata didn't say a word to Yasch about what happened in the curling rink. She didn't speak to anyone about this Yeeat Shpanst with the pink wild rose in his dark suit who made a speech, fell down, and febeizeled himself right when Schneppa Kjnals was trying to make him live up again with that plunger. Oata didn't say a word, not even to Haustig Neefeld waiting for them when they came home from the baseball game. Oata tried to look Haustig Neefeld in the eye, but he just looked away and talked only with Yasch like she wasn't even there.

Oata didn't know what to do, but for sure she didn't go into the house while Yasch and Haustig made the deal for the truck. No, Oata stayed outside under the yard light and looked the truck over carefully along with Doft and Frieda and she caught Haustig glutzing at Frieda's green hair. Though Haustig was trying not to let on that something was wrong, Oata saw his hand tremble when he folded Yasch's credit union cheque into his shirt pocket. Oata thought of offering to drive Haustig home by saying that she wanted to neighbour with Pienich

Neefeld about something, just so she could check out with him what had gone on in the Gutenthal Curling Rink. But Haustig wouldn't look her in the eye, and Oata started to shiver a little over what she would see if he did. Besides, what would Pienich Neefeld think if her neighbour, Oata Siemens, brought her man home in the middle of the night when there was a moon rising through the oak trees along Mary's Creek?

Then, as Yasch and Doft drove Haustig Neefeld home, Oata heard the low brumming of an airplane in the sky. "Sounds like Bulchi Wiebe," Frieda said beside her. "Maybe visiting by Schneppa Kjnals's Mama again."

Oata laughed a little, and as she put her arm around her green-haired daughter she remembered Adelaide Thiessen advertising for a husband, a husband who had never answered the ad, and now green-haired Frieda was going to be bridesmaid for Adelaide's daughter, Thecla, with cherry-red hair spiking up like a rooster comb. Oata wanted to ask Frieda if she had seen Thecla at the baseball game, but a strange shiver stopped her as they stepped through the opening in the Chinese elm hedge onto the planks leading to the cement step. She remembered how, during the curling rink meeting, she had seen Thecla in her bedroom sticking her tongue out at her naked reflection in the mirror, and even as Oata reached to open the screen door she saw Thecla again in front of the mirror wrenching her skinny freckled body into gruelich shapes as she chanted:

Iesaak, Shpriesack
Schlenkjafoot
Schleit siene Brut
Em Kjalla doot.

Oata shivered as she switched on the kitchen light and sat down at the table. She hugged herself as she stared at Thecla, so close Oata could count the goose pimples on her naked skin.

"You want coffee, Mom?"

Oata saw her reflection in the dark window looking out to the garden. An embroidered rose in the tablecloth pressed into her elbow. Something else was trying to seep into her brain out of the darkness on the other side of the glass. "Fellow Canadians," she mumbled, "this is a dark day for Canada."

"What's that you said?"

"Huh? Oh, nothing."

"You want coffee?"

"Uh, no. I think I'll just go to bed."

11 BEETFIELD CHORUS

Nah yoh, who won the ball
game?
Wasn't there, had to wash my hair.
Sweet shampoo good for getting
mosquitoes to come.
Not beer shampoo. Mosquitoes don't bother me
with beer shampoo.
Beer is for drinking
after Prachadarp wins
the baseball game.
Prachadarp won?
Yep, Gutenthal was just a holy error all evening.
First Base Banman
almost knocked
himself out chasing
foul balls and slipping
on a banana peel.
So who was eating banana by the
baseball game anyways?

Yeah, bananas only make the mosquitoes worse.
Not like oranges. Oranges keep mosquitoes away.
                    Yeah, sure and tomato juice is
                    good for skunk perfume.
Haustig Neefeld sold his truck.
                    The one Needich Neefeld used for
                    picking up girls?
Same one, sold to Yasch Siemens late in the night after the
ball game.
          So?
Pienich Neefeld said her man was all white in the face when
he came home from selling the truck, white as a wedding dress
in the sun.
                         Washed white as snow.
                         So who will drive Haustig Neefeld's truck
                         you think?
          Maybe Yasch.
                                   Maybe Doft.
Maybe Frieda.
                    Maybe Oata.
     Oh mensch, these rows are long.
                         Yeah, will we ever finish this
                         field?
It's not August yet. What's the hurry?
                              Yeah, we all got a
                              tough row to hoe.

12

Politicks sipped Pinklich's dandelion wine, hardly even noticing the taste. He hadn't felt this way since his father's death when, for the first few days, the world had been like the television pictures running in front of his eyes, and he hadn't been able to muster up enough energy to get up and switch the television off and bring the real world back. That's how he felt now, shaken by Yeeat Shpanst's heart attack in the curling rink, shaken by the strange vanishing, and the thought that his heart attack, too, might come before he had done something really useful with his life.

When the local news finished, Politicks set down his wineglass and reached for the pencil and note pad on the end table. The LOTTO 6/49 machine appeared on the screen, and like he did every Saturday night Politicks wrote down the numbers as the six balls popped out of the machine and rolled down the chute. This time he wrote down 36 15 20 27 13 49. Politicks never got very excited about the LOTTO 6/49, for he spent only a dollar each Saturday afternoon when he went to the Gutenthal Store for the mail. And he always played the same numbers, numbers he had decided would be his lucky numbers, numbers that all had something to do with his wife, Pinklich, who liked to go to bed early on Saturday nights and never even noticed him writing down the winning numbers when they rolled down out of the machine. It was just one of those little secret things that a man had to do.

Politicks himself was usually pretty dozy by this time on a Saturday night, especially when the glass he was using for the dandelion wine was an eight-ounce tumbler, and what with his brooding, the numbers he was copying from the TV didn't really sink in at first. Often he didn't even bother to check them against his ticket because he always played the same numbers, but as he got up to turn the TV off he suddenly looked at the note pad again. Then he switched the tri-light lamp to high. 36 14 21 27 13 49. Politicks's heart started to clapper. Thirty-six was Pinklich's brassiere size. She had told him that the time she sent him to Fruelied Fashions in the Flatland Mall to buy her one when he was going to town anyways to get some combine parts. Fourteen was how old Pinklich was when Politicks first noticed her sitting on the desk in the grade 10 room showing off her fishnet nylons on the day John F. Kennedy was shot. Twenty-one was how old Pinklich was when they had tried out her Virginia Slims cigarettes and her new birth control pills the same evening Trudeau invoked the War Measure Act. Twenty-seven was the waist size of Pinklich's wedding dress and forty-nine was the year Pinklich was born. Only the thirteen made no sense. Politicks's sixth number was the most secret of all, the one he would have the hardest time to explain if he had to. That was the number three, the number of girls he had made love to in his life. He was sure he hadn't won the jackpot, maybe the five out of six pot, but he reached for his wallet anyway. When he held the ticket under the lamplight his heart almost did stop. Where he expected a three he had a thirteen. He had all six numbers. "All six fuckin' numbers," he heard himself say, which was strange for him because he just wasn't a swearing man.

There had to be a mistake. But no, all six numbers matched up with the numbers he had copied down. He reached into his pants pocket and found the game card he had marked his numbers on. Sure enough, for some reason he had marked thirteen instead of three. Whatever the reason for his mistake, he had made it, not the machine. "All six fuckin' numbers," he heard himself say again. He couldn't remember how much the jackpot was. He just never paid that much attention to it. He turned toward the hallway door, then stopped himself from calling Pinklich. Carefully he slipped the ticket into his wallet. Then he locked the wallet in the drawer of the small writing desk in the corner.

In the bathroom he turned on the taps and let the tub fill up to the overflow drain, then lowered himself into the almost scalding water. As the heat worked its way through his body his mind wandered at will until he dozed off. He shook himself awake and scrubbed himself with the soapy washcloth, washing hidden nooks and crannies more carefully than he had for a long time. Then he lay back until he felt the water cooling off. He pushed the drain-plug lever with his foot and enjoyed how he got heavier as the water drained away. When the tub was empty, Politicks reached up for the hand-held shower head, pulled back his foreskin and let the water pulse against the purple head of his penis. He shut the water off and dried himself, shaved carefully, brushed his teeth twice, then walked naked into the bedroom.

Pinklich lay on the bed, her thin nightgown open in the heat. Politicks pulled a feather from the pillow and stroked her leg with it, and as they made love in the heat, slowly, endlessly, he had a vision of tall grass growing beside a shallow creek, and as Pinklich reached back around his ass to stroke his balls just before he started to come he saw a buffalo grazing in the tall grass beside the creek. He recognized the clump of willows behind the grazing bison on the banks of Mary's Creek where it cut through the back forty of his very own farm. Pinklich cried out as he thrust deep inside her and she squeezed and squirmed as his orgasm rendered him helpless. He almost told her about the lottery but he was panting too hard. Pinklich pushed at him and he rolled onto his back, and before he could go soft she straddled him and rode him until she collapsed on top of him in a sweaty heap. He didn't come again, but Pinklich did, and it was only after she began to snore on his shoulder that he slipped out like a wet noodle.

PART TWO

It's the told story that affects the national interest. A waved flag has more power than a statistic.
—Koadel Kehler, the teacher's son

13

"**Y**ou had to drive to Haustig Neefeld's place for a Farmers' Union notebook?"

"And a carpenter's pencil."

"And a carpenter's pencil?"

"Yeah."

"Now, right in the middle of thrashing?"

"Yeah."

Later, Oata would write in her Farmers' Union notebook with the stubby carpenter's pencil that at first she really thought there was a mosquito between the pages and didn't want to believe that the buzzing could be words trying to meddle their way in between the verses right there where she had been reading the Beatitudes in this Good News Testament, well, sort of reading, but mostly glancing at the little drawing of the people going up the mountain. Oata hadn't been sure if she liked this different kind of Testament where, instead of, *Blessed are the poor in spirit,* the way she knew it off by heart, Jesus was saying, *Happy are those who know they are spiritually poor,* but when Oata got to where it said, *Happy are you when men insult you and mistreat you,* these mosquito kind of words started buzzing right there on the Testament page.

Even when she glanced up through the windshield and saw Yasch waving with both his arms and she hurry stepped on the clutch and turned the key to race the truck across the stubble to line it up under the auger spout so that Yasch could empty the hopper without stopping the combine, the mosquito words still kept buzzing from the Good News Testament where she had thrown it down on the dusty dashboard beside the Farmers' Union notebook Yasch had found in the glove compartment when he bought the truck from Haustig Neefeld the same night Yeeat Shpanst had febeizeled himself. Haustig Neefeld was a Co-opich kind of guy who had believed in the Farmers' Union, and there was still a sticker in the back window with three sheaves leaning together in a stook and three sheaves fallen down with some words underneath, and while the barley was pouring down into the truck Oata liked to sing the old hit-parade song with the same words, "United we stand, divided we fall." And in the hot barley dust blowing over the cab Oata felt happy, united with Yasch, moving together with him until the auger rattled empty and she stepped on the clutch and the combine pulled ahead, swallowing the swath and blowing strawdust across the harvest sky.

But the Testament was still buzzing, so she picked it up and as she read, *Happy are you when men insult you and mistreat you and tell all kinds of evil lies against you because you are my followers. Rejoice and be glad, because a great reward is kept for you in heaven,* the words buzzed like a mosquito over hot skin on a sleepless night, buzzed loudest right after *insult you and mistreat you.* So she read it out loud, only this time she stopped right after *mistreat you* and the mosquito voice buzzed so loud inside her head she had to open her mouth to let the words out: *I for sure wasn't happy when the boys in school used to call me names. I for sure wasn't happy when they locked me in the beckhouse at recess time and nobody let me out when the teacher rang the bell. I for sure wasn't happy when Forscha Friesen told Ask the Pastor that I was making Yasch do sinful things when I was with him only engaged. I for sure wouldn't be happy if Yasch gave me one with his fist in the eye the way some women I know get it and are afraid to come to church on a Sunday morning.*

Yasch was waving her to come, so she swallowed those words until the truck and the combine were fuscheling together with the pouring grain and she could say, *I for sure wouldn't be happy if Yasch talked to me like I was a mother dog and kicked me in the ribs because the soup was too hot, and I wonder me if Kunta Klassen's wife is happy when he comes home from worrying in the beer parlour about the farm credit loan interest and calls her a bitch because the supper she has been holding for him has gotten cold. Does she rejoice? Is she glad enough to collect that reward in heaven? If she is not happy, will she still get to go?*

When the combine auger rattled empty again Oata drove the load to the yard. It was good, she thought, that Yasch's Muttachi was looking after the children, because otherwise they would be bizzing around the truck cab and getting their arms caught in the auger and stuff like that. Didn't you hear what happened to that Schroeder family by Yanzeed where the four-year-old bengel lost his hand in the auger when he dropped his little shovel into the chute and reached in to get it back? Was that mother happy? Can a person get to heaven only if she is happy to be unhappy?

Later, Oata would write in her third or fourth Farmers' Union notebook how it was right after she wrapped the starter rope around the pulley that her fingers got so itchy she wanted to hold ice, until she scrambled to the cab and rummaged around in the glove compartment for the carpenter's pencil and wrote down in the Farmers' Union notebook the words the mosquito-buzzing voice from between the pages of the Good News Testament was telling her. With that flat wide pencil made to write on a two-by-four Oata wrote down the words that rushed out from her mouth when the truck and the combine and the pouring grain had been fuscheling together and lots more things, too, so there were only two pages left over in that Farmers' Union notebook when the point of the carpenter's pencil got too dull to write anymore. That's when she heard the auger motor sputter and die.

When Oata hurried behind the truck she saw she had forgotten to open the chute and that all the barley was still in the box. On the field the combine lights were already blinking on and off, and then yet she spilled some gas onto herself when she was filling the auger motor tank. It was really scary that first time it happened, she would write later when she was a little bit more used to it, because how was she going to explain it to Yasch that right in the middle of augering the barley she had had to write down with a carpenter's pencil in a Farmers' Union notebook arguments a buzzing mosquito was having with a page in the Good News Testament, and yes, she would admit it later in her notebooks, she tried to kill that buzzing mosquito. Yes, she slammed that Good News Testament closed and slapped the seat with it twelve times before she drove back to the combine. But that day Yasch never said a thing because he was worried if he would ever be able to sell his grain, or if he would have to pay the elevator to take the crop off his hands, so he didn't even ask, what for, when she wanted his pocketknife so she could sharpen the carpenter's pencil, and she sat down in the cab and wrote in the notebook, *Happy are you when you ask and receive without being asked, what for.*

Later, in the fourth or maybe fifth Farmers' Union notebook, Oata would write how she stayed awake with the notebook and carpenter's pencil in her hand waiting for a mosquito to buzz over the bed. But the buzzing words wouldn't come and she started wondering if even anything had happened in the cab of Haustig Neefeld's truck. It was so quiet in the bed with just the fan blowing and she lay there in the hot night waiting, wondering, thinking until her head ached, and she went downstairs for an aspirin, only when she got downstairs she didn't switch on the light, or go to the medicine cupboard, and the cement step outside was cool, and the gravel hurt her feet across the yard.

It was so still, like a coffin, she would write in the Farmers' Union notebook, but in the dusty cab light she made herself reach for that Good News Testament on the dashboard, and when she paged to the Beatitudes, her heart wanted to stop. At the same time it wanted to clapper ninety miles an hour. The mosquito was there. Squashed right on the people heading up the mountain to hear the Beatitudes. The mosquito legs almost fit in with the lines of the drawing, where someone was being carried up the mountain. Except for the blood on the facing page. A drop of blood smeared over *Happy are you.* The mosquito was dead. It didn't buzz.

Back in the house, Oata found only one aspirin in the bottle.

"Couldn't you write those words down on a calendar page with a ball-point, or in your recipe scribbler in the evening?"

"No. It has to be a Farmers' Union notebook."

"And a carpenter's pencil?"

"Yeah, a carpenter's pencil."

"Now, in the middle of thrashing?"

"I'm sorry, Yasch, but when those buzzing words come and my fingers start to itch I almost die with craziness until I get that carpenter's pencil in my hand and write in the Farmers' Union notebook. I can't help it, Yasch."

"Well, maybe . . ."

"You think I should maybe go see the doctor?"

"Well, I don't know, I mean, if you feel sick maybe, but it is thrashing time and if you tell the doctor that a mosquito is telling you to argue with Bible verses, that could be scary . . . what do you think?"

"There's nothing wrong with me, Yasch. I just have to write some words down sometimes."

"In a Farmers' Union notebook with a carpenter's pencil."

"Yeah, but I should be okay till thrashing is over because Pienich Neefeld gave me a dozen new ones left over from when Haustig was on the Farmers' Union board."

"I guess that should be okay then, I mean, if you're not feeling sick."

"No, I just have to write."

Later, in the fifth or sixth notebook, Oata would write that she had never loved Yasch so much as right then when he climbed back up on the combine, somehow understanding without understanding, and Oata thought for sure she would make it up to Yasch in the night, but the hot upstairs could have baked bread even with the fan from the Co-op's blowing over the bed, and besides Yasch had been too tired to even snore.

But Oata herself couldn't sleep and at first, as she lay there naked on the bed beside Yasch with the Co-op's fan blowing hot air over her breasts, she thought it was just the heat. One heat drives away another, her mother used to say when she was cooking-in jars of vegetables in the August kitchen, and yes, Oata thought maybe she and Yasch could have driven away one night heat with another. Only, that wasn't keeping her awake.

Feeling sexy had never stopped her from sleeping. She wrote later, when she wasn't afraid anymore to write her secrets, that she slept better if she was feeling sexy. It was the fucking that would wake her up. Oata wrote in the Farmers' Union notebook that when she was feeling sexy it was like she was a blooming flower and that sometimes she just liked to stay that way, instead of being plucked and stuck in a jam jar of water with an aspirin in it so she would still look like she was blooming even when she didn't feel like it anymore. Oata had read in the *Cosmopolitan* magazine by the hairdresser's how some women have all this frustration because they can't get to the big O three times a week along with their three-times-a-week aerobics class and it all sounded quite interesting, especially some of the practice exercises this one article had recommended. For sure Oata would never have said that sex wasn't important to her, but at the same time she couldn't say that it was a frustration. Besides Yasch was a morning man and so getting a cheerio to start off her day was not a problem.

Oata wrote later that as she lay there wide awake in the blowing hot air she felt very much alive. All summer she had been feeling poor in spirit, so poor there had been some days she had hardly made it through. And she couldn't say why exactly during this warm green summer the world seemed so black and white, with more black than white. The summer made Oata feel like those films Schacht Schulz used to show in the Gutenthal school, mostly black and white, especially if they were about schwierich things like wars and fires and coal mines, and Oata would always remember this one film where some gruelich thing had happened like an earthquake and all these brick buildings were crashed down and there were people fallen under those bricks. Some police had been rescuing with a dog and Oata could still see how they found one man with just his head sticking out and how they gave him something to drink from a canvas water bag just like her father, Nobah Naze Needarp, used to take along to the field. And another place in the film they showed a boy maybe fifteen years old clawing out from under the bricks, screaming, his hair falling over his face, his clothes all ripped and one bare foot all blood, and Oata had sure been scared as the boy almost jumped out of the film into the Gutenthal School. And another thing Oata remembered from that same film was a girl, a young woman really, wearing a dark dress with short sleeves, scrambling herself over a steep pile of fallen bricks and stone and she could hardly stay up on her feet with those open-toe high heels on, and Oata couldn't remember exactly, but she thought the girl had had glasses on, too, glasses that were hanging crooked on her face. And then, as Oata lay there naked in the hot night beside Yasch, the beetfield voices started schwietering about what had happened since the Prime Minister's dark day for Canada speech and Yeeat Shpanst's febeizeling himself.

And even before she heard the mosquito buzzing over the blowing fan, Oata rutsched herself backwards so she could lean her shoulders against the cool headboard and she raised her knee in the harvest moonshine and reached the Farmers' Union notebook and the carpenter's pencil off her mother's old white chair beside the bed.

At first she wrote about the Prime Minister's speech and Yeeat Shpanst's febeizeling himself. She wrote how she sneaked glances in church at Haustig Neefeld and Tape Deck Toews, but they'd had such schwierich looks on their faces that she was scared to talk them on. Politicks Paetkau and his wife, Pinklich, hadn't come to church yet after that dark Saturday and Hippy Pauls and Schneppa Kjnals usually weren't there anyways. That Cora Lee Semple woman with the notebook wasn't from Gutenthal and Oata didn't read the *Winnipeg Daily Witness,* though there were some along the Post Road who got it delivered every day. Thecla Thiessen's people went to a church in town, if they went at all, or sometimes Knibble Thiessen would load his whole family in the car and drive across the line to a gospel church where he had lots of States of America patients. Oata had hinted that Frieda should invite Thecla over for faspa so they could talk about the wedding, but so far it hadn't happened even though Frieda's bridesmaid dress was almost finished. So Oata hadn't had a chance to talk about this Yeeat Shpanst business with the red-haired girl.

But Oata had asked Frieda about Thecla and how she was feeling and did it still seem like maybe Thecla wouldn't go through with the wedding. Frieda seemed more mixed up than ever about that. She told Oata that Thecla seemed a bit different in the last while. She was laughing most of the time in a comfortable way it seemed, as if something had been decided in her head that had been bothering her before when she had laughed a lot, too, but sounded like she wasn't quite comfortable with it. At the same time, Frieda said to Oata that Thecla's eyes sometimes shone as if somebody had turned a light on inside and Frieda had said, so quietly Oata could hardly hear it, "Don't say nothing, Mom, but I just have this feeling sometimes that maybe Thecla is on something, though I sure don't smell nothing in her room when I'm there."

"How would you know what it smelled like?" Oata wanted to know, thinking that now she had another thing to worry about.

"You know, Mom. I would be able to smell something different in her room, like if she was smoking grass or something like that. Last year by the borsch supper there were some guys from Prachadarp smoking grass behind the curling rink and I smelled it then."

"They were doing that behind the Gutenthal Curling Rink?"

"Yeah, Mom."

"Was Doft with them?"

"No, Mom."

"Well, you tell me if you ever think Doft is doing such a thing. People can go mental if they start taking drugs."

"Oh Mom, people go mental these days even without smoking grass. Besides, I told you, I can't smell anything at Thecla's place. Please don't start a gossip column about this. I really don't think she is doing drugs."

"I hope not, and for sure don't you let her talk you into doing anything like that."

"Of course not, Mom. I wouldn't touch the stuff. I shouldn't have said nothing because now you'll be thinking that Thecla is a dope addict. It's just that you asked about her and . . ."

"You think there is something wrong?" Oata said when Frieda hesitated.

"Yeah, I guess."

Oata had been quiet for a few minutes wondering what to say next because she felt that this drug business had come between them, that Frieda wouldn't want to confide in her if she got so suspicious about everything she said. "Maybe Thecla is taking pills from the doctor for something. You know, like some women take Valium because of their nerves. Adelaide had to take nerve pills after the baby was born and she couldn't find a man to marry her, even after she advertised in the *Producer* for a husband. For the longest time, till Thecla was old enough to start school, Adelaide couldn't make it through the day without flying on those Valium pills. It was only when she got that job in Emerson at the bank that she started to get over it. Sometimes these things run in the family."

"Mom! I hope not!" Frieda said, and then they had both shoved that thought out of their heads as best they could.

Beside her in the hot bed, Yasch, naked too, was still so silent that Oata almost put her ear to his chest to see if his heart was still beating, the way she used to do when they were first married. She would wake up in the night and Yasch would be so still beside her she figured he was dead, and a couple of times she had woken him up, and the last time she had done that he had barked at her, "If I'm dead, then let me be dead already!" So Oata didn't put her ear to Yasch's chest, but as she lay there she wondered what Frieda, her green-haired daughter, would say if she told her about the buzzing mosquito from the Good News Testament in the cab of Haustig Neefeld's old truck. What would Frieda say if Oata told her how she had felt herself seeing into Thecla's bedroom even as she sat at her own kitchen table? Would Frieda be scared of what was running in the family?

And then, as she leaned back on the bed beside Yasch with the notebook resting on her knee, she thought of Politicks and Pinklich Paetkau not showing their faces in the Gutenthal Church after Yeeat Shpanst febeizeled himself, and before she knew it that carpenter's pencil was writing itself into the living room where Politicks Paetkau brooded in front of the television, sipping Pinklich's dandelion wine, writing down his winning 6/49 numbers. Thinking about what she could do with millions of dollars made Oata miss part of Politicks's bath, and then when he walked naked into the bedroom she wondered if she should make that pencil stop, make that marriage bed into a closed coffin.

Of course they missed church the next morning, Oata wrote, chuckling to herself. Almost she put the carpenter's pencil down so she could roll on top of Yasch to remind him that he had shares in a marriage bed, but then she heard the front door open and close. Doft was home and it was late for him to be coming home. She would have to say something to him in the morning to let him know that he still had parents, but as Doft crept up the stairs in his stocking feet she remembered how when she was driving the truck full of barley to the yard she had been thinking how good it was that Yasch's Muttachi was looking after the kids. Oata hadn't thought it strange at all to be thinking like that when really her kids were too big to be bizzing around a truck cab, and if they were over by Yasch's Muttachi's place it was because the old woman needed help, not because the grandchildren needed looking after.

Shivering, Oata reached for the summer quilt and covered herself, wondering if even the Good News Testament mosquito would be able to tell her what to write down about that. But then, as her brain started fuhlenzing between her thoughts, she saw Politicks Paetkau again, following Pinklich out of their bedroom. She saw Pinklich turn and kiss Politicks on the lips before she slipped into the bathroom and closed the door behind her. She saw Politicks go naked down the stairs, out the back door, to piss off the stoop. Oata thought he would turn around and go back into the house after he finished, but instead he stepped into the grass and began to walk away from the house to the west. And like in a film running backwards a sunset appeared, growing brighter and brighter until Oata saw Politicks Paetkau step onto a beetfield.

A sugar-beet hoe was planted blade up at the end of the third row. Politicks Paetkau ran his thumb along the edge of the blade, then pulled the handle out of the earth, and wiped the dirt from its smooth end. He began weeding the third row, deftly separating double plants, thinning, two hoe-blade widths between plants, quickly cutting the tiny roots under the soft earth, squinting against the setting sun, smelling the soil, smelling the beets, the mustard, the dandelions, thinking he had to get to the other end of the row and back before he could call it a day. Then Oata saw someone else on the field, a shadow at the far end against the setting sun. As the figure got closer, she saw it was a man weeding toward Politicks, a black shadow against the sun weeding toward him in the next row. A man, a man with a hat, a dark hat, weeding quickly, faster than Politicks Paetkau, faster than the Leeven boys, faster than the Ukrainian from Gardenton who weeded for Zamp Pickle Peters.

Politicks Paetkau leaned on his hoe to watch this weeder, to neigbour a few words with him. On a beetfield a person stops to neighbour a few words. The shadowy weeder's hoe moved like a piston, steady, slice slice, push a double, slice slice, push a double, the weeder's back poker straight, neck bent, sweaty felt hat tilted, checked shirt buttoned to the top, police suspenders straight and tight, pink wild rose stuck in the breast pocket, sleeves rolled up the forearm, weeding quickly, steadily, slice slice, push a double, slice slice, push a double.

"Howdy, nice day if it don't rain!" Politicks's voice echoed over the field. Then slice slice, push a double, slice slice, push a double. "Weeding by the row or by the hour?" Slice slice, push a double. Why this guy won't talk? From Paraguay maybe? Can't speak English? Then right beside him in the next row, Politicks Paetkau smelled the sweaty clothes, he smelled the sour breath, he smelled cold earth. And then words. He heard words, Flat German words, "Paetkau, kjikj den curling rink plautform unja!"

"What you say?" Politicks turned to hear the man's words again. But the weeder vanished, *pfft,* just like that. Politicks Paetkau on the field alone turned back to the setting sun, and his heart clappering almost stopped. The shadowy weeder hoed at the other end of the field again, hoed toward him in the next row. Politicks shivered in the evening heat as the weeder hoed toward him, slice slice, push a double, slice slice, push double. "What you say?" he shouted. The shadow weeded furiously, slice slice, push a double, slice slice, said nothing. "What you say?" Politicks shouted again. Push a double, slice slice, push a double. He smelled the sweat, the sour breath, smelled the cold earth. "What you say?" Slice slice. "Paetkau, look the curling rink platform under!"

"What you say?" The weeder vanished, *pfft,* just like that. Politicks Paetkau turned his eyes to the setting sun, again the shadow weeded toward him, slice slice, push a double, slice slice, push a double. "What you say?" Politicks stepped into the next row. "I'm going to hold you up this time," he muttered. "What you say?" The shadow weeded, slice slice. Politicks smelled the sweat, smelled the sour breath, the cold earth. "What you say?" Slice slice, push a double. "Stop! What you say?" The weeder kept on coming. Politicks stood right in the weeder's way. He turned to catch the weeder's chest with his naked shoulder. The weeder spoke again, calmly, coldly, "Paetkau, look the curling rink platform under." The weeder didn't stop. He never touched Politicks Paetkau. But he didn't stop.

Politicks threw down his hoe and flitzed away over the rows. The weeder spoke behind him, calmly, coldly, "Ekj sie Yeeat Shpanst, Paetkau. Kjikj den curling rink plautform unja! Ekj sie Yeeat Shpanst!"

Oata laughed into the hot night as her carpenter's pencil wrote Politicks Paetkau clawing away from that beetfield, naked back to the house, back to Pinklich starting to snore on their bed, and she wondered if Politicks remembered that long-ago beetfield yeschwieta helping the time go by on those half-mile rows under the hot hot sun.

Who?
That blue car there.
Which blue car?
That one over there.
It has driven by here two times already.
You don't know who that is?
No.
Never saw that car before.
(whisper) That's Yeeat Shpanst.

Oata wondered if Politicks still figured there was no such person as Yeeat Shpanst, mayor von Altbergthal. Did Politicks figure he was just somebody made up by Laups Leeven on that beetfield, the other badels playing along to nerk the girls, and then in the falltime they always had a ready essay-writing topic for English at Knackzoat Collegiate? Oata wondered if Politicks remembered how he even wrote about Yeeat Shpanst's pig wedding on the grade 10 departmental exam and passed with a 52 percent, and he bragged that he must have gotten full marks for that essay because he had left out the sight poem and the questions about Henry Before Part V because Politicks figured reading Shakespeare was too much like reading the Bible and he could already do that in Sunday School. And then Oata wondered if Politicks remembered who had fed him the name Yeeat Shpanst on that long-ago beetfield, and she tasted rainbow ice cream on her mind's tongue and she had a last dozy idea that just maybe she could write her way out of this black and white summer all by herself.

14

Later, Oata would write that she should have felt scared on the next Sunday after dinner when she found her mother sitting up on the back of the Lazy Boy chair in the corner of the mental home common room with the remote control switching thing in her hand. The television was on *Newsworld* and the screen showed a Mohawk Warrior with his handkerchief over his face and a machine gun in his hand, nose-to-nose with a soldier hardly old enough to shave himself. Oata's mother glutzed at the TV with the remote control gripped like a doll or a butcher knife, Oata thought, like the time when Doft was two and he took the butcher knife from the cupboard and was holding the blade in his little hands and Oata had never talked so softly and warmly and motheringly as she did then to convince Doft to put the knife down easy on the floor. Oata couldn't understand why her mother would be holding the remote control like that, especially to keep the channel on the news, when over the years if the patients in the mental home had argued at all, they had argued over watching *Edge of Night* or *All My Children* or maybe *Hymn Sing,* but she had never heard about them arguing over watching the news. And her mother mostly hadn't been interested in the television at all.

And when Oata's father, Nobah Naze Needarp, had still been alive, whenever they had come to visit, her mother was always sitting in the common room corner with the checkerboard. If she was playing with another patient, she would be dringent to finish the game before she would pay any attention to them. She would say, "Wacht, ekj mott eascht daumbrat schpaeluh." And afterwards, when the visiting hours were over and they were driving home in the '51 Ford, Nobah Naze Needarp would complain about that fedaumpte brat, that damned board his wife in the mental home always wanted to play when he came to visit. And she wouldn't even play it with him, only with one of the patients or with Oata. And Oata sat in the front seat of the '51 Ford looking out the window while her father complained beside her, and she had wished she could visit her mother by herself to see if she would just want to play checkers then.

Even then, when she was only nine or ten years old, Oata was able to feel that her mother wasn't at all comfortable when Nobah Naze Needarp came close. But what could a person do if she was only ten years old and couldn't drive a car herself to the mental home to see her mother? Nobah Naze only visited on Sundays after church and they would stop by Sleeveless Mary's Drive Inn and have a hot dog to eat and a small 7-UP in a green bottle to drink, even if by Sleeveless Mary's they had hamburgers and chips, too, and soft ice cream. One time Oata had asked Nobah Naze for a hamburger and chips instead of a hot dog, but when he went to Sleeveless Mary's window he ordered the hot dogs and 7-UPs just like always and Oata knew for sure that she shouldn't even think about asking for a soft ice cream cone because it was fifteen cents, and ice cream cones you could only get by Hi-Way Inn on the way home where they would give a double decker for just five cents. Oata always waited in the car while Nobah Naze went into Hi-Way Inn to stand in the lineup, and she watched the other people and their kids coming out licking double decker ice cream cones they had picked out themselves and Oata wished she could go into the Hi-Way Inn and pick out a chocolate or a cherry cone or maybe a rainbow, only Nobah Naze always bought vanilla one Sunday and then fruit the next.

Except one Sunday it was so hot that even Hi-Way Inn didn't have any ice cream left when they came by from the mental home. Even now when Oata was staring at her mother holding the remote control she could still see her father, Nobah Naze Needarp, holding open the Hi-Way Inn door for a short-legged man with a double decker rainbow cone in one hand and a banana in the other, and Oata's heart had clappered with the wish that maybe all the vanilla and fruit was gone and her father would have to buy rainbow cones. She watched the man walk to a funny looking blue car called a Henry J and she saw him reach the rainbow double decker through the car window to his wife on the woman's side, and for a second Oata had dreamed that he was reaching the rainbow cone in through the window of her '51 Ford, reaching the cone to her, and she had closed her eyes so she could taste it better on her mind's tongue. Then she heard her father open his door and even before she could open her eyes he said, "Such a schendlich hot day and Hi-Way Inn has no more ice cream." Before Oata's heart could even stop clappering, Nobah Naze Needarp had pointed at the blue Henry J car and said, "That Yeeat Shpanst there believes yet he is the mayor von Altbergthal!"

Oata had seen how disappointed her father was and had thought maybe this would be a good time to suggest that they should go to the Dairy Dell on the 14A and have soft ice cream instead. Nobah Naze had been thinking maybe the same thing because he drove very slowly along the highway, so slowly some cars even honked them behind, and Oata thought for sure her father would turn in by the Dairy Dell. He even stuck his arm out to signal a turn, but then Nobah Naze saw two motorcycles and these two schuzzels leaning black leather jackets against the Dairy Dell window on such a schendlich hot day that Hi-Way Inn had no more ice cream. They had police kind of caps on, too, the kind called motorcycle caps in the old days before the government got all like communism and made everybody wear safety helmets on a motorcycle and seat belts in a car. But in those days in a '51 Ford there were no seat belts or signal lights even, and motorcycle drivers used police caps. When Nobah Naze saw those schuzzels he said, "With motorsickles yet I don't need to eat soft ice cream," and so he hurry speeded up along the 14A and Oata's chin pressed her arm down on the window glass sticking up out of the door, and she let the green fields blur by as the wind blew through her hair and her mind's tongue licked that Yeeat Shpanst's last five-cent rainbow double decker. The next Sunday Hi-Way Inn had raised a double decker to ten cents so Nobah Naze Needarp only fuddahed himself single-decker cones after that.

But now her father had been gone for so long Oata sometimes hardly even remembered him, and her mother hadn't once played checkers since the day the nurses told her that Nobah Naze Needarp had died. And in the years since then Oata had thought that her mother could maybe leave the mental home and live in the world again, and for sure the doctors sometimes said she was making progress, but never quite enough. Even when Oata had wanted to bring her mother home for Christmas day, it seemed like she always got a bad flu and couldn't come. And for sure, what with marrying Yasch and having the children, and making a go of the farm that was half hers and half still her mother's, Oata herself had been so busy sometimes she had tried to get a mental home visit over with quickly. But always a person had to stay at least till five minutes after visiting hours.

But here was her mother perched on the back of the Lazy Boy chair in the mental home common room with the television remote control in her hand, muttering as she glutzed at the Mohawk Warrior nose-to-nose with the army soldier on the screen. She was muttering just loud enough for Oata to make out the words, "Where is he? Where is he now when we need a leader to get us out of this? Where is the bugger with his smooth talk? Looking in the mirror, blow drying his hair? Where is he now that we've got real trouble?"

"Who, Maam? Who are you talking about?" Oata glanced around at the couches and Lazy Boy chairs all empty, the other patients peeping around the corner from the hall. Hups Hilbraunt, who used to play checkers with Maam, stepped his way carefully into the common room. He was carrying a small wooden nail barrel with a long swatch of hair hanging like a horse's tail from the centre of the hide stretched over the top.

"Oata," he said hoarsely. "Sei lat dei frueiss nijch emol daut TV up pausse."

"You mean, Maam won't let them watch TV?"

"Blouss news. All the time blouss news on. No *Edge of Night* or *Hymn Sing* even. It's Sunday today and no *Hymn Sing*."

A younger woman Oata had seen before but didn't know by name stepped out from behind Hups Hilbraunt. "Yeah, now already for two days she keeps the remote control herself and watches all the time news. How come they have to have news on all the time anyways?"

"Where is he now? Where is the bugger when we need him? Can't he see we're in trouble?" Oata's mother raised her voice to drown out the complainers inching their way into the common room hoping maybe Oata could convince Maam to give up the remote control, or at least to switch away from *Newsworld*.

"Maam, who are you talking about? Who do you mean?" Oata stepped closer. Her mother turned and stared into Oata's eyes.

"Fellow Canadians, we cannot escape history. A house divided against itself cannot stand. Where is the bugger now?"

"See, Oata. See how she's talking crazy! And she just wants to watch out for the news."

"Ha!" Oata's mother turned on a roller-haired woman holding a pack of Cameo cigarettes in her orange polished fingers. "In the kingdom of the blind the one-eyed man is king."

A house divided against itself cannot stand. We must watch the news. We must see!" She turned her eyes back to the TV screen. A reporter losing his hair in the front was talking dringently into a hand microphone and then they showed a parade of cars going over a bridge and then people were throwing stones at the cars, and Oata's mother cried out, "See! Where is the bugger now when such is going on? We must see this! The dice of God are always loaded. The news. We must see the news! It is the absolute right of the States to supervise the formation of public opinion. That's what the bugger said. Now where is he?"

"Who are you talking about, Maam? It's just the TV. It's not happening here."

Her mother stood up on the soft cushion and Oata noticed the forties high heels and charcoal nylons and for a second the girl from the black and white film scrambled herself over a pile of fallen bricks through Oata's head. Then Oata recognized the shoes. Her mother had worn them that one time they had gone to Sawatsky in Winkler to take off a family picture.

"It is happening here," Oata's mother declared. "Such is happening in our country and we can't get even away if after three days men grow weary of a wench, a guest, and rainy weather. Where is the bugger when we need him?"

"Maam! Where are you getting these words from? You have never talked like this before. Now give me the remote control and let your friends watch *Hymn Sing*."

Oata's mother tottered on her high heels, almost sinking through the cushion, then she sprang down to the floor and stood broad-legged in front of the television. She waved the remote control. "Listen people, listen to what the bugger said, listen!" She smoothed the lapels of her housecoat and began to recite the Prime Minister's dark day for Canada words, waving the remote control like Shtemm Gaufel Friesen leading the singing in the Gutenthal Church. And as Oata's voice harmonized with her mother's she felt the patients from the corridor gather around her in the common room and their voices murmured along like a whole church full of people saying "Our Father which art in Heaven," only it was a prayer with no God listening Oata thought, but it seemed hartsoft important to say these words along with her mother, like it was important to turn underwear inside out to rub the lye soap on the brown streaks to wash them white as snow.

"Public opinion wins wars. Why should we subsidize intellectual curiousity? I prefer the dollar sign, the symbol of free trade, therefore, of a free mind. All things obey money. The stupid speak of the past, the wise of the present, fools of the future."

Saying the words along with her mother and the other mental home patients made Oata feel free, free the way she had felt when she was maybe thirteen or fourteen and she had forgotten her overshoes in the Gutenthal Church, and when she went back to get them on the Sunday afternoon she walked down the aisle, up behind the pulpit, and sang Marty Robbins's "Don't Worry 'Bout Me" song into the microphone. Her voice had bounced itself out of the loudspeaking boxes all over the walls and the empty benches and there had been nobody to tell her not to sing because she was sliding off the tune, and it had felt so good, so free, she thought she was going to fly.

"And I say to the provinces, you may have all that the hen lays, except for the eggs. And I say to the aboriginal people, you may have all the freedom and self-government of a dog at the bottom of a well. When the rooster crows on the manure pile, the weather will change or stay as it is."

The other patients murmured along, forgot about watching *Edge of Night* and *All My Children* and *Hymn Sing,* and out of the corner of her eye Oata saw Hups Hilbraunt set his wooden keg on the floor and kneel in front of it, and as he stretched the swatch of hair up from the hide cover and rubbed it between pinched fingers to make a growling brumming sound, Oata felt a power building up in the room, a power like yeast pushing the dough up out of the loaf pan.

"If you buy what you don't need, you will soon need what

you can't buy, and this country could not survive with a policy of unfettered free trade, but that was so long ago, it is hardly true anymore. I'm not denying anything I didn't say."

The on-call doctor and the big nurses and the Sunday orderly came into the common room when they were halfway through the Prime Minister's dark day words a second time, but the chanting was too powerful to interrupt, and later Oata would write that when they got to, "Give me your tired, your poor, your huddled masses yearning to breathe free," she heard the Sunday orderly reciting along with them. She was sure about that because the Sunday orderly was a bass singer in the Community Cantata Choir and his voice had been like a basement under this house of words her mother was building in the mental home common room.

Later, Oata would write in her Farmers' Union notebook that as her mother began the Prime Minister's dark day words a third time, she had felt like something hartsoft wonderful was going to happen, something maybe a bit scary but hartsoft wonderful, and then a horn honked outside, a horn honking a long blast and a bunch of short little blasts and a long blast again, like if maybe a wedding car was driving past with a schuzzel best man nerking the bride and groom as they drove from church through town to Sawatsky's Studio. But the honking blasts didn't pass away like a wedding car would, just got more dringent, and Oata later thought it had sounded like some music she had once heard by mistake on CFAM during the *Evening Classical Concert*. For a second Oata's mother froze with the remote control pointed to the ceiling and in that second of stillness the horn honked once more

BLAST BLAST BLAST

BLAAAAAST

and for another second the whole world was still. Then Oata's mother swung the remote control down through the air and shouted: "FELLOW CANADIANS, WE CANNOT ESCAPE HISTORY. A HOUSE DIVIDED AGAINST ITSELF CANNOT STAND!"

And with a kick of those forties high heels, Oata's mother led all those mental home patients marching from that common room outside onto the green grass cut short like an undertaker's carpet. Oata followed her mother and the patients through the crab apple orchard chanting at the top of her lungs: "I MUST . . . CONSTITUTE THIS COUNTRY. EITHER IT COMES WITH ME, OR IT BREAKS! FOR OUR COUNTRY, WRONG IS RIGHT!" Oata followed her mother's dancing heels, her mother who hadn't kicked up any joy since her wedding evening on the school yard playing the wedding games on the dewy grass by the light of the moon and the headlights of cars, the black high-heeled shoes hidden by the white hem of the wedding dress, the white hem soaked by the endless circling in the dewy grass, the dancing heels leading the mental patients through the crab apple orchard, leading Oata through the fallen crab apples, chanting: "FOR WHEN MEN ARE WELL-GOVERNED, THEY NEITHER SEEK NOR DESIRE ANY OTHER LIBERTY. THE BULLET IS STRONGER THAN THE BALLET!" Dancing through the apple orchard, skidding deliciously on fallen Trail apples, fallen green pie apples, fallen mulchy crab apples, to the white picket fence cutting the mental home off from the road allowance.

Oata's mother rose at the white picket fence, rose up over the sharpened pickets and descended on the other side. Oata saw her mother dance up the side of the ditch to the open door of the waiting Lazy Leisure Camper Company van. It was the biggest Lazy Leisure Camper Oata had ever seen, and each mental patient in turn climbed over the stepladders on each side of the white picket fence, and scampered up the ditch to the waiting open door. Suddenly, Oata's mother's voice echoed from the funnel-shaped loudspeakers mounted on the van roof: "GIVE ME YOUR TIRED, YOUR POOR, YOUR HUDDLED MASSES YEARNING TO BREATHE FREE, THE WRETCHED REFUSE OF YOUR TEEMING SHORE, SEND THESE, THE HOMELESS, TEMPEST-TOSSED, TO ME, I LIFT MY LAMP BESIDE THE TRUE NORTH STRONG AND FREE. O SAY, CAN'T YOU SEE?" Hups Hilbraunt's brummtupp rummeled behind the words, brumm brumm, rummel rummel, fortz fortz.

Oata, panting, stopped on the first step of the ladder. Her mother's voice, now joined by the voices of the mental patients, repeated the revolving chant of the Prime Minister's dark day for Canada words and Oata felt herself pulled up to the next step. Then she stopped again. She looked ahead of herself, looked at that open waiting door on the Lazy Leisure Camper big enough to hold a thousand chickens, looked at the short-legged man behind the steering wheel, saw the elevator heel on the pointed jet boot on the brake pedal, and Oata let her eyes go up the short legs, up over the knees of the bright purple pants, up past the hem of the flowered Hawaii shirt hanging over the sucked-in belly. Knowing already what she would see next, she looked at the pink wild rose blooming on the Hawaii shirt and she looked up higher at Yeeat Shpanst's waiting face, his tongue licking a double-decker rainbow cone, and she wanted to follow her mother into the Lazy Leisure Camper and at the same time she wanted to touch the grass again, step on a crab apple fallen to the ground. Yeeat Shpanst honked,

BLAST BLAST BLAST

BLAAAAAST!

Oata didn't move. Her mother's voice called through the funnel loudspeakers: "I OFFER NEITHER PAY, NOR QUARTERS, NOR PROVISIONS; I OFFER HUNGER, THIRST, FORCED MARCHES, BATTLES, AND DEATH. LET THOSE WHO LOVE CANADA IN THEIR HEARTS AND NOT WITH THEIR LIPS ONLY, FOLLOW ME. IT'S NOT THE SIZE OF YOUR CAUCUS, IT'S HOW YOU USE IT." Oata still didn't move. The door of the Lazy Leisure Camper closed, and with the puff of air brakes and a diesel drone the van pulled away down the government road allowance, leaving Oata frozen on the stepladder inside the white picket fence, her eyes straining after the van until it vanished in the dust. Brumm brumm, rummel rummel, fortz fortz.

Later, Oata would write in her Farmers' Union notebook that she laughed as she suddenly thought about that Cowboy President of the States of America who had called on the people to sing "Born in the USA," like that boy from Springstein camp sings on a tape, and Oata figured for sure that States Cowboy President had never even listened to the words of that "Born in the USA" song because Oata had read the words one day on Doft's little tape-box liner notes, words that hadn't had much good to say about being born in the States of America. And so Oata laughed, figuring if the mental home patients were driving around the country in a Lazy Leisure Camper chanting the Prime Minister's dark day for Canada words through the funnel loudspeakers, maybe people would think they were campaigning *for* the Prime Minister.

Oata laughed up into the white marshmallow clouds floating in the bright blue August sky until the tears dripped off her cheeks and she stumbled down from the stepladder so she wouldn't spear herself on the sharpened white pickets her mother had climbed over so easily. Yes, Oata wrote, it had been a powerful feeling of bread dough rising over the sides of the loaf pans. And without knowing what it all meant, just trusting and glorying in that hartsoft gruelich scary feeling, Oata stumbled and skidded through the fallen crab apples under the trees in the orchard, and she wanted to say something to the Sunday orderly and the two big nurses and the on-call doctor standing on the undertaker's carpet lawn trying to decide which high psychiatrist words they should use to explain themselves, and Oata wanted to say to them, "Now you know what it feels like!," but she was laughing so hard, her gruelich joy bubbling over, and so she just hurried herself past them to the door the Sunday orderly had propped open with the janitor's four-buckle overshoe.

Why she did it, Oata could never explain, but she kicked the four-buckle overshoe out of the way, and as she pushed open the inner door, the outer door locked behind her.

In the common room the TV was still on, still tuned to *Newsworld*. Oata laughed over how her mother had somehow not pressed any buttons on the remote control as she waved it around, leading the patients in chanting the Prime Minister's dark day for Canada speech. But then she stopped short.

"Maybe you should have waited, Maam. There's the bugger now!" Oata quickly swallowed a laugh and stepped closer to the TV. The Prime Minister walked across a platform to a pulpit with maple leaf flags drooping on each side, his back stiff, legs moving like he was a wind-up toy soldier, and Oata saw how the Prime Minister used his left hand to smooth the lapel of his suit jacket all the way down to the buttons, just like her mother had smoothed out her housecoat lapel before she started her chant.

The Prime Minister stepped between the drooping flags. He didn't smile. He didn't tell a joke about the opposition's sexy disqualifications for public office. His voice didn't even sound like a warm radio announcer on a lazy afternoon purring to housewives at their ironing. A fist hammered on the outside door. Oata crouched in front of the TV.

"The government," the Prime Minister started to say, but a small frog stuck in his throat so he stopped to sip from the water glass beside the pulpit. "The government had an answer for Canada. The provinces had an answer for Canada. It was a good answer. A good answer. A good answer to glue the knot in the tie that binds our country together. The government had a good answer for Canada."

The Prime Minister sipped from the water glass again, and as the fist kept hammering on the outer door Oata wondered if it really was water in the glass. "A good answer for Canada. We had a done deal. But . . ," the Prime Minister's teeth gritted themselves like somebody smaller than he was had gotten the better of him. "But we live in a great democratic country, and there are those in our midst who claim that not only did they not like our answer for Canada, they claim they never heard the question." Here the Prime Minister almost smiled and Oata figured maybe he would tell a joke, but those lips tightened around his teeth again. "There are those who claim they never heard the question because a question was never asked, and if it was asked, it was asked behind closed doors by eleven men duly elected by the people of Canada, and there are those in our midst who think that is not democratic enough. And then there are those whose understanding of history includes no knowledge of the past and they claim there was no need to ask a question at all!"

The hammering on the outer door was getting louder, and as the Prime Minister sipped water again, knuckles knacked on the side window, but Oata didn't look away from the TV. The Prime Minister put down his glass, reached inside his suit jacket and pulled out a pair of eyeglasses. When the eyeglasses were slanted across his sweating face he gritted his teeth and looked up, and Oata thought he was looking straight into her eyes. That's what she thought, it felt like he was looking straight into her eyes. Mostly TV people pretend to look out at you but really look at something just a little to the side and a little bit above the place where the people's eyes are at home. But this time it felt like the Prime Minister was looking straight through those slanted eyeglasses into Oata's eyes and she had to make herself look straight back as he said to the people of Canada: "We live in a democratic society. This government is committed to democratic principles. Therefore, though we had an answer for Canada, we will begin anew. We will give the people of Canada an opportunity to have their voices heard. We will determine if there is a question to be asked. We will determine what the question will be. We will determine what the answer will be. We will ask the question. We will let you answer. And not even the door to the PMO washroom will be closed!"

And as Oata stared back into the Prime Minister's eyes she felt something change deep inside her somewhere, like the change in a pump handle when the soaked pump leather seals the cylinder and sucks the first ploomps of water into the empty pail.

"We will consult all Canadians. We will consult every rooster crowing on the manure pile. We will consult every dog at the bottom of a well. We will consult the mountains and the trees. We will consult the rivers and the lakes. We will consult the tundra and the plains. We will consult from shining sea to shining sea to shining frozen sea. Send us your faxes. Call our 800 number. Present briefs to our forums. Attend our weekend conferences. Hold your own forums in church basements. Hold block parties. Talk about our Canada at garage sales and fishing derbies. Tee off for Canada at the golf course. We will have a great debate. We will leave no opinion unturned until we have reconstituted this country! Prepare to find the question!" And then, as Oata feared the knacking knuckles were going to break right through the double window glass, the Prime Minister repeated his dark day for Canada chorus: "GIVE ME YOUR TIRED, YOUR POOR, YOUR HUDDLED MASSES YEARNING TO BREATHE FREE, THE WRETCHED REFUSE OF YOUR TEEMING SHORE, SEND THESE, THE HOMELESS, TEMPEST-TOSSED, TO ME. I LIFT MY LAMP BESIDE THE TRUE NORTH STRONG AND FREE. O SAY, CAN'T YOU SEE?"

And Oata found herself chanting his words again as she turned away from the TV in the common room and skipped down the hall to the front doors of the mental home and the hammering fists got quieter and quieter until she couldn't hear them at all anymore.

15

"I saw him today," Oata said quietly, looking around the waiting room into each eye in the circle. For one eyeblink, nobody spoke; for the next, they all talked at once.

"Who?"

"What you mean?"

"You saw . . ."

"Today?"

"Alive?"

"Where . . ?"

"When?"

"Who?"

"Yeeat Shpanst," Oata said and she told them with a rush of wind what had happened that afternoon at the mental home. Then she closed her teeth down on her tongue even though she felt like a balloon tire pumped up far too full. Haustig Neefeld sat almost straight across from her in the circle of nine and Oata wondered if the mosquito in the Good News Testament had ever argued words with him when he was driving along in the grain truck. But the mosquito was something else again, and right then, biting her tongue, Oata wasn't sure there was a connecting rod between the mosquito and these people who had come to the Gutenthal Curling Rink on this August Sunday afternoon to a meeting nobody had called.

Without warning, Thecla Thiessen stood up, her cherry-red rooster hair trembling on top of her head. "We want to die dancing!" she said. "They can't kill all of us! We want to die dancing!"

After thirty seconds of stillness, stiller than the water that runs deep, all talked at once, even Cora Lee Semple who had never said a word in the Gutenthal Curling Rink before, even she spoke and didn't write anything down. And the gist of what they said in that thirty-seven seconds of everybody talking at once was something like this—at least, both Oata and Cora Lee wrote down the exact same words later, Oata in her Farmers' Union notebook and Cora Lee on her steno pad that rested so beautifully on her knee: WELL, IF THE BUGGER IS GOING TO BOTHER US WITH A QUESTION, LET'S SURE AS HELL MAKE HIM LISTEN TO THE ANSWER! That's what they said, even those who maybe weren't sure if they believed in hell or not.

"How can we do such a thing as that?" Hippy Pauls asked.

"We want to die dancing. They can't kill all of us."

At first they thought it was Thecla Thiessen repeating her words but she was gazing at Barbara, who had lifted off her little black mosquito netting hat and rested it on her crossed knee. Barbara slipped off her sunglasses and spoke again through those dark chokecherry-red lips, "We want to die dancing. They can't kill all of us."

For a moment Oata saw her mother leading the mental home patients up the stepladder, over the sharpened white pickets. In the back of her head she heard that "Lord of the Dance" song the hippies from the Bible College brought home to the Gutenthal Church way back when she and Yasch were first married. And in the same flash Oata remembered how after the Prime Minister made his dark day for Canada speech she had felt like she maybe wanted to die, but now she knew that if she had to die she wanted to die dancing. Even King Herod hadn't been able to kill everyone, and for a second that salami woman danced through her mind with John the Baptist's head on a plate, but Oata quickly let her dance right out through the bone behind her ear where she had her hair pinned back with a bobby pin. The people in the circle weren't Baptists anyway, they were mostly Anabaptists, and Oata grinned as she also wondered who the bobby was with a pin for a last name, but she didn't worry about her dancing thoughts because she wanted to die dancing, and then a mosquito bit her beside the bobby pin, right through to the bone. This was no laughing matter. If the bugger was going to bother them with a question, how could they make him listen to the answer?

Politicks Paetkau cleared his throat, looking away from the stocking run peeking out from under Cora Lee's steno pad. "You know," he said, cowering almost, the way he used to in the political science seminars where others who had no ideas but expressed them anyway took up all the time. "You know," Politicks said again, glancing down at Cora Lee's knee, and then up at her finger gripping the pen. Afterwards Cora Lee wrote that Politicks's words had come out "like a firm sigh": "You know, the way our country is today, I feel like I've lost my political stripe."

The stillness ran deep again for a second. Then Tape Deck Toews said, "Yeah, I think I know what you mean. Like when I was young I was a Marty Robbins fan and I could sing all the words to his gunfighter ballads and the radio announcers used to call him Mr. Teardrop. But then when I was older already I read a magazine about Marty Robbins where it said that he was a real right-wing Republican who was for the Viet Nam war and against doing stuff for poor people and civil rights, and I have never been able to listen to his songs the same way. Even after he grew his hair long and tried to look like a hippy it made things too muzharich for me, and I think what you mean, Politicks, is that it seems like the old songs that used to help us get from one end of the beetfield to the other on a hot day just don't seem to work anymore. And what makes it such a Weltschmerz is that a person can't see any new songs coming from anyplace to help us."

Oata almost said that listening to Marty Robbins sing "My Woman, My Wife" had helped her get through some hot days, but before she could make a fool of herself, Hippy Pauls said, "You mean, we need a new Dylan to sing us a new song?"

"Or a Leonard Cohen," Barbara said.

And then Oata changed her gear so fast she surprised herself. "Listen!" she said, pulling the bobby pin from behind her ear where the mosquito had bitten her. She scratched the bite, then spread the prongs of the bobby pin with her teeth to fasten her hair to her skull. "We have to talk about what has happened here in this Gutenthal Curling Rink. We will never find a new song for ourselves if we don't talk about it. I feel like I've lost a stripe, too, or a will or whatever it is, but something has happened here and like you said, Thecla, I want to die dancing."

Oata paused, but nobody argued any opposition to what she said. "Now, Barbara Spenst," Oata went on, looking at Barbara who was playing with her sunglasses and her black hat on her knee. "Is that your right name? You are Yeeat Shpanst's wife?"

Barbara slipped her sunglasses back onto her face and slowly pulled her left glove off, finger by finger, before she replied. "Partner," she smiled, as she began pulling off the right glove. "Significant other. I'm Barbara Arachnik."

"You mean you're living common-law with Yeeat Shpanst?"

"We live together." When Oata didn't say anything right away Barbara added, "George, or Yeeat as you people call him, never got divorced from his wife. She wouldn't give him one." Barbara looked around the circle to check for understanding of her situation, then she set her black hat on her head, letting the mosquito netting fall over her dark sunglasses to her chokecherry lips. Oata worried that this Barbara Arachnik was going to get up and walk out the door because of her common-law question, and the last thing Oata wanted was for this Barbara to walk out the door because she oyahed herself about something.

"Barbara," Oata said. "Please don't take offense." She paused, wondering herself if she had said it right, then she went on. "Barbara, we have to figure out if we are all crazy or if something real has happened here. And the only way we can do that is if we put all the things we know for sure in front of us and then maybe we can figure out the things we don't know for sure. Does that make any sense?"

The people in the circle didn't say yes, they didn't say no, but they didn't hold their noses at the question neither. Oata sniffed the air carefully, so carefully nobody noticed, and then she went ahead.

Later, Oata wrote that the mosquito must have been helping her because while she talked there was this quiet buzzing behind her ear, a vibration in the bone where the mosquito had bitten her, like a hippy kind of vibe, and even much later, when she was trying to make sense of all this by writing it down in her Farmers' Union notebooks, she wasn't altogether sure if the vibes had been good or bad. But sometimes blind faith was all a person had left.

"Barbara," Oata said, "tell us already for sure what is going on here. Are we crazy? Is Yeeat Shpanst real or is he a ghost?" There, it was out in the open, the question that Oata needed answered. Haustig Neefeld lifted his John Deere cap from his knee to his head. Politicks Paetkau lifted his cap too, but dangled it from his forefinger. Hippy Pauls scratched himself deep inside his bird's nest beard. Tape Deck Toews thought about his missing cassette tapes, the missing proof. Cora Lee Semple bit her lip, nervously skeptical. Oata's question seemed almost as much of a nuisance as the Prime Minister's question. Thecla Thiessen wished that a ghost would explain it.

Barbara uncrossed and recrossed her legs, set her mosquito-net hat on her knee, and pulled her sunglasses off as if she needed remove her mask before she could be believed. She folded her sunglasses into her purse and pulled out a piece of Kleenex. For a second Oata had a crazy thought that Barbara was going to wipe her makeup off with that Kleenex, but Barbara just rested her hands on her purse with the Kleenex balled in her fingers. "You won't believe this," she said. Later, Hippy Pauls couldn't get her trembling mouth trying to smile out of his mind. "I don't know. You live with a man for seven eight years. You travel around the world with him. You listen to his vision of the world every day. And then he's gone. *Pfft*. Man's life's a vapour full of woes. He cuts a caper and down he goes. I loved that man, sinfully even, you might say, but I loved him and I really believed he had a vision that we need. I really believed that, given time and opportunity, he would provide us with the song we are yearning for. I still believe it. I can't explain what happened here that night. I was just like you, listening to his inspiring speech when he collapsed. And then he vanished. Like a mosquito or a puff of smoke. But I can't believe he's gone. I don't believe he's gone." She looked at Oata. "And now you say you've seen him again. It must be true. It needs to be true. We need George. We need Yeeat Shpanst to help us with the question. He is our only hope!"

The stillness that followed ran deep, too deep for Mary's Creek in a dry August. But Barbara did not confess all, did not share what she had seen, what she had felt as she drove home through the night after Yeeat Shpanst vanished. Barbara did not share how it had felt to grip the steering wheel with eight arms, how she had screamed when she looked in the mirror, how each night sleep would not come until she crawled into the banana bunch on the ornamental tree in the solarium. Barbara didn't confess the pain of hearing Oata describe how Yeeat Shpanst had returned to pick up a bunch of crazed mental patients and had ignored her. That bum. She almost stood up to yell, "There is no Yeeat Shpanst! Let's go for a drink and get on with it." But the dread of returning to the banana bunch in the solarium kept her seat pressed to the hard stacking chair. She set her little hat on her head, pulled a handful of black yarn and a silver crochet hook from her purse, and began crocheting rapidly, her eyes darting around the circle.

Something had been lurking at the edge of Oata's brain, and when she noticed Politicks Paetkau glancing at the stocking run that had spread open across Cora Lee's knee cap, she remembered Politicks running naked from the beetfield, but before she could wonder what he would do, Barbara blurted out, "The black book! Yeeat Shpanst's black book. If we are going to make a new song to help us through these times, we need Yeeat Shpanst's black book!"

"What do we want with it?" Oata asked, so quickly she surprised herself again, cutting Barbara off without knowing for sure what it was she was trying to say. Then Oata's tongue took over, even as her eyeballs glanced back and forth between Politicks and the platform like she was watching a ping pong ball: "I mean, sure maybe there is something important in Yeeat Shpanst's black book. We all were in this waiting room when something wondrous happened here, something none of us can understand yet, or even try to explain. If we could, we would have pluidahed it all over the place like it was good news or something. Now sure, it feels like it maybe is good news. It sure felt like good news to me when I saw my mother leading those mental patients over the picket fence into Yeeat Shpanst's camper van. I'm willing to believe. But believing isn't enough. Right now, even after what has happened, we don't know if there is anything to believe in. We don't know if Yeeat Shpanst really has something important to say. I mean, we only heard maybe ten per cent of a speech before he febeizeled himself right in front of our eyes. Barbara, did you ever read in his black book?"

Barbara's chokecherry lips turned almost white. She slowly shook her head, a strip of black netting dangling from her crocheting fingers down over her rhinestone nylon leg.

Oata swallowed some spit and went on. "I don't want to say that Yeeat Shpanst's black book isn't important. It could easy be that what is written in that black book is just what we need to know. Now Barbara, you saw Yeeat Shpanst writing in that black book?"

"Oh yes, I woke up lots of times in the middle of the night and he'd be sitting at the desk writing in the black book. When he noticed me watching him he would say he was writing speeches for the campaign."

"But you never read what he wrote in there?"

"No, I respected him too much to invade his privacy like that."

"Did he ever talk about what he was writing in his speeches?"

"Well, sure, he was always talking about his vision for the country's future. I mean, that's what our life was. We were searching for answers in a new world order."

"And you think the answers are in Yeeat Shpanst's black book?" Politicks asked, sounding like his voice needed a squirt of oil, and Oata wondered how long Politicks would pretend not to know where the black book was.

"Of course," Barbara said, uncrossing and recrossing her legs again. "George's whole vision is in his book. You would have heard it all, had he not been. . . ," here she hesitated like she could be stepping too far out over the mud puddle, "had he not been called."

How could they argue with words like that? All the Gutenthallers in that circle of chairs knew the language, knew about being called, and even if they sometimes twieveled inside their heads about who was really doing the calling it was hard for them to argue out in the open with such words, even Politicks and Hippy who had learned themselves pretty high in university. And actually, it was Hippy who most wanted to side with Barbara about the importance of the black book. He wanted the reassurance of having a text. Hippy had even checked his grandmother's dandelion wine recipes against such texts as he had been able to find. Such was the burden of learning high.

But Oata questioned the importance of having the black

book. Not that she didn't want to believe in the black book or even Yeeat Shpanst's vision of the country. But ever since Eaton's had substituted her a dress completely different from the one in the catalogue picture, Oata had some twieveling doubts about written text, unless of course she had written it herself. And according to that text, it was Politicks Paetkau who had been called to look under the platform.

She had an ally. When Oata came right out and said, "Maybe the black book is important, maybe it has in it only a list of women he will phone when it's time to vote for him, but we can't wait till we find that black book. We can't wait for that," Cora Lee Semple backed her up.

"That's right. You heard what the Prime Minister said this afternoon. We can't wait for a black book to deal with that."

And so it came to pass on that hot August Sunday that the people in the Gutenthal Curling Rink forgot all about faspa. Nobody asked for a cup of coffee or peanut butter and jelly smeared double on a home-baked two-back bun. Nobody asked for another thick slice of vine-ripened tomato. Nobody asked for fresh farm cream to pour onto a slice of scratch chocolate cake.

Nobody even got up to go to the toilet. Tape Deck Toews did go to his Carpet Cleaning and Audio van to get his tape recorder. He set it up on a tenth chair in the centre of the circle. He ran an extension cord to the outlet behind the platform. He made sure he had blank tapes and he checked that the mike was working.

Cora Lee Semple started off by reading from her steno pad the notes she had scribbled down during Yeeat Shpanst's speech. Oata added what she remembered from the speech, though later she wrote that she had mixed in some of the stuff that the buzzing mosquito in the Good News Testament had said, too.

Haustig Neefeld told the tape recorder that he had been worried about the RCMP and their Sputnik infrared satellite camera that could count the aphids on a stem of green wheat, so he hadn't heard exactly what Yeeat Shpanst had anyways said.

Hippy Pauls said that pink wild rose on Yeeat Shpanst's lapel bothered him and he couldn't help wondering if Yeeat Shpanst's vision could possibly just be recycling from the More Debt or Social Credit Party which used to brag about how good it was in Alberta because of the oil wells. Barbara right away jumped in with both high heels to say that the wild rose was a symbol of the prairie and not just Alberta, and to hold the wild rose against Yeeat Shpanst would be like saying the buffalo had only been in Manitoba and just in Saskatchewan would three sheaves of wheat grow number one hard. Oata schmuistahed herself a little behind her hand as she listened to Barbara get excited because, even though a person could still hear the English from Ontario in her voice, she was starting to sound like living seven years with Yeeat Shpanst from Altbergthal was seeping through.

Schneppa Kjnals would have liked it if Barbara had kept on talking with her eyes full of fire because she was giving him a feeling like he was being wrapped up in threads, but she only argued that one thing and then all eyes were on him. He was a bit knocked sideways by this because he had never thought it was his job to actually listen to what was being said on a platform. He had always thought his place was to watch out for everything else while other people listened and so he really hadn't heard a single word Yeeat Shpanst had said. All he could do was tell how in his dreams at night he still heard the fortzing plunger on the bare planks after Yeeat Shpanst had febeizeled himself.

At first Thecla was a little shy, what with her rooster-red hair and all these older people around her, but then she swallowed and said, "It was cool, what he said, you know, that stuff about the prostitutes in free trade zones and the Barbie doll workers getting a bonus if they get their tubes tied. I mean, I never thought about stuff like that before, and man, he just made my head spin with that stuff about being discarded by an electronics factory, and I was thinking about millions of stereos and TVs and radios and computers and stuff all made by women who will be chucked out on the streets to be prostitutes after their eyes and their brains and their fingers are all warped with soldering transistors and computer chips, just so we can listen to Madonna. Talk about revenge for the atomic bomb. Man, I never heard another word the dude said until he like collapsed and split."

Politicks Paetkau wanted to tell Thecla about what was happening in the poultry industry, how free trade forces would put all poultry production and processing in the hands of three or four conglomerates situated in areas where labour laws had no protection for workers. He wanted to tell Thecla that working in an electronics factory was probably paradise compared to working in an eviscerating plant preparing chicken for take-out buckets and barrels. He wanted to describe the poultry plant in the southern States where the employers had locked all the doors to prevent alleged pilfering and twenty-five workers died when a fire broke out. Politicks wanted to say these things, but instead his heavy tongue mumbled, "We have to bring the buffalo back." And he thanked his lucky stars that nobody had heard him, because Politicks was in no way ready to explain what he meant by this sentence that had rumbled up from nowhere.

Tape Deck Toews started to talk about the Gutenthal Curling Rink Accord and about what he called the trickle sideways theory and he said, "What good is it to have a humungous tractor if you then have three people with nothing to do? When we didn't need horses anymore we sent them to the glue factory, but what are we going to do with the people?"

Haustig Neefeld said it bothered him how the CPR was tearing up the railroad tracks and then a farmer had to buy a bigger truck—and for sure he wasn't going to drive twenty miles to the elevator with half a load—so the municipal road system was getting all ploughed to hell by these overloaded trucks and then taxes had to go up again, and did those Ottawa *empties* ever think about that? And Oata thought Haustig Neefeld sounded almost like her Yasch or even her dead father, Nobah Naze Needarp, when he said that there had to be a better way to farm than with all these GRIP, GRAB, and

GRUB programs. And Politicks Paetkau said, yeah, the depopulation of rural areas was a crisis and that's where he thought Yeeat Shpanst's idea of using the Gutenthal Curling Rink Accord as a model was a good one. "Without that Curling Rink Accord, this waiting room could very well be a pig barn or maybe even a hydroponic marijuana farm!"

On and on they talked through that August Sunday afternoon, and the waiting room, cool at first, got warmer and warmer. Haustig Neefeld and Politicks Paetkau set their John Deere caps on their heads for a while, and then, when the sweat leaked down, hung them on their knees. Oata was sweating so much she wished she was skinny like Barbara and Cora Lee or even a toothpick like Thecla, but then she saw a drop of sweat running down the dark nylon stocking on Barbara's leg and for a moment she could hardly breathe. But Tape Deck Toews kept changing the tapes and pushing the record buttons and they kept talking and talking, and all the time the question that wasn't a question yet kept hanging over them like the smoke from Barbara's cigarette that she just had to smoke already with all this hot talk going on. And for the first time in ten years Politicks Paetkau, too, felt like smoking, though he didn't break down to bum one off Barbara. He didn't really want to smoke anymore, but there was something about what was happening in the Gutenthal Curling Rink waiting room that called for the ritual that smoking cigarettes with a group of friends used to provide before smoking became politically incorrect. Politicks Paetkau didn't really argue with the Flat German Minister of Health who had implemented many anti-smoking programs, but he sometimes wondered whether the desire to live forever was a higher value than the desire to share the ritual of smoking a cigarette in the company of friends on a spiritual occasion. And without thinking, he found himself murmuring, "Perhaps when we bring the buffalo back."

At first Politicks Paetkau thought he had dozed off into a dream, for as soon as he murmured, "Perhaps when we bring the buffalo back," he heard a distant rumble, faint as his whispered murmur, calm like a unison Lord's Prayer mumbled by a radio church congregation. Then the mumble murmur picked up a galloping rhythm like thundering hoof beats, and Politicks Paetkau thought he was dreaming of the buffalo stampeding back. An explosion of thunder blacked out the lights. Lightning flickered through the far door of the curling rink, thunder cracked again, and rain rushed down on the roof, followed by a deafening clatter of hail. But before anyone could cry out, before anyone could open the door to check on the storm, their breath caught and their eardrums wanted to burst as they were pummeled by the roar of a thousand trains, the boom of a million jets breaking the sound barrier. Yet even in that bullering rummel, Oata wrote later, she heard the water being sucked out of the toilets. Hippy Pauls remembered the strong ozone smell just before the curling rink lifted off its foundation up into the funnel cloud swirling over their heads. For a long moment they gaped up into the spinning darkness, smelling gas, choking, blinking as flashes of lightning zigzagged up and down the dark sides of the funnel. Oata managed to expel a scream as she felt the sucking force of the updraft, and then the concrete slab waiting-room floor lifted the circle of nine into the swirling blackness.

They all screamed then, a primal unison scream cut off when a jagged arc of lightning seared over their heads, singeing Thecla's red-rooster hair. And then the speed of the swirling cloud stopped their breath again as they were sucked upward in a widening spiral suddenly agonizingly slow, their chairs on the concrete slab at the funnel's edge orbiting the updraft.

It was Cora Lee who first realized that their chairs were fixed to the floor. It was as if the force of the whirlwind fixed them in place, like lovers pressed against swing-backs on a merry-go-round at the fair. Cora Lee pointed down through the huge swirling circle to the earth passing beneath them. Haustig Neefeld was the first to recognize Flatland. He saw the high school, the mall, the railway tracks, and the elevators. He felt the twister stretch, reach down, grope around.

Paralyzed, he feared for the people below. Then he became fascinated, curious about what the tornado would choose.

Like a celestial pachyderm feeding on the earth, fussy, picky, expanding and contracting, raising and lowering its funnel snout, the twister hovered over the town, dropped suddenly and sucked up the boarded-up post office, swept up a section of railroad track, then slurped up the Pool elevator Haustig Neefeld had stared at, but left the Cargill elevator unscathed, swept up some more track, then scooped up the CPR station. Politicks Paetkau watched with intrigue and terror as he saw the swirling circle hover over the federal government building and then, like a salesman demonstrating the precision of his vacuum cleaner, the snout deftly snorted up the Unemployment Insurance wing where his wife, Pinklich, worked. His initial panic was slightly calmed by the thought that it was Sunday. The buildings twirled upward, past the wide-eyed passengers on the concrete slab, and Cora Lee looked back down just as the twister sheared off a wing of the hospital, then hopped back over to the railroad track, slurping it up like long spaghetti, rails, ties, spikes, and trestles, before it lifted and headed northwest. Within seconds they were hovering over Portage La Prairie, and with two hissing sucks the Campbell Soup plant and the air force base were snatched and slung upward past them on the slab.

"Look!" Cora Lee shouted. The twister hovered over a battery factory in Winnipeg and in a flash of lightning it was gone. Faster than FAX they hovered over Morden and the Tupperware factory was gone. A second later the twister had scooped up a razor blade factory in Ontario. Lightning flashing, the funnel cloud hopped over Ontario and Quebec, slurping up 1500 jobs here, 2000 jobs there, 1300 jobs there, spinning off another 7500 jobs there, then for a break swept the country from coast to coast to coast clawing back old age pensions and family allowance payments. Lightning zigzagged through the gyrating funnel cloud, and Haustig Neefeld saw the States of America President swing his golf club at a ball and say, "We're gonna kick some ass!" The golf ball landed in the pine trees, and then ten million TV screens swirled through the tornado flashing video-taped barricades, men with masks and AK-47s, overturned police cars, soldiers nosing Mohawks, cars driving over a bridge, and hundreds of people throwing stones, smashing the windows, smashing through the roofs, an old man dying. And then the lightning flashes speeded up and the circle of nine was surrounded by an endless exploding blitz in a swirl of yellow-ribboned computer calm voice-overs: Operation Desert Shield, precision bombing, pre-emtive strikes, lateral damage, smart bombs, patriot, scud, desert Hitler, Qatar, Gulf, Gulf, Gulf, Operation Desert Storm, Stormin' Norman Schwartzenegger, and then just as suddenly the flashing ceased and the tornado decided to get down to business and began sucking up things in earnest.

The circle of nine on the cement slab shuddered as the funnel sucked up Parliament Hill, the railways, Newfoundland codfish, CBC, Canada Council, the Maple Leaf Flag, the prairie sky, the Arctic Ocean, snowmobiles, the Bay of Fundy, the Peggy's Cove lighthouse, Niagara Falls, the RCMP, Margaret Atwood, Wayne Gretzky, the Wood Buffalo herd, the whooping crane, Medicare, peace keepers, ice breakers, Hudson Bay, Lake Superior, Plum Coulee, Batoche, Queenston Heights, the Vegreville Easter egg, Twillingate, the Queen on a horse, the Montreal Forum, the Rocky Mountains, the Giant Yellowknife Mine, the St. Lawrence River, the Queen on a moose, Hecla Island, the Big Nickel at Sudbury, the Stratford Festival thrust stage, the Gas Station Theatre, Rainbow Stage, the Westfield grain auger factory, the Canadian Wheat Board, the Queen on a Ski-doo, the Dogrib language, the National Film Board, UIC, the minimum wage, *100 Huntley Street,* the Bank of Canada, the Gutenthal Credit Union, the Business Council on National Issues, the Charter of Rights and Freedoms, Molson Canadian beer, wild rice, the Mackenzie River, Baffin Island, Robertson Davies, the Toronto Stock Exchange, Olympia and York, Maara Haas, Mordecai Richler, *Prairie Fire,* Eaton's, the National Arts Centre, Macintosh apples, the CN tower, Mount Royal, Portage and Main, the Bluenose II, Eastend, Neepawa,

Heisler, Morris, Clinton, the Toronto Islands, the Milton Acorn Poetry Festival, Peter Gzowski, Ovide Mercredi, Kakabeka Falls, "Suzanne takes you down," Gertrude Story, the Musical Ride, *Paper Wheat, Mon Oncle Antoine,* KD Lang, *Smoked Lizard Lips,* and the diamonds in the Northwest Territories. And the pieces of the country swirled, turning and turning like a sleeve caught in a power takeoff.

Suddenly they were engulfed by a blizzard of worms, each worm forming an upside-down hook. And there was no turning away. Some Canadians tried to hold their noses to keep the worms from crawling up, and someone said No, someone else said Yes, and another said Maybe, and another said I need more information and was smothered in worms, and there was a Yes here, and No there, a No No No over there and a Yes Yes over here, and ten Nos on that side and six Yeses on this side, and in spite of the noise of a thousand trains and the explosion of a million jets breaking the sound barrier, the boom of ten thousand precision bombings, the poof of 157 Patriot missiles missing 156 Scuds, the tumult of Yeses and Nos and Undecideds rose above the whirling din, YES-NO-UNDECIDED, YES-UNDECIDED, NO-UNDECIDED, YES-NO, YES-NO-UNDECIDED, NO-YES, UNDECIDED-NO-YES, YES-NO, NO-YES, YES-NO, YES-NO.

"YES!" Politicks screamed.

"NO!" Oata yelled back.

"YES!" Barbara shouted.

"NO!" Haustig hollered back.

"YES!" Thecla hissed.

"NO!" Cora Lee barked back.

"YES!" Tape Deck rasped.

"NO!" Schneppa Kjnals howled back.

"YES!" Hippy cheered.

"NO!" Barbara growled back.

"YES!!"

"NO!!!"

"YES!!!!"

"NO!!!!!"

"YES!!!!"

"NO!!!!"

"YES!!!!!"

"YES!!!!!"

"LOOK!!!!!"

Oata pointed up. The lightning was zigzagging across the inside of the swirling funnel cloud, lighting up millions of children working at taco stands, while crusty bureaucrats handed out K-Y jelly to the unemployment lines. And then Thecla cried, "We're back on the ground!" The spinning mouth of the funnel cloud lifted above them as the slab of the waiting room floor settled down into the rectangle of bare dirt in the grass. They sneaked quick glances at the landscape around them before their gaze was hauled back up into the heart of the tornado where the pieces of Canada swirled above them, still intact, still not shattered, waiting to be dropped.

Later, when they were able to speak, Haustig Neefeld and Thecla Thiessen said they saw two grinning men turning a big crank that was causing the whole tornado, something like *Wizard of Oz,* Thecla said. But right then all they could do was gape upward, mouthing *Yes* and *No* at random as the Gutenthal Curling Rink settled down over them onto its foundations. For a few seconds they sat in the darkness, the bare-naked light bulbs still out, the door still shut, their ears still plugged with the rumble of a thousand trains, the explosion of a million jets breaking the sound barrier, the poof of 157 Patriot missiles missing 156 Scuds in a Desert Storm. Then they heard only their own veins throbbing.

16

After a long minute a chair scraped in the darkness and footsteps whispered over to the platform. The table and the portable pulpit crashed against the wall as the front of the platform was lifted, and a faint beam like a dying firefly bobbed about underneath. Then the platform dropped back into place and a dark figure with a tiny flashlight sat on the end plank and focused the flashlight on an open black book.

For a moment there was only the sound of thundering hearts. Then Politicks Paetkau began to read and his voice strangely calmed the pounding pulses.

And a man in the land of Them, north of the land of Us, lived in a small house with a large yard. And his name was Castor, after the busiest animal in the land, and his wife was Maple, after the sweetest tree in the forest. Castor was proud indeed to possess Maple's beauty and he thrived on his enjoyment of her loveliness, at once wild as an eagle on a cliff or an elk in a mountain meadow, and tame as an orchard of peaches or a field of wheat. Their lovemaking could be as thunderous as a stampede of bison or as silent as a pickerel escaping a hook in a cold lake. Their relationship could be frigid as a Barrenland whiteout or steamy as a mosquito-filled marsh. They loved through dust-blown drought and hoisted their piano upstairs in flood time. Castor worshipped Maple, whether she was dressed in lace petticoats or manure-spattered Wellington boots. And it was said that Castor treated Maple well. He was concerned about her health and did his best to avoid potholes in the road when she was pregnant. And he shared some responsibility for the upbringing of the children, certainly more than most of his close neighbours did. For many years Castor and Maple lived happily in their small house, enjoying the freedom of their large yard, and the world saw their way of life and said that it was good.

In the land of Us, to the south of Castor and Maple's happy home, stood an enormous white table with carved Greek column legs and the biggest men in the world sat at the table and played cards for high stakes. And their every whim was catered to by young nubile maidens, sun-bronzed, lettuce-fed, scantily clad in blue, red, and white. And Castor saw the men with their cards, saw the servile maidens, and he longed to sit with the big men at the table, longed to play his cards close to his chest, longed to risk all to win all. And so, with his beautiful pale Maple timidly holding back, Castor stepped over the line into the land of Us and approached the poker table. For a time he watched the cards being shuffled, dealt, played, drawn, and discarded. He watched the stacks of chips exchange hands, watched the maidens display their bronzed cleavages as they bent to offer cocktails, mixed with the world's finest spirits, and cigars illegally imported from an equatorial island. And Castor saw the fine silk suits, the rings on the players' fingers, the plush chairs they sat on, and, at intervals, how a player would follow one of the bronzed maidens out through the red velvet curtains behind the table, only to return a while later, grinning, confident of winning, ready to risk all. And Castor longed to join the table.

After clearing his throat three times, Castor managed to catch the attention of the dealer, a man called Jag, which Castor was to learn later stood for John Abraham George. Jag looked at Castor with curiosity, then asked what he wanted. Castor, flustered by the opportunity, blubbered that he would like to join the card game. Jag eyed the cut of Castor's suit, the tie with the maple leaf on it in honour of his wife, the hands calloused from a canoe trip down a rushing northern river, and the look in his eye was slightly disdainful, especially when he spotted a bloodstain on Castor's left pant leg—a reminder that Castor had bandaged a farmer's hand cut by a swather knife. But the same eyes that sneered slightly at the bloodstain spotted the toes of the soft leather Gucci loafers Maple had given Castor at Christmas, and the sneer transformed into guarded interest. "You wish to join the table?" Jag asked. "Yes, I would like very much to play your game," Castor said, with just a slight quaver in his voice. "You must be willing to risk all to play at our table. It is risky, but it will be a level table," Jag said. He looked Castor up and down, then looked over Castor's shoulder at Maple holding back as if she might be planning to slip into the shadows of the forest. "And you must bring your lovely wife."

And so it came to pass that Castor joined the marble table after he had coaxed and threatened and coerced Maple to cross the boundary line from their wonderful yard into the land of Us, and he handed her over to the eunuch in charge of the maidens. He was given his stack of chips and dealt the cards by the dealer, Jag, and the game went on and on, with Castor's stack of chips rising and falling as the fortunes of the game rose and fell, and his heartbeat quickened with the thrill of playing with the big boys, drinking the finest cocktails served by the maidens with bronzed cleavages, and he felt positively global in spirit and joy as he played his hands, sometimes winning, sometimes losing, always competitive, always thrilled, winning losing, always ready for another deal.

And he had no regrets, not even when he saw Maple, his pale-skinned Maple, dressed in blue, red, and white, her cleavage snowy in contrast to the bronzed lettuce-fed maiden who bent over his shoulder, nibbling his ear at the end of a losing hand, and he followed the maiden through the red velvet curtain into the Bostonian Room where he discovered why England slept and he gained a new profile in courage. He returned to the white marble table with the carved Greek column legs, sat in the plush chair, stacked his chips, was dealt back into the game, winning and losing, competitive, global.

On it went, and never once did Castor look back over his shoulder at his little house in the land of Them, north of the land of Us. Until his eyes began to blur. When he groped for his chips he found he had only five chips left. He tried to look over his shoulder to his little house; he looked around the room to see if he could spot Maple, and he thought he saw her disappearing through the red velvet curtains into the Bostonian Room, but he wasn't sure since, after all this time at the white marble table, Maple had lost her paleness and was as lettuce-fresh as the other bronzed maidens, and Castor counted his chips again and he looked around the table. But there was not a wink, not an eye capable of producing a tear, and he felt lettuce breath in his ear and a bronzed bosom pressing into his arm, and he heard the whisper, the sultry whisper, "Go on, the next hand will be your lucky one. You'll clean up the table!" Castor nodded to the dealer and received the cards as they were dealt, but the last of the royalty was flushed and Castor's last chips disappeared into the banker's pouch.

Castor pleaded with the banker to lend him enough chips to get back into the game and he looked around the table at his fellow players for support, but the faces were all stone and Jag said coldly, "You're finished kid, you're toast. Now beat it." Castor couldn't believe the treatment he was getting and he protested, but was quickly thrown out of the establishment by two steroid maidens. When he called for Maple to come, they just laughed and said they'd never heard of anyone by that name.

And when Castor walked dejectedly toward his little house in the land of Them, north of the land of Us, he found it was no longer there. Us just went on and on forever it seemed. On and on Castor plodded, looking for the little house with the large yard, on and on under the light of a double rainbow coloured gold, on and on and on, and Castor began to panic and he began to run and he ran along endless garbage-covered pavement under the arched golden light which obliterated sun, moon, stars, and auroras, and then he stepped on a silver bullet beer can and it stuck to his soft leather Gucci loafer, and he ran clunk clunk clunk down the pavement, desperately hoping to find the northern edge of the endless land of Us. Slipping on a pile of half-eaten burgers squelched in mustard and relish and ketchup, he skidded into a garbage can and dumped it over himself as he sprawled against the middle base of the double golden rainbow.

And as Castor brushed the garbage off his face, his hand grasped what seemed to be a magazine, and under the arched golden light he saw the title, *History Gallery: The Girls Who Used to Live Next Door,* and Castor turned page after page, sickened as he recognized girl after girl after girl from the lands on all sides of the land of Us and far beyond, and in the middle, folded in the centre, with a staple perforating her navel, he found Maple, spread out, bronzed, only her breasts and her crotch still the snow white that he had loved so much before he joined the poker table.

By the rushing waters of a south-flowing aquaduct, Castor lay down and wept.

And all eight of them got so lost in their heads it took them maybe a minute to realize that the story was finished and the waiting room lights were back on and that Politicks Paetkau had febeizeled himself—just like Yeeat Shpanst.

PART THREE

. . . only nowadays, what with posthole modern stories, a person isn't supposed to have beginning middle and end, and then yet realism is supposed to be dead, except if it's magic and resists meaning and is mythological and reflexological on itself with unwilling beliefs getting snapped at by police suspenders. It seems like we want to be fooled, but at the same time we want to know that we are being fooled, and then we want to know how we are being fooled, so we can better enjoy being fooled. It's like reading Everything You Always Wanted to Know about Sex but Were Afraid to Ask *while making love under fluorescent lights on a stainless steel counter. Of course now there is* AIDS *so probably none of this is true anymore and a person going to write a posthole modern style book should hurry it along before Generation X decides to help the neo-conformatives to propel us forward into the past to the social at the Darwin Community Hall.*

—*Koadel Kehler, the teacher's son*

17

As she drove away from the curling rink Oata said to the windshield wiper, "Isn't it always like that? Every time there is trouble in this world that needs to be talked about a man reads us from a black book and our voices get stopped up in our throats like sausage in a sealer jar."

She shivered like a hailstone big as a grade-A large egg even after two weeks in the fridge, and she thought of her mother standing in her high heels on the Lazy Boy chair in the mental home common room gripping the TV remote control in her hand. And she wanted to crawl in someplace, the way two-year-old Oata had crawled inside her mother's coat in the storm when the car got stuck in a snowbank and her father, Nobah Naze Needarp, was shovelling outside and the snow had been blowing itself across the car lights and her father had been a shadow dancing in the blowing light. Oata crawled into the warm dark under her mother's coat, stayed there even after her father crept back into the car and started it rocking forth and back, almost jerking Oata down to the floor. Oata fell asleep under the warm coat after the car ploughed through the snowbank, and her mother the next morning complained how her back was gruelich sore because she had carried Oata into the house all the way up the stairs into the bed.

Oata shivered, wondering if for her mother the mental home was like the warm dark under the coat. She felt all stoppered up like sausage in a jar, afraid if she spoke she would say something crazy, that she would let it out from under the bushel that she had crazy thoughts in the head even after having been read to from a black book by Politicks Paetkau sitting with a flashlight on the platform in the Guten-thal Curling Rink waiting room, Politicks who had then febeizeled himself. Oata was glad it was already dark enough to switch the car lights on. The lights pointed a way at least, so she could see without being watched. She felt the car light beams reaching out and her fingers itched in torment when she turned into her own driveway and the lights shone along the Chinese elm hedge. She inched the car forward, closer, closer, closer, until she was right behind the open box of Haustig Neefeld's former grain truck, and she thought she had febeizeled her brain for sure. Farmers' Union notebooks, a whole truck-box full.

Oata crept out of the car and tiptoed to the back of the truck. She saw. She reached in. She clutched. She pulled back. She flipped through the blank pages of one Farmers' Union notebook. Somewhere in the black sky she heard the whirling roar of the tornado but when she raised her eyes from the notebook she just saw the other notebooks, piled higher than the reach of the high beams. Her fingers found the flat hardness of a carpenter's pencil, freshly sharpened. Oata flattened the notebook on the iron edge of the truck box and by the light of the sealed beams behind her she began to write.

Later, long after the sealed beams had sucked the juice from the car battery, long after the carpenter's pencil was sharpened to a little stub she could barely pinch with her fingers, long even after Thecla's wedding, Oata would write that when she was leaning over the notebook on the truck-box floor she had wanted to write about her mother waving the TV remote control. She had wanted to write about Yeeat Shpanst and his Lazy Leisure Camper Company van. She had wanted to write about the Curling Rink meeting and the pieces of Canada swirling around in a tornado dangling question-mark worms in front of their faces. Oata had wanted to write about this so she could try to understand what was going on and prove to herself that she hadn't febeizeled her brain.

And no, there wasn't any mosquito buzzing her what to write, though later, when she dared to think about what she was doing, she wrote that she had felt like her brain hadn't had much say in her writing. She felt like her whole body was pushing itself into her thumb and forefinger, pinching the carpenter's pencil, kjritzeling grey marks onto the little note-book pages. Her body strong, pushing the grey marks out onto the little notebook lines, and even as her brain still tried to write what had just been happening, her body pushed her pinched pencil to write the future with lead from the past.

No mosquito from a Good News Testament buzzed her what to write. Just her body, her own body carrying up jar after jar of canned pickles and chicken legs, beets and raspberry preserves, chokecherry syrup and crab apples, cooked-in sausage and mustard pickles, peaches and pears, string beans and watermelon from the dark earth cellar crammed full. Pint jars, quart jars, half-gallon jars of canned corn and peas, komst borsch and rhubarb jam sealed with wax, bing cherries that matched the wine sofa and beef jars upside down on their lids, fat risen to the bottoms. Sweet pickles, garlic dills, million-dollar pickles, bottles of ketchup with slivered onions. Carrots buried in pails of sand. Bacon-baited rat trap under the smoked ham hooked to the floor joists. Jar after jar, rat trap after rat trap clunked up the musty earth-cellar steps and pressed themselves onto the short lines of the Farmers' Union notebooks on the grain-box edge as the sealed beams behind her drained the juice from the car battery. Jars perfectly sealed, fruit fresh; jars with bad rings, grey mould like mouse fur or dust balls under a bed. Apples wrapped in blue paper, later a wipe of pleasure after the *Free Press Weekly* funnies. A cabbage head wrapped in a flour sack in December. The cool discarded linoleum on bare feet. The sudden dark of accidentally switched-off light, the wondrous dark between light and scream. Potato sprouts curling around an ankle. Pale butter in a wooden mold. Pale butter rose molded by the carved wooden lid of the one-pound butter box. Pale butter rose shaved, carried gently on the wedding knife tip to the bran-speckled bun on Adelaide Thiessen's faspa saucer. Freckled cheeks grinning at Oata, two girls feeding themselves faspa at Knibble Thiessen's dining table, wedding china, wedding knives and spoons from the red velvet chest. Pale butter rose set beside the Sunday jar of raspberry jelly, wedding blade smearing double. Biting tips off green dill-pickle tongues, two girls alone on a Sunday afternoon at Knibble Thiessen's table. Oata tripping on the doorsill, wrecking her ankle, Adelaide smelling of Abadalduc liniment playing bonesetter behind the curtain off the sitting room, Adelaide's freckled fingers knibbling everything except the wrecked ankle, "just like my Dad," Adelaide said. Oata not so sure it was good, Adelaide's fingers knibbling, for sure Knibble Thiessen had never knibbled a wrecked ankle higher than a stocking. But Oata hardly ever talked to anybody except her father, Nobah Naze Needarp, now that her mother was in the mental home and Nobah Naze had laid himself down on the wine sofa after they came back from the visiting hours and Oata walked in the garden and Adelaide Thiessen came riding along on her balloon-tire bike and asked her to sit on the boys' bar. Adelaide wobbled Oata all the way to Knibble Thiessen's place and they had faspa and played knibble behind the curtain.

It only happened that one time and even years later, when she thought she understood all it could have meant, Oata couldn't say that playing knibble with Adelaide Thiessen had bothered her any more than eating faspa off the forbidden wedding dishes had. Only when she got home she remembered how Adelaide had fuscheled as she knibbled Oata's thigh, fuscheled, "You got a key for your room?"

"What you mean?"

"You're old enough to need a key for your room." Then Adelaide had laughed loud and long till tears came and Oata had thought Adelaide's laughter hadn't been a funny hah hah at all, not at all. Nobah Naze Needarp already in the barn milking when Adelaide stopped her balloon-tire bike and Oata slid off the boys' bar and ran to the house to pull on her barn clothes before her father could schell her out. But before she climbed upstairs, she clawed through the junk drawer in the kitchen until she found a skeleton key.

Oata never knew if she had understood Adelaide right; only once, about a year after the faspa in Knibble Thiessen's house, did Oata hear a slight rattle of her doorknob in the middle of the night, then Nobah Naze's feet shlorring across the linoleum to his room. Only once, but the key stayed on a ribbon around her neck, until after her father's funeral.

A mustard jar of peach jam. A crock of headcheese, hearts, tongues, and pickled pigs' feet. Five Old Colony maple syrup jugs of dandelion wine, even the one they drank the only time Adelaide came over for faspa on a Sunday—Oata, emboldened by Adelaide's presence, pouring three little glasses of wine from the maple syrup jug, one for her, one for Adelaide, one for her father, Nobah Naze. Solemnly, they sipped the wine, even Adelaide stifling the laughter that usually gurgled up from her throat every few minutes. Nobah Naze chewed his buttered bread and sipped his Postum as if deep in thought, with no time for young girls. But after Adelaide had gone Nobah Naze said, "Nie vada doat Tiessuh uhyeseffa to faspa invituh!"

One can of Klik. A Libby's Sweetened Orange Juice can full of Klik keys. A pinched Klik key scraping chicken shit from the treads of the white runners to wash in the tub of soapy water behind the house. A soft whistle from the oak trees on the garden edge. Desirable Delia in a black raincoat, rubber boots, straw hat. Oata stepping bare feet across the cucumber patch, snagging overalls on the barbs of the wires Adelaide Thiessen spread apart for her only friend, the black raincoat falling open, the pleated skirt stretched over skinny

Adelaide's rounded belly lifting the hem over freckled knees. Oata fingering the L-shaped rip in Nobah Naze's overalls, Nobah Naze under the hump of yellow clay in the churchyard.

At first Oata thought her friend had smeared on too much eye shadow, but then she saw that the dusky circles wouldn't wash off, not even with the gurgle in Adelaide's throat, the hah hah hah that was never quite funny.

"Who is he?" Oata whispered, so softly, hardly heard over the dry oak leaves fuscheling under her bare feet.

Adelaide's laugh gurgled, but she turned away before she said, "A guy." Oata wrote that she almost gurgled back, "Me too," and that her hand slipped through the slit at the side of her father's overalls and grasped a handful of her fat stomach which hid the secret she already knew. The secret she would have to get a man to confirm so she could break the news to Yasch.

"Who?" she whispered, later writing how close and distant her friendship with Adelaide Thiessen had been, how Adelaide had been her only friend in Gutenthal all those years she lived alone with Nobah Naze Needarp before she snagged Yasch. And they had been so close together, spiderwebs joining them, yet they hardly saw each other because Adelaide went to the next district school, and though Adelaide never talked about the other kids there, Oata for sure thought that Adelaide Thiessen must have lots of friends and just had time to visit Oata maybe once or twice a year. So it didn't seem strange to her at all to have to ask her friend, "Who?"

Adelaide gurgled again. "A guy," she said and then she turned back to face Oata, her freckled face made up into a smile, an eyelash-blinking kind of smile that almost fooled Oata again into saying, "Me too." And Oata wrote that the only thing that stopped her from saying, "Me too," to her friend Adelaide, with some guy's rounded belly straining at her pleated skirt, had been the Klik key still pinched in her fingers. She held it up, a little startled, and Adelaide saw it too.

"Oh," Adelaide gasped, a freckled hand over her mouth. "I never thought of that kind of key!"

And Oata, somehow wanting to bring them both back down to some manageable earth, said, "Yeah, it's good for getting the dirt out from cracks."

"I guess it would be," Adelaide said, letting her laugh gurgle from her throat again, and for a few minutes they talked about their gardens, and then Oata crawled back through the barbed-wire fence and picked a baseball-small watermelon from the patch. She cracked it on a fencepost, broke it open and handed a chunk to Adelaide. Wordlessly, they gnawed out the red flesh, spitting flat seeds, smearing watermelon juice all over their faces, letting it leak down their chins, onto the clothes stretched over their bellies.

"I never thought of that kind of key!" Adelaide said again as she flung the watermelon rind into the bush, and then she waved and shuffled off, the crackling oak leaves fuscheling something Oata hadn't been able to understand.

A whole night full of jars writing themselves up from the earth cellar, Oata moving the flat edge of the carpenter's pencil along the short lines of the Farmers' Union notebooks, stopping from time to time to scrape at the lead with the pocketknife she had never given back to Yasch, until her fingers pinched a stub shorter than a .22 shell.

In the dewy harvest dawn Yasch and Doft shovelled the empty notebooks into gunnysacks and piled them neatly in the garage. Oata stacked the filled notebooks carefully in a wooden apple box, carried it into the house, and set it down beside the Singer sewing machine. Frieda looked up from the stove where she was frying eggs for breakast but she never asked what was going on, not even with her eyes. At the breakfast table Yasch said it was always best to switch off the headlights after a person had parked the car because Co-op batteries weren't like those flashlight batteries on TV that could keep a rabbit hopping for a week without stopping. That's all he said, and Oata went out to the garage after breakfast and brought a sack of notebooks in to her sewing machine and scribbled jars up out of the earth cellar until mid-afternoon when the phone rang and she heard Frieda tell Thecla

Thiessen that sure she would come over to help her try on the wedding dress.

Later, Oata would write how that afternoon, as she sat at the Singer sewing machine pinching the carpenter's pencil over the notebooks writing one jar after another out of the earth cellar, she had this strange desire to gain weight. Not that she had suddenly seen a bony maroni reflection when she looked into the mirror behind her eyelids. No, not that, though when she looked at the full-length mirror hanging beside the sewing machine she saw a reflection that would easy fit into most clothes a person would see schluffing through the Flatland Mall or any city slicker Wal-Fart. And it wasn't that she was suddenly very hungry, for she had figured out a long time ago that hunger was mostly in the brain, like that summer replacement doctor had said about sex, ninety per cent between the ears and ten per cent between the legs, only with hunger the brain often didn't figure out that it was satisfied until it was too late. No, it wasn't hunger that gave her this strange desire to gain weight, at least not a hunger for eating. Later, Oata wrote how she sat there with a Farmers' Union notebook spread out on the closed sewing machine lid, her bare feet pressed down on the iron holes of the treadle, writing with the pinched carpenter's pencil while the whirling tornado droned somewhere up in the sky, and she just felt too small. She felt as if she wanted to grow like bread dough rising from the pan so she could wrap herself around this world full of me onlys telling the me toos that there isn't enough for everybody.

And as the tornado droned somewhere high in the sky swirling those pieces it had picked up from the ground, Oata felt herself stretching after Frieda riding her bicycle to Knibble Thiessen's place and climbing up the stairs to Thecla's bedroom with the muzharich mirror on the antique dresser where the wedding dress lay spread out on the four-poster brass bed, the room that had once been Adelaide's room. Thecla, shivering in her off-white camisole, hearing the tornado's drone, too, while downstairs in the lean-to porch the wringer washing machine chanted:

Iesaak, Shpriesack
Schlenkjafoot
Schleit siene Brut
Em Kjalla doot.

Oata saw Thecla looking into the rusty mirror seeing not her cherry-red spiked hair singed by the tornado lightning, but seeing the sandy waves of hair on Politicks Paetkau's head as he sat reading from Yeeat Shpanst's black book on the platform in the curling rink waiting room, and Oata tried to reach into Thecla's head to see what the attraction was with those sandy waves of hair and the sing-song Flat German preacher's kind of voice Politicks had used to read the story, but before she could figure out that attraction Frieda knocked on the door. Thecla said, "Come in." Frieda opened the door, stepped in, and Oata saw the two girls throw their arms around each other and hug each other for a long time, the cherry-red spiked hair pressed against the apple-green pixie cut, two friends squeezing each other.

Oata wondered what it felt like, to hug a friend like that. She wondered what would have happened if she and Adelaide had hugged that way, wondered what would have happened if anyone had hugged her in those days of the Sunday afternoon drives to the mental home, wondered what would have happened if she had hugged her mother as she played daumbrat checkers with Hups Hilbraunt in the mental home common room in those days when they didn't even have a TV in there, wondered how come she hadn't hugged her mother. What had stopped her? What was it that could make a person afraid of touching another person, even her own flesh and blood? And Oata wished she was bigger so she could understand this, understand the jars coming up out of the earth cellar, understand Thecla's head, understand Adelaide draining the wringer washer in the lean-to porch letting the wash water flow out through the plastic pipe, out to the roses blooming in the tractor tire beside the house, Adelaide staring into the tub of the washing machine, watching the little eddy swirling at the drain hole, gasping at the flash of gold caught in the grate, Adelaide reaching in to the dregs of the wash water, pinching the ring between her fingers and holding it up to the light, staring at the glistening clear stone cut to sparkle light that wasn't its own, Adelaide trembling, biting her lip, pinching the ring, turning away without shutting off the pump motor, stomping into the house, up the stairs to Thecla's room, Thecla and Frieda just coming out of their embrace. Adelaide brandishing the ring, her voice stopped up like sausage in a jar, Thecla gaping, then shrugging, Frieda puzzled, fearful, wishing she was at home with Oata.

Outside, in Knibble Thiessen's driveway, Kjnirps Iesaak Klippenstein's Trans Am horn cut through the tension and Thecla reached out and plucked the ring from Adelaide's hand and slipped it on her ring finger, wrinkling her nose at the wash water smell, then scrambled into a pair of ripped jeans and shrugged her head and arms through the holes in a black sweatshirt with a faded KISS on the front.

Oata heard the heavy footsteps tramp up the stairs, saw the half cigarette smoking between grime-lined fingers, smelled the mix of sweat and BRUT on the stubbled chin, saw the hair sticking out past the collar like a yellow crow's tail, and she felt half of Thecla's body warming itself into a sweat while the other half shuddered and leaked little ice diamonds. Oata wanted to reach out to Adelaide, wanted to reach in to discover what it was that was keeping her from wrapping her arms around Thecla and slowing her down, letting her know that it was alright to pause at the door, that a person didn't have to pass through before she was ready. As Kjnirps Iesaak Klippenstein knocked his smoking knuckles on the bedroom door, Oata heard again a little louder the droning of the tornado high up in the sky someplace and she wondered whose tornado that was anyways, wondered if it was just something kjriezeling through her head like the beetfield yeschwieta about Yeeat Shpanst, wondered if she had invented all this like a bad dream, wondered if like a dream this tornado swirling the pieces of Canada up in the sky was just some kind of warning or if it was something already happening for real. Suddenly her arms chilled cold with longing. She jerked on the sewing machine stool, jerked because she felt a hand on her shoulder. She turned around. Nobody was with her in the sewing corner of the bedroom she shared with Yasch, her lawfully wedded spouse. On her notebook page she saw Adelaide jerk from the touch of a hand nobody could see as Kjnirps Iesaak Klippenstein opened Thecla's door, leaned against the dark oak doorjamb, and blew a smoke ring that spiralled into the bedroom and hung itself on the spikes of Thecla's cherry-red hair.

Oata stood up from the sewing machine stool and smoothed some of the wrinkles out of her day-old Sunday dress as she looked at herself in the full-length mirror, saw her bare feet, almost thought about panty hose, ran her fingers through her hair, then reached for the kerchief hanging over the back of her mother's old white chair beside the bed, tied it under her chin. She stuffed a handful of Farmers' Union notebooks into her purse, stuck a new carpenter's pencil behind her ear, and walked barefoot out to the car. The hood was up and she heard the hum of the battery charger. Oata stopped. A sharp gravel stone pressed into her instep. Her mother was not in the mental home anymore. She had run off with Yeat Shpanst in a Lazy Leisure Camper. Oata shuddered as she wondered why she had never asked her mother, "Who is this Yeeat Shpanst anyways?" Then she shuddered even more at the thought that she might never again get a chance to ask, never again get a chance to wrap her ice-cold arms around her mother.

18

Haustig Neefeld saw the shadow looming over his barn from beside the dark oak trees along Mary's Creek. He knew what it was even though he hadn't switched on his lights when he left the curling rink and he didn't switch on his lights now that he was home. He didn't drive out past the barn along the field road toward the shadow. He didn't look at it twice. Seeing was believing and he didn't want to believe. He had seen too much.

The yard was dark. The sky was cloudless and black. He, too, heard the tornado's whirling drone above him. His wife, Pienich, hadn't left the yard light on for him. She had maybe gone to bed before it was altogether dark and she wouldn't want to waste the hydro just for him. It was good that the yard light was off. Haustig Neefeld didn't want to see. The eyes were too easy to fool into believing. He wanted to touch, to feel, to grab and grip.

He didn't switch on any lights in the house. He took his shoes off beside the kitchen door and then remembered how he had slipped on the stairs in his stocking feet on the night he sold his truck to Yasch Siemens, so he pulled off his socks, and his bare feet felt good across the cool floor to the stairs. He let each step press into his soles, send warm shivers up his legs. He thought he should maybe go to Knibble Thiessen's to get his feet rubbed again. At the top of the stairs he stopped, his heart clappering just a bit too fast, his lungs feeling a bit sticky, like a plastic garbage bag that didn't want to open. He gripped the round ball of the newel post and waited till he was idling even again.

In the bedroom he opened his belt buckle so carefully even he couldn't hear the little brass prick hit the buckle frame. He slipped his pants down his legs along with his underwear. The floorboards creaked, but the vague mound of darkness on the bed didn't stir, except for a faint breath Haustig thought he heard in the pause before he unbuttoned his shirt. In the darkness he stared at the quilt covering Pienich, the squared quilt that always reminded him of thirty-six quarters of farmland.

Haustig Neefeld slipped his naked body into the empty half of the bed without touching his wife and he let his back sink into the mattress. He shrugged his head into the pillow and closed his eyes. The shadow loomed out of the darkness of his eyelids. A shimmering shadow, darker than the black August night, trembling. Haustig Neefeld opened his eyes and looked at the ceiling boards, a dim white even in the dark night of the room, the V-joints straight black lines from wall to wall. Forty-one boards if he counted the half board by the window which had been schelped narrower to fit. He closed his eyes, and again the shadow shimmered up from the darkness and he saw even the pointed peak against the cloudless sky. Haustig Neefeld blinked open his eyes again, and after he counted the forty-one V-joint ceiling boards sideways back and forth, he turned himself on his side and stuck his nose into the tuft of loose hair sticking out from the kerchief Pienich always tied around her head for going to bed. He smelled a sniff of the green apple shampoo Neddy's wife had given her for a Christmas present. His penis touched the nightdress where it was pulled tight around her seat. Her knees were pulled up together and Haustig pushed his knees up so she was sitting on his lap. He lay that way for a few minutes thinking they were like two spoons lying together in the drawer. His eyes closed, but blinked open as soon as he saw the tall, pointed shadow again.

His penis stirred against the warm bottom of the flannel poajchem nightdress Pienich wore even in summer heat. He put his hand on her hip, then slowly moved it down so he could slip it under the hem of the nightdress to the inside of her thigh. Pienich didn't move and he nuzzled his nose into the tuft of hair sticking out from her kerchief and he kissed the hollow place on her neck. He let his hand move upward slowly in the soft warmth and still she didn't move, and as he stared into the darkness past her earlobe his fingers found the soft flannel poajchem between her legs and Pienich moved her leg slightly and said, snoring as she talked, "Mensch, wowt wesst du met dei fuest enne futz?" Her words made him remember long forgotten times and Haustig ylipsed his hand into the opening she made when she moved her leg. He moved his lips from the hollow place on her neck to her earlobe poking out from under the kerchief and as he nibbled on it he pushed himself as close as he could, and Pienich snored at him again, "Mensch, dei hoade stang puakst mie em hingarenj!" But Haustig wasn't going to close his eyes to face the shimmering shadow looming in the cloudless night, and when he started to ylips his fingers under the flannel poajchem underpants, Pienich shifted herself over onto her back. "When already, then already!" she snapped. Haustig shuddered, felt trembling all around him. He wished that the shadow would fall, make an end of it.

Pienich's hand touched his arm. In a soft long-ago voice she said, "Jungkje, traak doch emol dei unjabecksi oot!" Haustig raised himself up to his knees and timidly drew the flannel poajchem down, leise rieselt der Schnee, his rough hands rubbing over the hairy calves as Pienich raised her knees. "Weetst noch wua auless ess, oola Neefeld?" she teased as he leaned himself over her, but Pienich didn't leave it up to him to find his own way in the dark, and anyways wood saws better if there is a person on each end of the saw. And with Haustig trying to blank out that looming shimmering shadow, the Sealy Posturpaedic mattress reached deep into its twenty years of guarantee to find some hidden springs and Pienich called out, "Pauss up, oola Neefeld, daut hoat kloappaht noch to nicht!" and then Haustig pooped out on top of her like a whale schlucksing for air on a Newfoundland beach and Pienich grunted from under him, "Dusent noch emol eent, daut jefft noch tvins!" With wide-open eyes Haustig Neefeld panted on top of his wife, wanting to believe that Pienich meant those playful words she hadn't said for so long. She pushed at him and he rolled himself off to his side of the bed and stared at the forty-one V-joint ceiling boards. Could he deserve to believe it? Beside him Pienich shrugged herself comfortable and then squealed, "Oh sure, jungkje, nue mott ejk dann wada enne moos schlope. Haft dei oola zack kjeen boddem? Dit ess meist so deep aus dei fifty flood!"

Haustig trembled, trying to find some words to say. Her hand touched his thigh, then gently cupped his sack of bottomless balls. He found no words. Pienich sat up and pulled the string for the overhead light. Through tears their eyes met without blinking. "It was just an elevator," Pinklich fuschelled as she pulled off her kerchief, letting her long hair fall over her shoulders. "We didn't need to let such a thing bother us for so long." Haustig shivered as she kissed him on the lips, the first kiss in twenty years. With her fingers she closed his eyes so dark there wasn't even a shadow.

But in the morning the Pool elevator glanced the sun off like a knife blade sticking up from the back field near the banks of Mary's Creek. Rusty railroad tracks ran to the east and to the west as far as Haustig Neefeld could see and the tears in his eyes muzhahed the vanishing tracks like heat rising from a black field in spring.

19

"Read to me," Cora Lee Semple said, tucking her feet under her on the sofa chair and raising her glass of red wine to her lips. Politicks Paetkau leaned forward on the loveseat and opened Yeeat Shpanst's black book.

"I'll try," he said. He lifted the ribbon marker from between the pages. For a moment the writing looked like meaningless scratches of ball-point pen, just like it had been each time he'd opened the book since the tornado. Then he felt a tiny vibration in his fingers and the ink resolved into clear writing. Politicks tooks a sip from the wineglass on the coffee table, glanced at Cora Lee, then began to read:

In the land of Them, north of the land of Us, there was a wealthy farmer with all his granaries filled with grain. The market price was good because there had been a poor crop in the faraway land of Yousur and so the farmer looked forward to increasing his wealth and spending the winter in the warm land of Us.

Now the wealthy farmer had a neighbour whose business was the production of eggs. It was a small operation, the hens still allowed freedom of movement inside and outside the barns, the neighbour unwilling to confine the hens to cages. The egg neighbour needed grain to feed his laying flock. He calculated his costs, building in a slight profit, just enough to sustain his operation and increase his family's comfort to a small degree, and then he approached the wealthy grain farmer with an offer to purchase grain and an offer to sell eggs to the farmer at what seemed like a reasonable price.

The grain farmer listened to the egg farmer's offer, tapping out figures on his calculator as he listened. When the egg farmer finished presenting his offer, the grain farmer played with his calculator for a few more minutes, and then he turned to the egg farmer and shook his head. The grain farmer told the egg farmer how much he could get for his grain if he sold it to the land of Yousur. He told the egg farmer the low price he would pay for eggs if he imported them from the factory farms in the land of Us. He told the egg farmer the difference in profits that would make.

The egg farmer looked at the grain farmer, asked to use the calculator, recalculated his costs, reduced his price and upped his offer, reduced his profit margin so that although his wife would have to wear her coat for another winter his children would still get new snowsuits. He handed back the calculator and presented the grain farmer with the new offer. The grain farmer played with his calculator for a few minutes again, then turned back to the egg farmer and shook his head. "Why should I lose so much profit to make this deal with you? It is the market. You can't go against the market. It's not economical."

"But I live just down the road. My eggs will always be fresh. My children play hockey with your children," the egg farmer said.

"It's the market. You can't go against the market. It's bad economics."

"And so the grain farmer sold his grain to Yousur and

bought his eggs from Us, and he expanded his farm and bought the latest machinery and spent winters in the warm southern parts of the land of Us, and he thought it was good.

But then one year the faraway land of Yousur had a bumper crop at the same time that Us had a bumper crop and the grain farmer in the land of Them had a bumper crop, and no one wanted to buy the grain and the grain farmer had no cash flow, and the egg factory farms in the land of Us wouldn't trade eggs for grain. The grain farmer was in trouble. The bank which had encouraged his expansion and his new machinery now threatened to foreclose. The grain farmer remembered the egg farmer's offer of a long time ago, so he drove over to his neighbour's place to make a deal. But the egg farmer was no longer there. The egg farm had become part of a corporate grain farm and the grain farmer discovered that his old neighbour had moved south to the land of Us to work for a corporate egg factory. "He couldn't fight the market. It was bad economics," said the CEO of the corporate farm. "Bad economics."

Politicks Paetkau saw the hairy-legged spider spin its silky thread as he gazed over Cora Lee's pink shoulder. She had collapsed back into her chair when he finished reading and he was waiting for her to comment on what she had just heard. Then the spider rotated slowly and Politicks saw the red hourglass mark on its belly, but before he could alert Cora Lee the spider grew and a moment later Barbara, the hartsoft beautiful journalist, stood at the foot of the bed buttoning up her black blouse to cover up the red camisole underneath. She yanked the black webbing from the ceiling, then sat on the edge of the bed and pulled her crochet hook from her black purse.

"I see you've got the book," she said as her gloved fingers began moving the crochet hook rhythmically. "My dear George's bedtime stories."

20

Simple Hein couldn't say if there had been a storm in the night. His ears felt thick like there might have been thunder, but sometimes he still had dreams about the army bengel setting off atomic bombs on the Martens yard across the sunflower field. Sometimes the dreams were so loud he got a headache, a headache so bad he had to go to the doctor for some 222s. Only the doctor always told him to be satisfied with aspirins and then by Brownie's Drug Store they would only give him the cheap welfare aspirin without words pressed into the pills. But this night he couldn't even say if he'd had a loud dream and his head felt funny like it had a hole where the headache should have been.

Most mornings the cool air woke him up, but this morning there was hardly any air at all under the bridge, and it was hot, like the air in a beckhouse or a granary with the door closed. Simple Hein figured that if it was so hot so early, it would be schendlich hot by dinner time.

All this before he opened his eyes. Simple Hein liked to listen to the world before he opened his eyes. He liked to smell the world and touch the air with his hands. This morning the air smelled a bit like a lightning storm, but Hein didn't think it had rained. A lightning storm smell was a cool smell and the smell in his nose was too warm for that. Too closed in for a morning smell under the bridge. Hein threw off the cowhide he slept under and waited for the air to cool his bare legs. The cool air didn't come. It didn't make sense. Maybe Simple Hein had slept in, had slept all the way till noontime like a lazy welfare on the bum. He listened. He couldn't hear anything, except his own breath. He hadn't heard a sound since he thought he heard some thunder when he woke up. He hadn't even heard a bird or the wind rustling the grass.

Simple Hein turned on his side, resting his cheek on a corner of the fur side of the cowhide. Slowly he opened his eyes to look where he had parked his three-wheeler bicycle just under the bridge. It was buried in ice. The whole opening of the bridge was blocked off by chunks of ice. Warm ice. Simple Hein turned over. The south side, too, was blocked by clear chunks, sun shining through, blurred, ice that wasn't melting, ice that looked dry. Funny hailstorm, Simple Hein thought. Maybe storm from south wind can bring warm hail. Simple Hein stood up and tiptoed over to the north opening. He touched the icy-looking stuff with his toes. It was warm. It felt familiar. Then he noticed something else. The shape was familiar, too, and each chunk had a metal point. Hein grabbed one metal point and pulled it free of the pile. Plastic pop bottle. Clear plastic pop bottle. Two litre. Clean. Brand new, it looked like. No label. No Coca-Cola or Orange Crush drops left at the bottom.

Hein pulled another bottle from the pile, then another and another. He found the handlebars and pulled his bicycle free. Then he remembered his pants and his shoes. He tiptoed back to his mattress and picked up his pants. He stepped his right foot in, then looked at both piles of bottles before he stepped his left foot in. He pulled the waist up and zipped and buckled and spiralled the long leftover belt around itself. He found his socks balled up on the ground beside his shoes. He marched back to the north opening. Using one hand like a wedge, dragging his three-wheeler behind in the other, and with lots of swearing, Simple Hein fought his way through the bottles to the far side of the ditch.

"Holem de gruel and scare yourself yet!" The mountain of clear empty pop bottles was piled up on his bridge so high that at first Hein thought it was as high as a Pool elevator, but when he looked to the sides he could see the pile was maybe only a couple of shoes higher than the hydro poles. "Dusent noch emol eent! Bottles coming out of my ears!" Simple Hein dragged his three-wheeler up the side of the ditch to the road. He looked up at the blue sky, pale blue with not a hail cloud in sight. He looked at the basket on the back of his three-wheeler. He looked at the gleaming mountain of bottles. He turned around and looked toward town three miles down the road. He scratched his chin and licked his left nose hole. He scratched his right armpit, looked at his basket again. He tucked his shirttail under his waistband, hitched up his pants, and wiped his hands on his hips. He backed up his three-wheeler, grabbed two bottles, hesitated, pulled them from the pile, froze, waited for the pile to slide. Nothing happened. Hein laid the two bottles in the basket. He grabbed two more and then two more, carefully building a load of bottles until he had to stand on his toes to set the last bottle on the peak.

Hein grabbed the handlebars. The load of bottles wobbled. Hein let go, studied his load, looked down the road toward town, looked at the pile on the bridge. Then he scrambled down the side of the ditch, fought his way through the bottles, gathered his twine collection from the nail above his mattress, fought his way out through the bottles again. Carefully, he tied down the load, so the bottles couldn't move even when he jerked the three-wheeler as hard as he could. "Solid as a Model D John Deere!" he said. Using his hands he measured his load and made a comparison with the pile. He counted on his fingers, scratched his head, "Tousand, maybe two tousand trips. Good training for Olympic game." Hein climbed on his bike and started to pedal toward town. He kept looking back to see if his load was still there. He couldn't see around his load to check the pile on the bridge. Simple Hein pedalled fast. He had a funny feeling down his backstring that this was a one-time opportunity, and if he didn't move fast, even those plastic bottles could melt and just febeizel themselves. Poof! He wondered if Three Rs Reimer by the Flatland Recycling Council would have enough money in the till so early in the morning to buy so many bottles, but that thought only made Simple Hein push harder on his pedals.

Then Simple Hein saw the dust. A big dust, like a five-ton grain truck, maybe Hutterites even. Now for sure his pile of bottles would febeizel themselves, poof!, just like that. And Hein shouted, "I knew it. Too good to be true. I knew it!" And he let his bike coast to a stop, shielding his face to fight off the dust that was going to drown him. But it wasn't a five-ton grain truck full of Hutterites that stopped beside him and honked. It was a bus thing. A bus thing like a Triple E, only gruelich bigger. With big funnels and TV aerials on the roof. Commenists from the States come to rest him up for stealing the bottles from by the bridge. He was going to get blown away, wiped out, knocked off. A back window opened. A package was shoved out. Atomic bomb for sure! Patriot Scud! Plastic explosive anyways. Hein covered his ears. The bundle that dumped down on the road was wrapped up in silver aluminum and plastic, but before Hein could let go his ears, two more bundles dropped down on top of the first one. No exploding. No dunnasche big bang and that's the end of Hein.

Then a voice rummeled out from the loudspeaker funnels on the roof of the bus thing: "HEIN. DO NOT SELL THE BOTTLES TO THE RECYCLING CENTRE. THESE BOTTLES HAVE A HIGHER PURPOSE. YOU HAVE BEEN CHOSEN TO HELP US DELIVER THE BOTTLE MESSAGES. YOUR COOPERATION IS VITAL TO THE FUTURE OF THIS COUNTRY. LISTEN CAREFULLY. HERE IS WHAT YOU MUST DO. THE MESSAGES ARE IN THE SILVER BUNDLES. PUT A MESSAGE INTO EACH BOTTLE AND CLOSE THE CAP TIGHTLY. STORE THE PREPARED BOTTLES IN THE MACHINE SHED ON THE MARTENS YARD, THERE ACROSS THE SUNFLOWER FIELD. DO NOT WORRY. NO ONE WILL STEAL YOUR

BOTTLES. IF YOU RUN OUT OF BOTTLES, MORE WILL BE PROVIDED. JUST DO YOUR PART. DO NOT STOP UNTIL BULCHI WIEBE LANDS HIS SILVER FOUND BROTHERS AIRPLANE ON THE MARTENS YARD. BULCHI WIEBE WILL HAVE FURTHER INSTRUCTIONS. DO NOT ASK ANYONE TO HELP YOU. DO NOT TELL ANYONE WHAT YOU ARE DOING. DO YOUR PART FOR YOUR COUNTRY. YOU CAN BE THE SOLUTION, SIMPLE HEIN."

With that, the bus thing honked and drove away. Hein got off his bicycle to watch how the bus would get past the pile of pop bottles on the bridge, but the dust covered everything over and when it cleared there was no vehicle on the road, just the pile of pop bottles glancing the sun off like a glass mountain.

When Simple Hein's heart slowed down to clappering normal, he started the work he had been given to do. He cut a slit in one of the bundles and pulled out a handful of narrow gold papers with red words on one side. He picked up a bottle and unscrewed the cap. He curled up the message lengthwise and stuck it into the bottle. The message dropped to the bottom. Hein screwed the cap back on and held it up to the sun. He puckered up his lips and reached into his pants pocket. He pulled out a marble, held it up to the sun. He gazed at the gold flower thing in the glass, looked at the bottle again. Simple Hein grinned and put the marble back in his pocket. He tossed the bottle toward his three-wheeler and reached for another.

It was lankwielijch work, ferrying the bottles in his three-wheeler basket to the machine shop on the deserted Martens yard; lonely, too, for nobody came down the road for a whole week. That, too, was strange. So close to town and nobody drove down his road. Simple Hein wondered if he wasn't still dreaming. It was a hot week, and though the work wasn't heavy like working by Zamp Pickle Peters at baling time, a man did get hartsoft thirsty in the summer sun and it was hard sometimes to stick to the job with so many empty pop bottles around. Hein couldn't help thinking how simple it would be to hurry pedal a load of empties into town and cash them in for a full cold Pepsi-Cola or C-Plus Orange. And for sure one afternoon Simple Hein did get a little dizzy in the hot sun, pedalling along the road watching the gravel stones flow by his front tire. Suddenly, the town was right in front of him. Only a quarter mile down the street, over the train tracks, around to the shipping door of the boarded-up post office where Three Rs Reimer collected pop bottles for the Flatland Recycling Council. Simple Hein could already see himself, loonies in his hand, pedalling his empty three-wheeler to Hi-Way Inn to buy a bottle of 7-UP, or Mountain Dew, whatever bottle in the cooler was the coldest.

But then, before he got to the train track, he saw the big bus thing coming toward him from the far end of the street. Simple Hein turned around so fast that, even tied down, his load pretty near spilled. He raced to the bridge never daring to look back. He had heard the story of Lotsof wife that looked back, and for sure he didn't want to be a salt pillow like Lotsof wife, especially not here so close to Dairy Doell's cattle crossing sign. When Simple Hein got back to his bottle pile the bus thing was gone, but it took his heart forty-seven minutes to clapper normal. Forty-seven minutes, Hein said later. He had measured it with his dollar secon'-han'-store pocket watch.

Still, the next afternoon it was even hotter, and Simple Hein was watching the gravel stones flow by his front tire when a brumming sound woke him up. Again he was going the wrong way, getting close to town, and a silver airplane was flying toward the Martens place. Simple Hein turned around thinking, Huy Yuy Yuy, the job is over at last, but when he got to the Martens yard the silver airplane hadn't landed. He didn't measure his heart slowdown this time, but he took his time unloading. The machine shed was getting pretty full and he wondered if he could even fit in all the bottles still left.

Then Simple Hein shivered. It fell him by that if he had tried to cash in by Three Rs Reimer maybe he would have gotten into trouble because of the message in the bottles. Simple Hein didn't like to read. Reading gave him a headache.

But maybe he should check this stuff out. He picked up a bottle, unscrewed the cap, tipped the bottle upside down and let the paper slide to his finger. It wasn't easy, but he got the paper out. He sat down on a rooster-chopping stump and flattened out the paper on his knee. He started to read sideways: I HA . . . VE A VIS . . . I . . . ON—I SEE MILL . . . I . . . ONS OF BE . . . ET . . . WE . . . ED . . . ERS, W . . . IT . . . H HO . . . ES SH . . . AR . . . PEN . . . ED, DESC . . . END . . . IN . . . G ON OUR CH . . . O . . . KING FIE . . . LDS, HA . . . C . . . KING A . . . WAY AT THE MUST...ARD AND THE WILD OATS, SE...PA...RAT...ING THE DO . . . U . . . BLES, FREE . . . ING THE S . . . WE . . . ET SU . . . GAR BE . . . ET TO FLOUR . . . IS . . . H AS WE WE . . . ED OUR WAY IN . . . TO THE FUT . . . URE. T . . . HERE, W . . . IT . . . H THE HELP OF GOD, I WILL LE . . . AD YOU!

On the seventh day Hein put the last golden message paper into the last bottle. He checked under the bridge and in the grass of the ditches on both sides, but he found no more bottles. He checked through the plastic that had wrapped up the messages. No more. Hein pedalled to the Martens yard, shoulder-checking every two seconds to see that the mountain of pop bottles hadn't returned itself.

He had to wiggle each bottle to get it in between the others already stuffed into the machine shed. When he picked up the last bottle he checked that the cap was on tight. He turned the bottle on its side, held it up above his head, and jiggled it gently so the red words lay flat against the side. He stammered his way through the verse one more time and he decided no, it wasn't a Bible verse, it wasn't in a Bible. He looked at the bottle. He smiled. He took the bottle in both hands, crouched, and threw the bottle high into the air. "NO!" he hollered at the sky. "IT'S A BOTTLE VERSE!"

That's when he heard the brumming airplane. Hein clutched the last bottle to his clappering heart. Bulchi Wiebe's silver Found airplane tipped its wings to circle around the Martens yard. Hein shuddered when it seemed the plane was going to fly away again and not even land and he even said a prayer because he just didn't want to pedal back to the bridge to face another bottle mountain.

Bulchi Wiebe touched down at the far end of the field road and the silver airplane roared toward the yard, dragging dust. Hein covered his ears as the plane rumbled a circle around the yard-light pole and taxied to a stop in front of the machine shop so that one wing rested right over his head.

"Well, G'day Hein," Bulchi Wiebe grinned as he helped his belly out of the cockpit. "I see there's no rest for the wicked. Good job, Hein. Good job. Be the solution."

If Bulchi Wiebe was expecting Simple Hein to answer his greeting he didn't show it. He just added, "Work, for the night is coming," and reached in behind the pilot's seat to pull out a tightly tied-up bundle of strings. He paced off ten baby steps behind the tail of the plane and carefully set the bundle down on the ground. Simple Hein stepped closer as Bulchi Wiebe knelt to unroll a folded net about ten feet long. Then he got up off his knees and began unfolding it sideways. Simple Hein couldn't help himself: "You going be fisher of men, Bulchi Wiebe?"

Bulchi Wiebe laughed. "You bet, Hein. We will show people how to be the solution." He spread out the left half of the net and unfolded the right. Then he opened a flap like on some trapdoor underwear and spread open a big pocket.

"Hunnerd bottles, Hein. I need one hunnerd pop bottles."

Hein looked at the bottle still clasped to his heart. He waved it in Bulchi Wiebe's face. Bulchi laughed again and said, "Drop her in the pocket and get me ninety-nine more!"

"Lucky for you I think so maybe I got ninety-nine bottle on han' today." Hein rushed to the machine shop, grabbed his arms full of bottles, and dumped them into the open pocket.

"That's the stuff, Hein, but don't hurry your feet off. I have to pack these babies carefully or we'll have no end of trouble in the air." In the second of stillness after Bulchi Wiebe's words Hein heard his heart shuddering. He had flown with Bulchi Wiebe before. When the hundredth bottle was packed Bulchi Wiebe closed the flap and sealed the velcro closer. Then he carefully threaded a thin cord through eyes in the velcro strips and stretched it out on the ground away from the net to keep it from getting tangled.

"One down and four to go," Bulchi said, and he spread open the next pocket. And so five hundred message bottles were packed precisely into the five pockets of the net bag. Gently they turned the bag over so the five trapdoors faced down. Bulchi attached a harness to rings on the net bag and to brackets on the underbelly of the plane. Then he threaded the five long cords from the pockets through little pulleys and fastened them to a row of hooks under the passenger seat.

"Okay Hein, up we go."

Bulchi Wiebe revved up the airplane engine, pulled out some knobs, and the airplane shuddered down the field road faster and faster and faster, louder and louder and louder, and Hein felt the bag of bottles jerk behind the plane. They lifted away from the ground and on the wheat field below Hein saw the shadow of the sack hanging from the shadow of the plane. The needle on a speedometer thing went up 3000 4000 5000 and Hein figured, Holem de gruel, five tousand mile an hour. Get ticket for sure! And then Bulchi Wiebe hollered, "We're gonna fly to Morden to drop the first pocket, and then hit Winkler, Plum Coulee, Horndean, and Rosenfeld on our way back! This is a test run, so we might as well do it over friendly territory, right Hein?" Hein moved his chin up and down and looked out of the window. He saw cars small as Dinky Toys driving along a highway and then he saw the Pembina Hills ahead of them, and when he saw the Morden Dam lake he felt Bulchi Wiebe turn the airplane and they circled so they would fly over the town of Morden. Bulchi shouted, "Get ready for number one!" and Hein reached down and put his hand carefully on the lever with the 1 on it and he looked over at Bulchi. Bulchi stuck his first finger in the air and Hein pressed the trigger and pulled back as far as he could. The plane jerked.

"Bombs away!" Bulchi Wiebe yelled, "Handy as in Chortitz!"

Hein looked out the window and saw the pop bottles hailing down from the airplane.

"Get ready for Winkler!"

A minute later Bulchi pointed two fingers in the air. Hein squeezed the trigger and pulled back the handle, felt the little jerk, and looked out the window to watch the bottle messages scatter to the ground. Plum Coulee, Horndean, and Rosenfeld came up almost as fast as enemies on a Nintendo game, and it was such fun that the plane was landing on the Martens yard before Hein remembered to turn green.

When they climbed out of the airplane Simple Hein figured they could call it a day. But Bulchi Wiebe checked the sun in the sky and called for more bottles. Before he could worry about it, Simple Hein found himself back in the airplane ready for takeoff. They flew farther west this time to drop the bottles on the unsuspecting Pembina Hills. Bulchi Wiebe signalled, Simple Hein pulled the levers and it was fun. When they returned to the Martens yard Hein automatically headed for the machine shop for more bottles. Three more times they loaded the net bag and took off. Then the evening got so dim Hein could barely make out the Martens yard as they came in for the landing, and when they hit the ground Bulchi Wiebe said, "Time to call it a day! Never got my IFR qualifications. That's okay. We are anyways the children of light, not so, Hein?"

"Light, for sure," Hein laughed. "Children? None that I know about."

Simple Hein started toward his bridge in the dusk, but Bulchi Wiebe called him back.

"C'mon, Hein. You're a working man now. You sleep under a roof. Just hang on while I put my baby to bed." Bulchi Wiebe tied down his airplane and neatly folded the net bag and stashed it behind the pilot's seat. Then he pulled out two rolled-up sleeping bags and a tiny red television and led Simple Hein to the old Martens farmhouse.

"We going to sleep here?" Simple Hein asked. "What about army bengel and his dad? They don't care?"

"Don't worry about them. They're long gone. It's all been arranged for us to use the house for a few days, just like the machine shed. Did anybody bother you about the machine shed?"

"Nope. You first person I see aroun' here for seven days. Funny thing. Seven days nobody come down road over my bridge. Seven days not see nobody. Almost like I was only person left in whole wide world. Like Adam before he got his rib ripped out. Seven days all alone. But you know, Bulchi Wiebe, never one time was I lonesome. Never one time. Only thirsty sometimes in the hot sun. Thirsty for two litre cold Coca-Cola."

"Good man there, Hein. When a man is busy with a purpose there is no time to get lonesome. But c'mon, there's cold drinks in the fridge."

And so they settled in each night in the abandoned Martens place. Each night Bulchi Wiebe opened the cupboard and pulled out a thresher loaf of fresh-baked homemade bulchi broot and a sealed pint jar of home-canned sucker-fish. And there was a dish of farm-churned butter in the fridge beside a two-litre bottle of cold pop. And always two huge ripe tomatoes in a bowl on the table. Each night they cut thick slices of bulchi broot, smeared it with butter and pressed forkfuls of home-canned sucker-fish into the soft, still warm bread. They sprinkled thick slices of tomato with salt and pepper. Bulchi Wiebe filled their tumblers equally until the pop bottle was empty. Only the flavour of the pop changed from day to day. There was nothing else in the cupboard or the fridge. Simple Hein knew, because once in the night he woke himself up a little thirsty so he sneaked to the fridge and there wasn't even frost in the freezer. And in the cupboard just a box of old-man-with-the-black-hat grits beside a Postum jar. In the mornings, bowls of grits steamed next to hot cups of Postum and a pint crock of milk, still warm from the cow. When they landed around noontime, a Bee Hive syrup pail full of roast-beef sandwiches always waited on the chopping stump beside a thermos bottle full of scalding coffee.

It didn't seem to bother Bulchi Wiebe and Simple Hein was scared to ask about it because the longer this thing went on, the more it seemed he was in some kind of dream. Because it was the strangest thing, he thought. Ever since he had woken up that morning and found his bridge covered up with pop bottles he hadn't seen another living person except Bulchi Wiebe. Not one living person, unless he counted the cars and trucks he saw when they were flying over a highway, but they never flew low enough to see people themselves. And though Simple Hein was used to being alone, it wasn't altogether comfortable to not see other people for such a long time. But he was scared that if he asked too many questions, Bulchi Wiebe might disappear.

Such things could happen. That much Simple Hein knew. Once upon a time Simple Hein had had parents. One day they had been loading all their stuff from the house onto the back of the truck and they had told him to go play with some kids on the street. And after he had looked all over town and only found kids that wanted to throw stones at him he went back to the house. The truck and his parents had febeizeled themselves and he was left all alone. So Simple Hein was just a bit scared that Bulchi Wiebe would disappear and leave him all alone. Not that it was scary to be alone. He had been mostly alone over the years and lots of times he had been alone because he wanted to be alone. It was better to be alone than to be someplace where he didn't fit, just like it was easier to walk barefoot than to wear shoes too big or too small.

One time Help All Heinrichs had taken him to Ha Ha Thiessen's store and bought him some new shoes that had been in the window so long the dust was thick as mouse fur. For sure, Hein had been happy to get new shoes and he didn't argue with Help All Heinrichs and Ha Ha Thiessen that sure they were very nice. Only the right shoe was a size 8 and the left one was a size 7 and even that would have worked, except that Hein's left foot was bigger than his right and so his new shoes were too loose and too tight at the same time, and it got really kompliziet trying to make sure he was wearing the new shoes when he saw Help All Heinrichs on the sidewalk because he didn't want him to think he wasn't dankbar for the new shoes. Besides, Help All would always invite Hein to come to church on Sunday and reach him a Bible tract. Hein would carefully slip it into his shirt pocket to read later, and after Help All drove away in his car he would pull out the tract and find the dollar bill inside. "I could be crazy, but not me I'm stupid," Simple Hein would say and whistle his way down the sidewalk.

Hein had tried living with other people. When his parents first febeizeled themselves, quite a few different families took him in to live with them and Hein tried to like it there, but somehow he could never be comfortable in people's houses for very long. Some people figured it was because he wasn't all there; others said it was because he had been born in a truck box when his family was moving through the States from Mexico and that being born outside in the open air like that had let the wildness touch him and so he would never be able to be comfortable in a civilized Christlich house. All Simple Hein knew for sure was that after he tried to live with people in a house for a few days he would have trouble breathing.

Still, Hein missed other people if he was alone too long, and if somebody like Help All Heinrichs or Bulchi Wiebe came along and paid him some attention Hein would try to make the relationship last as long as possible. At least now that he was older the hockey team bengels weren't interested anymore in taking his pants off and playing with his sausage and eggs. Homo fairies everyone of them. That's why on TV they didn't want women reporters to come into their dressing rooms. Still, Hein liked to go to hockey games and Flood Funk would let him sweep the floors after everybody was gone, and Hein would often find dropped money under the stands. And at a hockey game, if he stood himself in the right spot, a hundred maybe two hundred people would say hi to him. Hi Hein. How's it going Hein? Who's going to win, Hein? How's she hanging Hein? Merry Christmas Hein.

This pop bottle business was pretty strange, but with Bulchi Wiebe along at least it wasn't scary. And it was quite comfortable in the old Martens house. It wasn't cluttered full with furniture and Hein had no trouble with his breathing, even sleeping in the same room with Bulchi Wiebe who snored like a D-9 Cat once he got going. It was almost like being in heaven, really.

Each day they flew farther to drop their bottle messages, and Hein loved watching the roads and the rivers and fields and train tracks flowing by below them. And at night they curled up in the sleeping bags on the floor and watched the *CBC National Journal* on the little red portable TV Bulchi Wiebe had brought in from his plane on the first night. After the news was over Bulchi Wiebe would click off the switch and in the dark room he would say, "Sweet Dreams. Up and at it bright and early tomorrow." And in a few minutes Simple Hein would be asleep.

21

Eaza Bone Peetash hammered in the last spike with three dings of the sledge hammer. Then he lifted his striped engineer cap and wiped the sweat off his forehead with a red polka-dotted handkerchief. He looked at the new rails he had laid down on the new ties. The rails were virgins, still rusty new, waiting for a train to polish the steel to a gleaming shine. It had been at least twenty-five, maybe thirty years since Eaza Bone Peetash had laid down new rails. Twenty-five years of fixing CPR tracks and this was the first time he had had to lay down brand new rails because old rails had febeizeled themselves, along with the ties and the top layer of roadbed. Just the length of track between the Cargill elevator and the Paterson, febeizeled, poof, gone, along with the Pool elevator that had stood in between. Eaza Bone Peetash sat down on the jigger and rolled himself a Player's cigarette with Vogue papers. Funny thing, the elevator febeizeling itself like that. And nobody able to tell him what happened, or nobody wanting to.

Eaza Bone had been away when it happened, taking

holidays on the VIA train through the Rockies, using his pass even though it nerked the CPR to still have oldtimers like him around with passes they had to honour, but Eaza Bone figured he wouldn't let them buy out his pass as long as the VIA train was running. Besides, he had gotten an extra couple of days of holiday out of it in a CN hotel because the VIA train was forty-six hours late coming through the Rockies, and no way would Eaza Bone Peetash let them put him on a bus instead. When he got back to work his first job was to put in this new bit of track. Nobody explained to him what had happened to the track or the elevator and Eaza Bone Peetash had learned long ago that life was easiest for him if he just did what he was told and didn't ask any questions or give any answers either. Now he was smoking his roll-your-own Player's on the jigger, happy that outside workers were still allowed to have a smoke.

For a few minutes he sat there watching cars cross the tracks and he noticed that quite a few were driving over toward the big church behind the Consumers Co-op Garage. Maybe there was a wedding on, he figured, and sure enough, when his smoke was too short to pinch between his orange fingertips, a cherry-red Toyota Camry all decorated with flowers bounced over the crossing. He thought it looked like the bride was driving herself and maybe going to be late for the wedding. Then Eaza Bone climbed up on the jigger, started the motor and clattered slowly down the track to his next job, which would take just long enough to allow him to sit down in the beer parlour at exactly three minutes after four-thirty.

A flatdeck trailer was parked on the spot where the concrete foundation of the Pool elevator had been. Even the ramps were gone, the ground level as if some Paul Bunyan had scraped up the whole works with a spade. But the annexes on both sides of the vanished elevator still stood, acting sort of like a shelter for the trailer. The Pool elevator yard was where the Free Church had always had their street meeting on Saturday night right after the stores closed. But since the Flatland Mall had opened, the main street was often like a ghost town and on this afternoon, after Eaza Bone Peetash clattered away on his jigger, for about five minutes there wasn't even a sparrow on a wire.

Then Barbara angle-parked her black Lincoln Continental against the curb in front of the old beer parlour that wasn't there anymore. She tilted the rearview mirror so she could touch up her lipstick. Cora Lee Semple parked her Hyundai Pony beside her and got out without checking in the mirror and walked around to Barbara's door. She was wearing her navy blazer over her pink skirt-shorts outfit. Her nylons had no runs and her running shoes looked freshly washed. Barbara dropped her lipstick into her purse, pulled down her black veil, and opened the door. The two women eyed each other over the door frame without speaking, then Barbara swung her black high heels to the pavement. As she closed her door Politicks Paetkau's Ford pickup pulled in on the other side of the Lincoln.

Barbara jingled her keys and opened the trunk. Cora Lee reached in and pulled out a long-legged wooden stool with a round seat. It was red. Barbara slammed the trunk shut, and without looking at Politicks Paetkau, the two women crossed the street to the flatdeck trailer, Barbara grabbing Cora Lee's elbow to steady herself as her heels tottered over the rutted elevator yard. Cora Lee set the red stool up on the trailer, grabbed the rub rail, and boosted herself up. She carried the stool to the centre, sat down on it sideways, and crossed her legs. Rust streaked the left leg of her pink shorts. Then she pulled her steno pad from her blazer pocket and scribbled on it, glancing from time to time into the elevator space between the two annexes. Barbara lit a cigarette and leaned against the flatdeck, occasionally waving at Cora Lee and pointing at something in the elevator space or on the raw annex walls which were a mixture of shredded tar-paper, weathered timbers, and streaked horizontals that could have made a picture in a modern art gallery. The women didn't speak, but seemed interested in the empty elevator space, pointing and scribbling, craning their necks as if trying to see the peak of the elevator. Then Barbara pulled out one of those disposable Fuji film cameras and snapped a picture of the space between the annexes.

Politicks Paetkau, the black book in his hand, sauntered over the rutted elevator yard. He studied the ground around the flatdeck as if figuring out where the thick cement foundation for the elevator had been. He looked up into the elevator space, too, pointing at different spots, and Barbara took more Fuji disposable pictures.

Tiedig Wiens came walking along the main street from where he had been having early faspa in the Flatland Motor Hotel beer parlour that now allowed women in. He saw these people by the trailer and he figured maybe they would know something about what had happened there, because nobody had anything to say about this febeizeled Pool elevator, not even in the parlour after three draft. So he schluffed his feet across the main street and looked up into the elevator space like these strangers were doing. A minute later, Holzyebock Hiebat stopped his gravel truck on the elevator side of the street and walked over to see what these people were looking at.

In the church behind the Consumers Co-op Garage the organ started playing the "Wedding March" loud through the open windows. Soon the elevator yard was full with people looking up into the empty elevator space between the annexes. The clerks from the Flatland Mall lined up outside the entrance watching their customers head across the main street to the elevator yard, and Sheklich Suderman from Fruelied Fashions said to Real Estate Regehr, "Too early for street meeting, not?" and Real Estate Regehr answered by looking her up and down and wishing his wife could wear an outfit like Sheklich had on, only his wife was at home, pregnant again with feet swollen up too big to fit into her shoes. That's the only answer Real Estate Regehr had a chance to make because Politicks Paetkau climbed up onto the flatdeck trailer and carried a black book over to the long-legged red stool. Cora Lee quickly got off the stool and after scanning the crowd jumped from the deck and landed on her feet.

"Could be a street meeting," Sheklich Suderman said, and she advertised her dress across the main street, only nobody was watching her except Real Estate Regehr, who decided to stand up straight and suck in his belly.

Politicks Paetkau sat down on the red stool and started paging in the black book. When he found the place, he crossed his legs and rested the book on his knee. Without looking up, he began to read in a quiet voice, but later people who were there said they had been able to hear even better than if there had been a whole bunch of loudspeakers hurting their ears.

In the land of Them, north of the land of Us, lived a boy named Donald who one Christmas morning found a toy train in his stocking hung by the chimney with care. Donald squealed with delight and eagerly fitted the sections of track together on the living room floor until the oval was complete. Carefully he set the engine on the track and then hitched up the coal car, the box car, the tanker car, the flat car, and the little red caboose. When all was set up he plugged in the transformer and moved the control switch. The black engine jerked forward, then stopped. The boy moved the switch again, and the same thing happened, but the train moved a little farther. The third time the boy moved the switch smoothly and the train set off on its journey around the oval track. After a few rounds of the track, the boy discovered that by turning the switch on the transformer he could make the train go faster or slower. The boy discovered that he could make the train go so fast the wheels of the cars would leave the track speeding around the curve. The boy set the cars back on the track and found that by turning the switch the other way he could make the train back up, and as he played he learned the coupler hitches worked just like the ones on real trains and that he could hitch up stray cars by backing up the train until the couplers hooked. And Donald was annoyed when his mother made him take the train apart and pack it away in the box before he went to bed.

Just before Politicks Paetkau paused to turn the page, Oata Siemens drove Haustig Neefeld's former grain truck along the main street, and even over the yueling sound of the old truck she heard Politicks Paetkau's quiet voice as clearly as she had on Sunday in the Gutenthal Curling Rink. By this time the curbs on both sides were parked full, so she stopped in the middle of the street, even with the flatdeck trailer. She reached a Farmers' Union notebook from the dashboard and pulled the carpenter's pencil from behind her ear.

Over the next few days Donald found that assembling the train each day before he began to play was more exciting than driving the train when it was all set up and he began to wish he had more track so he could build a bigger railroad. So he emptied his piggy bank and went to a toy store having a Boxing Week Blowout and invested his life savings in a T-crossing and enough track to expand his railroad from an oval into a figure eight. That kept the railroad game exciting until New Year's Day when Uncle John came to visit.

Uncle John sat on the davenport sipping holiday Scotch and watched Donald set up his figure-eight track and run his toy train. And Uncle John got a gleam in his eye. "My boy," he said as he dropped fresh ice into his empty glass, "I can see a vision!"

"What do you mean, Uncle John?" Donald asked.

"My boy, one must dream great dreams. I see a railroad track running from one end of this room to the other, with branch lines veering off to every nook and cranny, with little stations and grain elevators and warehouses and towns and crossings and trestles and tunnels through the mountains all the way to the sea."

"But Uncle John, I have no more money to buy more track and all the other things you want," said Donald.

"Ach, my boy, come to your Uncle John." And Uncle John emptied his glass of Scotch down his throat and pulled out his wallet. "Here's a fifty dollar bill. I'm investing in your railroad. I expect to see results the next time I visit you."

"YOH!" a voice shouted over the still sound of Politicks Paetkau turning the page. Politicks didn't look up, but he paused just long enough for people to turn and see a young bengel with long dirty hair wearing a Ski-doo suit that looked like it had dragged under a harrow for a hundred and sixty acres. He had two gold rings bommeling from his right ear. Funny, Oata later wrote in her notebook, how she, too, saw the Ski-doo suit and the earrings before she saw the sign on a stick the bengel was carrying, a sign that said in big red letters, YOH on one side and NEH on the other. But Politicks Paetkau's voice carried quietly to each ear on the Pool elevator yard, even to those behind him on Eaza Bone Peetash's newly laid rails, and even to the ones buying free air by the Consumers Co-op Garage on Railway Street on the other side of the tracks. Politicks's voice carried quietly but so strongly that the people in the crowd hardly noticed Tape Deck Toews and his wife CD tiptoe around the corner of the south annex with little video cameras on their shoulders, and those who felt the camera being pointed at their faces stared even harder at Politicks Paetkau reading from the black book on the red stool in the middle of the trailer where the Pool elevator once had been.

Donald was very excited, but when he went back to the toy store after New Year's Day the Boxing Week Blowout was over and he had to buy his track at inflated prices. Still, when Uncle John came by a week later, he was impressed and he invested another twenty dollars in Donald's railroad. And Donald got intensely involved in planning his routes around the living room and careful purchasing at the toy store. He even learned to shop around for the best deal. But most exciting was coming up with a new proposal in anticipation of Uncle John's next visit. Donald shrewdly determined that proposals were more favourably received after the second glass of Scotch than before the first. And so Donald built the longest, most complicated model railroad that any boy had ever built, and he was as proud of himself as Uncle John was proud of him.

"YOH!" the earring bengel yelled. But Politicks Paetkau just went on, his quiet voice floating on the barely moving air, between the annexes, over the tracks, across Railway Street, past the Consumers Co-op Garage, in through open windows. "NEH!" the bengel shouted, pumping his YOH-NEH sign on a stick up and down, not bothered at all that CD and her camera were right in front of him like a black eye.

But then Uncle John died, and it was found that he had died in debt, and Donald's father had to pay for the debts. Things got rather tough for Donald's railroad. Sections of track, rail cars, and transformers began to break down. At first Donald found money to maintain his system, and even to update it as new engines and transformers came onto the market. But keeping the system going wasn't nearly as exciting as building it had been, and without Uncle John's dream Donald began to lose interest. Instead of checking out the railroad section at the toy store, he found himself eyeing the radio-controlled model airplanes and 4x4 trucks. Before long, he was buying planes and trucks, and gradually he began tearing up lengths of track to make room on the floor for his new toys. Piece by piece, branch line by branch line, he removed his railroad from the living room, until there was barely enough track left to complete an oval. Still, from time to time Donald tired of his planes and trucks, and he would sit down with his railroad and tinker with it until he got it running around the oval track a few times.

Sometimes he would remember the clink of ice in the Scotch glass and Uncle John's hearty voice saying, "My boy, one must dream great dreams. I see a railroad track running from one end of this room to the other, with branch lines veering off to every nook and cranny, with little stations and grain elevators and warehouses and towns and crossings and trestles and tunnels through the mountains all the way to the sea." Sometimes Donald even had to wipe a tear from his eye.

Oata heard the ending of Politicks Paetkau's story clearly, uninterrupted, in one smooth piece. It was like a wind on a field that couldn't be stopped no matter what a person did, no matter how loud a person shouted. Even the earring bengel who shouted "YOH" and then "NEH" to match Politicks Paetkau's every second word couldn't stop the wave of the story. And each person in the Pool elevator yard heard every word as clearly as if it had been peace be still.

But at the same time, between the periods and the capitals, between the commas and the subordinate conjunctions, between the articles and the nouns, between the nouns and the verbs, Oata wrote in the Farmers' Union notebook with the flat carpenter's pencil how Politicks Paetkau's words floated in the almost peace-be-still air in the elevator space between the annexes, over the tracks across Railway Street, past the Consumers Co-op Garage, in through open church windows. The cherry-red Toyota Camry taped full of flowers screeched to a stop beside Oata's truck and Thecla Thiessen jumped out in her lacy white wedding dress, her rooster-red hair still singed black from the lightning in the tornado, and she danced between the people listening on the Pool elevator yard, danced between the periods and the capitals, between the commas and the subordinate conjunctions, between the articles and the nouns, between the nouns and the verbs, scrambled up the wheel onto the flatdeck, and knelt at Politicks Paetkau's feet to hear what little was left of Uncle John's dream.

It was an interlude of bliss, and Oata paused in her writing for maybe an instant too long, she later wrote, and there was a honking of horns and screeching of brakes, and then Kjnirps Iesaak Klippenstein and his seven pastel-blue best men clambered onto the trailer. Politicks Paetkau sat on his stool, red-faced, chewing his lips, frantically looking around for Cora Lee and Barbara, but Cora Lee was scribbling on her steno pad and Barbara was lighting a cigarette, one eye closed against the smoke, the other eyeing the faces listening to the story.

Thecla knelt adoringly at his feet, pleading to follow him, to assist him in his mission, enraptured by Politicks Paetkau and his sandy hair, his voice that had penetrated all the way into the church and rescued her before she could say, "I do," so enraptured that she didn't notice the pastel-blue tuxedos closing in on them until Kjnirps Iesaak Klippenstein reached out to grab her.

Politicks Paetkau spotted the tuxedos, saw his chance, and leaped from the flatdeck, twisting his ankle as he landed. Barbara and Cora Lee helped him across the Pool elevator yard, his arms hooked around their necks, but the crowd didn't notice. Thecla tore away from Kjnirps Iesaak Klippenstein's grasp, charged through the circle of pastel-blue tuxedos and leaped off the edge of the trailer.

BLAST BLAST BLAST

BLAAAAAAAST!

The Lazy Leisure Camper rolled down the track on retractable train wheels.

BLAST BLAST BLAST

BLAAAAAAAAAAAST!

The door opened as the Camper screeched to a stop. Yeeat Shpanst, wild rose on his Hawaii shirt, grinned as Thecla scurried up the cindery slope. The cherry-red wedding sandal flew from her right foot and caught Kjnirps Iesaak Klippenstein smack on the boutonniere. Thecla never paused, never looked back, and danced up the step into the van.

BLAST BLAST BLAST

BLAAAAAST!

Moving before the door closed, the Lazy Leisure Camper clattered down the track faster than any CPR train had ever done.

Oata closed her Farmers' Union notebook, stuck the carpenter's pencil behind her ear. As she reached for the ignition key she wondered if she had written it right, but before she could bother herself too much with that she saw her green-haired Frieda running toward her on the main street in the apple-green bridesmaid dress they had stayed up till three o'clock to finish. Oata cleared her head to listen to the story Frieda was going to tell her, because a story is always best if it feels like you are hearing it for the first time.

But just before Frieda stepped on the running board of Haustig Neefeld's former truck to open the door, a brumming noise drowned out even Oata's thoughts. Bulchi Wiebe's silver Found Brothers FBA-2C buzzed over the main street dragging the sack net. And as the people stared upwards, a flap opened and a hundred bottles hailed down through the air. The plane circled back over the main street and another flap opened and more bottles hailed down. Five times the flap opened and when the plane flew off a bottle had hailed down for each person standing on the Pool elevator yard, and one dropped into Frieda's arms. Oata wanted to drive away. She wanted to get out of town ahead of the crowd so she could enjoy listening to Frieda's story while they were driving, but she waited as Frieda waved the bottle for Tape Deck Toews's video camera. Oata remembered Tape Deck saying how important it was to get a video record of whatever activity they did, how that was the way to create a myth nowadays.

Frieda climbed her green excited bridesmaid self into the truck cab and Oata drove away, but when she stopped by the first stop sign she hurry wrote in the Farmers' Union notebook that she had just seen the earring bengel and his Flat German YES-NO sign climb into a grey Volkswagen with Schneppa Kjnals.

22

"I feel like a virgin," Frieda whispered so Oata could hardly hear.

Oata looked over at Frieda staring ahead through the windshield at the double-dike grass that matched her green hair and green dress, and Oata thought she looked like a sunflower plant not blooming yet.

"What?"

"Like a virgin. That's how I feel."

"Well, for sure, that's how you feel. You're only fourteen. You should feel like a . . . Frieda? What?"

"Oh, Mom, I don't mean sex. I mean . . . like a . . . foolish virgin. You know, like in the Bible, the five foolish virgins waiting for the bridegroom to come."

"Oh yeah, that kind of virgin," Oata said, and her heart clunked just a bit as she hurry glanced away from the Good News Testament still lying on the dashboard. The virgins who were late for the wedding because they went to buy oil for their lamps. The foolish virgins who missed the bridegroom.

"What would one bridegroom want with ten virgins at his

wedding anyways?" Frieda turned her freckled face to her mother, and though Oata's heart clunked again, she felt happy that Frieda hadn't filled her lamp with oil yet. Still, it was one thing to argue with Bible verses in your own head and something different to hear your virgin daughter asking questions nobody could answer. For a second she remembered Preacher Janzen's wife, Luella, coming to visit a couple of weeks after Yasch and Oata's justice of the peace wedding story had sifted through Gutenthal like Purity flour. Luella had come alone, her brown hair waving down to her shoulders like the picture in Adelaide Thiessen's Bible where Jesus looked like he had gone to the hairdresser's. Preacher Janzen didn't have enough nerve to come visit himself, for sure not to hint that they should do things right and get married in the church, too, or at least get themselves dedicated. Anything to get themselves in through the door. That's what Oata had heard sifting between the words coming through Luella's smiling teeth. Ready or not, the weighty thing was to get in through the door.

"What would one bride want with seven virgins? Seven pastel-blue virgins."

"What?"

"Oh, just the seven best men. Kjnirps Iesaak Klippenstein rented them pastel-blue tuxedos. Didn't you see them chasing Thecla?"

"Oh, yeah," Oata said, and for a second her nose argued with a sneeze as smoke curled up from the justice of the peace's daughter's brown-stained fingers as she bent her rolled hair over the table to sign the witness line on the marriage papers. The cigarette hand had let go of the top of the pink housecoat to steady itself against the table and Oata thought the pink lapel that fell open had had a smear of peanut butter on it. The justice of the peace's wife had kept her apron on, but she had quickly run a brush through her hair when her man called her to come sign while Yasch was kissing Oata on the lips right after they put the rings on each other's fingers. Actually, if the girl's cigarette smoke hadn't almost made her sneeze, Oata hardly would have noticed the witness business. The idea that they needed witnesses for such a thing just hadn't figured into their thinking as they had fuscheled in Oata's bed on that rainy evening after she told him about the baby. What she and Yasch had figured out together hadn't needed anybody else's advice or permission. Still, Oata never gave a thought to the possibility that she and Yasch could just have put the rings on each other's fingers themselves after breakfast and sailed her belly with little Doft inside through the winter and into the spring without any papers signed, or, as she thought when she was writing about it in her notebook, they could even have dropped their rings in the Salvation Army Christmas kettle when they had gone shopping by Polo Park. Who knew what such giving might have done? Oata hadn't needed a feed-the-five-thousand wedding, but she had still wanted rings on their fingers and papers signed for when little Doft was ready to slip himself into the world.

And for sure, when Oata had seen Luella, the preacher's wife, through the window pulling the chain on the woodpecker door knocker, she had hurry run upstairs to the jewellery box on the dresser to put on her rings before she opened the door. A diamond and some gold on a finger sticking out from the ear of a Tuesday morning coffee cup quickly took care of Luella's wifely obligations, and since Luella had interupted Oata in the middle of cutting up noodles, it didn't take long for her to offer to lend her the automatic noodle-making machine the Janzen family had given her for a wedding present. During the second cup of coffee Luella confessed that if she had her way she would just as soon make noodles with a good sharp knife because a knife was less bother to wash afterwards, and having a good sharp knife in her hand had a feel to it that you couldn't get from turning a crank on a machine.

For an eyeblink Oata remembered all the wedding presents she and Yasch didn't get because they hadn't had a big wedding in the church, but then she thought of Pug Peters and Sadie Nickel coming home from their honeymoon and finding a truckload of barley augered into their bedroom right on top of the brand new DeFehr bedroom suite Ha Ha Nickel had bought for them. For sure, the baseball team would have done such a thing for Yasch, too, if they had known about their wedding beforehand. No, Oata didn't think she and Yasch had done it the wrong way even if Yasch's Muttachi had complained that at least they could have invited her to the wedding, and sometimes Oata had wondered if she had been unfair to her mother in the mental home. For sure, she herself wanted to be there when Frieda would get married, and that's when Oata started wondering if she had written this right. Should she have let Politicks Paetkau's words carry all the way down Railway Street, past the Consumers Co-op Garage, in through the open church windows to Thecla's ears? What was Adelaide Thiessen thinking as she still sat there in the empty church staring at where the wedding had been? What was she thinking as she sat there alone with her white-gloved fingers clutching the little white purse full of Klik keys? And then Oata remembered the words running through Thecla's head.

> Iesaak, Shpriesack
> Schlenkjafoot
> Schleit siene Brut
> Em Kjalla doot.

And she was sure now she had done right by letting Thecla run from the wedding, and whether it would have been better to let Thecla act out the wedding she had been dreaming in front of the muzharich mirror on her grandmother's dresser was a question of taste and community standards. And plot, too, maybe. Would Yeeat Shpanst have been so willing to open his Lazy Leisure Camper door on the train tracks for a bride running naked? And what was Yeeat Shpanst anyways doing with Thecla Thiessen in his camper van? What was Yeeat Shpanst doing with Maam and the mental patients? Try as she might, Oata couldn't write herself inside that camper van.

But now Frieda was feeling like a foolish virgin, and as Oata looked along the double dike, along the strip of weeds between two tire tracks, weeds tall enough to wind themselves around the drive shaft of a low car, the green grass speckled with rusty weeds in the deep ditch carved into the land, she thought about those Bible men who had covered rocks with their coats to make pillows in the wilderness and dreamed about ladders to the sky, and she wondered what would happen if people could go back, not to the Old Testament fields with their flocks of sheep, no, but to the Gutenthal grass, taller than people, and lie down with their ears to the unploughed ground. What kinds of dreams could be dreamed then? What kinds of weddings would that give?

Oata reached for a fresh Farmers' Union notebook and pulled the carpenter's pencil from behind her ear and though she wanted to go back to the Gutenthal grass, taller than people, and lie down with her ears to the unploughed ground, her body pushed that pencil back to an Old Testamant field. A bloody baby lay naked on a patch of barren ground, Oata wrote, words flowing with the steady rhythm of memorized verses recited for gold stars. She filled four notebooks with writing, passing each one to Frieda as it was filled. Frieda saw her mother's writing trance and read Oata's writing for the first time, was astonished by her mother's strange words, frightened, and yet by the third notebook, even as the words became more shocking, she began to feel a comforting relief, the way a person feels after a sliver has been squeezed from a swollen finger.

Oata passed the fourth notebook to her daughter and stuck the carpenter's pencil behind her ear. She stared ahead along the double dike, feeling the throbbing veins in her writing hand slow down and relax. She had a flicker of a thought of what her story could mean if it was misread but then she, too, felt the comforting relief Frieda was feeling. For a moment she saw the virgin Gutenthal grass, taller than people. Then the dusk settled over the truck and Oata exclaimed, "Meyall, what is loose with us? Look, how schemma it is already! We have to get home to cook supper."

But Adelaide Thiessen was still in the Flatland Church sanctuary, her white-gloved fingers clutching the little white purse full of Klik keys. And she wasn't alone. Oata hadn't seen Knibble Thiessen at first when she was still sitting on the double dike with Frieda in the truck cab, but later, as she lay in bed listening to Yasch having a bath downstairs, she saw his shadow standing in front of the pulpit, hands stretched out to give away a bride. And as Oata lay there seeing Adelaide on the front church bench in the evening shadows, she wondered if her friend could hear the far droning of the tornado in the sky.

Why had it had always been so hard to speak with Adelaide about the real important things. Why always so many riddles? Why had Adelaide's mother, Mrs. Knibble, been almost more of a shadow than Oata's mother in the mental home? Then Oata saw Mrs. Knibble's faint shadow at the end of the church bench waiting for Knibble Thiessen to finish his giving away and come to sit down beside her on the bench. As Oata heard Yasch's footsteps climbing up the stairs, she felt herself staring at the refusing whites of Knibble Thiessen's eyes in the dark sanctuary of the Flatland Church and she shuddered as she thought it might be better to be given away than to be kept in the wrong jar between two shadows.

Yasch's bathtub body slipped into bed beside her, and even as they discussed the world with body language, Oata remembered the nightmares she had had about Uganda and Idi Amin and the taste of human flesh in her mouth, raw livers and sautêed hearts, her scream in the night waking the children in their beds across the hall, waking Yasch in the bed next to her, waking to the sheets wet with her sweat and the taste of the burning meat, burning flesh, and she thought of Isaac almost burning on the altar. She smelled the dead calf burning on the manure pile, saw Nobah Naze Needarp poking at the burning flesh with the pitchfork to make it burn better, and she wondered what it smelled like when the prophets were making burnt offerings to God, burning the goats and the sheep and rams on the altars, and it never made any sense to her that people would burn all this good meat on a pile of stones and she could never understand why Cain and his vegetarian offering weren't good enough for God. What must it have felt like to bring something special of one's own to give to God and then not have the smoke rise up to heaven like the smoke from his brother's burning meat?

One day Oata and Tusch Toews had been nature hunting in the bush around the Gutenthal School. Oata had collected a whole bunch of different kinds of grass that she had found in the unploughed strip between the bush and the flax field and she had found some interesting flowers, too, that hadn't seemed like weeds to her. But Tusch had caught an orange butterfly in her long skirt and the teacher had killed it with a drop of alcohol and pinned it through the head to fluffy cotton in a chocolate box and covered the top with some clear plastic. He hadn't even looked at Oata's grass and flower collection and the other kids had laughed at her weeds and said they should spray her with 2-4-D. Oata had wished for a butterfly, too, but she knew in her heart that the plants she had collected weren't weeds, not weeds at all. In the spring she had gone early in the morning to get the cows with her mother, and after they had walked down the cowpath through the oak trees to the open pasture, her mother had stopped and bent down to stare at some purple flowers growing beside a clump of snow. Oata had reached out to pick a flower, but her mother had grabbed her hand and shaken her head, *no,* though she never told Oata why she shouldn't pick this flower way out in the cow pasture when she had never cared if Oata had picked marigolds and gladiolas from the tractor-tire flowerbed in front of the house, or if she had picked pailfuls of dandelions and played butter under the chin all day long.

Had the 2-4-D killed them or the cows eaten them all? Why had her father, Nobah Naze Needarp, never told her the names of the many grasses that grew in the strips of land too narrow to plough? Had he even known what these different grasses were called? It seemed that all of the weighty things had been brought along from Russia, even the weeds, and she laughered herself over her mother's story about Hippy Pauls's great-grandfather, Dandelion Pauls, who had brought dandelion seeds over from Russlaunt in his felt burr socks. After Oata's different grasses had dried out in the pocket of her school jacket, she had sneaked a Redbird match and a syrup pail lid out to the pasture and knelt on the spot where she thought her mother's purple flowers had been in the spring. She arranged the grasses on the lid and struck the match on a stone. How she had loved the smell of the burning grass.

In her mind's nose Oata smelled smoke, cigarette smoke, then grass smoke, and as Yasch poosted out on top of her she giggled, thinking their love had started a fire. Then shuddered as she thought of her mother and Thecla Thiessen driving around in a Lazy Leisure Camper with Yeeat Shpanst while a tornado kjriezeled the pieces of Canada around. Oata's head began to spin as she felt the mouth of the tornado hovering over her and she clung to Yasch who pinned her to the sheets until she dozed off. But when he rolled over she woke and heard Politicks Paetkau's mumble, "We have to bring the buffalo back." Oata heard the twister rampaging through the night, saw it reach through the open truck window and snatch her four notebooks from the dashboard.

23

For the first few nights there was nothing much on the CBC *National Journal,* nothing that a person would remember the next morning. Then one night the Prime Minister came on and told the people of Canada that he was creating the Citizens' Future Forum. He had appointed a famous person Simple Hein had never heard about to be the Chair. This famous Chair was a guy with a wide-brimmed hat and a long black Zorro coat and his name was Al Seasoner. So right away Pierre Anchorbridge and the pundits put on their schwierich faces and wrinkled their foreheads and used lots of big words to try to predict what Seasoner and his Forum would hear as they went around the country listening to what the people said about the question that needed to be asked so it could be answered with the answer the Prime Minister already had shoved up his sleeve.

And to prove their determination to hear all points of view, the first thing the Forum did was charter two helicopters from Edmonton almost all the way to the Arctic Ocean so they could hear what the Bathurst Caribou herd had to say as it headed across the Barrenlands to the trees for the winter. It was quite a show, what with two helicopters for the Forum people and their staff all getting six hundred dollars a day plus expenses, and then yet the medium people chartered all the yellow Twin Otter airplanes in Yellowknife so they could take pictures and make reports to the people of Canada about what the Seasoner Forum was learning from the Bathurst herd.

It was such a hartsoft gruelich important thing that the whole CBC *National Journal* team chartered themselves a Hercules transport plane so Pierre Anchorbridge could put on a parka and broadcast the whole *National Journal* with the Bathurst Caribou herd running past behind him and then, of course, he had to talk with satellite TV phone to people in Ottawa, Toronto, Washington, and Morton's Harbour to hear what the pundits thought the caribou herd was saying to the Seasoner Forum. So Simple Hein and Bulchi Wiebe never actually got to hear what any of the caribou said, if they said anything at all, because the only time Pierre Anchorbridge turned away from the camera to actually look around himself he had a *Journal* reporter standing by with a live caribou leader interview, only it had taken her so long to find a parka with fur of the right colour to match with her hair and pink lipstick that the caribou had already hurried themselves over the river and all she could find to interview was a musk-ox, and the musk-ox wasn't talking.

The next night the Seasoner Forun was in a different part of Canada and the CBC *National Journal* was back in Toronttawa, and it was announced that a half-dozen regional CBC stations were getting closed down because of budget restraints.

And so it went, day after day, as Bulchi Wiebe and Simple Hein flew over the country dropping their loads of bottle messages on the Canadian people, and each night they lay back in their sleeping bags watching Pierre Anchorbridge tell the country where the Seasoner Forum had been listening to the people and sometimes he even told a bit about what the people were saying to the Citizens' Future Forum, but that didn't happen much. Most of the time just the pundits said, "I don't know," or "It's hard to predict," or "This is what I think they are saying," and for sure it mostly sounded like they didn't see their job as telling people what they were hearing so much as trying to tell the people what they should be thinking about all this.

But then one evening on the *CBC National Journal* there was a bit of a surprise. It wasn't on the news exactly. In fact it took the news people three days to find out about it. The surprise was in the commercial between the *National* and the *Journal,* the commercial for pretend States beer in a silver can. As the silver can was shooting across the screen like a bullet it suddenly changed into a two-litre pop bottle, and Yeeat Shpanst, standing in front of his Lazy Leisure Camper, caught it in his arms like a football. With the pink wild rose blooming brightly on the breast of his Hawaii shirt, he recited: "I HAVE A VISION—I SEE MILLIONS OF BEETWEEDERS, WITH HOES SHARPENED, DESCENDING ON OUR CHOKING FIELDS, HACKING AWAY AT THE MUSTARD AND THE WILD OATS, SEPARATING THE DOUBLES, FREEING THE SWEET SUGAR BEET TO FLOURISH AS WE WEED OUR WAY INTO THE FUTURE. THERE, WITH THE HELP OF GOD, I WILL LEAD YOU!"

"Ha ha ha, that's the stuff!" Bulchi Wiebe chuckled in his sleeping bag. "See, Hein? We are the solution."

Simple Hein wasn't sure what a solution was but for sure it made him feel important to see his pop bottle and the scary big camper van right there on the TV. Then, from out of the funnel loudspeakers on top of the Lazy Leisure van, like children at a Christmas concert, came the words: "FELLOW CANADIANS, WE CANNOT ESCAPE HISTORY. A HOUSE DIVIDED AGAINST ITSELF CANNOT STAND. IT HURTS JUST AS MUCH TO HAVE A TOOTH EXTRACTED AS TO HAVE IT PULLED OUT. YOU CAN'T DIG COAL WITH BAYONETS." And Yeeat Shpanst stood there grinning, with his chest puffed out, holding up the two-litre pop bottle with the golden message inside. "LET US BEGIN BY COMMITTING OURSELVES TO THE TRUTH. IT IS THE ABSOLUTE RIGHT OF THE STATES TO SUPERVISE THE FORMATION OF PUBLIC OPINION. PUBLIC OPINION WINS WARS. WHY SHOULD WE SUBSIDIZE

INTELLECTUAL CURIOUSITY? I PREFER THE DOLLAR SIGN, THE SYM-
BOL OF FREE TRADE, THEREFORE, OF A FREE MIND." And Yeeat
Shpanst began to repeat his bottle verse again: "I HAVE A
VISION—I SEE MILLIONS OF BEETWEEDERS . . ," but he was cut off
as the control room people woke up and handed the TV back
to the *National Journal.*

For the next three nights Yeeat Shpanst and his two-litre
bottle verse hijacked the States beer in a silver can. Then the
news people found out about it and Pierre Anchorbridge
reported unexplained signal interference in the broadcasting
system not only on the CBC but on all the TV news shows, even
imported cable programs, and as he was turning to the Chief
Political Correspondent for details the *National Journal*
blinked off the screen and Yeeat Shpanst came on again. When
his bottle verse was finished, the van drove away and left a
young woman in a flowered sundress standing in a park beside
a double stroller with identical twin boys sucking on Winnipeg
Jets baby bottles. The woman held up a two-litre pop bottle
and recited the bottle verse and when she was finished she
said, "I BELIEVE THE VISION OF THE BEETWEEDERS IS A MESSAGE
TELLING US TO BE WARY OF FREE TRADE AND THE CORPORATE
AGENDA. IT IS TELLING US THAT WE MUST RID OURSELVES OF THE
MULTINATIONAL PARASITES WHO ARE KILLING OUR PEOPLE. WE MUST
PUT PEOPLE BEFORE CORPORATE PROFITS!" Reciting voices like an
angel chorus schowelled around the woman as she grinned
and waved her bottle while her twin boys waved their Jets
baby bottles and spritzed Enfalac all over themselves: "I OFFER
NEITHER PAY, NOR QUARTERS, NOR PROVISIONS; I OFFER HUNGER,
THIRST, FORCED MARCHES, BATTLES, AND DEATH. I OFFER THE END
RUN; GOVERNMENT BY FOOTBALL PLAYERS. LET THOSE WHO LOVE
CANADA IN THEIR HEARTS AND NOT WITH THEIR LIPS ONLY, FOLLOW
ME. IT'S NOT THE SIZE OF YOUR CAUCUS, IT'S . . ."

Pierre Anchorbridge came back on the screen and with a
very red face apologized for the technical difficulties and went
on with the news and reported again how the Seasoner Forum
was crisscrossing the country holding hearings to hear what
the ordinary Canadian had to say. Al Seasoner himself, in his

wide-brimmed hat and Zorro coat, called upon the poets of the country to speak to the Citzens' Future Forum to use their word power to support a new vision for our great nation. Simple Hein thought for sure the *Journal* next would have four poets talking on the square TVs they have on the CBC wall but instead a curly haired hippy with glasses on talked about how a States wolf dancing movie was hartsoft better than a States Ninja Turkey 2, and Hein fell asleep without ever seeing a poet on TV.

Each day Simple Hein and Bulchi Wiebe flew farther and farther. They dropped bottles on the Rocky Mountains and around the Great Lakes. They bombed the CN Tower in Toronto and the Saddle Dome in Calgary. Back and forth from the Martens machine shed to the farthest reaches of this fair land the little Canadian-built Found Brothers FBA-2C ferried load after load of pop bottle messages, dropping them like manna from the sky, and where the little plane couldn't go the wind helped out, blowing the floating bottles like tumbleweed over fields and floods, rocks, hills, and plains. And each day as they loaded the net bag Simple Hein figured they would run out of bottles for sure, but there were always leftovers when Bulchi Wiebe packed the five hundredth bottle into the last compartment and fastened the velcro closers. Then they would take off and float over the land until they reached the targeted destination. And every night the TV news would be interrupted at some point by an ordinary citizen holding a bottle, reciting the beetfield vision, and then testifying as to what it meant personally. And Bulchi Wiebe chuckled and laughed and cheered at each new interpretation, and it didn't bother him when some of the interpretations contradicted each other.

Even Simple Hein could see that if one person said that weeding beets meant free trade was good and then the next day another person said that weeding beets meant free trade was bad, then there could be an argument over truth. But that's how it went. One night a man in a fourteen-piece business suit would say sincerely, like a radio pastor, that the beetweeding was a symbol of action against big government and regulations so that the God-given forces of free trade and the free market could create the nearest thing to heaven, yes they will. The next night a Member of Parliament would explain that the beetweeding was the settlement of the constitutional question so that politicians would be free to deal with the problems of the economy. And then on another night a woman would say that the beetweeding meant a removal of the patriarchal structures of society to free women and children from the stranglehold of men. But then a few nights later another woman would hold up a pop bottle and shout that the beetweeding meant clearing the garden of the feminist ideas now destroying the family. And Simple Hein almost cried in his sleeping bag the night a little boy all alone beside a creek full of garbage said in a tearful voice, "We got to clean up the pollution."

Bulchi Wiebe cheered each new interpretation, punched his fist into his hand, and said, "Right! Be the solution!" And each morning they loaded up the net bag with more bottles and took off for Hinton, Alberta, or Melfort, Saskatchewan, or Dildo Run in Newfoundland. They were hovering over Rae Lakes, NWT, when the first snow of the season fell, and Simple Hein's eyes got very big when Bulchi Wiebe pointed at the little lake where a man had fallen down to the ice from a plane one time and he was sure happy to curl up in his sleeping bag in the Martens house on that particular night.

That, too, was the night when there was new news for a change about the Citzens' Future Forum. It was quite a problem for the TV people to have new news that they hadn't rigged up themselves, and you could see in Pierre Anchorbridge's face and in the faces of the reporters with pink lipstick or dark moustaches how exciting it was to have new news. But they were also hopping around with frustration because they couldn't get any sex, lies, and videotape to show to the people guarding their TV sets at home. They couldn't even get any sound bites. All they could get were some interviews with people who knew other people who said they had been there.

What Simple Hein made of it was that two things were

going on that the news people and the pundits and the politickers didn't know about. One was a humungously shindasche holem de gruel hartsoft big camper van driving around the country holding hearings, inviting the people to come into the van to say their piece about the kind of country they wanted to live in. There were reports that people who had visited the van came out wearing wild roses on their chests, but a *Newsworld* reporter who had tried to interview a woman with a wild rose on her breast got squirted in the eye. People wearing wild roses were unwilling to speak to medium people. Some pundits speculated that the van was the same one in the interfering TV signals, but despite a joint task force of top technical people from all networks, the experts had still not determined how these messages were penetrating the broadcast system. And the problem was growing, too. Not only were newscasts being interrupted. Sportscasts, soaps, game shows, and even Bart Simpson were interrupted regularly, often at the one dramatic moment in an otherwise dreary program. Even the newspapers heard about it and then the tabloids in the grocery stores ran cover stories about aliens invading earth through televison. One of the foreign tabloids reported that the phantom hearings van was accompanied by a woman in high-heeled shoes who warmed up the audience by leading it in a chant of the Prime Minister's dark day for Canada speech, and the pundits were in a quandry as to whether this was a secret weapon of the Prime Minister's side of the campaign or whether it was a treacherous treasonous activity on the part of the *Royal Canadian Air Farce* satirizing the most serious crucial moment in the history of the nation.

The second item of new news was that apparently some non-Toronttawa based reporters who actually encountered genuine ordinary Canadians in the course of gathering the news had discovered a phantom dark-horse politician making thunderous well-received speeches from the platform of a flatdeck trailer. Unfortunately, Pierre Anchorbridge had to say that sex, lies, and videotape were still unavailable on that story.

24 BEETFIELD CHORUS

Doesn't this row have
an end? Or this field?
It's already almost
October.
Makes no sense.
Keep weeding. It's a tough row to hoe, but we'll get to the
end.
Sure, and then we just have to
tough it back to the other end.
Makes no sense.
It's almost Halloween!
And still weeding
beets. Can't even get a
suntan.
What you need to be brown for anyways?
Weed faster. It's a global trend. There's nothing we can do.
It's reality. Don't you watch the *National Journal?*
Nah, I just watch
Roseanne if I'm not out.

Makes no sense.

        What already? Makes no sense.
Makes dollars for somebody, you can betchur
boots and win a 6/49.

That's the real world. There's nothing we can do. It's just the
way the economy is. Just weed faster.

        To run away in a wedding dress.

            Who? What?

Didn't you hear?

            Yeah, you deaf or something?

Yeah. Kjnirps Iesaak Klippenstein standing in front
of the preacher with seven blue best men ready to
get welded together till death do us apart and his
bride claws out just before the "I do."

            You mean in the
            church and everything
            all ready and people
            crying and taped
            flowers on the cars?

        To run away in a wedding dress.

Yeah, and Kjnirps Iesaak Klippenstein and his
seven best men chased her to the street meeting
by the febeizeled elevator, but she got away.

        To run away in a wedding dress.

            Kjnirps Iesaak Klippenstein
            singing the blues.

No values nowadays. Too much welfare. Unemployment
cheaters. Poverty line too high.

        To run away in a wedding dress. Why
        didn't she at least take it off? Makes no
        sense.

            What you mean?

Yeah, a bride has to keep her clothes on, even if
she's running away.

Values. No values nowadays. Too many caught in the saftey net.

        Listen. You don't understand. She still has
        it on.

What? Who? What she
has on?

The dress. She is still wearing the dress,
two weeks after.

How you know that?

Yeah, how you know that?

I saw her . . .

Saw her in the funnies?

No, I saw her. I know it was her. On the
television.

No way!

It was on a Maxi-Thin commercial during
Kids in the Hall when all of a sudden this
bride with cherry-red rooster-comb hair
comes running on this grassy field full of
flowers and a shiny object drops out of
the sky and she catches it and it looks flat
like a book wrapped in silvery stuff like a
survival blanket from Canadian Tire . . .

You mean like
Madonna's book?

Madonna reads books?

Madonna has a picture
book all wrapped in
silver stuff so little
boys don't smear their
peanut butter fingers
over the pages in the
store.

Leave Madonna and her underwear out of
this. Thecla catches this silvery thing and
holds it to herself like a baby and she
looks out from the TV and says, a loonie
is a loonie is a loonie.

So? I could have told
you a loonie is a
loonie.

Not in the States. It's only seventy-five cents there.
But why is she still wearing the wedding
dress when she ran away from the
wedding? Why didn't she put on
something else already instead of
shlepping the train through the dirt?
How come a bride dress has a
train anyways?
Listen. Eaza Bone
Peetash is gone.
On strike again probly. Damn unions.
No, he's gone. They
found his jigger with
the motor still running
by the Buffalo Creek
bridge, but no Eaza
Bone.
No, that's not true, in Rosenfeld
I heard that the jigger is gone
too.
Maybe CPR just abandon another track. Can't make
money without a crow.
Crow's nest or crow banker?
Subsidies have no place in a global economy. We just have to
be competitive. Tighten our belts.
But the wedding dress. Makes no sense.
A loonie is a loonie.
Except in a family trust.
Speaking of family,
they say Adelaide
Thiessen and her
father and Mrs.
Knibble are still in the
church waiting.
Huh?

25

During the next few evenings Simple Hein and Bulchi Wiebe, curled up in their sleeping bags, watched reports of government officials and network presidents and ombudsmen ordering investigations. The phenomena disrupting the land were treated as a near crisis, and Hova Jake Harder of CSIS was put in charge. In an exclusive *Fifth Estate* muckraker rebroadcast on *Midday, 24 Hours, W5, Canada AM, America's Most Wanted,* and MTN *Pulse News,* Hova Jake revealed that by using the latest psychographic findings based on the most sophisticated CSIS polling information, right or wrong within four percentage points nineteen times out of twenty, a forensic profile of the phantom politician had been constructed. The phantom politician didn't make normal speeches. No, this phantom read stories and sometimes even poems from a black book. Sometimes he declaimed his words, sometimes he sat on a chair and read softly so audiences had to cup their ears to grasp his words. CSIS suspected that the phantom politician might be a poet deluded with the apparent success of poet-politicians in the torn iron-curtain countries. Hova Jake even had a police artist computer sketch which came on the screen and then changed itself to show the possible ways that a poet might look.

The next night the *National Journal* showed the Chair of the Canada Council hauled before a Senators' Committee to explain how come the Canada Council Reading Program would give money to a subversive lunatic, for how else could a poet afford to crisscross the country giving readings? And the night after that the TV showed the Chair of the Canada Council and the Public Readings Officer on their hands and knees with the finely printed lists of official Canada Council approved readings spread on the Chair's office carpet floor. But even with a magnifying glass they couldn't find a match for the curly sandy-haired man with the black book who was causing such a stir. The computer data base housing all Canada Council grant applications and plot outlines since the Council's formation in the fifties showed not one clue, though the names of all poets and fiction writers whose applications had been turned down by juries more than once were handed over to Hova Jake for thorough investigations. The editors of *Canadian Forum, This Magazine, NeWest Review, Briarpatch, Frank,* and *Canadian Dimension* were taken out for beer in seedy downtown karaoke bars. But none could offer a clue as to who this man was. CSIS operatives dug deeper and bought furtive glasses of draft beer for editors of literary magazines: *Prairie Fire, Grain, Dandelion, Malahat, Geist, Prism International, Quarry, Paragraph, Fiddlehead, Canadian Fiction Magazine, Open Letter, Capilano Review, Fireweed, Gasp, Antigonish Review, Canadian Author and Bookman, Descant, Event, Exile, Matrix, Blood & Aphorisms, New Quarterly, Prison Journal, Windscript, Raddle Moon, Rampike, Room of One's Own, Scrivener, West Coast Line, Whetstone, TickleAce, Zymergy, On Spec, Zygote,* and *Secrets from the Orange Couch.* Not a clue was uncovered, though for two days there were tremendous beating hearts at CSIS headquarters and in the Prime Minister's Office as manicured fingers perused the back issue of *Border Crossings* containing Lorna Crozier's vegetable poems. And yes, a record number of poems were read into *Hansard* as various caucuses took stands against vegetarianism.

The unapproved TV bottle-verse spots caught the eye and ire of the CRTC who suspected evangelical religious broadcasters, and despite the fact that CRTC investigators became regular churchgoers and at least a dozen had conversion experiences, the phantom politician-poet remained elusive and unidentified. A would-be politician who avoided television was a complete bafflement to the medium people.

Yet the phantom politician-poet existed, and a few broadcast journalists managed to track down his meetings, only to discover that their equipment failed to work in his presence. There was an unidentified source of interference when they attempted to record the man on video or audiotape. It was as if he was protected by a Ronnie Star Wars shield which scrambled all electronic signals, including those required by cellular phones. Yet, the man's own voice, his reading voice, carried to the crowd without a PA system. At the same time, some witnesses maintained that there was a pair of TV people who always showed up in a Carpet Cleaning and Audio van.

Then a breakthrough occurred when a print journalist who hadn't forgotten how to take notes with a pencil managed to get a coherent story on the man into the newspapers. The high point of interest for the sex, lies, and videotape people was that the man was being introduced by a young woman with spiked cherry-red hair wearing a white wedding dress who passed out tracts containing the politician-poet's message after the reading was over. But instead of reading from the tract in their news reports, the medium people engaged a retired police artist to come up with a composite drawing of the bride based on what people who knew people who had attended a flatdeck poetry reading thought had been seen. However, when this police-artist drawing was put on the screen, some people thought it looked like a cross between the Minister of External Affairs and the Prime Minister's wife, and others thought she looked like a cross between the woman George Bush said he didn't fool around with and Howard Cosell.

And each day Simple Hein and Bulchi Wiebe flew that Found Brothers FBA-2C airplane, dropping their endless supply of bottle messages on the country, never running out of fuel. Each night they retired to their sleeping bags to watch the CBC *National Journal* before they fell into dreams full of sleep.

26

Schneppa Kjnals was on the Trans-Canada going east, getting close to Thunder Bay, after a short stop by Kakabeka Falls where in the mist the earring bengel had tried to show him the face of the chief's daughter who had sacrificed herself over the falls in a canoe to trick the enemy Sioux. Suddenly the traffic came to a stop as dead as a lineup of cars behind a car trying to make an illegal left turn at 4:30 on a Friday afternoon at the crazy corner in Winnipeg.

At first Schneppa Kjnals figured it was an aboriginal barricade of angry people tired of being dismissed with another slippery study or convoluted commission, but then, as he followed the earring bengel and his YOH-NEH sign through the stopped cars, he saw Terry Fox's statue above the heads of the crowd. He combed through his brain to see if it was an anniversary of the day Terry Fox gave up his one-legged run across the country on this very spot. Then the sing-song voice came floating over the parked cars and craning necks, and as he threaded his way through the crowd after the earring bengel, he could hear the words as clearly as if he had been sitting in the Gutenthal Church wearing Happy Heppner's grandfather's hearing aid connected to the pulpit microphone.

27 A POLITICKS PAETKAU
FLATDECK READING

In the Land of Them, north of the Land of Us, the people
built themselves a sacred trust. A sacred trust is a thing that
is built because it is good for all the people. A sacred trust is
a scary thing. A sacred trust is like sunshine scaring monkeys
in a long-ago jungle.

When the sacred trust was first mentioned in the Land of
Them, there were many who said it was an indecent proposal.
Many saw red. Many saw collective farms. Many threatened
to pile their families into their trustworthy station wagons and
move to the Land of Us. Some even did that. Some never
returned to the Land of Them. Some only returned for surgery.

But the sacred trust was built and it was strengthened and
reinforced as the years went by. The people of the Land of
Them became proud of their sacred trust and most agreed that
even though the Land of Them had no palm trees or irrigated
deserts growing lettuce, it had a sacred trust that made it the
most wonderful land in the world. It appeared that the whole
hockey team, so to speak, the right-winger and the left-winger,
the centre and the goalie, the defencemen and the coach all

agreed that the scared trust was a good thing for the people of Them. And the fans in the stands had no inkling that all was not well with the sacred trust. After all, the whole team kept saying that the sacred trust was the most important thing in the Land of Them, north of the Land of Us.

In the Land of Us the people had no sacred trust, though they had palm trees and irrigated deserts growing lettuce. Often people in the Land of Us looked at the sacred trust in the Land of Them with envy. Of course, there were those who said a sacred trust was an indecent proposal. Many saw red. Many saw collective farms.

At the same time, there were rumours about *those* in the Land of Them who looked with envy at the palm trees and irrigated deserts in the Land of Us and wondered what made the difference between the two lands. And some of *those* in the Land of Them concluded that it was the sacred trust that made the difference. The sacred trust was the reason there were no palm trees or irrigated deserts in the Land of Them.

Still, even when some of *those* came to power, they continued to praise the sacred trust, made ringing speeches about the importance of the sacred trust. And the people of the Land of Them were reassured that even *those* would not destroy the sacred trust. However, when some of *those* made their ringing speeches in praise of the sacred trust, they began slipping in words like *restructuring* and *efficiency* and *competitiveness*. But the people had faith in *those* in charge, though many started to feel small irritations about the sacred trust, small uncertainties, a minute change in flavour, the way some people will tell you that Coca-Cola nowadays doesn't taste the same as it did fifty years ago. And occasionally someone would say out loud that something was happening to the sacred trust, that she was sure the trust was getting smaller, that it was leaning a little on the right-hand back corner. And right away some of *those* would vehemently deny that any such thing was happening, though they did use the *restructuring* and *competitiveness* words more and more each time they rose to defend the sacred trust.

But the sacred trust became less satisfying. Burned-out light bulbs were seldom replaced. Snow wasn't cleared off the front steps. Broken windows were boarded up instead of being repaired. And people who tried to use the services of the sacred trust found that the people who were to serve them seemed very brusk and bureaucratic, sometimes even downright rude. Lineups got longer and longer and service was only received after getting past a series of lower officials who kept saying, "I don't believe we can help you, but if you are prepared to wait . . ." And then the service received by the persistent was usually only a shoddy halfway measure, and people became exhausted by the ordeal of trying to benefit from the sacred trust.

And then one day some of *those* in positions of power said in a TV news special that the Land of Them could no longer afford the sacred trust and therefore it would be knocked down. And the exhausted people remembered all the lineups and waiting and rude behaviour and unsatisfactory service, and they sipped the Coca-Cola that didn't taste the same as it used to and pressed the button on the remote control to watch ducks and sharks playing hockey on desert ice.

28

Schneppa Kjnals wouldn't have argued that Politicks was at his best when he did that reading on the flatdeck parked in front of the Terry Fox statue overlooking the sleeping giant lying in the mostly frozen bay. It wasn't exactly beetfield weather, and Politicks Paetkau was shivering on that red stool as he read from Yeeat Shpanst's black book, twitching each time the earring bengel pumped his sign on a stick and shouted, "YOH!" and then "NEH!"

It was after the second or maybe third "YOH-NEH" shout that a movement caught Kjnals's eye behind the Terry Fox statue. Thecla Thiessen in her wedding dress climbed over the spiked fence that keeps the tourists from falling down into the mile of bush that separates the highway from the CPR tracks and the sleeping giant bay. A piece of her train caught on a spike but she tore herself free. Kjnals saw the silver package in her hand as she climbed onto the flatdeck, one cherry-red wedding shoe still on her foot. The bengel shouted "YOH!" as Thecla knelt at Politicks's feet and rested the silver bundle on her lap. Kjnals raised his binoculars when the "Sacred Trust" story ended. Thecla looked like she was begging something from Politicks, only now that he wasn't reading Yeeat Shpanst anymore his voice didn't carry out to the crowd's ears. Cora Lee Semple and Barbara crowded in. Cora Lee reached out for the silver bundle, but Thecla wouldn't give it, and then the whole scene interrupted itself with a holler louder than a drunk at a hockey game. A pastel-blue arm holding up a cherry-red high-heeled shoe shoved itself through the crowd from the east. "THECLA!" the voice hollered again. Thecla whirled around, saw Knirps Iesaak Klippenstein and his seven pastel-blue best men pushing through the crowd who were wondering if they should stick around in the wind shivering off the sleeping giant bay for another story.

Thecla raised the silver bundle over her head, and through his binoculars Kjnals saw her look right into his eyes. As soon as she saw him she spotted a parting of the Red Sea path through the crowd and jumped from the flatdeck and flitzed through this Red Sea path waving the silver bundle. Kjnirps Iesaak Klippenstein sprang after her. Holding their noses like naked boys leaping into a dugout, the seven pastel-blue best men followed. Red wedding shoe cradled in his hand like an egg in a spoon relay, Kjnirps raced after Thecla. Schneppa Kjnals stood paralyzed and he figured for sure Kjnirps was going to catch his bride when he heard a horn honk behind him. He looked over his shoulder thinking it would be Yeeat Shpanst and his Lazy Leisure Camper. But he was wrong. It was a small school-bus load of models in wedding dresses who had come to the Terry Fox Lookout to do a Winter Wedding White photo session for *Bride* magazine. The brides rushed past Kjnals, engulfed Thecla, and stopped Kjnirps Iesaak Klippenstein and his seven best men in their tracks by holding up their stocking feet to try on the red high-heel Kjnirps Iesaak held in his hand. Thecla broke free of the brides and grabbed Kjnals's arm.

"Which way's your car?"

Thankful for the rubber padding on the bumpers of other people's new cars, Kjnals turned his car around and headed back down the highway, ready to race all the way to Kenora with this red-haired bride, but Thecla yelled, "Turn left at the first corner!" Kjnals swung onto Holden Avenue on two wheels, and as soon as the vw tilted back onto all fours Thecla yelled, "Turn east at Strathcona!" Schneppa Kjnals lost a hubcap around that corner and as he floored the accelerator a thought flashed through his head that he might find a replacement at Prell Doell's Salvage Sales in Gutenthal. Then the CPR tracks loomed ahead. "Stop! Stop! Let me off!" Leaving ten thousand clicks of tire wear on the pavement, Kjnals stopped the vw ten feet from the rails. Thecla jumped out of the car, still holding the silver bundle, and on one red high-heel fled toward the tracks just as Eaza Bone Peetasch and his jigger came rattling along from the west. Without letting the jigger slow down, she jumped on beside him. She waved back at Kjnals, and then the jigger disappeared around a curve into the Ontario bush.

By the time Kjnals got back to the Terry Fox Lookout, the one-legged runner looked very alone in the wind shivering off the sleeping giant bay. Schneppa Kjnals stepped on the accelerator and a few minutes later going up a hill, he passed Tape Deck Toews's Carpet Cleaning and Audio van in the slow-traffic keep-right lane. But the earring bengel was no-where to be seen. Kjnals drove on, worried about the earring bengel freezing to death in his Ski-doo suit. Then, just as he was thinking he should turn around and go back, he overtook the *Bride* magazine school bus. The earring bengel's YOH-NEH sign was pressed up against the back window.

29

It was a Sunday evening. Bulchi Wiebe and Simple Hein had celebrated the day of rest by dropping their pop bottle verses on churches only and now, after eating their simple supper of a loaf and canned sucker-fishes, they were relaxing early in their sleeping bags. Darkness had fallen as they watched *The Road to Avonlea* on the little red TV waiting for the *CBC Sunday Night Movie*. But when *Avonlea* was over, loud drumming and trumpets brought on Pierre Anchorbridge: "TONIGHT A CITIZENS' FUTURE FORUM NEWS SPECIAL. WHAT IS THE ORDINARY CANADIAN SAYING OUT THERE? WE TAKE YOU LIVE TONIGHT TO THE TINY CURLING RINK IN GUTENTHAL, MANITOBA, WHERE THE SEASONER COMMISSION IS SITTING TO GATHER THE VIEWS OF THE AVERAGE CITIZEN."

"Holy doodles!" Hein squealed. "You hear dat, Bulchi Wiebe? Gutenthal on the *CBC National Journal!* Must be I'm crazy!"

"Heh, heh, heh," Bulchi Wiebe chuckled. "See! We can be the solution!" They leaned toward the TV trying to see past Pierre Anchorbridge to the Gutenthal Curling Rink in the background, but Pierre Anchorbridge didn't want to let the people see until it was absolutely necessary, so he kept talking to these pundits from Toronttawa while Al Seasoner and his CFF people got out of their Grey Goose Circle Tour Bus and filed across the gravel to the curling rink door.

"There's Haustig Neefeld!" Hein exclaimed.

"For sure, he's got the keys for the curling rink!"

"And Hippy Pauls!"

"Still can't afford razor blades!"

"Hey, who's driving Haustig Neefeld's truck?"

"Didn't you know? Yasch Siemens bought that truck from him."

"Look. Oata is driving the truck!"

"Well, sure, it's the nineties!"

"And Yasch is carrying a scribbler in his hand."

Then the CBC control room someplace switched off Pierre Anchorbridge and showed the inside of the waiting room where Al Seasoner and the Future Forum had seated themselves behind the folding table up on the platform. The curling rink pulpit rested on another table down on the floor. Bright lights glared for three big TV cameras on wheels and microphones dangled down like snakes in the Garden of Eden. Gutenthal people crowding in looked lost in their own curling rink. The outside picture showed lots more Gutenthallers trying to squeeze in. But there was no more room and for sure no time to switch the hearing into the ice part because the *CBC National Journal* was showing the whole thing live. But Lectric Loewen and Tape Deck Toews had rigged up loudspeaking boxes and floodlights on the baseball backstop and soon all the bleachers and all the baselines were full with people.

"Hey, there's Hingst Heinrichs!"

"There's Schacht Schulz!"

"There's Ha Ha Nickel!"

"There's Zoop Zack Friesen!"

Simple Hein and Bulchi Wiebe were so busy looking into the TV for people they knew they didn't even hear Al Seasoner's opening remarks, and then they almost fuhschlucked themselves when they saw who was standing by the little pulpit with Oata sitting on a chair beside him.

"Yasch Siemens? Talk politics in front of the people?"

"Sure, why not? He gave a testimony in the church once."

"Is that so? When?"

"Long time ago. But people don't talk about it."

"Listen! He's starting to talk."

Yasch Siemens looked down at Oata for a second, cleared his throat, and started to read from the scribbler page on the pulpit: "Mr. Al Seasoner and the rest of the Future Forum members, I welcome you to the Gutenthal Curling Rink. My name is Yasch Siemens and beside me is my wife, Oata. We farm a half-section here in Gutenthal, mixed farming, with a small hog operation. Me and Oata are just quiet farmers and nobody ever phones us up to ask us if the Prime Minister should go up or down on his poll, or if the Finance Minister should be in a mental home. Still, when we heard that your Citizens' Future Forum was coming to the Gutenthal Curling Rink, me and Oata figured we should come here and say what we think about this country."

"C'mon Yasch, you tell 'em good!" Hein cheered and then he cupped his ear with his hand and leaned closer to the TV.

"So I phoned on the dial phone to 1-800-66-FOR-UM, and this guy who sounded like maybe he was a Russlenda German from Yanzeed answered the other end and right away wanted to know my name, address, and postal code. Now, I know already that in Canada nothing can move if you don't give your postal code."

Bulchi Wiebe punched Simple Hein's shoulder and said, "That's the stuff, Yasch. Tell 'em what it's like for the little guy."

"Sure enough, three weeks to the day, came the Citizens' Future Forum Discussion Kit. There was the *Official Pamphlet*, the discussion points, a *Guide to Leading a Group Discussion*, a *Group Report* form, *Individual Report* forms, an *Invitation*, a postage-paid *Envelope*, and *Signs* to put up on telephone posts. Oata hung the *Guide to Leading a Group Discussion* on a nail beside the toilet paper roll."

Simple Hein and Bulchi Wiebe listened with all four ears and their noses, too, as Yasch told how he and Oata had their very own Citizens' Future Forum at home with Politicks and Pinklich Paetkau on All Saints' Day in the afternoon. They cheered each time Yasch told that Al Seasoner another thing about how it was for the little guy in this country.

"Now, I'm not a history professor, but the way Politicks Paetkau explained it, the reason we have a country called Canada at all is because John A. Macdonald and the Fathers of Confederation didn't want the United States to take over all of North America. That's why John A. sat with his wife on the cowcatcher of the CPR train through the Rocky mountains with a glass of whiskey in his hand, a glass without even a bottom line."

Simple Hein watched and listened, his ears and eyes open so wide he felt like he hardly had anything else left on his face. He saw Oata give Yasch one with her elbow and Yasch turned to her and said: "Oh, yeah, Oata, I know I'm supposed to talk about Quebec, too. No, I wouldn't forget to do that. You know, Mr. Seasoner, I'll bet in the last few months you have heard a lot of people complain about having French shoved down their throats, and if Quebec wants to go, let them go already and let us get on with making a buck."

And Bulchi Wiebe punched Hein on the shoulder again when Yasch explained how the Flat Germans were losing their language.

"So I can understand why French speakers are worried about losing their language. I'm worried, too. I mean, already, there are a whole bunch of Canadians who think Coors Light is beer."

"Hey hey hey," laughed Bulchi Wiebe. "Hey hey hey."

"So, I would have to say, yes, I am in favour of bilingualism in this country, though I know I may find a dead orchard frog on my windshield for saying this too loud. But, Mr. Seasoner, I see that you have taken your jacket off and you have loosened your tie, so I know I will have to stop talking soon."

So Yasch Siemens told the story about how the Gutenthal

Curling rink had been saved from the artificial ice rink in town, and Simple Hein listened very hard because he had been at that meeting, too.

"And we signed the Gutenthal Curling Accord. Now only the skips have to use corn brooms, the others use what they like. And Pinklich Paetkau suggested a parallel accord, so now we have prizes for 'artistic impression' in sweeping. I have to say that, for me, there is something special about a corn broom in the hands of a woman curler, right from the way she whacks the dirt off the bottom of the rock, to the way she balances herself as she lifts the rock in a backswing, then glides along with the rock to the hog line with her broom raised like an angel's wing. Then the slap of the sweepers' brooms is one of the sweetest sounds in the world. Thank you, Mr. Seasoner, for listening to us, and oh yeah, I almost forgot. Politicks Paetkau phoned just before we came here and he said that for sure I should tell you: We have to bring the buffalo back."

"Heh heh heh!" Bulchi Wiebe clapped his hands as Yasch sat down beside Oata. And right away Pierre Anchorbridge and his Toronttawa pundits tried to make head or tail out of what Yasch Siemens had said to the Seasoner Forum, but the curling rink waiting room was still in the picture in the background, and then it looked like Pierre Anchorbridge was getting buzzed in his ear plug and the control room switched Pierre Anchorbridge and his pundits right out of the picture. A row of people had lined themselves up on the platform behind Al Seasoner and each person held up a big green sign with a red tinsel letter on it.

"Hey hey hey," Bulchi Wiebe laughed as he figured out that the letters spelled, "Seasoner's Greetings." The people in the line began saying up a verse like children at a Christmas program, only these weren't children. No sir, not children, and Simple Hein recognized some from the time Help All Heinrichs took him to the mental home and thought maybe he could leave him there. But the mental home doctors had seen what Help All was trying to do, so while Hein was playing daumbrat checkers with Oata's mother, one of the big nurses had made

Help All Heinrichs fill out an application form and he almost checked *himself* into the mental home.

So Hein recognized Oata's mother in the middle chanting the Prime Minister's dark day for Canada speech the loudest, all the way through, right from "FELLOW CANADIANS, WE CANNOT ESCAPE HISTORY" till "THE TRUE NORTH STRONG AND FREE. O SAY, CAN'T YOU SEE?" And then Oata's mother, with a TV remote control in her hand, climbed up on the table, her high heel almost stepping on Al Seasoner's fingers. She started conducting the people in the waiting room and they chanted the speech along with her, and when they got to "AND I SAY TO THE PROVINCES, YOU MAY HAVE ALL THAT THE HEN LAYS, EXCEPT FOR THE EGGS," Oata's mother jumped from the table, landed on her high heels lightly as a cat, and the line of mental patients clambered over the table after her, and Al Seasoner and his people wondered themselves if maybe the buffalo had come back the way this Yasch Siemens guy had talked about.

The people in the curling rink waiting room chanted the Prime Minister's dark day for Canada speech louder than the loudest verse at one of Schacht Schulz's Christmas programs:"BUT ALL THINGS COME TO AN END—EXCEPT A SAUSAGE, WHICH COMES TO TWO ENDS. AND I SAY TO YOU WITH ABSOLUTE SINCERITY, WHETHER I WILL OR NOT, I MUST . . . CONSTITUTE THIS COUNTRY. EITHER IT COMES WITH ME, OR IT BREAKS! FOR *OUR* COUNTRY, WRONG IS RIGHT!" And the people rose and followed as Oata's mother marched her chanting mental home patients out through the waiting room door, through the patch of pigweed across the gravel driveway to the ball diamond. The people on the bleachers and the baselines rose and joined in the chanting as Oata's mother stood on the pitcher's mound conducting the mass choral speaking choir, and Schacht Schulz chanting along in the crowd figured that if just once he had had this crowd for pupils he would have beaten Winkler for sure in the Speech Arts Festival."FOR WHEN MEN ARE WELL-GOVERNED, THEY NEITHER SEEK NOR DESIRE ANY OTHER LIBERTY. THE BULLET IS STRONGER THAN THE BALLET." On and on they chanted, over and over, and then just as the CBC cameramen were trying to wheel one of their big cameras out the curling rink door,

BLAST BLAST BLAST

BLAAAAASSST!

The CBC cameraman dollied after Oata's mother and her mental home patients as they chanted from the baseball diamond up the driveway to the road, the crowd of Gutenthallers chanting along behind them. The door of the Lazy Leisure Camper opened and Oata's mother skipped lightly up the steps and disappeared. The mental home patients followed and the door closed.

BLAST BLAST BLAST

BLAAAAAASSSST!

Later, when the CBC cameraman played his tape he had the Gutenthal Curling Rink, he had the baseball field, he had the road, but no mental home patients following a crazy chanting woman and no Lazy Leisure Camper driving away down the road.

In the Martens house Bulchi Wiebe and Simple Hein stared at Al Seasoner and his Citizens' Future Forum sitting with faces white as dough. Then a cameraman tiptoed up behind Al Seasoner and stuck one of those little earplugs in his ear, and Pierre Anchorbridge's face was on the screen again and he was asking Al Seasoner if he could describe for the viewers what had just happened in the Gutenthal Curling Rink. Seasoner moved his jaw and the camera picked up his tongue moving around inside the open mouth but not a word came out. Then Pierre Anchorbridge tried to say in words what the people watching the TV could see for themselves: that Al Seasoner looked like he had febeizeled his brain.

The TV control-room switcher managed to slip in half of a silver bullet States beer commercial before it was cut off by pounding drums and trumpets with a bagpipe and a bugle thrown in. The CBC announcer who never shows his face sang out like a homemade chocolate cake drowned in farm-fresh cream: "FROM OTTAWA, THE RIGHT HONOURABLE PRIME MINISTER OF CANADA." The Prime Minister climbed out of his black limousine and to show how hartsoft important this speech was he had on a Team Canada hockey sweater and no tie. He went up the Parliament Hill steps two at a time to a flatdeck trailer parked on the top step. The Prime Minister jumped up on it and sat down on a chrome chair. Two CBC girls scampered up to him. One threaded a clip-on mike under his hockey sweater while the other placed a black book in his hand. The Prime Minister's lips formed a five-flavour Life Saver ring:

There are those who love this country, this competitive country, global in vision, self-reliant and open for business, there are those who love this country. There are those who serve this country, forgo executive salaries for meagre honoraria, bend their ears to the whispered needs of the average Canadian, tirelessly traverse the country in search of the will of the people, there are those who serve this country.

There are those who abuse this country, this open, generous, giving country, there are those who abuse this country. There are vandals in this country, vandals wantonly wreaking open havoc on the businesslike, competitive, global consultation processes of the lovers and servers who seek a level solution to today's economic realities, there are vandals in this country.

There are nationalists in this country, who appeal to your patriotism by dredging up the past, who are too stiff-necked to thrive in a changing world, who wish to drag you down with them, there are nationalists in this country. There are alarmists in this country, mired in ideology, refusing to see the need for a realistic redrawing of the poverty line, a redrawing that would eliminate food banks, there are alarmists in this country. There are terrorists in this country, who use the mask of free speech to disrupt the speech of others, who put modern technologies to sinister use to manipulate the sensationalist media, to manufacture dissent, there are terrorists in this country.

Just watch me, I will not negotiate with a gun at my head,

just watch me. By the powers invested in me by the multitudes in the lobbies of this land and beyond, I authorize CSIS and the RCMP to search out the perpetrators of the heinous crime that has been done in the Gooding Doll arena today, and I call on the good people of Newfoundland to aid and abet the authorities in tracking down those who have brought shame to your great land of cod! It is no shame to fall down, but to stay down is. So when already, then already! I have a vision—I see millions of beetweeders, with hoes sharpened, descending on our choking fields, hacking away at the mustard and the wild oats, separating the doubles, freeing the sweet sugar beet to flourish as we weed our way into the future. There, with the help of God, give me your tired, your poor, your huddled masses yearning to breathe free, the wretched refuse of your teeming shore, send these, the homeless, tempest-tossed, to me. I lift my lamp beside the true north strong and free. O say, can't you see?

"Hey hey hey!" Bulchi Wiebe punched his fist into his hand. "Hey hey hey!" He punched Simple Hein's shoulder as they tried to see Gutenthal one more time, but the TV picture just showed flying silver beer cans, maxi-pads, and a man talking with a hemorrhoid in his mouth.

"Ouch, that hurts!" Hein said, grabbing his shoulder. Bulchi Wiebe punched his shoulder again. "Hey hey hey! Tomorrow we bomb our bottles on Ottawa!"

30

How come Oata let Yasch make a speech to the Seasoner Commission was something she wondered about, too, as she sat beside Yasch on the woman's side of the car going home from the Seasoner Forum. For sure, after all the stuff she had been writing in the Farmers' Union notebooks with a carpenter's pencil, she would have had lots to say. And it wasn't because she was too shy, not after the way she took over leadership in the curling rink waiting room just before the tornado. Though it is true that to take leadership behind closed doors is a different thing altogether than to do it where everybody can see you operate. Even in school Oata had figured out how all that phoney respect Koadel Kehler, the teacher's son, got in class or on the Christmas concert platform wasn't worth two macaronis once he was with the other schuzzels in the bush behind the school, schuzzels like Forscha Friesen or Johnny Cake Pauls who had lots of influence as long as they could "hide it under a bushel no," like in that song Shtemm Gaufel Friesen made them sing in Sunday School.

Oata smiled as she remembered that Halloween when Koadel Kehler's parents left him home alone to look after the trick or treating and he decided to pass out pickling onions wrapped in apple papers so they looked like candies. It was the kind of thing his Woody Allen grandfather, Kjrayel Kehler, might have done. A funny idea, but kind of boring to do actually, except when he heard Nettie Neufeld swear on the road after she bit into an onion in the dark. But then, when he only had a handful of onions left over in his grapes basket, some schuzzel pulled the switch by the yard-light pole and the house went dark. So Koadel took the flashlight to go out to switch the lights back on. He figured the schuzzels would be hiding in the dark watching to see who would come out to put the light back on, but when he opened the door and shone a light out, a dressed-up person was standing sideways on the porch, a person dressed up so much Koadel couldn't see who it was.

Slowly, the face turned into the flashlight beam and Koadel sucked in air with a wheezing sound almost like rusty hinges and, at the same time, stumbled backwards into the porch, smashed into his mother's deep freeze, and knocked over the grapes basket, spilling the pickling onions. The screen door slammed closed and the person stepped closer and looked at him through the screen. A pretend low voice said, "Fear not, for behold, I knock on the door of thine heart." The person knocked lightly on the screen door. Koadel straightened himself up and aimed the flashlight through the screen. The person had hair and a beard made from string mops, old ones, all grey from floor water, and Koadel almost sneezed from that dirty mop smell. Between the beard and the hair, the face was made from brown old woman's stockings with black circles drawn on for eyes. "Peace, be still," the pretend low voice said. "Come unto me." By this time Koadel was embarrassed already, so he stepped closer like he was brave. But then the person opened the screen door and the pretend low voice said, "Kehler, baler," and then a girl's voice squeaked, "Shit in the trailer!"

Koadel jumped after her as she slammed the screen door in his face, but now he was mad like a man fooled by a woman, and he banged through the door and caught the girl with the flashlight beam just as she ran around the corner of the house. Koadel chased after her, his flashlight shining on the gunny sacks she had sewed into some kind of Old Testament man's dress for herding sheep, and even though she was bigger Koadel ran faster and just before she got to the ditch he reached out and grabbed the grey-mop hair. The mask caught on her chin and she jerked to a stop. She screamed as it slipped over her face and came loose in his hands. She shoved back at him with her rump and then she whirled around and Koadel staggered back. He shone the flashlight in her face and screamed. In his hand he had hair, beard, and face. Cackling in his flashlight beam was a white skull: "Kehler, baler, shit in the trailer!" Hands clawed at him, hands in gloves with ripped fingers, hands milk white with red streaks. "Kehler, baler shit in the trailer!" the voice cackled again, and the person rushed at him and ripped the hair and beard mask away. Koadel's heart almost clappered to a stop. "Kehler, baler, shit in the trailer," the voice said again, normal now, playful, not even teasing. Koadel's flashlight beam flickered from his shaking hand. The person turned around again. White fingers reached up slowly and peeled off the skull made from the leg of combination underwear. A painted clown face, kind of smeared, grinned at him, and Oata said again, "Kehler, baler, shit in the trailer." Then she turned and shuffled through the ditch and onto the road, and in the trembling beam of Koadel's flashlight she slipped the skull back over the clown face, pulled the beard and hair over the skull, and stalked off to rule the world.

PART FOUR

31

Long after Simple Hein had forgotten his bruised shoulder, Bulchi Wiebe would remember that boast about bombing Ottawa, and even longer after that he would think about what he had left out of his boast. Bulchi Wiebe had forgotten what he was bombing the country with. He had forgotten that he wasn't playing a game; he wasn't just littering. But Bulchi Wiebe had lived in a free country all his life and in a free country a person doesn't expect to get shot at for dropping a verse on the land, especially if the verse doesn't even have any religious sex in it. So he had no feeling of apprehension in the morning as he and Simple Hein prepared for their mission to Ottawa.

Simple Hein felt particularly good because he actually saw the back wall of the machine shed as he brought out the five hundred pop bottles Bulchi Wiebe packed into the net bag for their Ottawa mission.

"Y'know, Bulchi Wiebe," he said as they closed the velcro flaps on the last pocket, "I think so maybe one . . . two . . . maybe tree more day and all bottle will be gone."

"Yep, Hein, our work is almost done. After today the rest will be relaxed, short trips close to home, Steinbach maybe, Plumas, River Heights, maybe one dump on Linden Woods. The end is nigh. The end is nigh. All done before Christmas."

And yes, even though it was late November the weather had been unusually mild and there was little snow. Still, Bulchi Wiebe took some precautions, insisted that Simple Hein dress warmly, put on the hydro parka and wind pants hanging in the Martens house that morning. "The old tub can get pretty cold in the wintertime," he said, "especially at six, seven thousand feet." But Bulchi Wiebe was in good spirits, and Hein sensed no hint of danger in Bulchi Wiebe's words. And it was a good flight, a quick flight with a brisk tail wind, and Simple Hein was thrilled as they circled the Peace Tower on Parliament Hill shortly before twelve o'clock noon Eastern Standard Time and he pulled all five levers in fairly quick succession and for a few minutes the Ottawa sky looked like a celebration as the five hundred bottles floated down around Parliament Hill. It happened so quickly that no TV crew was alert enough to get a shot of the bottles actually floating in the air, and Bulchi Wiebe buzzed over the Ottawa rooftops so low that the Canadian Forces radar was unable to pick him up in time to react.

"Heh heh heh!" Bulchi Wiebe exclaimed through the headphones into Simple Hein's ear, exclaimed so loudly that Hein had to take the headphones off to scratch inside his ears with his little finger. They flew northwestward for a while, a little slowly because they were heading into the wind. They didn't say much, except at intervals Bulchi Wiebe would holler, "Heh, heh, heh!" and Hein would have to scratch inside his ears again. Things looked like they would turn out fine, they would make it back to the Martens farm without incident. Later, Bulchi Wiebe would argue with himself that all would have been hunky-dory if it hadn't been for the goose.

One of Bulchi Wiebe's pleasures during the bottle missions was to show Simple Hein the landmarks that towns in Canada had erected to give their communities some distinction. They had seen the welded wild rose at Roseisle, the monstrous Ukrainian Easter egg at Vegreville, the sharptail grouse at Ashern, Sara the camel at Glenboro, the Russell bull, the frog at St. Pierre, the mosquito at Komarno, the Viking at Gimli, the Big Nickel at Sudbury, the lobster at Shediac, the twenty-eight-foot oil can at Rocanville, the prairie lily at Parkside, but neither Bulchi Wiebe nor Simple Hein had ever seen the goose at Wawa. Bulchi Wiebe checked his flight map and realized that by veering just slightly from his flight path they could fly right over Wawa. And so he did that, and cooked his goose, so to speak.

Simple Hein was dozing off when Bulchi told him through the headphones to start looking for the goose. Bulchi Wiebe knew it was beside the highway so he dropped to a thousand feet above the four-lane pavement. They looked down, saw the town, flew past the town, but they saw no goose. "It's gotta be there, Hein!" Bulchi yelled through the headphones. "It's gotta be there!" Bulchi followed the highway for a few more minutes, then began to circle back. Hein looked down at the forest, and then the rows and rows of houses. "Look, Bulchi Wiebe! Lots airplanes down there!"

That's when the first bullet pinged through the flap on the left wing. "Holy shit!" Bulchi yelled through the headphones boring right through Hein's head from one ear to the other. "It can't be!" Another bullet pinged through the tip of the left wing. "Gott im Himmel, they're shooting at us! Airplanes, you say? We're over PETAWAWA! No wonder we can't see the goose!"

Bulchi Wiebe wrestled with the wheel stick, yanked at levers and rocked his feet on the pedals and pulled buttons out, pushed other buttons in while the airplane rocked and veered and Simple Hein chucked up a week's worth of canned sucker-fish as the airplane pointed down.

"Take it easy, Hein," Bulchi Wiebe shouted through the headphones, "I'll get her down. I see a lake over there. It looks frozen!" Bulchi Wiebe ripped off his headphones and straightened out the plane and even Hein thought it felt almost normal, but he kept his eyes pinched shut. Then he felt the bump as the wheels hit the ice, felt the skid, then heard Bulchi Wiebe cheer, "We made her, the ice is holding! We made her, Hein!"

Hein raised his head, opened his eyes, saw treetops and sky whizzing by, and then Bulchi Wiebe screamed, "OH NO!" Ice crackled louder than the airplane motor and the plane jolted down abruptly, and for the first time they figured out what seat belts are for.

"You okay, Hein?" Bulchi shouted.

Hein didn't move for a second, then ripped off his headphones to hear better.

"Good!" Bulchi shouted. "We got to get out of here before she sinks!"

32

On Victoria Island in the Ottawa River a bottle fell into the lap of a child sliding out of the mouth of "The Frolicking Beaver," a sculpture made of stove-length logs cemented together to look busy. The child, wearing a white snow suit covered with red maple leaves, was coming down the beaver slide for the ninety-seventh time when the bottle landed in his lap. His mother was sure of the number; she had been counting as she stamped her feet in the snow, shivering in the lace-cuffed long johns and mini-skirt she wore with a short leather jacket. Snow suits were not stylish for teenaged moms. And who would have thought a twenty-minute excursion to the beaver slide would turn into a marathon to set a Guiness World Record while she froze. At least the kid wasn't scream-ing, though the look in his eye each time he whooshed to the bottom and ran around to the back again suggested that he knew he was bugging her. But she was as stubborn as her son and was determined to make him beg to stop and go home. So she had been counting the trips down the slide as she stamped her Bi-Way runners in the snow. Ninety-seven times down the slide would be something to brag about at Moms and Tots on Tuesday.

Then the bottle dropped from the sky into the child's lap. The child hugged the bottle and whooshed to the bottom of the slide. "Look, Mommy! I got a bottle." But before the young mother could say, "Come, show Mommy," the child felt the bottle tug. It was a gentle, but firm tug, like grandpa's hand when they walked down the sidewalk together, a tug that pulled him along at just the right speed for his four-year-old legs. The bottle tugged him along the path that wound through the bushes, and before his mommy could catch up to him, he had reached the steps leading up to the sidewalk over the Portage Bridge. His mommy felt the tug of the bottle, too, and she followed her son, without panic, feeling like she had stepped onto a moving sidewalk.

On the other side of Portage Street an elderly gentleman was walking a basset-beagle near the totem pole. He, too, felt the tug of the bottle, as did two spandex-clad joggers running around the perimeter of the island. By the time the child crossed the bridge to the south bank of the Ottawa River he was leading a parade of about fifty people. By the time he got to the Ottawa River Parkway he had over a hundred followers. By Wellington Street his followers had doubled again. As the crowd approached the Garden of the Provinces five high school truants smoking on the "Twelve Points in a Classical Balance" sculpture tossed away their cigarette butts and sauntered over to shadow the procession, lurking among the frozen fountains, but drawn steadily onward with the crowd now joined by the staff flowing out of the National Library and the National Archives, some clutching dusty diaries not due to be made public for another thirty years. As the child passed the Canadian Phalanx monument under the Memorial Arch his followers were joined by other groups who had caught two-litre pop bottles falling from the sky. A patient from St. Vincent Hospital, brandishing a bottle and his intravenous stand, led a dozen patients who had been out on the hospital steps smoking when the bottles fell.

The crowd marched past Louis St. Laurent sitting on his bench facing the civil servants streaming out of the Justice Building. The staff and children from the daycare centre in the basement of St. Andrew's Church lined up on the sidewalk and hitched themselves to the daycare director's mountaineering rope. They set off alongside the crowd, past the Currency Museum, and laughed at their reflections in the cold, glassy Bank of Canada windows, laughed and pointed at the green copper roofs of the Parliament Buildings reflected behind them. They marched past the Postal Museum on the right and the West Block of Parliament on the left. "Oh, no, not again!" shouted the boy from the beaver slide, whose mommy had finally been pushed close enough by the crowd to clutch the peak of her son's snow suit hood. The boy followed the bottle's tug through the open wrought-iron gates, across the cracked pavement of the driveway, past the circle of provincial crests surrounding the Centennial Flame, onto the snow-covered lawn of Parliament Hill.

Over in Hull, across the river, a young man pushed a shopping cart along Promenade du Portage. Three aluminum pop cans, two brown beer bottles, and one No Name bottle lay on the bottom of the cart. The young man wore a black Reebok jogger on his left foot, and a green and purple Nike high-top on his right; neither shoe had laces. His Canadiens hockey jacket had a jagged rip in the back and his matted shoulder-length hair looked like it would change colour if it touched water and shampoo at the same time. He had heard the drone overhead, but you don't find bottles by looking up at airplanes. At the corner of Aubrey and Promenade du Portage he stopped and gazed at the snowplow sculpture. He had read the title "Open and Closed Wall No. 45" many times but it always reminded him of the snow plow his father used to drive in the Gatineau Hills. A two-litre pop bottle was stuck in the V of the snowplow. The young man pushed his cart up to the sculpture and reached for the bottle. It was unlabelled, with a gold strip of paper inside. He dropped the bottle into the cart and felt the cart tug at his hand. At a brisk but comfortable speed the cart with Simple Hein's bottle pulled the young man along Promenade du Portage, down Boul Maisonneuve, onto Victoria Street, past the sculpture "Amour" which resembled a mushroom on a smooth potato resting on a piece of leg bone.

Civil servants began streaming out of the Place du Portage buildings to follow the young man and his shopping cart down Victoria onto Laurier Street. Workers at the E.B. Eddy plant broke for lunch early to link up with the tourists and curators streaming out of the strange and wonderful curves of the Museum of Civilization to join the procession as it surged onto Boul St. Laurent. They spread onto the street, cutting off vehicle traffic as they followed the young man and the bottle past the Hull Marina onto the Alexandra Bridge.

Over the grey waters of the Ottawa River Samuel de Champlain beckoned them with his astrolabe as they approached his pedestal on Nepean Point. Hardy buskers who had planned an unauthorized noonday concert in the Astrolabe Theatre found themselves drawn out of their cavern to join the multitude surging into Major's Hill Park, past the Royal Canadian Cannoneer preparing to fire the nine-pound Noonday Gun. A group of understudies from the National Ballet rehearsing an experimental dance around a sculpture of three-dimensional puzzle pieces pirouetted and pistoleted their way into the crowd flowing past Colonel By with his pointed plumed hat, sword straight down his leg, best foot forward on his pedestal overlooking the Rideau Canal he built to protect against an American invasion which never came by water, or land for that matter, but came nonetheless when Colonel By was long dead, came by invitation.

The crowd surged on into the shadow of the Chateau Laurier Hotel, past the wooden Japanese fan sculpture known as "Twist One Point Five," on around the Mackenzie Avenue side of the Chateau Laurier onto Wellington St., past a weighted down, earth bound, sweating, one-legged Terry Fox, over the canal bridge, past the twenty-two snow-covered soldiers scurrying under the angels of peace and freedom on the arch of the National War Memorial in Confederation Square. They pushed past Sir Wilfrid Laurier, bald forehead round, coat open, tight hand on hip, left foot forward, marching to free-trade defeat. They trampled past Sir Galahad, erected in honour of Mackenzie King's friend, Henry Albert Harper, who lost his life trying to save a young woman from drowning, and surged in through the wrought-iron gates, past the Centennial Flame, onto Parliament Hill.

Southwest of Dows Lake in a stable of the Central Experimental Farm the Royal Canadian Groom was currying the Royal Canadian Horses in preparation for their daily exercise. The Royal Canadian Queen hadn't ridden in the Royal Canadian Carriage in Canada since 1982 when she came to sign the patriation of the Royal Canadian Constitution with Pierre Elliot Trudeau. No one had sat in the plush leather seats of the black and gold trimmed Royal Canadian Carriage since then, though the groom polished and oiled the conveyance weekly and once a month used it for an actual practice with the Royal Canadian Horses. When Simple Hein's beetfield verse bottles fell on Ottawa, the Royal Canadian Groom was preparing for his monthly rehearsal with the real Royal Canadian Carriage.

There was no written law and there was no common law that said only the Royal Canadian Queen could rest her royal hams in the royal carriage. In fact, the groom had been lobbying his MP to encourage the Governor-General to use the carriage to ride to the Throne Speech ceremony, and last summer he had suggested a daily carriage excursion from Rideau Hall down Sussex Drive to Parliament Hill to provide an aesthetic complement to the Royal Canadian Bear Hat Changing Guards. But Governor-Generals had either Cadillac tastes or Volkswagen tastes, depending on whether the appointment had been made to reward loyal service or to neutralize opposition. And Prime Ministers now demanded bullet-proof limousines just like States of America presidents.

So the groom was a little startled to be handed a gold-embossed note as he was hitching up the Royal Canadian Team to the Royal Canadian Carriage, a note instructing him to pick up an important passenger on Prince of Wales Drive at the railroad tracks. That it was a Royal Canadian Mountie on a horse, complete with scarlet tunic and Smokey the Bear hat, who handed him the note was surprising, too, but it only made sense, for any time the Royal Canadian Carriage was used there were always plenty of mounted Mounties on hand.

Fortunately, the groom's ceremonial uniform had been freshly delivered from the Royal Canadian Cleaners the day before, and in no time at all he was ready to go. He tapped the rumps of the four Royal Canadian Horses and they pulled the carriage out of the Royal Canadian Coach House and fell in behind a pair of Royal Canadian Mounties carrying lances adorned with Simple Hein's bottles instead of red and white pennants. Two more Mounties, bottle-tipped lances erect, took up positions behind the Royal Canadian Carriage. They cantered up a service road and turned onto the National Capital Commission Driveway to Prince of Wales Drive. The well-oiled Royal Canadian Carriage barely clattered on the pavement, and the groom felt the horses' eager tug on the harnesses as they approached the railroad tracks. The forward Mounties halted before the tracks and the carriage stopped behind them. The groom cupped his ear to listen for a train. The Mounties sat expressionless, their moustaches unflickering. As the groom climbed down to take up his position beside the front wheel of the carriage he expected a whistle, or the clanging of a bell, the chug chug of a steam engine. Certainly, for such an occasion they would use the antique steamer from the Museum of Science and Technology.

When the jigger appeared over the bridge crossing the canal at the end of Dows Lake, the Royal Canadian Mounties frowned and their gloved forearms brushed against their Sam Browne holsters. But there was no panic as the jigger clattered toward them, gradually revealing the operator, a man in an engineer's cap, and a feminine figure dressed in white. The

Mounties and the groom took in the situation, quickly understood and adjusted their thinking, relaxed their moustaches, their slightly tensed fingers, almost smiled when the jigger stopped in the middle of the crossing and Eaza Bone Peetash climbed down to lend Thecla Thiessen a gallant hand in her descent from the jigger. Her cherry-red hair spiking up like a rooster comb reminded the groom of the Royal Canadian Fergie for a moment, but the white wedding dress was too frayed at the hem and certainly hadn't just come from the Royal Canadian Cleaners. And the groom didn't think Fergie would arrive on a Royal Canadian Visit wearing only one cherry-red shoe. Thecla's big toe stuck through her once-white wedding stocking. In her white gloved hand Thecla clutched a flat bundle wrapped in silver plastic. The Mountie who had been transferred from the P-project recalled how they had almost seized the book in question until a memo had come down from the Royal Canadian Commissioner informing them that said item was corporately correct.

Thecla scampered gracefully across the pavement to the coach, the shoeless foot hardly causing a limp. The groom moved too slowly, and she climbed up into the carriage before his white gloved hand could assist her. Thecla sat back on the seat, the silver bundle on her lap. A shout was heard from the end of Dows Lake where the tracks cross the canal and a file of sweat-suited runners jogged over the railroad bridge. The leader in a bright yellow suit waved an object high in the air like the golden boy running naked on top of the Manitoba Legislature. The lead Mounties brushed their holsters with their gloved forearms and made as if to move out, but Thecla said, "Wait!" The Mounties froze their moustaches into terse frowns and watched the runners approach. It was the Carleton University women's track team. The leader was waving a bottle, the gold paper strip inside flicking from side to side. By the time the Carleton women reached the carriage, three other groups of joggers were running down the bicycle path that cuts through the experimental farm, one group led by a former Royal Canadian Governor-General, each leader waving a Simple Hein bottle. The Royal Canadian Mounties quickly assessed the situation, adjusted their thoughts, relaxed their moustaches, and gently spurred their horses to lead the Royal Canadian Carriage across the tracks with timing so precise that the joggers never had to break stride. On the seat of his jigger Eaza Bone Peetash rolled a cigarette and eyed the procession without analysis or judgement as it moved along the road that follows the Dows Lake shore.

The Royal Canadian Carriage clattered politely under the Bronson Avenue Bridge onto Queen Elizabeth Driveway. Thecla waved across the Rideau Canal at ten outdoor smokers and four motorized wheelchairs lounging in front of Perley Hospital. The patients waved back and began a parallel procession on their side of the canal, quickly picking up three candy stripers, two interns, six nurses, and an X-ray technician. They crossed over the Bank Street Bridge to join Thecla as her carriage clattered into Lansdowne Park.

That's when the Royal Canadian Carriage was first spotted by skaters on the Rideau Canal. Five would-be speed skaters scraped to a stop and spun around faster than hockey players to shadow Thecla as she rode past Bill Reid's bronze "Killer Whale," up under the Pretoria Bridge where students from Algonquin College on skates and on foot joined the parade. People streamed from the surrounding streets onto Queen Elizabeth Driveway, calmly, steadily, no shoving, no trampling. They passed under the Queensway Bridge to the bend at the University of Ottawa where they picked up suddenly alert students from a political science seminar who had been dozing while a columnist from *The National Newspaper* was doing a postmortem on a scheme that had died of *vox populi*. The canal became crowded, but all the skaters were headed in the same direction, calmly, no collisions, up past Lisgar Collegiate and under the Laurier Bridge, past the Provincial Court of Ontario which emptied of black-robed lawyers and judges and handcuffed innocents unable to resist Thecla in the Royal Canadian Carriage clattering into Confederation Park.

The Mounties led the carriage between the giant bent-sausage pipe sculpture called "Traffic" and the "Kwakiutl Totem Pole," between the Colonel By Memorial Fountain, the red, blue, yellow, and green "Homage à Samuel Beckett," and the "South African War Memorial" paid for with pennies from thirty thousand school children, past the soldier leaning on an upside-down rifle shooting himself in the foot in the Northwest Rebellion, on under the Mackenzie King Bridge. The crowd surged past the National Arts Centre and the Daudelein statue which didn't know if it wanted to be an animal or a machine, past five men and a woman "Balancing" on a big letter Y, through Confederation Square, past the twenty-two snow-covered soldiers huddling under the National War Memorial.

The Royal Canadian Carriage dashed across Wellington Street to the East Gate of Parliament Hill, cutting off a dark limousine, and the Royal Canadian Groom remembered how he had never even received a reply to his polite invitation to give the Prime Minister's wife and her children a ride in the Royal Canadian Carriage last summer.

The Royal Canadian Standby Chauffeur (Montreal) was thinking of his daughter's birthday party which he was missing because the Royal Canadian Official Chauffeur (24 Sussex) had jumped limousines the day before to accept a position as driver for the leader of the Creme de Separateur Party. The traitor had complained of exhaustion from driving in both official languages and claimed he was losing his soul. So Standby Chauffeur (Montreal), who was from Niverville, Manitoba, and had been driving in unofficial languages for most of his life, suddenly found himself the Chief Driver and Door Handle Polisher at the Prime Minister's wife's disposal on the very day he had promised his daughter he wouldn't miss her birthday party again. Last year, he had had to miss the party because the Prime Minister's mother-in-law's bridge team had entered a charity bridge tournament in Hull and Standby Chauffeur (Montreal) from Niverville had been pressed into service.

The Prime Minister's wife emerged from the front door of

24 Sussex Drive with the two children. Standby Chauffeur (Montreal) opened the rear passenger door. The Prime Minister's eight-year-old daughter tugged on the chauffeur's sleeve and asked, "Did you know Carmen San Diego is a lesbian?" Before he could reply, she scrambled into the limousine after her brother. The Prime Minister's wife brushed against him as she stepped into the car and Standby Chauffeur (Montreal) stifled a sneeze. He was allergic to French perfume since dousing himself with his Aunt Nettie's *Evening in Paris* collection when he was still in diapers. Now he preferred an unscented woman. He closed the door politely, ignoring the smoky grey flash of expensive nylons as she crossed her legs in the back seat.

As he opened the driver's door he glanced up just in time to catch a two-litre pop bottle plummeting from the sky. He looked at it curiously, the gold strip of paper inside reminding him of the Bible verses the Niverville Sunday School teacher had passed out each week. He felt a strange tug as he clutched the bottle. It seemed to pull him into the driver's seat. Carefully, he laid the bottle on the floor, then adjusted his mirror. The Prime Minister's wife was talking on the car phone and the children were engrossed in a hand-held video game.

Everything seemed normal as they passed Rideau Gate at the Governor-General's residence and crossed the bridge over Rideau Falls and city hall island. By the time they reached the National Research Council, though, an unusual number of pedestrians crowded the sidewalks on both sides of the street. People were filing out of the Pearson Building and the chauffeur wondered if there were emergency fire drills going on. By the time they reached the Ottawa Rowing Club something was definitely amiss. The pedestrians had spilled off the sidewalks, and by the time the limousine approached the National Gallery of Canada the street was jammed.

The Prime Minister's wife asked, "What's going on?" through the intercom.

"I'm sorry, ma'am. I received no briefing from security about any parades." He honked the horn, but the pedestrians didn't even glance at the limousine. He could not stop the car. He could not back up. He could not escape down a side-street. He could just inch forward in unison with the crowd.

People streamed onto Sussex from the Royal Canadian Mint and the War Museum. Major's Hill Park was an ocean of humanity. The crowd carried the limousine past Notre Dame Basilica and the Canadian Ski Museum. The Prime Minister's wife's voice was anxious over the intercom which had a short in the wiring somewhere, causing irritating static. Standby Chauffeur (Montreal) decided to brave the French perfume and he lowered the window separating him from the passengers. The children were chanting:

"O Canada Day."

"Will there be fireworks, Mommy?"

"Is Daddy going to tell jokes to the people?"

"Is Daddy going to sing 'that's what you get for loving me?' "

The Prime Minister's wife sounded frantic on her phone: "What do you mean he's disappeared from the Commons? He can't even fuck me without CSIS watching and you say he's disappeared from the House of Commons?"

Like an ocean wave or the Titanic steaming toward the iceberg, the multitude carried the limousine onto Wellington, past the Chateau Laurier, over the Rideau Canal.

"Look Mommy! The Queen!"

Thecla and the Royal Canadian Carriage cantered out of Confederation Square, parting the waves of pedestrians like Moses parting the Red Sea, and cut off the limousine.

"Mommy, is this the surprise you promised us?"

"O goody, the Queen. Is she going to stay at our house?"

"She can have my bed."

"No, mine."

"No, not yours. You wet your bed last week."

"Mommy, he's telling lies about me."

"Shush, kids! Something's happened to Daddy!"

33

That's when the Noonday Gun went off. Two hundred thousand people lifted their wrists, then glanced up at the clocks in the Peace Tower. It was exactly twelve noon Eastern Standard Time. The universe was unfolding as it should and a west wind was unfurling the maple leaf flag. The Royal Canadian Carriage crossed Wellington Street in front of the Prime Minister's wife's limousine, in through the East Gate of Parliament Hill. The Royal Mounties escorted Thecla behind the East Block. She waved the silver package at Sir Wilfrid's round forehead, then counted MPs' cars angle-parked against the Royal Canadian Curbs. When she waved at the determined statue of William Lyon Mackenzie King, the Noonday Gun went off again. Thirteen senators woke up in the red chamber. "Halt!" she cried at the statue of John A. Macdonald. The Royal Mounties allowed their moustaches to curl slightly as they accommodated Thecla's innocent interest in the Father of Confederation holding important papers in his hand. But Thecla hardly gave Sir John A. a glance. Her eye was caught by the bare-shouldered woman seated at the foot of the pedestal regally brandishing a staff with a flag as full-bodied as a crinoline petticoat. The Noonday Gun fired again. "Onward, ho!" Thecla commanded. The Royal Mounties adjusted their moustaches and escorted the Royal Canadian Carriage behind the Centre Block of Parliament.

The Prime Minister emerged from the dark cave-like south arch of the Peace Tower between the lion and the unicorn and gloated at the multitude on the Hill. Even Canada Day 125 hadn't brought out such hordes. It was an opportunity not to be missed. The flatdeck trailer was still there on the top step. All he had to do was climb up and be himself, be human, tell a few jokes, be one of the boys and the little suckers would be eating out of his hand. Real communication, that's what was needed, real face-to-face man-to-man communication. No more filtration by the media with their unflattering camera angles and edited clips. Let the people see him unhandled, unmanaged for once, and they would love him with their hearts as well as their fearful ballots.

The Noonday Gun boomed again just as he scrambled up onto the flatdeck. It was a more powerful boom this time, a boom that carried from the Hill over the Langevin Block, quivered the Bank of Canada building, rattled coffee cups along the Sparks Street Mall. The needles on the Richter scales at the Canadian Centre for Remote Sensing shivered a jagged line on winding graph paper. Skiers halted for a microsecond during their descent down Mont Ste-Marie in the Gatineau Hills. The crystal ball on Mackenzie King's museum desk clouded faintly, and beside it the porcelain dog wagged its tail. The multitude became still. You could have heard a loonie drop in freshly fallen snow. The Prime Minister stepped to the centre of the flatdeck trailer and for a moment had a wild urge to yell to the multitude: "Give me an F. . . !" But he remembered just in time that the old fuddle-duddie was a fading memory best unresurrected in this global age. So he stuck one hand in his trousers pocket like a father fishing for his kids' allowances and spoke calmly to the crowd: "The government is like a family where the wife and the children have lost control of spending . . . spending way beyond their means . . . accumulating debt. Now the time has come to pay the debt, to cut back and control spending."

In the brief pause after his opening words, a faint clatter echoed from around the corner of the Centre Block and a woman's whispered voice carried through the air with such eerie force the skiers whizzing down Mont Ste-Marie experienced a slight stutter in their descent and the sparrows on the ruins at Kingsmere stopped chirping as the woman's words rattled their eardrums. "Who benefited most from all that borrowing?"

The Royal Canadian Mounties with lances erect at their sides led the Royal Canadian Carriage around the corner of the west end of the Centre Block. Thecla, cherry-red hair spiked high, clasped the silver bundle against her chest, the neckline of her white wedding dress pulled down to bare her freckled shoulders. The carriage halted in front of the flatdeck trailer, and with one red high-heeled shoe and one open-toed white stocking foot she leapt from the carriage, landing on the flatdeck two feet away from the Prime Minister. His hand seemed stuck in his pocket as he looked to the Royal Mounties for help. But the Royal Horsemen moved out and escorted the Royal Groom and the Royal Carriage around the curve past the East Block, and the multitude divided to allow the conveyance to pass on its way back to the stables.

"Who collected all that high interest? Have those people who had money to lend you, have they paid their taxes?"

The Prime Minister looked at this creature before him. She was young, red-haired, freckled, like Antoinette, the first girl he . . . ah, this wouldn't be so hard to handle. "My child, you do not understand. These are complex issues. These are complicated global competitive times."

"Who has all this money? What are they doing with this money?"

"Why, they are investing it, buying and selling it."

"They are lending it out, right?"

"That's right. Now you are beginning to understand."

"Why, then, aren't they creating jobs with it?"

"Well, you see, my dear, it's the state of the economy. We have been in a global recession."

"Oh. Now, an economy, is that something like a Monopoly game?"

"Yes, my child, now you understand, the economy is like a Monopoly game. I loved to play Monopoly when I was a boy. I learned so much about economics and business."

"And a recession is like a Monopoly game when one player has all the money and all the properties and all the houses and hotels?"

"Yes, my child, that would be a deep recession . . . a very deep recession."

"So the problem is to get the game started again?"

"That's right. You are getting to be a real smart girl."

"Well, if you want to get a Monopoly game started again you put all the money back into the box and then pass out the same amount to every player and the game gets going again."

"Well, in a game it's okay to do that, but in a real economy to take away all the money and give the same to everybody, well, we just can't have that, you know, that wouldn't be corporately correct . . . that would be communism."

"Oh, and I thought communism was lots of barbed wire and secret police scared of books and Bibles. But in Monopoly if you play it all the way to the end until one player has it all, the only way to get the game going again is to take it all away from the winner and give everybody a fresh start."

"Well, in a game, yes, but in the economy there are market forces."

"In a market, people buy and sell, right?"

"Right."

"And if nobody buys, then nobody can sell either."

"Right."

"Then the market doesn't work, so you have a recession?"

"Right."

"The people with no money can't buy, right?"

"Right."

"And the people with all the money aren't buying because they already have everything they need, right?"

"Well . . ."

"One time in the Gutenthal Curling Rink we had a Monopoly game during the bonspiel. And to keep the game going for a long time we changed the rules a little."

"Well, sure I did that when I played Monopoly with my friends at the cottage when our parents were out at a party across the lake, but, my child, in the real world we can't just change the rules. There are global market forces as powerful and unalterable as the journey of the sun through the sky and the rhythm of the ocean tides. To interfere with these global forces is tantamount to arguing with the Creator of the Universe. Why, I read in the *Reader's Digest* just the other day . . ."

"Have you read this?"

"Ah, the Madonna book. Well, a man in my position is extremely busy and to take the time to read such a book would not be the most material way to spend my time . . ."

"This is not the Madonna book. Here. You could say it's an alternative way to play Monopoly in the real world. The silver plastic just protects the book in case it drops in the snow."

"Well, as I said, I'm a busy man, but perhaps I can have my Executive Assistant assign a member of the staff to read it and report on it."

"With all due respect, sir, I do think you should read it yourself. I will be voting in the next election and I think there is something you need to understand."

"Of course, my dear, let me shake your hand. I ask for your support to keep this great country of ours on the right track."

"Listen. I read in the newspaper that in this country there are 118,162 corporations with combined profits totalling twenty-five billion dollars who did not pay corporate income tax in 1987. Is that true?"

"Well, maybe in 1987 . . ."

"You mean, you fixed that so it isn't true anymore?"

"Well, you see, with a corporation it's different, uh, it's . . ."

"Doesn't it bother you to see all that profit untaxed when you have such a big deficit?"

"Well, uh, it's not really untaxed, uh, you see, the corporations are just deferring their taxes for a while, as is allowed under the law."

"Oh. Um, deferred taxes, huh? Deferred means put off till maybe later?"

"That's right."

"And that's legal?"

"As legal as kissing third cousins."

"Hmmm . . . then how come a couple of years ago when my grandfather put off filing his income tax return till September the RCMP showed up at his door with a summons and after in court he had to pay a fine?"

"Well, um . . . ah, probably he hadn't incorporated his business. That would make a difference."

"Oh, yeah, now I remember. In grade 11 business law we learned that if you make your business into a corporation your business gets all the rights of a person but doesn't have the responsibilities of a person by herself or all the same risks, and Goofy Goertzen said to the teacher that a corporation sounded a bit like a gang of bullies beating somebody up on the school yard and then all saying they didn't do anything."

"Well, uh, it's not exactly like that . . ."

"But you think it's fair to make a woman pay GST when she buys Kotex but not a corporation that makes millions in profits?"

"Well, you could . . ."

"Use a handful of moss? Is that what you're saying? Is . . ."

But before Thecla could finish her question and before she could press the silver bundle into the Prime Minister's hand, the Noonday Gun went off again so loudly swallows' nests shattered and the frozen mud and straw poured from the Peace Tower gargoyles. Five hundred thousand people checked their watches and glanced up at the Peace Tower clocks. It was exactly twelve o'clock noon, twelve-thirty in Newfoundland. In the hush that fell, the Peace Tower bells played Rick Neufeld's "Moody Manitoba Morning." The Prime Minister looked out over the multitude and gestured at Thecla to move out of the way. He recognized the tune, he had heard it years ago at the Velvet Glove in the Winnipeg Inn when he had treated his secretary to dinner with the Five Bells because she loved to hear their "How you make me quiver" song and he remembered the Winnipeggers had clapped loudest for "Moody Manitoba Morning." Maybe he could win this audience by singing this old favourite with them. Maybe his critics were right. To keep singing "When Irish Eyes Are Smiling" suggested a colonial mentality. But even as the Prime Minister gazed out at the multitude gathered on the Hill, with "Moody Manitoba Morning" ringing in his ears, he quivered in his soft leather loafers.

Like a zipper sliding down the back of his wife's gown after a successful dinner with the President of the States of America, the ocean of people at the Centre Gate was parting without a whisper. At first he couldn't see clearly, then at the Centennial Flame he spotted a woman in black dividing the crowd with a black gloved hand. A woman in pink shorts and a navy blazer followed with a tall red stool. Behind them a rumpled sandy-haired man clasped a black book to his chest.

Later, Politicks Paetkau remembered that his mind had been blank as he followed Cora Lee Semple's white Reeboks through the crowd parting in front of Barbara and closing behind him. His mind was always blank before a reading. He had no idea where the book would open, no idea what he would read to his audience. Even reading in bed with Cora Lee never prepared him for what would happen in an actual public reading. In bed with Cora Lee he would reread the stories he had already shared with his flatdeck audiences. The new stories remained a blurred scribble until he was seated on the red stool and the crowd had hushed so the turning leaves of Yeeat Shpanst's black book could be heard clearly by the farthest hearing-impaired member of the multitude. Then Politicks Paetkau would read. And the words he read were always as strange and startling to him as they were to the people who heard him.

He had no opportunity to analyze his story, to accept it or reject it, to try to make it fit into some mold prepared in his mind by sales motivation seminars or Report on Business columnists or eco-terrorist pamphlets left behind in dentists' waiting rooms. Afterwards, after a reading, when he stretched out on the worn blankets of dusty motel beds, listening to Cora Lee reread that day's story while Barbara dangled from the ceiling displaying the red hourglass on her abdomen, spinning silk, the words he had fed the audience from the flatdeck felt right. Then, after Cora Lee had dozed off and Barbara had disappeared into a dark corner of the ceiling, he would quietly call Pinklich to let her know that he was okay, that he loved her and would be home as soon as he could. He didn't tell Pinklich about reading in bed with Cora Lee Semple while Barbara the black widow dangled overhead on a silken thread. Trying to explain that would have been more troublesome than confessing to adultery and Politicks Paetkau could affirm on a stack of Bibles without perjuring himself that during this whole campaign with Cora Lee Semple and Barbara Arachnik not once had he committed adultery, not even in his heart. It just wasn't that kind of situation. In fact, the only time he even got an erection on this trip was when he was talking to Pinklich on the phone late at night after Cora Lee and Barbara were asleep.

So Politicks Paetkau had no idea what he was going to read when Cora Lee scrambled onto the flatdeck trailer and set up the red stool. She gestured to the Prime Minister and Thecla Thiessen and they sat down at the front of the trailer, hugging their left knees as they watched Politicks sit on the red stool. Cora Lee dangled her left leg over the edge end of the trailer and rested her steno pad on her bent right knee.

Politicks shrugged his shoulders and shifted his bum on the stool, hooked his right heel on the lowest spindle, and opened the black book. The rustle of the pages silenced the sparrows on the ruins at Kingsmere, halted the skiers on Mont Ste-Marie in mid-slope, filled the crystal ball on Mackenzie King's museum desk with a thundercloud. Like *Guiness Book of World Records* dominos, the multitude sat down on Parliament Hill and melted the snow. At Politicks Paetkau's first words, the tulips bloomed in the flowerbeds over the underground heating ducts.

34 A POLITICKS PAETKAU
FLATDECK READING

The land of Them, north of the land of Us, was ruled by a wavy-haired legal man of fair mind. In his youth he had devoted his energies to saving innocent men from the gallows. As ruler, his speeches caused citizens to straighten their spines, proud of their differences from the land of Us. And the rule of the wavy-haired legal man of fair mind appeared to be good.

However, the rich and the powerful of the land, with the help of their bean counters, complained that their taxes were too high, that it was difficult for the rich to get richer under the unfair tax system. So the rich and the powerful sent an emissary, an old friend, in fact, to the wavy-haired ruler to plead for a Ruling Commission to investigate the unfairness of the tax system. To make it easy for the wavy-haired ruler to grant their plea, they recommended that the most respected bean counter in the land be appointed to head this commission. They also hinted that the wavy-haired ruler might find it difficult to get his picture into the newspapers during the next election if such a Ruling Commission was not set up. And so the wavy-haired ruler granted the plea, which, in any case, seemed a good thing to a legal man of fair mind.

The pre-eminent bean counter was Kevin Clerk, a man well-versed in the needs and desires of the rich and powerful. He was also an honest man. He accepted the wavy-haired ruler's plum appointment as Chairman of the Ruling Commission Investigating the Fairness of the Tax System, although down in his heart, from his years of counting beans for the rich and the powerful, he felt that there wasn't much wrong with the tax system as it was. He thought the rich and powerful were perhaps protesting a little too much.

However, Kevin Clerk was an honest man, and when an honest man opens his eyes he does not blink, no matter what he sees. Kevin Clerk examined the tax system, slowly, meticulously, turning his practised bean counter's eye to every aspect of the tax laws, and he was startled at what he found. The rich and the powerful were correct. The tax system was unfair—to the majority of the citizens of the land of Them. He found that in the labyrinth of the tax laws and regulations and court rulings a dollar was not a dollar was not a dollar. He found that in most cases a rich man's dollar was defined as unearned by the sweat of his armpits and therefore untaxable, whereas the poor man's dollar was always earned by the sweat of his armpits and therefore taxable. Kevin Clerk found that the system was unfair because the rich and the powerful were not paying enough in taxes while the poor were paying too much, and he reasoned that for tax purposes a dollar should be a dollar should be a dollar, no matter how earned, and he further reasoned that although the taxes of the rich and powerful would rise with the implementation of his recommendations, in the long run the economy of the land of Them would be better for it.

And so Kevin Clerk reported his findings and his recommendations to the wavy-haired ruler and the citizens of the land of Them. And the newspapers shrieked "Make the Rich Pay!" and "A Dollar Is a Dollar Is a Dollar!" and the citizens of the land of Them almost heard the message, but the rich and the powerful screamed, "Traitor! Make the rest pay!" and they threatened to take their unearned dollars to the land of Us without giving the wavy-haired ruler a penny for his next campaign.

Kevin Clerk attempted to reason with his former friends whom he had always considered to be reasonable men, but to no avail. So he ended his days in disgrace, while the typewritten pages of his report gathered dust in the ruler's vault like a Bible behind the iron curtain.

35

For a moment all was still. Then the porcelain dog next to
the cloudy crystal ball on Mackenzie King's museum desk
barked. Not loudly, just a healthy annoying yap. The sparrows
on the ruins at Kingsmere chirped and flew away. The skiers
frozen on Mont Ste-Marie resumed their descent. The Noonday
Gun fired once more. The multitude on Parliament Hill erupted
in tumultuous applause and scrambled to its feet, waving
Simple Hein's two-litre pop bottles with the golden beetfield
verses. The needles at the Canadian Centre for Remote Sensing
went wild. Samuel de Champlain on his pedestal on Nepean
Point lowered his astrolabe to the proper functional position.
More swallows' nests shattered in the Peace Tower gargoyles
and cascaded to the ground.

Thecla Thiessen placed the silver bundle in the Prime
Minister's lap. She whispered in his ear: "No, sir, this is not the
Madonna book. It is Kevin Clerk's forbidden text. The text
commissioned by your mentor, the wavy-haired legal man of
fair mind!"

But before the Prime Minister could protest, before he

could tell this child to leave him be and go home to change her diapers, before he could get to his feet and disappear in the tumultuous applause for Politicks Paetkau's reading, the crowd began to chant the bottle verse: "I HAVE A VISION—I SEE MILLIONS OF BEETWEEDERS, WITH HOES SHARPENED, DESCENDING ON OUR CHOKING FIELDS, HACKING AWAY AT THE MUSTARD AND THE WILD OATS, SEPARATING THE DOUBLES, FREEING THE SWEET SUGAR BEET TO FLOURISH AS WE WEED OUR WAY INTO THE FUTURE. THERE, WITH THE HELP OF GOD, I WILL LEAD YOU!"

BLAST BLAST BLAST

BLAAAAAAAAASSSSST!

The horn of the Lazy Leisure Camper cut through the cold Ottawa air like ice cracking on a great northern lake. All of Ottawa was awakened, except for fifty-three senators still nodding over their desks in the Red Chamber and the Royal Canadian Right Honourable Leader Opposite slumped in his easy chair in Stornoway where he had dozed off in front of the television wondering how come he never saw himself on the *National Journal* or even *Newsworld*.

BLAST BLAST BLAST

BLAAAAAAAAASSSSST!

The horn honked louder than a thousand Manitoba wedding cars heading from churches to Sawatsky's Studio. The blast rippled over the land with more speed and power than CNCP Telecommunications and Roy Rogers Cable and Cello-Fax Phone. The blast was heard by the goose at Wawa. It was heard in the old-growth forest on the Queen Charlotte Islands. It rattled a drilling rig in the Beaufort Sea. It woke up an actor playing a French soldier at Fort Louisbourg. Robots in auto plants in Oshawa hesitated just enough to cause future recalls of cars. The iron ore mine in Schefferville, Quebec, reopened.

Oata Siemens heard it in Gutenthal as she paused at the kitchen table to chew on the end of her carpenter's pencil, a Farmers' Union notebook spread out in front of her between two stacks of notebooks, the empty ones on the left, the filled ones on the right. She gazed through the square panes of the window overlooking the snow-covered garden at the white-faced black-eyed heifer staring back at her from beside the bird feeder. The corner pane reflected the TV from the living room where Yasch and Doft were watching the hockey game. Bluejays pecked at sunflower seeds and frozen leftover porridge, daring the heifer to raise its nose to the bird feeder. Oata lowered the carpenter's pencil to the pages of the Farmers' Union notebook and saw the Lazy Leisure Camper inch through the crowd on the driveway curving past the West Block up Parliament Hill toward the Prime Minister still clutching the silver Kevin Clerk Tax Reform Text beside Thecla Thiessen on the flatdeck trailer. Politicks Paetkau sat on the red stool, fingers poised to turn another page in Yeeat Shpanst's black book.

BLAST BLAST BLAST

BLAAAAAAASSSSSST!

The horn cut through the Nashville yowling of an afternoon karaoke cowboy in the bar at The Senator in Saskatoon, interrupted a publisher's rep's gossip about M&S and HarperCollins at Sutherland Books in Regina. In Victoria the girl with the Bottecelli face spilled capuccino on expatriate prairie knees. The Oilers hockey team tripped on their practice pucks as the blast resonated through the West Edmonton Mall where shoppers dropped merchandise and streamed to the exits. The camper inched up the Hill and stopped in front of Politicks Paetkau. The horn blasted once more. The snow slid from the roof of the covered bridge at Wakefield, Quebec, and the bronze bare-shouldered woman at the base of John A. Macdonald's pedestal dropped her flagstaff and reached out for a cello.

A rumble reverberated from the funnel speakers on the camper, a low, rummeling, blood-stirring, earth-toned growl, a brumming, fortzing, shuddering sound heard by ears but felt by feet on the ground, by seats on the grass, a sound, a vibration, like thundering buffalo hooves and chugging trains hauling boxcars of wheat, a vibration that shivered bones and made loggers' arms yearn to hug trees. The sound faded out like a pause for breath and in the hush the million ears on

Parliament Hill heard the soft quavering of a bow drawn across a cello string pressed to the fingerboard by a bronze finger, trembling.

The Lazy Leisure Camper opened and Hups Hilbraunt stepped down carrying his Flat German brummtupp friction drum. Like a twelve-year-old boy he scrambled himself up onto the flatdeck trailer and set down the nail barrel brummtupp right in front of the Prime Minister and Thecla Thiessen. Stretching out the swatch of horsetail tied to the centre of the cowhide head, Hups began to rub it up and down between pinched fingers and the rummeling, brumming, fortzing sound schowelled all over Parliament Hill.

But that was only the beginning. Oata's mother led the other mental patients out of the camper van all wearing red and white Mary Maxim sweaters and fur hats, like Pierre Eliot Trudeau wore when he walked in snowstorms. All carried 8-Ender curling brooms over their shoulders. In milk-spattered four-buckle overshoes they stomped down the steps to the Parliament Hill lawn melted clear of snow by five hundred thousand sitting people. The crowd cleared a space, and with Hups Hilbraunt and the brummtupp keeping time, Oata's mother began to chant: "FELLOW CANADIANS WE CANNOT ESCAPE HISTORY!" And she marched up and down with her 8-Ender curling broom over her shoulders, stomping her four-buckle overshoes in perfect time to the chant and the fortzing beat of the brummtupp, leading the other mental patients in perfect formation all the way through the Prime Minister's dark day for Canada speech. The second time through, the citizens on Parliament Hill picked up the chant, even a bunch of Royal Canadian Fur Hat Changing Guards who had been roused from their cribbage game in the barracks by an unexpected bugle call and had arrived at the main gate just as Oata's mother and the mental patients began their marching chant. By the third time through, the chant and the brummtupp were rummeling and fortzing all the way from Green Gables by Cavendish Beach to Howe Sound in BC and Igloolik in the High Arctic. Even the Prime Minister on the flatdeck chanted along with his own speech, a speech he had never even written himself, and he was thinking for sure that never again would he hire himself a speech writer who had taken a correspondence course from the Famous Writers' School paid for with a grant from Alberta Culture; he was thinking maybe he should have hired that person from the League of Canadian Poets who had been writing him letters about really weird stuff like Public Lending Right and exempting books from the GST; at the very least his next speech writer would have lived the Sage Hill Writing Experience in Saskatchewan; no more Harbourfront types for him.

Oata was writing so fast that she came to the end of the notebook at the same time the carpenter's pencil lead was worn flush with the wood, and during the moment that she reached for a new Farmers' Union notebook and pulled a fresh carpenter's pencil from behind her ear, every television screen hooked up to the Roy Rogers Cable Company wires flickered for a second, then went dead. Such a stillness hadn't been heard in the land since King Eddy 8-Ender fell off his throne to go chasing after Bart Simpson's Auntie Wallace. Even the hydro lines between Brunkild and Sperling stopped humming in the cold prairie air.

36

At Stornoway the Royal Canadian Leader Opposite had stripped to his sleeveless undershirt and sat gripping a bottle of Molson Canadian as he watched a hockey game between players with red stockings and players with blue stockings. An organ played high in the arena loft but there was no cello. A blue player shot the puck into the red goal and the organ sounded like a herd of horses galloping up a mountain. The Leader Opposite looked away from a States beer commercial, set his empty Canadian into the case behind his chair, and pulled out a full one. But when he had twisted the cap off there was no hockey game on the screen. Instead, the pin-striped blue Minister of Deficits, wearing newly cobbled shoes, stood in the Common House with a thick sheaf of papers in his hand. And this is what he said as the Leader Opposite tipped back his beer waiting for the hockey game to resume: *O Canada, see your abominable conduct. Your father was Uk and your mother was Fran and when you were born your umbilical cord was not tied. You were not bathed in water and sprinkled with baby powder. You were not diapered in leak-proof Pampers. No one cared for you enough to do any of these things and you were thrown out on a few acres of snow in your own filth on the day you were born.*

The Leader Opposite burped and pressed a button on the remote control. A pretty blonde woman with red lipstick stood at a lectern in front of a WOMAN, REALLY banner saying, . . . *filth on the day you were born. I came by and saw you kicking helplessly as you lay in your own blood on the few acres of snow and I decreed that you should keep on living in your blood. I tended you like a maple tree in the forest and you throve and grew. You came to full womanhood; your breasts became firm and your hair grew, but you were still quite naked and exposed.*

He pressed the button again and a man in a Hugo Boss suit with the legend Royal Corporate Monopoly Players said: *. . . naked and exposed. I came by again and saw that you were ripe for love. I spread my Pierre Cardin trench coat over you and covered your naked body. I plighted my troth and entered into a pre-nuptial agreement with you, and you became mine. Then I bathed you with scented water to wash off the blood; I shaved your legs and armpits; I painted your toenails; I fitted you with nylon stockings and sandals of dugong-hide; I fastened a control-top girdle round you and dressed you in fine red lace. I adorned you with jewellery: bracelets on your wrists, a chain round your neck, a ring in your nose, pendents in your ears, and my stylists molded your hair with French mousse. You were adorned with gold and silver, and clothed by Alfred Sung and Ralph Lauren with fine silks and brocade. Fine pasta and honey and olive oil and sushi were your food; and I gave you daily workouts in my chain of fitness studios and you became a great beauty and rose to be a First Lady. Your beauty was famed throughout the world; it was perfect because of the splendour I bestowed on you.*

The Leader Opposite would have switched the channel sooner except that the Hugo Boss suit looked a bit like the guy who had married his sister and then broke her nose when she confessed to him that she had voted *no* when he had told her to vote *yes*. But now he flipped the channel and a woman in front of a CLOSED PERMANENTLY sign on a chain-link gate said: *Relying on your beauty and exploiting your fame, you played whore and offered yourself freely to every passerby. Your spread your Alfred Sung garments on vandalized bus shelter floors and there you committed fornication. You pawned the splendid gold and silver jewellery that I had given you, and mail-ordered scanty garments from Frederick's of Hollywood; you sent for battery vibrators and inflatable dolls from sleazy magazines in the Land of Us with which you committed fornication. You covered your lovers with your Ralph Lauren robes, and you massaged their round mouse ears with my oil and burned my incense in honour of their turtle shells. The food I had provided for you, the fine pasta, the oil, the honey, the sushi, you set before them as an offering of soothing odour.*

Oata was so yralled up in her head wondering what would happen on Parliament Hill that she didn't notice there was a problem with the television until she heard Yasch say, "What the dukkat is loose with the TV?" Oata looked at the television reflected in her kitchen window and when she squinted she could suddenly see the picture as clearly as if she was in the living room, a picture of a row of men in suits behind a table with microphones and glasses of water. Off to the side, a long-haired bearded man wearing a sweatshirt with the words Artists Rescue Them was pointing to a television on a wheeled cart and the screen showed lots of striped and starred flags, shooting, exploding cars, and women's clothes ripped off by men with dark faces who hadn't shaved or washed their clothes in Tide. And the artist said: *The sons and daughters whom you had borne to me you took and sacrificed to these images as their food. Was this slaughtering of my children, this handing them over and surrendering them to your images, any less a sin than your fornication? With all your abominable fornication you never recalled those early days when you lay quite naked, kicking helplessly in your blood on the few acres of snow.*

"Oh no!" Oata said as she recognized the words from her stolen notebooks. Doft clicked the channel changer and the screen showed the States of America President shaking his finger at third-world ambassadors, sounding like a cross between a John Wayne cowboy and a Rocky 4 boxer: *Woe betide you! After all the evil you had done you set up a couch for yourself and erected your own shrine in every open place. You built your shrines at the top of every street and debased your beauty, offering you body to every passerby in countless acts of harlotry. You committed fornication with your lustful neighbours, the Evil Empires, and provoked me to anger by your repeated harlotry. I stretched out my hand against you and reduced your territory. I gave you up to the will of your enemies, the Philistine women, who were disgusted by your lewd conduct.*

In Stornoway the Leader Opposite flipped channels and saw a national union leader raise a fist, shouting: *Still unsatisfied, you committed fornication with the Assyrians, and still were not satisfied. You committed many acts of fornication in a land of free traders, and even with this you were not satisfied. How you anger me! You have done all this like the headstrong hooker you are. You have set up your couches at the top of every street and erected your shrines in every open place, but, unlike the common prostitute, you have scorned a fee. You adulterous wife, who receives strangers rather than your own husband! All prostitutes receive presents; but you give presents to all your lovers, bribing them to come from far and wide to commit fornication with you. When you are so engaged you are the very opposite of those other women: no one runs after you, and you do not receive a fee; you give one!*

On the next screen, sweat poured off Struttin' Steve Stropp's evangelical face as he hammered the air with his black Bible and sneered: *Listen, you harlot! Because of your brazen excesses, exposing your naked body in fornication with your lovers, because of your abominable idols, I shall assemble all those lovers whom you charmed, all whom you loved and all whom you turned against. I shall gather them in from all around and turn them against you; I shall strip you before them, and they will see you altogether naked.*

The Leader Opposite felt like he was in a bench-clearing brawl during the Stanley Cup as every channel showed another enraged public figure shouting the same words. A corporate executive railed at his unionized workers: *I shall bring you to trial for adultery and murder, and I shall give you over to blood spilt in fury and jealousy.* A cabinet minister harangued a jobless crowd in front of the Unemployment Insurance office: *When I hand you over to them, they will demolish your couch and pull down your shrine; they will strip off your clothes, take away your splendid jewellery, and leave you stark naked.* The Leader Opposite even saw *himself* in the Common House threatening the Prime Minister: *They will bring a mob to punish you; they will stone you and hack you to pieces with their swords; they will burn down your houses and execute judgement on you in the sight of many women. I shall put a stop to you harlotry, and never again will you pay a fee to your foreign lovers.*

Then on every screen in this fair land the Minister of Deficits flashed a smile and said in a gentle, seductive, fireside pastoral voice: *Then I shall abate my fury, and my jealousy will turn away from you. I shall be calm and no longer be provoked to anger. You never called to mind the days of your youth, but enraged me with all your doings; I in turn have brought retribution on you for your conduct. This is the word from the Throne.*

Oata tried to scream, "No, that's not what I meant at all. It's not a blueprint for living!" But no words would pass her lips.

Across the land, viewers kept flipping through the channels and every channel, even the channels the Roy Rogers Cable and Cello-Fax Phone Company usually scrambed, carried the same scourge from anti-patriarchal feminists and pro-life family valuists, from cable television companies presenting maple leaf arguments to the CRTC and Native leaders calling for redress, from farmers protesting unfair subsidization of foreign wheat and a writer standing in front of a chain bookstore calling for anti-dumping action against foreign corporate cultural products. The viewers couldn't act. Their fingers stayed pressed on the scan buttons and the screens flipped past their stinging eyes, the same speech whipping their ears with new words and phrases slipping into the story, repeating themselves like a broken record over and over *productivity racist tighten our belts lazy cheaters* over and over *globalization politically correct free market deregulation you had it too good for too long we must pay now it's your fault but it will trickle down no pain no gain there must be incentive to work again* over and over and over again.

The Leader Opposite tried to switch off the television but pressing the off button had no effect. He rose from his chair and slammed in the off switch, but the screen kept flashing. He reached to pull the plug and found a permanent steel-covered cable growing out of the wall to his television. He covered his eyes, but the flashing screen would not go away. His brain had been cabled by a remote laser surgical strike. He stumbled back to his chair and fumbled for another beer. The bottles had been replaced by cans of Coors Light, and in a few minutes the Royal Canadian Leader Opposite's cabled brain had no recollection of ever tasting the full-bodied, sweet, slightly skunky, glorious burp of a Molson Canadian during a *Hockey Night in Canada* between the Canadiens and the Leafs.

37

"NO!" Oata screamed, as she spotted the pastel-blue tuxedos on the Peace Tower observation deck looking down on Thecla. She jabbed her carpenter's pencil at the notebook page but it wouldn't move; it refused to make a mark. She saw Thecla gazing at Politicks's sandy wavy hair, her head full of more arguments with the Prime Minister, oblivious to Kjirps Iesaak Klippenstein dangling the cherry-red wedding shoe above her head. The sun set behind the West Block of Parliament, leaving the Peace Tower clocks like double moons in the dusk. Then fireworks exploded in the Ottawa sky.

At first the five hundred thousand people on the lawns of Parliament Hill thought the fireworks were being fired from rafts on the Ottawa River but soon realized that the fireworks were not shooting up but dropping from the sky. For a few minutes the sky was filled with common patriotic Roman candles, Catherine wheels, flowerpots, and assorted sparklers and skyrockets, and the people thought the spectacle was in honour of Politicks Paetkau's reading. But then a spectacular

Catherine wheel altered form and became a Skydome-sized televison screen. At first the screen showed Politicks Paetkau pausing on the stool on the flatdeck, his fingers poised to turn the page of the black book on his lap. But before he could move, a flowerpot dropped from the sky and formed into another television screen showing the Minister of Deficits repeating the abandoned baby on the few acres of snow speech. Before Politicks Paetkau could turn the page, a steady *bloonk bloonk bloonk* filled the air, each *bloonk* placing another Skydome-sized television screen in the sky. In the time of a gulped breath the screens formed a complete circle around the horizon. *Bloonk bloonk bloonk.* A second circle built upon the first, then a third, like the snow blocks of an igloo, up and up and up, until the entire dome of the sky was covered with television screens, and the only stars to be seen were Hollywood stars and stars with stripes, but even those were outnumbered by mouse ears and turtles and hamburgers and toilet paper and family values at Toys R Us.

The multitude on Parliament Hill craned their necks, squinting for a screen made in their own image. A segment of the crowd spotted a maple leaf flag and for a brief second their cheers drowned out Bart Simpson outinsulting Roseanne, for an instant even overcoming Arnold Schwartzenegger's kindergarten guns. Then someone shouted, "It's upside down!" The crowd booed and the red maple leaf vanished altogether replaced by a Somali teenager talking excitedly beneath a double golden rainbow about a sushi-loaded kiloburger taco pizza.

Then all the screens blanked for a split atomic second. Two thousand and one Strauss brasses and kettle drums spoke Zarathustra and a vista of grassy hillsides appeared on all the screens quickly uniting into one domed picture. Slowly the Panavision camera zoomed in on one of the hills and then closed in on a figure resting its head on a coat-covered rock. Black gothic-style letters appeared on the grassy background:

Robert De Niro
Kim Bassinger
in
Ezekiel 16
The Score Easy Remake

It had been one thing for Oata to hear the words from her four notebooks used as weapons, but to see them acted out by Robert De Niro on Kim Bassinger was like going through a car wash with sand blasting out of the nozzles. Even the Score Easy ending where Robert De Niro shrunk into a newborn babe and crawled into Kim Bassinger's lap and starlight shone on his curly hair, white as wool, didn't make Oata feel any less whipped and battered.

Outside her window Oata heard the black-eyed heifer lowing, and on Parliament Hill she saw Politicks Paetkau force his eyes down from the televison sky. He focused on the handwritten words of Yeeat Shpanst. He opened his mouth and took a breath. From far away, as if buried down in the bottom of the deepest sea, he heard

Blast blast blast

blaaaast!

Before he could speak even one word, Cora Lee and Barbara were pushing him off the flatdeck trailer. "Don't look up! It's our only chance! Don't look up!" The door of the camper was open, Yeeat Shpanst still behind the wheel, honking.

BLAST BLAST BLAST

BLAAAAST!

Politicks Paetkau stumbled up the steps with the women behind him. Oata's mother scrambled her troop of mental patients off the Parliament lawn into the van, all except the young woman with the rollers in her hair and the Cameo pack in her orange-painted fingers who had wanted so much to watch *Edge of Night*. The Score Easy Movie Special over, she was frozen with her neck craned to a part of the sky where she had found three screens with *Edge of Night* and she didn't even hear the final

BLAST BLAST BLAST
BLAAAAASSST!
from Yeeat Shpanst before he closed the Lazy Leisure Camper door and drove off Parliament Hill, out through the empty streets of Ottawa. All inside were stiller than the water that runs deep and in the stillness they heard a fluttering rumbling sound, and one of the mental patients asked, "Where is Hups Hilbraunt with that brummtupp?" but like the two-by-twos on that long-ago ark they didn't let themselves think about all those who had been left outside as they set off down the Trans-Canada Highway.

On the flatdeck trailer Thecla sat prepared to argue again with the Prime Minister who gripped the silver bundle she had pressed into his hand. Then they heard the fluttering sound and the Prime Minister relaxed. He had toured the Peacemaker helicopter factory and the engineers had demonstrated the hardly noticeable white noise muzak sound of these choppers. At last he was going to be rescued from this strange event on Parliament Hill. Definitely an investigation into the National Capital Commission Celebrations Branch would determine who was responsible for this debacle, and definitely attrition would take place, silly service contract or no silly service contract. Hups Hilbraunt heard the fluttering helicopters, too, but he was in such a daze with that television igloo sky above him, he just started to play the brummtupp again as he watched a gospel music video baby formula commercial on a screen above him. Like a hummingbird, a Peacemaker heli-copter hovered over the Peace Tower.

Thecla screamed as her red wedding shoe plopped into her lap and the helicopter sank into the spot where the camper van had been. She jumped up as Kjnirps Iesaak Klippenstein and the seven pastel-blue best men scrambled onto the flatdeck. She whirled, looking for an opening.

Kjnirps yelled, "Stop her! That's my bride!" The Prime Minister swung the silver Kevin Clerk report and clunked Thecla on the side of the head. Thecla staggered backwards into Kjnirps Iesaak's arms.

"Get her to the church on time!" the Prime Minister shouted. "Use the chopper!"

The helicopter lifted so the cargo door was level with the flatdeck and Kjnirps Iesaak Klippenstein carried his bride over the threshhold. The seven best men scrambled in after them and the flattering whirlybird lifted out of sight.

A second helicopter settled into position. A dozen Royal Canadian Flyswatters jumped out, and in less than a tick of the Peace Tower clock Hups Hilbraunt had been handcuffed with a plastic tie-lock closure and hustled into the chopper, the silver bundle and the brummtupp quickly slipped into large clear evidence bags. The Prime Minister stepped into the cargo door, then turned for a quick wave at Parliament, but the Flyswatters scrambling after him blocked his view. With hardly a ripple the Peacemaker helicopter rose up the height of the Peace Tower. As it reached the pinnacle a banana peel splattered on the flag, clinging to the maple leaf like a yellow spider. The chopper soared up over the Peace Tower and became a tiny speck on a television picture of children in a Kurdish refugee camp holding three-litre pop bottles singing, "Coke is it!"

The multitude on Parliament Hill was so numbed by the bombarding television pictures they didn't notice that the Prime Minister had disappeared. They forgot that at one time there had been a live human voice reading live human words in the living air, forgetting that at one time there had been many living voices instead of many screens controlled by one deadly star.

At her kitchen table in Gutenthal Oata Siemens broke her carpenter's pencil into three pieces and ripped the Farmers' Union notebook in two. Outside she heard the lowing of the black-eyed white-faced heifer, waiting for her beside the bird feeder in the dim December evening. She brushed the ripped notebook out of the way and reached for a fresh one. She opened the notebook to the middle stapled page and flattened it to the table with her hand. Then she pinched the pointed tip of the broken carpenter's pencil and started to print like a beginner going to school for the first time on Friday afternoons.

Iesaak, Shpriesack
Schlenkjafoot
Schleit siene Brut
Em Kjalla doot.

When she finished she read her words through her tears and she shuddered colder than she had ever shuddered before.

Isaac, Shucksack
Stumble foot
Beats his bride
In the cellar dead.

But then she heard the whirling drone of the tornado above her head and she looked back to the multitude on Parliament Hill stunned by the television sky. "NO!" she screamed. The black-eyed heifer turned from the bird feeder and stared at her through the window. "NO!" she screamed again. The heifer turned and ran off bawling through the garden. "NO!" Oata scraped the germs off her tonsils. On Parliament Hill the little boy who had fallen asleep on his mother's lap started to cry. His mother took her eyes off the television sky, looked down on her son and screamed, "NO!" On the other side of the hill the ragged young man with the shopping cart yelled, "NO!" The Royal Canadian Standby Chauffeur (Montreal) remembered his daughter's birthday party, "NO!" The Prime Minister's wife shouted, "NO!" into her cellular phone. The Royal Canadian Fur Hat Changing Guards barked, "NO!" Five hundred thousand people on Parliament Hill screamed, "NO!" The statue of John A. Macdonald raged, "NO!" On Mackenzie King's museum desk the porcelain dog yelped, "No!"

Suddenly Oata's mother and the mental patients appeared on all the screens in the television sky. "Altogether now!" Oata's mother commanded. "One—two—three!"

NO!

The force of the NO rushed up from Parliament Hill, up from the Great Lakes, up from the St. Lawrence River, up from the tundra, the Maritimes, the Prairies, up from the Rock of Newfoundland, the mountains and the old-growth forests on the Pacific Coast, sending up vibration after vibration into the television sky, radiant beams to heaven afar. The screens began to pop and go dark, one by one, until the great dome of the sky was black. The people held their breath, waiting for the first pin-pointed stars to signal the cheer of victory.

But the stars had no chance to prick through the black sky as the tornado swirled above the land with the roar of a thousand trains, the sound of a million jets breaking the sound barrier, and then the maw of the twister opened wide above their eyes and flashes of lightning revealed the pieces of Canada swirling above them, tattered, shell-shocked from centrifugal force. The multitude gasped with hope. Then the twister swung away to the west, leaving the Ottawa sky pitch black except for the double moon of the Peace Tower clocks under the banana flag.

From far to the west a tremendous clatter echoed over the land as the tornado slowed its spin and let its trusted cargo crash to the ground. Over the clatter and clash a deep voice laughed, "Too late, suckers!" and a sudden wind blasted the house and Oata felt an icy wind swirl past her. Then she heard a door slam and she breathed in a whiff of green apple perfume.

"No, Frieda! Stop! Stop!"

38 BEETFIELD CHORUS

Br-rrr-rr-rrrrr! My
fingers are blue!

Stick 'em in your armpits!

Won't help. I got
icicles there already.

I told you to put your parka on, but you nevers
listen!

Who anyways heard of
weeding beets with a
parka on?

Who evers heard of weeding
beets when its almost time for
Joseph and Mary and the esel
in the Betlehem stahl?

We have to finish the field!

Why for? The ground is frozen.
The weeds are frozen, the beets
are frozen, and the snow is a
foot deep. Why for?

Oh, my feet are just
ice!

You asked yourself for it. Beach sandals on a
frozen field! Halter top with jeans cut off over
nylons! Where is your common sense, meyall?

Felt burr socks and
trapdoor underwear is
sure good style.

So what are you? The Flat German Madonna?

Like a virgin ma dunna and blitzen would
wear the trapdoor underwear over her
clothes. Then it wouldn't be underwear
no more. Heh heh heh.

Weed faster! Then you won't get cold! Stop whining and
cheating!

Why for? Why for are
we doing this?

Don't you know nothing?

More than you!

Don't you nevers watch the *National Journal?*

Is that before *Roseanne* or after?

The news, dummkopp! The CBC *National Journal News!* With
Pierre Anchorbridge.

Not me. I just listen to CFAM or maybe
C-fry Weather Eye.

So anyways, there's no
TV on this beetfield.

Whoevers heard of TV on a
beetfield?

Rudy Reimer has TV and VCR in his
Versatile cab.

Br-rrr-r-rrrr-rr! Even with long johns and hockey
socks on it is still freezing today. Maybe Willy will
give me a Ski-doo suit for Christmas.

You mean you will still
be weeding beets after
Christmas?

What else? We must finish the field. Don't you anyways watch the *National Journal?*

But if I know my Willy he will go in by Fruelied Fashions in the Flatland Mall and those women will blink their eyesiepers at him and he will pick out something so thin and flimsy and too small to fit a person over three months old. He will call it a Teddy, but it'll only be bare and won't have any fur.

How come, Serena, you are weeding beets anyways? You nevers used to in the olden days.

It's too cold to talk about.

We must finish the field! On the *National Journal* they say . . . And I shiver myself blue even under two quilts and the electric blanket and even my Willy can't warm me up!

Weed faster! Grip that hoe handle on tight with both hands and hack harder and faster and the ice will break and the weeds will cut. Weed faster!

There is no ice today, the snow is sticky! A person can't weed beets fast in sticky snow!

Powder snow is worse! Powder snow is worst!

Specially if you have to break the icy crust through and the hoe blade gets stuck in a too-small hole.

Even my Willy can't warm me up and it is so cold and the row is so long and the thermos of coffee is at the other end of the field.

Oh shit, now I got a hole in my panty hose. Weeding beets in winter is a sin.

Oh, you just stop already with your kahyinkering. Your hearts will bleed yet all over the white snow. You have to live in this world the way it is, not the way it is in a Niemols Nevers Land. These are tough times. You have to put in a winter thermostat.

Oh, yeah. And in the summer you promised us global warming and that if we thought it was hot on a beetfield we still had a few things coming. And now . . .

On the *National Journal* they say it is only a temporary setback, a global restructuring. It will warm up, but who could predict that Filipino volcano. Besides, we are on the right track.

And what kind of a track is that? The same track that Haustig Neefeld dreamed himself up by his elevator?

The beetfield! Don't you nevers watch the *National Journal?* The Prime Minister! I have a vision—I see millions of beetweeders, with hoes sharpened . . .

I don't see any millions of stupids like us on this cold cold field breaking our hoes on frozen beets.

And melt your cold cold heart. I don't have a television. I don't see millionaires.

Oh, that wind is blowing through this parka like it was thin as Willy's Fruelied Fashions Teddy without fur.

What's that?

Where?

There, blowing across the snow.

We have to finish the field!

Looks like an ice chunk tumbling. A tumble ice.

We have to finish weeding the field!
  Where? I don't see nothing!
    Watch out! It's coming right at you!
  OW! Right on my frozen leg!
      What is it?
   Grab it!
    Got it!
      What is it?
   Let's see!
Give it here!
     No way, I caught it!
  It hit me. It's mine!
Give it here!
      What is it?
    Pop bottle.
  Two litre. Empty.
 The five cents is mine!
    It's not empty. There's some
    paper in it.
     Take it out.
 If it's money, it's mine. It clunked me on the leg!
Give it here!
    I got it out. It's got words on it.
     What's it say?

Give it here!
  Read it already.

    I have a vision—I see millions
    of beetweeders . . . hacking
    away at the mustard and the
    wild oats, separating the
    doubles . . . as we weed our
    way into the future. There,
    with the help of God, I will
    lead you!
See, just like on the *National Journal!* The Prime Minister . . .
    Doesn't say nothing about the
    Prime Minister here!

Don't you understand dummkopp? That verse proves that
we're on the right track. Weeding beets is the right way to go!
Don't you understand? That's why we're here!

                              Let's see. Where does
                              it say we have to
                              freeze our putoots off
                              on a beetfield in
                              winter? I quit!
You can't quit!

                              Says who?
On the *National Journal* they say this is the only way to
recovery. We have to tough it out. It's the only way we can
compete. Otherwise we'll be shut out of the market.

          Holem de gruel! What's coming now?
          Ski-doos!
                    Two Ski-doos.
                              Hurray! They're
                              coming to take me
                              away ha ha ha ha!
Hold your hoes ready. On the *National Journal* they say there
are terrorists.

          Hey, that looks like Tape Deck Toews!
                    And that's CD, his wife, with him.
                              CD who can wear size 5?
They have weapons!
          Just TV cameras, stupid!
TV cameras? You mean like the *National Journal?*

          Tape Deck Toews and CD? For sure not the
          National Journal. They don't even have real fur on
          their parka hoods.
How would you know so much?

          Just because I don't wet my pants over it doesn't
          mean I never watch the *National Journal*.
                              Hey, they want to see the bottle!
                              The bottle?
                              Yeah, they want to film us with
                              the bottle.

Film us?

                    Yeah, they want us to read the
                    message out loud.

For crying out loud! On the *National Journal* yet! I told you
we were on the right track!

        But my hair is all frozen with icicles!

                    And I got a hole in my
                    panty hose.
             C'mon, let's read it already.

Here, let me see!

                    Altogether now.
      Oh well, what can you do. I have a vision . . .
. . . I see millions of beetweeders, with hoes sharpened . . .
                . . . descending on our choking
             fields . . .
                    . . . hacking away at
                    the mustard and the
                    wild oats . . .
             . . . separating the doubles . . .
    . . . freeing the sweet sugar beet . . .
        . . . to flourish . . .
                    . . . as we weed our
                way . . .
           . . . into the future . . .
      Holem de gruel, we did it!
See, I told you we are on the right track!
                    Listen!
        What?
              Hear that?
     Hear what?
                    The voices!
I told you! Just like on the *National Journal!*
        Holem de gruel, it is schowelling all over the
        himmel from one end to the other.
                . . . the dice of God are always loaded . . .
                    . . . in the kingdom of the blind
                    the one-eyed man is king . . .

. . . I offer the
end run;
government
by football
players . . .
. . . one dog does not change a bone with another . . .
. . . In this world we have people, turtles,
and three-sided iron files . . .
. . . all things come to
an end—except a
sausage, which comes
to two ends . . .
. . . The bullet is stronger than
the ballet . . .
Where are the Ski-doos?
Gone!
Gone mit zuh vint!
So quickly gone. I wanted to ask when we'll be on
what channel.
Just watch the *National Journal*. You'll see.
It's getting too dark to see.
Ouch, I almost hacked
my toe.
Look!
What?
There! The light!
Well, it's Christmas, dummkopp!
For Christmas it should
be a star. Mit fife spitze
ecken!
What is that?
Must be government!
Government?
Well, for sure! Who else would put up a
buffalo light?
So high, a green
buffalo in the sky.

Hey, you hear that?
What?

Holem de gruel, that's noisy!

I don't hear nothing.

Can't you smell the
ozone?

Ouch! My ears!
Dunna noch emol eent!
Something's smashed up for
sure!

39

When the Christmas lights lit up the Pool elevator nobody was more surprised at what he had done than Haustig Neefeld, himself. And if anybody had told him that at his age he would be so dringent in bed that on Thanksgiving Saturday evening Pienich would at last put her foot down and say that even Gott im Himmel had a day of rest, he would have thought the person had febeizeled his brain. But it was true, on Saturday nights now Pienich went to sleep in Neddy's old bed so she wouldn't be all poosted out for church in the morning. Though on Sunday evening she was always back in the right bed again.

Haustig never would have thought when the GST bribe money cheque came in the mail that Pienich would endorse it herself and cash it by Fruelied Fashions in the Flatland Mall and come home with a shopping bag full of new Sunday clothes and even a little black hat with mosquito netting hanging down over the face. And then yet Pienich had gone to the hairdresser's and not only had she cut off her hair for the first time in her life, but she got holes poked in her ears, too, and now yet on weekdays she always had something bommeling from her ears and Haustig, though he teased her about having fish hooks in her ears, had to give in that Pienich was quite something to see. And on Sunday for going to church Pienich would lightly touch her lips with lipstick crayon, but not enough to start a whole pile of fuscheling while Klaviera Klassen was playing the piano.

And yes, Pienich had picked him out a made-to-measure suit at the Men's Wear store, and as Vaumst Voth's daughter, Vaumstje, measured him it flitzed through his head that he was maybe buying his coffin suit. And before he could even shudder himself over that he remembered shouting in the curling rink before the tornado lifted them off the earth: "THEY CAN'T KILL ALL OF US AND I WANT TO DIE DANCING." And he felt so good that when Vaumstje raised herself up from measuring his inseam she gave him a funny look and then sort of checked herself over to see if maybe the oola fortz had been glutzing in the wrong place. But the smirk stayed as he wondered if Pienich would go so far as to actually get up and dance with him. And then he started to shudder, scaring little Vaumstje Voth almost to call 911.

On his way home from the Flatland Mall Haustig Neefeld stopped by Jake Esau's place and borrowed his forty-foot extension ladder. And when he was loading off the ladder beside his Pool elevator he thought of something else and drove away again. But not before he had gone into the house where Pienich was baking Christmas cookies for Neddy's children and taken her around the waist from behind and said, "I am you so good!" Pienich stuck a piece of raw cookie dough in his mouth and told him to be satisfied with that in the middle of the day. Haustig chewed the sweet dough and held her without letting his hands claw where they weren't supposed to. Then he went out of the house without saying anything about dancing and drove away off the yard.

As he drove along the road he looked at the stubble poking through the snow on the fields, counted the cattle standing in feedlots, and noticed who had left cultivators parked in the fields. But he felt like he wasn't really seeing these things, that what he was driving past wasn't altogether real for him, or that maybe *he* wasn't altogether real, and he felt like he was a pencil drawing a follow-the-dots picture, one that was so kompliziet a person couldn't see what it was going to be until it was all the way finished. When he had shuddered in Vaumst Voth's Men's Wear store he had thought of borrowing Jake Esau's extension ladder, and then when he loaded it onto his car roof he thought he would load it off by his Pool elevator, and then when he did that he thought of Prell Doell's Salvage Sales and he didn't have a clue what he would look for once he got there.

But at Prell Doell's place he felt like he could see through the ten-foot high used board fence the municipality had made Prell build around his junkyard. What Haustig Neefeld saw was the town of Vanish Creek from in the Pembina Hills. He saw the town of Vanish Creek the way it was before he and Pienich were married, on that Sunday they had driven west through the Pembina Hills, farther than they had ever driven from home alone before. They stopped in Vanish Creek by a Chinese cafe and he and Pienich sat in a booth sipping 7-UP through wax paper straws out of little green bottles.

Pienich suggested that Haustig should put some nickels into the jukebox and play some songs, and he played with her fingers on the table while they listened to the songs and looked in each others' eyes and didn't even notice the Chinaman drying the last cup over and over again, smiling at them. Until at last Pienich sucked at her straw and it made that empty shlurpsing noise, and she turned around. "Look it that! It's almost dark! I'll be late for milking!"

The sun had sunk behind the Pembina Hills when the Chinaman put his last cup on the rack so he could take the fourteen cents from Haustig for the two 7-UPs. They stepped out onto the cafe steps and they stood, Haustig with his arm around Pienich, and stared at the coloured lights hanging across the main street like Christmas lights on washlines, and even after they got into the car they sat for a while staring at the coloured lights and then they drove slowly along the main street where it curved over a bridge and up a steep hill, and at the top Haustig parked the car on a little field so they could watch the coloured lights.

When Haustig Neefeld said, "I want the coloured street lights from Vanish Creek," Prell Doell gestured with his head and led him past piles of grain elevator two-by-sixes, rows of shiplap and V-joint ceiling boards, sections of wrought iron fences, stacks of fence pickets, pails of nails, crates of telephone insulators, bundles of wooden shingles, sections of steel granary bins, and an old municipal dredge with its long boom laid down like a giraffe gone to sleep and the scoop shovel lying at the end of the cable like a dead tired tongue. The coils of sockets leaned against the Vanish Creek Town Convenience which Prell Doell had decided to keep intact as a backup for Bill's Beckhouse Rentals during the summer festival season. Next to the seven coils of sockets, each coil long enough to stretch across a main street, stood a dozen bushel baskets of coloured bulbs. "I'll take 'em all," Haustig said. Prell Doell just nodded and pointed out a path snaking its way through the junk where Haustig could back up his car.

After loading up, Haustig stepped in by the office and watched Prell Doell type some stuff on a computer thing that said Radio Shack TRS-80 Model 4D on it. Prell Doell noticed him watching and said, "Best computer ever made. Handles six disk drives and never mixes them up. Can't even donate them to a mission field in a third world country." Haustig Neefeld wasn't sure what Prell Doell was talking about, but watching him type on the computer reminded him about that Sputnik satellite infrared camera that could count the aphids on a stem of wheat, so he asked Prell Doell if he had any of those lying around, and Prell said, "Not yet, but I won a tender to take apart the first C from the CBC."

When Haustig got home he automatically drove to the elevator, and before he knew it he had leaned the forty-foot extension ladder against one corner and was climbing up. He got so busy attaching the string of lights to the edge of the elevator he didn't notice how high he was until Pienich called up, "OOLA NEEFELD, WAUT DEIST DU DOA SO HUACH?" For a long second Haustig Neefeld remembered he was scared of heights, that his son, Neddy, had always climbed up to change the yard-light bulb while Haustig held the ladder down on the ground. After Neddy went off to Chartered Accounting school Haustig tried to climb up the ladder himself but he got so shakery and shittery half-way up he had to creep down and confess to Pienich that he was scared, and Pienich said if he would hold the ladder then she would do it, and she had. But now he was up at least fifty feet high on a forty-foot ladder and he hadn't even thought about being scared. He hadn't even noticed the forty-foot ladder getting longer and longer each time he climbed down to get more wiring, but during that long second after looking down at Pienich he shuddered so much he was afraid the ladder would start sliding across the side of the elevator like a windshield wiper.

Then the elevator seemed to shudder, too, and for another long second he was driving his car alongside the elevator, inching along the government road allowance on Heinrichs the Mover's biggest timbers, Pienich beside him, Neddy in the back seat, the new Sealy mattress tied to the roof, and Haustig staring up through the windshield at the top of the elevator. Suddenly the elevator shuddered and Haustig Neefeld jumped out of his car without even taking it out of gear and flitzed away, leaving his wife and son in the shuddering elevator's shadow.

When he came back to the car, Haustig met his son's eyes for a second, felt him see deep into the dark empty hole inside him, and he knew Neddy would never quite believe him anything after that, that he would never be able to take the strap to his son again no matter what he did because Haustig Neefeld would never again be able to hit hard enough for his son to feel it. And Haustig never touched Pienich or quite looked her in the eye until the shadow scared him into reaching out in bed that August Sunday night after the tornado had bedoozled the world.

"FASPA! OOLA NEEFELD!" Pienich called from far below. And Haustig Neefeld noticed it was getting almost too dark to see and his stomach was hanging crooked. So he climbed down and Pienich led him by the hand into the house.

It was in bed that night that the buffalo lit up in his head, and for the first time since that August Sunday night Haustig stopped before he was finished and Pienich patted his softening penis and said, "Daut's okay, oola Neefeld. Dit zent ye nijch de Olympics. And for a change I can sleep dry."

In the morning Haustig drove to Prell Doell's Salvage Sales and said, "Buffalo." Prell Doell scratched his neck, typed on his TRS-80 Model 4D, and signalled Haustig to follow him. From behind an Edenburg Swine Club Float he pulled out a wire frame shaped like a buffalo. "Good stuff," Haustig said.

The ladder kept reaching higher as he strung the lights up the sides of the elevator, along the edges of the roof, top and bottom as well as the peak. Finally, with a pulley and a long rope, he hoisted the wire buffalo frame strung with green lights to the top. Without a quiver he set the buffalo into place and connected the wires—well, not completely without a quiver, for there was a second when he thought he heard a voice whispering in his ear, daring him to throw himself down from the pinnacle, but it seemed as if Haustig had already faced his demons and he shouted, "THEY CAN'T KILL ALL OF US AND I WANT TO DIE DANCING!" And as a reply, he thought he heard Pienich shaking out the mop on the porch steps singing, "Daunce, daunce, wuaever you may be!"

And then Haustig couldn't wait. He had to try out his lights. He shouted down to Pienich, "PLUG EMOL DEN YALEN EXTENSION CORD EN!"

"WAUT SAJCHST, OOLA NEEFELD?"

"PLUG DEN EXTENSION CORD EN! DEN YALA! DOA BIEM SHTAUL!"

"FUATS UPUH SCHTADE! OBAH LOAT ME EASCHT EN AVAROCK AUN TRAKJE!"

The minutes that it took Pienich to throw on her overcoat, step into her barn four-buckles and shuffle through the snow across the yard seemed an eternity, what with the cold breeze whispering temptations into his ear, planting doubts, testing his faith. What if this whole electricity business wasn't true anymore? What if people stopped believing that power could move along a wire for a thousand miles from a waterfall someplace and make light? What if that was a story that just didn't work anymore? What then?

"PAUSS UP, OOLA NEEFELD! ECK PLUG DIE NUE EN!"

"READY!"

The green buffalo lights blinded him for a second and then Haustig heard a faint rumble, like maybe far thunder, or angels singing bass. Pienich shouted from the barn, "HOLEM DE GRUEL, OOLA NEEFELD! DAUT ZIT SHTRAUM!"

And Haustig Neefeld looked down the strings of coloured lights, each bulb a clear pure light like a little candle burning in the night and not one bulb from the Vanish Creek main street was burned out, and Haustig felt himself sweating in his underwear, as if he was wrapped in an electric blanket, and he heard Pienich shout to him, "OOLA NEEFELD! HAST DU DIE ENJEPLUGGED? DU SHIENST AUS NE HARLIJCHE MONE!"

He heard the rumble again, the far thunder, the angels singing bass, and he stared off into the east through the green buffalo lights, remembering Politicks Paetkau's mumble about bringing the buffalo back. Then he heard the whistle. At first he thought it was the howl of a wolf, it was such a long-ago sound, then he heard it again, followed by the faint chug chug chug, and saw a single pinpoint of light, coming.

"YOU HEAR THAT, OOLA NEEFELD? IS THAT A TRAIN?"

"FOR SURE, THAT'S A TRAIN!" Haustig shouted. "AND NOT A DIESEL NEITHER!"

Chugga-chugga-chugga-chugga-wooo-wooo-wooooooo -woo-woo. The pinpoint of light came closer. Chugga-chugga-chugga-chugga-chugga-woo-woo-woooooooo-wooo-wo o. Closer closer, rumble rumble, thunder, angels singing bass. The elevator shuddered. Haustig Neefeld braced himself like he was standing on a moving sled, and he heard Pienich call, "PAUSS UP, OOLA NEEFELD. BREN DIE DEH BULB NICHT UHT!" The elevator vibrated like a hayrack clattering across a stubble field and the train whistle pierced Haustig's ears and he saw the black shadow with its one piercing eye getting closer, getting closer, wheels clattering the rails. He saw the cloud of black smoke, smelled the coal, heard the clanging bell.

Haustig looked down on the top of the train clattering through the glow of the elevator lights and spotted two figures flattened on the roof ladder of a boxcar. The figures sat up, and over the rumble of the train Haustig heard, "Jump, Hein!" A moment later Simple Hein and Bulchi Wiebe rolled in the soft snow beside the track. They lay motionless for a few seconds and then Bulchi Wiebe helped his belly up out of the snow and hollered at Pienich who was running toward them: "PLUG OUT THOSE CHRISTMAS LIGHTS. HURRY!" Pienich whirled herself around and fled back to the barn. She had never in her life yet disobeyed a man who hollered like that.

The elevator went dark and suddenly Haustig Neefeld remembered he was afraid of heights. Bulchi Wiebe and Simple Hein held the forty-foot ladder while Pienich climbed up the eighty feet to the edge of the elevator roof and coaxed Haustig Neefeld to come to her the way she had all those years ago in Haustig's futtachi's car on the hill looking down on the coloured lights of Vanish Creek. Rung by rung Pienich guided each foot down the ladder, rung by rung by rung, all the rungs on a forty-foot ladder extended eighty feet high.

Later, Haustig wasn't sure exactly when the flattering noise started clappering in his ears, but by the time his foot touched the ground the whole sky was vibrating with helicopters and Haustig Neefeld thought he was inside the swirling funnel cloud again as Pienich took him by the hand and said, "Come, oola Neefeld, that's enough for one day." As she put him to bed he felt the twister slow down like a merry-go-round at the end of the ride and all night long he dreamed he was tumbling out of a gruelich big chute into Prell Doell's salvage yard, and he didn't even think to wonder about Bulchi Wiebe and Simple Hein until Hova Jake, the CSIS man, came to breakfast the next morning.

40

"Mosquito, where are you now anyways?" Oata muttered as she peered through the little patch scraped clear on the frosted windshield. "How come this truck has no heat? How come this truck has no oomph? I could walk faster with high heels on a ploughed field! *Too late, suckers,* he said. *Too late!* Oh Frieda, help Thecla to stop herself. Help Thecla to say, I don't! There must be another way!"

Oata glanced through the tiny frost shield on the right side window, saw a pinpoint of light. Haustig Neefeld's yard light, she thought. Suddenly the Pool elevator was outlined in coloured lights with green bulbs making a buffalo on the roof. "Is that what Politicks Paetkau meant when he said we have to bring the buffalo back? Is that the only kind of buffalo that can be brought back?" The road rumbled under the wheels of the truck. The elevator lights went out.

"Oh please, not another tornado!" Oata cried. "Maam! What about your Yeeat Shpanst? How can he let this be?" The darkness was so black it sopped up the light from her sealed beams only inches in front of the truck. She felt the tires swerving in the ice-packed ruts. But she couldn't stop. She had to get to the Flatland Church. There was a wedding to interrupt. Why was the truck crawling like a turtle even with the accelerator pressed to the floor? "Oh Maam, where are you? Can't your Yeeat Shpanst help anymore?" And then Oata wondered about what she had just said to her mother who wasn't even there. She had said, "Can't your Yeeat Shpanst help anymore?" "Your Yeeat Shpanst" she had said and she wondered why, except that it felt right somehow, and she wished she could ask her mother, "Who is Yeeat Shpanst anyways?" And she wondered if she would ever see her mother again, her mother and the mental patients driving all over the countryside in a Lazy Leisure Camper with some Yeeat Shpanst.

Snow fell into the patch of light between the truck and the blackness, and even the red blinking TV tower lights on the other side of the States ditch were out. Oata pressed her foot harder on the accelerator feeling the tires gliding along the icy ruts as snowflakes blew across the lights, thickening until all Oata could see was powdery light. The rumble got louder and louder until in the swirling snow the truck swerved like it was going to be lifted off the road. "Oh Maam! Is there no way out of this? Can the bugger get away with it again?" Outside the truck Oata heard the roaring, the deafening clatter. The wall of powdery light cleared away, and even as Oata felt the foot-to-the-floor speed of her tires in the icy ruts she was blinded by oncoming lights.

BLAST BLAST BLAST

BLAAAAAAAASSSSST!

Oata steered hard to the right, stiffened her legs against clutch and brake pedals. The truck tilted and crunched into the snow-filled ditch. Gasping against the seat belt, she stared through the frost shield into the side mirror and watched the taillights of the Lazy Leisure Camper receding behind her. The brake lights brightened, stopped for a moment, dimmed, then moved out of sight.

Blast blast blast

blaaaaaaaassssst!

Chugga-chugga-chugga-chugga-wooo-wooooooo-woo-woo, clang-clang-clang-clang. A blur of boxcars flashed by her headlights. Oata closed her eyes. The clattering train faded into the low throbbing of her truck motor. Funny that the truck hadn't stalled when she hit the ditch, she thought as she hugged herself trying to squeeze together some warmth, and she wanted to crawl under her mother's coat as her father shovelled the car out of that long-ago snowbank. Sudden pounding on her side window shook her awake. A fur hat topped a grinning face shrugged into the collar of a red Mary Maxim sweater. "Maam!" Oata grabbed the door handle and pushed. The door was blocked by snow.

"Wacht, meyall!" her mother called. "I'll sweep some snow away with this curling broom."

Oata undid her seat belt and shoved her shoulder against the door. The door opened a few inches but not enough to let her get out.

"Maam, I think there's a shovel in the box."

"For sure that would be better than this shtramel broom."

Oata heard the clang of the aluminum shovel as Mamm unwedged it from between the cab and the grain box.

"How did you get here anyways?" Oata called through the narrow opening.

"I made that Yeeat Shpanst let me off. He was just going to drive away and leave you here in the ditch. Shove yourself against that door again."

Oata gave that door an NHL body check, then grabbed for the steering wheel as she nearly landed heista kopp in the snow. She pulled herself upright and stepped out, breaking through the crust, and sinking past her knees.

"Pauss up, meyall. I'm too old already to shovel snow all the night through."

Oata scrambled up out of the ditch and and klunked her knee on the shovel as she threw her arms around her mother.

"Wacht, meyall. Let me stick the shovel in the snow first. It's no use being each other good, with a shovel sticking between." And so in the dark night beside Haustig Neefeld's former truck stuck in the ditch their hearts beat each to each through Oata's barn parka and her mother's red Mary Maxim sweater. For a wild second Oata thought maybe they could turn into salt pillows and stay in that embrace forever. Then the truck motor stopped.

"Maam," she whispered. "We can't just stay here. We'll freeze."

"For sure, meyall," her mother laughed. "But we still have a bit of heat left inside us. I mean, we're not just skin and bones."

They clung together for a few more minutes and then Oata noticed the truck lights flickering.

"The battery's going dead. I better switch the lights off."

"Well sure, we don't need the lights anymore. The moon is coming out."

Oata stumbled through the ditch and switched off the truck lights.

"How are we going to get out of the ditch, Maam?"

"Oh, leave it for your men to deal with. Why else do you have them anyways? Come on, let's start walking. We have a lot of stuff to talk over."

Oata took her mother's arm. Maam carried the 8-Ender curling broom over her shoulder, and for the distance between two hydro poles they listened to their overshoes shlorring on the ice-packed gravel road.

"Who is Yeeat Shpanst anyways?" Oata asked the question so quietly she was almost surprised that her mother heard it over the shlorring of their overshoes on the road. Maam swung the 8-Ender curling broom off her shoulder to let it drag behind her in the icy track and laughed a voiceless breathy laugh, a *laechelnd* kind of laugh that shivered Oata all the way back to Sarah in Abraham's tent, shivered her even more when she thought of her mother in a Lazy Leisure Camper with a man in a Hawaii shirt who could febeizel himself one day and then show himself again the next. She looked sideways at her mother in the moonlight, sideways at the front of her mother's red Mary Maxim sweater. It looked as flat as it always had.

Maam whacked her on the behind with the broom and

laughed her *laechelnd* laugh again. "Ach meyall, you don't have to worry yourself about such a thing with Yeeat Shpanst and me. Besides, with so many crazy people inside one camper, such schmausing would be a more schwierich thing to get away with than junge lied holding hands in the choir loft by a Sunday Night Christian Endeavour. Besides, now that black widow Barbara is back together with him, he can't even *see* an old woman with a red curling sweater on. I had to almost take the broom to him so he wouldn't dump me off by the mental home fence with the others, so yralled up he was with this black widow Barbara and her chokecherry lipstick, with rhinestones on her nylons yet."

Maam stopped talking and let her *laechelnd* laugh echo over the snowy fields and Oata tried to scramble words together to make a question, not just one question, but a whole catechism of questions, but they passed by two more hydro poles before she could ask again, "Who is Yeeat Shpanst anyways?"

"Your father, Nobah Naze Needarp, always wanted to know that, too."

"My father?"

"Yeah sure, Nobah Naze Needarp was your father."

"Well, I guess, Maam. Who else could it be?"

Her mother laughed, only not *laechelnd* now like Sarah in Abraham's tent. She laughed like she was maybe swallowing tears. "He never wanted to believe me that."

"What didn't he want to believe?"

"He never wanted to believe me that he was your right father."

"But why not? Even a blinguh kooh with a blindfold on could see that I looked like him. For sure I never ordered my 200 pounds fat from the Eaton's Trienkje catalogue!"

"Oh Oata, how can a mother talk about such to her daughter?"

"Such what?"

"Such stuff that is supposed to stay hidden under the flour-sack underskirts and thick brown stockings."

"Oh." Oata thought for a second about Frieda feeling like a foolish virgin. "But Maam, if a mother and her daughter can't talk about such things, how is anyone supposed to learn anything?"

"Ach meyall, I know I know, only knowing isn't the same as doing, and I still don't know how I can say this to you even when I want to already. It's so funny really." Her *laechelnd* laugh crackled over the moonshiny snow.

"What's so funny about my father not believing you that I was his daughter?"

"Ach Oata, that wasn't funny one bit, not one bit. What was funny was *who* Nobah Naze figured your father was." The *laechelnd* laugh burst out again as if Maam couldn't stop herself.

"Who, Maam?"

"Yeeat Shpanst."

"What do you mean by that?"

"Nobah Naze Needarp thought Yeeat Shpanst was my lover."

They walked without speaking past another hydro pole before Oata could bring herself to ask, "Was he?"

"Not the way Nobah Naze thought. But once he got Yeeat Shpanst on the brain there was no bringing it by to him that Yeeat Shpanst was just a boyfriend I dreamed up for myself when I was twelve years old."

"You mean Yeeat Shpanst is just a made-up dream?"

"Yeah sure, only I wrote letters to him in my five-year diaries that nobody was ever supposed to read. And then Nobah Naze caught me writing one day and grabbed the diary away from me. When he read about Yeeat Shpanst he got a laupsijch idea that this was a real person in Altbergthal or someplace and to his dying day he figured this Yeeat Shpanst had got there ahead of him. For sure, it didn't help when you decided you had to get born six weeks early. There was no bringing it by to him then that Yeeat Shpanst was just words on a page."

"If Yeeat Shpanst is just words on a page, then who is that man driving around in the Lazy Leisure Camper van?"

"You can see him, too?"

"What you mean with such a question?"

"You can see Yeeat Shpanst?"

"Well yeah, Maam, I can see him, too."

"Ach meyall, such wasn't supposed to happen. That's why I went to the mental home."

"You mean Nobah Naze didn't make you go there?"

"Oh no, even with not believing me that you're his daughter he wanted to have me cook and clean for him and keep his bed warm."

"And you couldn't do that . . . not even for me?"

"Ach meyall, I tried, and at first it seemed to work. I had you and on a farm a woman always has it druck, and writing in my diary helped me get through the day and Nobah Naze was dringent in the bed and I thought that was a good thing even if he was a little rough sometimes. It made me feel wanted, only Nobah Naze was so worried that another man would look me on that he would hardly take me visiting by neighbours, and sometimes on a Sunday after dinner if people came visiting he would stand by the door and tell them that I was sick in bed and soon people didn't bother to try anymore. Then I noticed one day that the lock on my five-year diary was broken and then quite often I saw that someone had been reading it. Oh Oata, I should have stopped writing letters to Yeeat Shpanst, but I had no one else. Sure, some would have said I should have prayed to God, and I did, but nobody had ever learned me to pray to God about what I could write in my letters to Yeeat Shpanst. How could I tell the God from the Gutenthal Church what it felt like when Nobah Naze got dringent rough in the bed? How could I tell God what I wanted it to feel like? I could tell Yeeat Shpanst in my diary. For me maybe that was my way to pray. At least it made me feel better the way a prayer is supposed to."

They walked past another hydro pole before Maam spoke again.

"Ach meyall, what could I do? After Nobah Naze started snooping in my diary he wouldn't leave me alone. Every night he had to fuck me. Fucking. That's what it was. It sure wasn't lovemaking. Maybe fucking isn't even the right word neither. He was punishing me . . . And I couldn't even cry out because I didn't want to wake you."

"Oh Maam!"

"And then one night after he finished and was snoring beside me I got up to go to the toilet. I could feel the blood between my legs. Even in the dark I knew it was blood. I went outside to the beckhouse. I can still remember the edge of the hole pressing into my seat. And the pain shooting up. Then I heard you crying in your bedroom. And I was standing over Nobah Naze who was snoring on his side of the bed. In my hand was the pig-sticking knife."

"Gott im Himmel, Maam!"

"Inside my head I saw what I was going to do with that knife."

"You were going to kill him?"

"Not just him."

"Me too? And yourself?"

"That's what I saw myself do."

"What stopped you?"

"Yeeat Shpanst."

"But what . . . you said he was . . ."

"Just words on a page of paper?"

"Yes, just words on a page of paper."

"Ach meyall, who would believe me that words on a page of paper can be so real? Real enough to stand up from the paper and stop a hand with a knife in it. How could I tell the mental home doctors that Yeeat Shpanst stepped out from my diary page, took my knife hand and led me out of that dark bedroom? He wrapped my coat around my shoulders and led me out to the car and sat with me through the night. His arms were so warm. For sure, I couldn't tell Nobah Naze such a story when he found me in the car in the morning. For one eyeblink when I looked into your father's eyes I thought I saw some sorriness there, but I could still feel the knife handle in my empty hand. I couldn't stay. Not even for you. For sure not for you."

Oata took a deep breath of frosty air and clenched her arm slightly to assure herself that her mother's arm was actually there linked with hers. She heard her mother's breathing, heard the overshoes shlorring along the icy ruts, felt the chill beginning to seep through her clothes. And yet, at the same time, she had an eerie double feeling of a flat pencil in her fingers pressing marks down on little notebook pages. If she squinted she could almost see her reflection in the square windowpane. She almost heard the black-eyed calf bawling beside the bird feeder. Her throat felt dry and she thought how simple it would be to get up and put the teakettle on the back element. She caught a lemon whiff of herbal tea steaming in the cup. So simple it would be, pleasant even, to sip tea and brood over what Maam had been telling her. Then her mother's arm clenched hers. There was a whole catechism of questions still to ask. A cup of tea would be too simple. Even this doubtful moment was confusing her thirst, deflecting the slurp of her desires.

"But what does it mean that I can see your Yeeat Shpanst, too? I never wrote him letters in a five-year diary or invented him for a boyfriend."

"Ach meyall, I'm just a crazy woman in the mental home garden slipping around on fallen apples."

"But if I can see this geschpenst, Yeeat Shpanst, does that mean I'm crazy slipping on fallen apples, too?"

"If I could tell you that I would be a mental home doctor, not a crazy woman. Anyways, we don't have time right now to reckon out if we are words on a page or if we are running loose after the ink leaked out of the pen. We are almost by Prell Doell's place."

"Prell Doell's? What for?"

"That's where Yeeat Shpanst took the others. It's the last stop on his campaign."

"What?"

"Didn't you hear that clanking clattering when the tornado passed over?"

"You mean you know about the tornado, too?"

"Ach meyall, sometimes we are all on the same page. Even in the mental home apple garden we couldn't get from that tornado away. FELLOW CANADIANS WE CANNOT ESCAPE HISTORY! But look, there's Prell Doell's place."

"But Maam, what does it all mean?"

"Trust and obey! Sometimes that's all a person can do. Looks like he dumped the others off by the gate and drove away with his black widow Barbara. But that's the way he's mostly been. In the end he would leave me to figure it out for myself. I wrote one time that he is like a hand hovering over the back fender when you are wobbling your first bicycle. See, Barbara isn't with them."

Politicks Paetkau was pounding his fist on the brown cedar gate of Prell Doell's Salvage Sales. Cora Lee Semple stamped her runners in the snow beside him. Schneppa Kjnals was looking for a lock to pick. Tape Deck Toews was pointing his video camera at Politicks pounding on the gate while his wife, CD, clapped her hands to keep warm. Hippy Pauls shivered with a bottle of dandelion wine in his hands.

"Hey hey hey! Be the solution!" Bulchi Wiebe pushed open the gate and beckoned them into the salvage yard. Oata hesitated for a second as she smelled lemon mint tea, then hurried after her mother. Bulchi Wiebe locked the gate behind them as they moved toward Prell Doell's office shack. Then Cora Lee yelled, "Look!" She ran past a pile of railroad ties to a gas station sign leaning against the yard-light pole. "Look! A White Rose sign!"

"What's White Rose?" CD asked.

"White Rose Oil Company. Just like Linda McQuaig talks about in her book. Canada used to own its own oil companies."

"You mean without a Petro-Can?"

"Yes, before we let Shell and Gulf in we had White Rose and BA and look, there's a North Star sign and over there a Royalite and look there, Johnny Roco says you can't buy a better gasoline."

"You mean Co-op wasn't the only gas a hundred percent Canadian owned?"

"No, and look over there! A case of Suncrest pop bottles!"

"Hey hey hey!" Bulchi Wiebe chuckled as he joined the group looking at a rusting Paul Bunyan sign leaning against a red CNR caboose.

"What's that from?" Oata wanted to know.

"Paul's Fifteen Cent Hamburgers." Hippy said. "The best deal in Winnipeg before McDonald's came and wiped them out."

"And downtown on Portage Avenue there used to be Kavanaugh's," Politicks said. "When we couldn't afford the Greeks on Ellice we would go to Kavanaugh's."

"Hey hey hey! That's the old stuff," Bulchi Wiebe said. "Wait till Prell Doell shows you his new stock. We had to kind of lay low while those helicopters were buzzing around, but with that blizzard dumping all that snow on us those Peacemakers figured Prell had shut down and moved his operation to Mexico."

Then the whole salvage yard was flooded with brighter light than they'd ever had at the Gutenthal skating rink for a hockey game. Blinking their eyes, they explored the yard calling out each time they found something else they thought had been dismantled for good, shredded, crushed, melted down.

"There's the Canadian Wheat Board!"

"I see the plans for the Avro Arrow!"

"The Vegreville Easter egg! A bit cracked but we could weld it!"

"Wow! I found the C from the CBC!"

"And here's the care from Medicare!"

"Holy smokes! Here's the Insurance for the Unemployment!"

"The minimum wage!"

"*100 Huntley Street!*"

"The Canada Pension Plan!"

"The Stratford Festival putting on a Harry Rintoul play!"

"And *Cruel Tears* at Rainbow Stage!"

"And *Saskatoon Pie* at Harbourfront!"

"I found Niagara Falls!"

"Here's the Canada Council Writer-in-Residence Program!"

"What are we going to do with the Business Council on National Issues?"

"I found the Clark Institute."

"That's okay then. Look, behind the Easter egg!"

"Yeah, the Economic Council of Canada and the Science Council, too."

"Here's Confederation and the Charter of Rights and Freedoms!"

"What's Prell Doell going to do with all this stuff?"

"Huh?"

"Well, what is he going to do?"

"What does he do with the junk he collects?"

"He sells it to whoever wants it."

"Would he sell it to us?"

"He let us in here didn't he? He wouldn't let the Peace-makers in."

"Can we afford this stuff?"

"We can't afford not to take back the nation."

"But can we do it? They have the helicopters."

"But we still have the ideas here."

"That's right, and we still have the black book."

"You never know when words will stand up and walk right off the page." Maam laughed her *laechelnd* laugh. "You never know what that Yeeat Shpanst will come up with next. Especially now that Barbara is back to write stuff for him."

"What you mean, Maam?"

"No leader worth his salt on the information highway writes his own stuff. Nowadays they all put the cart before the horse. Push comes to shove, a person could say."

"Where'd you get that from, Maam? From black widow Barbara?"

"Oh no, meyall, I like to still write my own page. It's still the only way for me. But listen!"

WOOOOOOOOOOO-OOOOOO-OOOOOOO-WOOOOO-WOO-CHUGGA-CHUGGA-CHUGGA-CHUGGA-CLANG-CLANG-CLANG-CLANG-WOOOOOOO-OOOO-WOOO. For the first time they noticed the tracks cutting through the salvage yard. From the west came the rumble and clatter of the train, shuddering the earth like a million buffalo stampeding in grass taller than people. The single eye of light lit up the rails, the binding ties. Oata thought of Jacob's ladder with angels climbing up and down and then she saw a buffalo cow on one side of the tracks lowing at her calf on the other side just as the train braked to a stop, showering the group in the salvage yard with sparks. Through the cloud of steam a red-nosed Sir John A. raised his glass from his perch on the cowcatcher of the Countess of Dufferin beside his wife, Agnes. "Load 'er up boys and take 'er back to the nation!"

Oata clenched her elbow to feel her mother's arm and came up empty. She felt the flat pencil pinched in her fingers. She saw her face in the window blended with the nostrils of the black-eyed heifer lowing on the other side. She looked at the heap of notebooks on the floor beside the table. She looked over her shoulder. She saw no hand hovering over her wobbling bicycle fender. Oata thought about making tea. She thought about what Frieda was going to tell her when she got home from Thecla's wedding. She wondered if there was an eraser in the junk drawer. She wondered if carpenter's pencil marks could be erased all the way.

41 BEETFIELD CHORUS

Yoh, did you hear?

Hear what?

Haustig Neefeld.

Haustig what?

They're letting Haustig come home today.

Home from where?

Home from Headingley. All charges dropped.

What charges?

What's the matter with you? You never watch the CBC?

The C is gone from the CBC.

Don't say such a thing! Can't you hear the helicopters?

What charges Haustig Neefeld dropped?

Theft of a Pool elevator over fifty feet high.

Dropped. Charter of Rights and Freedoms. If something drops on your land from the sky you didn't steal it.

Well, I guess.

Don't guess so fast. Simple Hein is still in
custody. They don't believe him that
those pop bottles just fell from the sky.
Well, he had no witnesses and besides he doesn't own that bridge.
And he was trespassing on the Martens
farm, they said.
Simple Hein in jail. I can't believe it.
I hope they take care
of him there.
So what's to take care of? He can just watch TV and eat three
meals a day. That's better than under a bridge.
You were on the hockey team when Hein was just
little, not?
What's that supposed to mean?
Yeah, what's that supposed to mean?
Listen. You hear that
helicopter?
Weed faster! Then they won't bother us.
Weed faster yourself! This is a beetfield, not a
concentration camp!
Look! It's right up
above!
Weed faster, I said! It's only the productivity patrol!
We weeded beets all through the winter. What did
we produce?
Hear that?
I only hear the flattering blades.
No, listen, behind the blades.
Weed faster. It's not funny! Be competitive! We have to show
the investors we appreciate them.
Oh, bite your tongue off already! Listen.
Hear that?
What?
Yeah, how we
supposed to hear with
such a flattering noise
in the air?

Listen.
You can hear it.
Yeah, I can hear them laughing.
See, they're laughing at us!
Weed faster. It's not funny. The investors want high interest rates and hard work.
I hear it! I hear it!
Laughing at us. Well, what about that?
Oh yeah, I can hear it now!
It's not funny. Weed faster. Don't you believe anything?
Ha ha, they're laughing at us!
But why? What's so funny?
It's not funny! They don't want unions and welfare.
You're right, it's not funny. They're laughing because . . .
We weeded beets all through the winter!
You got to increase productivity! Weed faster!
They're laughing because . . .
We were stupid enough to believe them!
Yeah, we believed them that there was no other way!
They got the free lunch!
There is no other way!
See! That's why they're laughing at us!
Laughing all the way to the credit onion!
Laughing all the way to the case of popular air!
Laughing all the way to the charter!
Now you're talking stupid. Laughing all the way to the charter!
Charter bank, dummkopp! Charter bank!

Say, what if the people chartered themselves a
bank?
　　　Now you're talking . . .
　　　　　Stupid, eh?
　　　　　　　Well, you can charter a
　　　　　　　Grey Goose Bus.
Yeah, and you can charter an airplane . . .
　　　　　　　Or a helicopter even.
　　　　　Yeah, you flattering whiplash
　　　　　twirler up there, you can
　　　　　charter a helicopter even!
Oh, you just can't see it! There is only one way! Weed faster!
You got to stay on the straight and narrow!
　　　　　How can we stay on the straight and
　　　　　narrow in a curved world?
Stop avoiding the issue.
　　　　　　　What's the issue?
　　　　　　　Charters.
Yeah, now if you charter a Grey Goose Bus, what
does that mean?
　　　　　Well, you can tell the bus to go where
　　　　　you want it to go, right?
Right, if you want to go to Mexico you can, or if
you just want to drive around all the darps
between the river and the hills you can do that.
　　　　　　Or you can go to the Black
　　　　　　Hills that aren't really black!
　　　　　　　Or you never have to
　　　　　　　go to the States of
　　　　　　　America if you don't
　　　　　　　feel like it.
Right! We would decide.
　　　　　But where would you tell a bank to go?
What's a bank got?
　　　　　Loonies!
　　　　　　Bucks!
　　　　　　　Charges!

And who decides what to do with the loonies,
bucks, and charges?
Well, the bank. Who else would decide?
Well, who else could decide?

Oh yeah, I think I see . . .
What is there to see?

Oh, you mean if we charter ourselves a
bank we could decide what to do with
the money?
Right! We could decide!

We could decide to use it in
bad weather and not just when
the sun shines!
Right!

But my dad said a
credit union was
supposed to do that.
Well, sure, but even a credit union can only go to
some places. To really help the people I would
want to charter the biggest bank, the Bank of
Canada!
Holem de gruel! Now you're talking like a communist yet! Only
lazy cheaters talk like that!

See! You believe them. That's why they're
laughing at us! They can scare you with a word
that has no meaning anymore!

Hey! What's that helicopter doing?

Oh it's dropping down
right on top of us!
Have those things got guns?
ow! my ears are bursting with that flattering noise!

Throw yourselves down flat on the
ground!
I told you not to talk like that!

Ouch, that wind is
tearing the shirt off my
back!

Dusent noch emol eent! How can they do this? It's a free country!

See! You don't want to believe!

See! If we had chartered our own bank sooner, this wouldn't be happening!

We will save our money in the bank of Gutenthal!

Hear that?

What? My ears are all plugged full.

We will save our money in the bank of Gutenthal!

They're still laughing at us!

See! You don't want to believe! There is no other way!

No! It's not the helicopter!

No?

We will save our money in the bank of Gutenthal!
We will save!
We will save!
We will save!

Look, the helicopter is flying away!

Really!

There it goes!

That was scary. I thought for sure we were going to die.

Now, I hope you have learned your lesson. It could be your last chance to weed faster!

Didn't you hear that song?

What song?

        The song that was laughing at the
        helicopters!

            Yeah, the song that scared the
            helicopters away!

No song can do that!

      That's what they want us to believe!

                We will save
                our

    money in the bank
        of Gutenthal!

           We will save our
               money in the bank
                  of Gutenthal!

    We will save our
        money in the bank
            of Gutenthal!
                We will save!
                  We will save!

Weed faster! No song can do that!

Look! Who's that?

        Who?

There on the next field.

    Oh him. That's just Politicks Paetkau.

What's he doing there? It's not his land.

      You don't have ears. The *National
      Journal* isn't the only information
      highway.

    Yeah, Politicks Paetkau won the LOTTO 6/49 and
    bought all the land along Mary's Creek.

So what's he doing with that funny looking machine?

      Seeding big bluestem.

Huh?

    Yeah, and little bluestem and blazing star.

Is that some new kind of canola?

      Oh no. Tall grass.

Tall grass?
                    Yeah, tall grass higher
                    than people.
Has Politicks gone mental?
        He's bringing the buffalo back!
                    Buffalo?
They'll never let him get away with it. Those helicopters will
be back.
                    I saw Thecla Thiessen.
        Where?
                    In the Flatland Mall on Easter Saturday.
I thought she was Thecla Klippenstein now.
        Did she still have on her wedding dress?
Well, I guess not, the wedding was before Christmas yet.
                    Oh, you think you know
                    everything!
And you think you have all the moral high ground to yourself.
                    Thecla had on ripped jeans and a Crash
                    Test Dummies T-shirt.
See, even married they still want to be hippies nowadays.
        Is her hair still spiking up?
                    No. And she is letting it grow out
                    Thiessen brown, but it is still cherry-red
                    from the ears down.
That would sure look good for getting a job in your charter
bank.
        Was Kjnirps Iesaak with her?
                    Yeah, and she had a ring around her left
                    eye the colour of a salamander.
        Avon doesn't sell that.
                    Iesaak Shpriesaak.
Schlenkjafoot.
        Don't say it!
                    Please don't say it!

AN ILLITERATE HITCH-HIKER'S GUIDE TO THE GUTENTHAL GALAXY

A DESSERT EATING IN PARTIAL FULFILLMENT OF THE ORAL REQUIREMENTS OF A PH.D. EASY

By Koadel Kehler, the Teacher's Son,
B.A.(Pass), Cert. Ed., B.Ed.(Old), M.Ed. (Sch. Admin.)

THESIS STATEMENT

The Flat German spoken in the Galaxy is peculiar to the community of Gutenthal which is located between the river and the hills just north of the big ditch that cuts us off from the States. Therefore, if the Flat German spoken is different from the Flat German you speak in your darp, that is the way it should be. Even in Gutenthal the people sometimes have difficulty understanding one another because each family has its own lexicon or Voca Bullary as Pug Peters used to say. The only historical pig latin root between Flat German and Pennsylvania Dutch is that Penzel Panna's sister who works by Dutch Bakery in Winkler is quite vain.

ANTITHESIS STATEMENT

When pronouncing these words use English phonic sounds; or whole language with roller bearing Rs; your pronouncement will either be cracked or funny.

SYNTHESIS STATEMENT

Health hazard warning: excessive use of this guide may turn flat German into Latin. Avoid inhaling.

Antidote: read three pages of *THE SALVATION OF YASCH SIEMENS* at the top of your lungs while riding on a tractor, followed by a silent reading chapter from *MURDER IN GUTENTHAL: A SCHNEPPA KJNALS MYSTERY* while sitting on the throne. If dizziness persists, try a round robin reading of the dark day for Canada speech. Reading the above-mentioned novels will also relieve itching caused by the discovery of words in the glossary not found in the text of *THE SECOND COMING OF YEEAT SHPANST*.

Unconfirmed side effect: persons in the tenth month of pregnancy are alleged to experience instant labour upon hearing Gutenthal flat German read for crying out loud.

PHRASES AND FROESES FUCHTIG AND OTHERWISE

Blouss news
    just news
Bren die deh bulb nicht uht.
    Burn yourself the bulb not out.
Chinga freow met sukka bestreit.
    Children's questions with sugar sprinkled.
Daut jefft noch twins!
    That gives yet twins!
Daut zit shtraum!
    That looks beautiful!
Dit ess meist so deep aus de fifty flood!
    This is nearly as deep as the fifty flood!
Dit zent ye nijch de Olympics.
    These are not the Olympics.
Doa biem shtaul.
    There by the barn.
Du shienst aus ne harlijche mone!
    You shine like a glorious moon!
Dunna noch emol eent.
    Thunder yet one time once.
Dusent noch emol eent.
    A thousand yet one time once.
Ekj plug die nue en.
    I plug you now in.

Fuats upuh schtade.
Now on the spot.
Haft dei oola zack kjeen boddem?
Has the old sack no bottom?
Hast du die enjeplugged?
Have you plugged yourself in?
Hoings laeva and butta brot.
Dog's liver and butter bread.
Mensch, de hoade stang puakst mie em hingarenj!
Man, that hard rod pokes me in the hind end!
Mit fife spitze ecken.
With five pointed corners.
Nu mutt ekj dann wada enne moos schlope.
Now must I then again in the fruit soup sleep.
Nun Danket Aller Gott.
Now Thank We All Our God.
Obah loat me eascht en avarock aun trakje!
But let me first a coat on pull!
Pauss up, oola Neefeld, daut hoat kloappaht noch to nicht!
Watch out, old Neufeld, that heart clappers yet to nothing!
Plug emol den yalen extension cord en.
Plug once the yellow extension cord in.
Portzelkje Fortzelkje Schpecka Droats Tien
New Year's fritters, natural gas, barbed-wire Tina
Sei lat dei frueiss nicht emol daut TV up pausse.
She lets the women not once that TV watch (in the
sense of guard).
Jungkje, traak doch emol de unjabecksi oot!
Boy, pull yet once the underpants out!
Wowt vell ye met me?
What will you with me?
Wowt deist du doa so huach?
What do you there so high?
Weetst noch wua auless ess?
Knowest yet where everything is?
Wowt wesst du met dei fuest enne futz?
What want you with the fist in the cunt?

AND A PADDLE ACROSS THE LEXICON

A

acred	tilled, worked; nowadays it would have to be hectared
allein	alone
Altbergthal	old mountain valley, alleged home of Yeeat Shpanst
am	him
angst	horror;(ahhngst; no connection with yuppie existential cord ehhngst)
ate	eat
audee	a dew; adios amighost
auless	everything
aus	as
Avarock	overcoat (skirt)

B

backstring	spinal column
badel	a male scoundrel mostly off-colour
bane	ceiling

beckhouse	bendover house
becksi	clothing for the bendover parts
becksisheeta	pants shitter
bedoozled;	
bedutzed	mentally fuzzified
beet	a piece
beluira	eavesdropper
bengel	boy, more innocent than a badel; the original namer of the Bengal tiger
best	(you) are
biem	by; at; during
bildness	picture, image (graven)
bizzing	buzzing, in constant motion
blaw	lowing as in 'the cattle are lowing'
bleed	shy
blift	stays; remains
blinguh kooh	blind cow; a children's game like blind man's buff
blitz	lightning; a flash
blous (blouss)	only; just
boddem	bottom
bommeling	dangling; especially from the ears
borsch	borscht
brat	board
bren	burn
broot	bread
bring it by	to explain
brumm	
(brumming)	a humming sound
brummtupp	a friction drum
brunen	brown
brut	bride
bulchi	loaf (of bread)
bulla (bullering)	to rattle, especially inside a sheet metal container
butterflowers	marigolds

C

Christlich	Christlike, but in a less positive sense than charisma
clapper	beat; rattle
clawed out (clawing out)	escaped
come back again burro	Flat German Mexican immigrant
cooked-in	home canning
Co-opich	overly zealous Co-op membership
cowfoot	crowbar
creamfat	cream gravy, a delicacy

D

Dank	thank; to say grace before meals
dankbar	thankful; Help All Heinrichs was always looking for Mr. Dankbar
dann	then
darp	an unincorporated village
daumbrat	dam(n) board; checkers
daut	there
deep	deep
dei	the
deist	do (you)
Dietschlaund	Germany
Dievel, Deivel	variations of devil
dit	this
doa	there
doch	then; yet, but
docht	thought
dola	dollar
doot	dead
dow-nix	a do nothing; a no goodnik
dowt (daut)	that
drankahma	slop pail; origins of German literary tradition Sturm und Drank
dringent	urgent, insistent

du	you
dukkat	meaningless expletive; rocking
dummheit	stupidity
dummkopp	stupid head
dunna,	
dunnasche	thunder
dunner and	
blitzen	thunder and lightning
dupsich	stupid
dusent	thousand
dreekauntje	three-sided; triangular

E

eaza bone	iron track
eent	one
eesht (eascht)	first
ei, eia	egg
ekj mott	I must; words spoken by the inventor of Mott's clamato juice
ekj sie	I am
em	in
emol	one time; once
endat	comes to an end; changes
enne	in the
ess	is
eyesiepers	eyelashes
ezel	donkey; mule

F

falls me by	occurs to me
faspa	afternoon coffee break on the farm
fat hen	a weed found in all Flat German gardens; some English grow it on purpose as portulacca
feadel	quarter
febeizeled	feschwunge; lost; vanished
fedajchtijch	suspicious; queer

fedaumpte	damned
feemaesich	bestially
feknutsched	crunched
feschwunge	vanished; lost; *febeizeled*
fiele	files as in iron files; tools used to create iron filings for magnetic politicians
fire evening	end of the work day
flitz	move very quickly
Foda	father
forsch, forscha	husky; a husky person
forsch, forscha	to inquire; one who seeks out information; had Forscha Friesen not been content as an an usher he might have become a detective instead of Schneppa Kjnals.
fortzes, fortz	methane gas emissions
fuddahed	ordered
france hose	a Frenchman
frate	animal mouth, to feed
frei, freid	joy
freiwilliges	freewillingness
frindschoft	relatives
fromm	pious
fruelied; frueiss; fruemensch	women
fuats	right away; immediately
fuchtig	furious; upset
fuest	fist
fuhlenzing	dozing
fuhschluck	mis-swallow; choke
funk	found
funkles	sparkles
fuschel (-ling; -led)	whisper
Futtachi	little Father
futz	cunt

G

gang	a room connecting the house and the barn
ganz geviss	absolutely positively sure
geschpenst	a ghost
glutz, glutzed	stare
Gott	God
gribble	mental activity; to figure; ponder
grote (groot)	big
grotestove	living room
gruelich	frightening; gruesome
grumsauling	grumbling
gute	good
Gutenthal	good valley; Gutenthaller wine is made from Gutenthaller dandelions first imported into Manitoba from Russia by Dandelion Pauls inside his felt burr sock in 1875.

H

hackel-wire	barbed wire
haft	has; have
handplaything	accordian
harlijche	glorious
hartsoft	extremely
haevel	a carpenter's plane; sometimes used to describe tremendous speed
heista kopp	heels over head
Himmel	heaven; sky
Himmelfahrt	Ascension Day
himmel-shine	heavenly light
himmelshtenda	telepost of the sky
hoade	hard
holem de gruel	exclamation of surprise; fetch the fear
holzyebock	wood tick
hon	rooster
hook on	to stop by
hova	oats

hova grits	oatmeal porridge
howd	had
Hullaund	Holland
huach	high
hund	dog
hups (hupsing)	jumping
Huttatolas	Hutterites
huy yuy yuy	expression of astonishment

I

in-leading	opening of the church service
invituh	invite

J

jeft	gives; also poison
jugend	youth
jugendverein	literally 'youth association'; a Sunday evening church service designed to put a monkey wrench in a young man's courting plans
Juide frei	Jewish joy; a bad pun on Jugendverein
jungchi	little boy
junge lied	an engaged couple

K

kammers you nothing	none of your business
katzenjammer	yowling of cats
kahyinkering	whimpering like a dog that has just been kicked
kjalla	cellar; basement
kjeen	no; none
kjnirps	a twirp
kjikj	look
kjrayel	tease; make fun
kjreit	crows, as in rooster song
kjriezeling	twisting, swirling

kjritzel	scribble, scrawl
kleenet	small
klingers	rings
kloot	a clod of dirt
klunked	clunked
knack	crack; hit
knackzoat	crack seeds; spits; sunflower seeds
knecht	hired man
knochenartzt	bone doctor
koata	a tom cat
kompliziet	complicated
komst	cabbage
kromm	bent, crooked

L

laechelnd	laughingly
lankwielijch	tedious; tiresome; long-whiling
laups, laupsijch	dolt; doltish
leise	softly; gently
let loose	to start up (an engine)
loaded in	invited
loat	let; late

M

maam	mom
me	me
meist	almost
mensch	man (human)
mest	manure
met	with
meyall	girl
middle road	a field road dividing sections into quarter sections
mist	manure
mist-acre	the nuisance ground; landfill site
mit zub vint	with the wind
mone	moon

moos	cold fruit soup
mousetail	foxtail grass
Mumchi	a wife; Mrs.
Muttachi	little mother
muzharich	
muzhahed	fuzzy; blurred

N

nah	well
narsch	the seat of knowledge
ne	a
needich	necessary; If you are necessary you should go to the beckhouse.
neh	no
neighbouring	to chew the fat
nerk	to tease
nicht, nijch	not; nothing
nie, niemols	never
nie vada	never again
noch	yet; but
nue	now
nutz you out	to get maximum use out of a hired hand's body and sometimes his soul

O

oabeida	worker; hired man
Oata	Agatha; as in Oata Christie the mysterious writer
obah	but
olden home	senior citizen's home
ooda	or
oola	old
Omchi	a husband; Mr.
onioning	crying
onntoofrade	discontented
oot	out
oppem	on the

ossentoata	a bull whip
ouster, oostre	Easter
outcall sale	an auction
ovenside	a leanto; a leanto used for cooking
oyah	peeve, agravate

P

pacht	rent
panz	belly
Panzenfeld	Belly Field; most residents drive Pontiac (Panzentecka) cars
pauss up	watch out
pesst	pissed
Pinjkste	Pentecost
pig wedding	pig killing bee
plautform	platform
pluida(h)	to gossip
pluida zack	a gossipping sack
ploomps	a splash of water
poajchem	flannel cloth
poosted	blew
postanack	parsnip
Prachadarp	Beggarville
prell	junk
proost	sneeze
puakst	poke (you)
Puggefeld	Frogfield
putoots	the parts that were created for sitting down —this made thinking possible

Q

qwaulem, qwauleming	billowing (smoke)

R

rosmack	order; to keep order
Reibtrommel,	
Rommelpot,	
Rubbeltrumm	rubbing drums, variations of the Brummtupp
rieselt	refers to falling snow
rummel	thunder
Russlaunt	Russia
Russlenda	Russians, especially Flat German Russians who fled to Canada after the revolution; Russlenda are largely responsible for the myth that all Flat Germans are great singers.
rutch	slide

S

saddle time	spring seeding
say up	recite
schacht	applied psychology, as in applying non-resistant force to the putoot of a child
schaps	a simpleton
scheia	a variation of scissors to make it rhyme with eia
schell	scold
schelped	to cut a narrow strip off a long board
schemma	twilight
schemmel	a roan as in 'Strawberry Roan'; check out John Weier's poems Ried Daut Bleivuh Schemmel
schendlich	disgracefully
schiltkjrate	turtles; shelled feast; used as an insult
schinkuhbein	ham legs; thighs
schinkuhfleisch	ham meat; schinkuhbeia would be Hamm's beer
schlax	long and flexible
shleit	beats, hits
schlenkjafoot	stumble-foot, club-footed

schlope	sleep
schlucks	a swallow
schluffs	
(*shlorring*)	drags (her feet); shuffles
schluhdenz	a slob
schowelling	echoing
schmallen	
Lebensweg	straight and narrow path
schmauntzup	Flat German yogourt full of boiled eggs, cucumbers, and green onions
schmaus	heavy lipstick-smearing face-chewing smooch
schmeikt	tasted; similar to schmecks
schmooz	to smooch lightly
schmuistahed	smirked
schnee	snow
schneers	pulls tightly
schneppa	to snoop; to sniff out
schpaeluh	to play
schuckel	swing
schuzzel	silly fellow
schwaecksing	skidding
schwengel	a lever; a crank
Schwiadochta	daughter-in-law
schwierich	troubled
schwieter	to chatter
seeper	to seep
seh (sei)	she
sei lat	she lets
shaftig	eager
shaubelkopp	beanhead
sheklich	fashionably dressed
sheet	excrement
shienst	shine (you)
shinda	
(*shindasche*)	a shoemaker; why it is used as a cussword in not clear but then logic is not one of cussing's strengths

shitts	a switch; a shut-off device
shlepping	dragging
shlurpsing	sound made by a combination of tongue, lips, and hot coffee.
shmuyng	extra heavy smooching, perhaps even going too far
shoevanack	Halloween vandalism
shpriesack	a chaff sack
shroutflint	shot gun; chopped feed gun
shrug	a nag (horse); Altlas shrugged, Trudeau shrugged
shteepa	to brace; to steady; to reinforce
shtemm gaufel	tuning fork
shtimm	voice, especially singing voice
shtollt	proud; conceited
shtramel	long narrow strip
shtroof	tart; not smooth; very dry (- 2 at the Liquor Commission)
shtrulling	squirting, especially milk into an empty tin pail
sich	herself; himself
siene	his
smeared on	deceived, cheated
snudder	nasal drip
snuddernose	runny nose
soldot, soldotten	soldier(s)
Sommerfelder	one of many Flat German church denominations, followers of the Elder from Sommerfeld
spitz poop	a big shot; a thief
stang	rod; bar
stick roses	hollyhocks
stoaw	die; starve
stoppered up	constipated
string yourself on	overexert yourself
strong	a heifer

Sylvester	New Year's Day celebration named after Pope Sylvester I
Sylvesterabend	New Year's Eve

T

tane	tooth
tea blooms	carnations
Tiessuh	Thiessen
to nothing	broken; dislocated
tubdewk	dish rag
trakje, traak	pull
truarijch	sad
truck	pulled
truff	hit
twievel	doubt, qualm

U

uck	also
uhyeseffa	wildlife, insects, weeds
unja	under
unjabecksi	underpants
upuh schtade	on the spot

V

vada	again
vaumstje	bed bugs
veah	was
verenichi	Flat German cottage cheese perogies smothered in rhubarb sauce
voa	will

W

wacht	wait
wada	weather
wan	when
washcumb	washing up basin
weetst	know (you)

weltschmerz	world pain; the weight of the world; an Atlas tire around one's neck
wesst	(you) want
What is loose?	What's the matter?
wie	we
winkle	corner; an addition to a building
wittet	white
write it on	charge to my account by writing it on the chimney
waut (wowt)	what
woata	water (just say it like the President from New Kennedy would have said it)
wua	where

Y

yankah	want, desire (root of the corrupt form hanker)
Yanzeed	the Flat German darp on the other side of the river
yeschwieta	high-pitched babble
ylips	slip; slide
yoh	yes
yowma	pity; whining like a locked up puppy
yralled (up)	enthralled, wide-eyed
yuelling	sound like a vacuum cleaner or a cowboy singing along with the cattle.

Z

zack	sack, scrotum
zamp	mustard
zell	shall
zirk	a gun grease fitting on a machine
zoop	drink, especially as an animal or an alcholic.

About the Illustrator

David Morrow is a freelance illustrator/designer who has been working in Winnipeg for thirteen years. He graduated from the University of Manitoba with a degree in Environmental Studies. In addition to illustrating book covers for Turnstone Press and Peguis Publishers, he often does 3-D prototyping for product design and styling. David Morrow currently lives in Winnipeg with his wife and three children.

Photo: Andrea Geary, *The Manitoba Co-Operator*

Armin Wiebe is the author of two novels, *Murder in Gutenthal* and *The Salvation of Yasch Siemens,* which was shortlisted for the Leacock Medal for Humour and the Books in Canada First Novel Award. He lives and writes in Winnipeg.

Praise for previous work:

"Armin Wiebe is a comic story-teller without equal in Canada today. Please hold your sides while reading."—Robert Kroetsch

". . . adds significantly to . . . an emerging mythology . . . on both sides of the double dike . . . Wiebe's two novels play an essential role in the larger story even as they offer delight in themselves."—*Border Crossings* magazine